Bill Hitchcock, successful banker, divorced womanizer, financial genius and confirmed cynic, thought himself lucky to be picked by the Saudi Arabians to mastermind the investment of their huge oil profits. Soon he found himself wheeling and dealing at the highest levels of government – and pursuing the beautiful Ursula Hartmann, daughter of one of the world's top scientists. But through her he learned of the offer that one of the Arabs' most powerful and dangerous enemies – the Shah of Iran – had made to her father to secure his services on a deadly (and deadly secret) project. A project which could prove fatal to Hitchcock's employers – and bring the world's economy crashing down in a collapse that would make the Crash of '29 look like Jackpot Day ... Paul E. Erdman, bestselling author of *The Billion Dollar Killing*, shows to the full his powers to take the reader right inside the armoured citadels of international politics and high finance in this gripping, frighteningly credible thriller of the dangerous connections between the worlds of big money and heavyweight political power.

'RIVETING' *Daily Telegraph*

'ERDMAN HAS DONE IT AGAIN ... A BLEAK, EXCITING LOOK AT THE VERY NEAR FUTURE' *Sunday Times*

The Crash of '79

PAUL E. ERDMAN

SPHERE BOOKS LIMITED
30/32 Gray's Inn Road, London WC1X 8JL

First published in Great Britain by
Martin Secker & Warburg Ltd 1977
Copyright © 1976 by Daisy Chain International, Inc.
Published by Sphere Books Ltd 1977
Reprinted 1977 (twice), 1978 (five times)
Reprinted 1979

TRADE
MARK

Set in Intertype Baskerville

Printed in Great Britain by
William Collins Sons & Co Ltd,
Glasgow

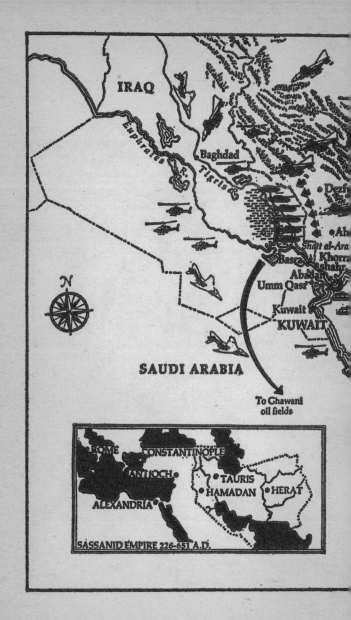

IRAQ

Euphrates R.

Baghdad

Tigris R.

Dezf

Ah

Shatt al-Ara

Basra al Khorra shahr

Abadan

Umm Qasr

Kuwait

KUWAIT

SAUDI ARABIA

To Ghawani
oil fields

N

ROME CONSTANTINOPLE
ANTIOCH TAURIS
ALEXANDRIA HAMADAN HERAT

SASSANID EMPIRE 226-651 A.D.

FOUR DAYS TO REBUILD AN EMPIRE

The shah's strategy for Iran's recapture of the Persian Gulf.

Teheran

IRAN

PERSIAN GULF

BAHRAIN

QATAR

Bandar Abbas

Straits of Hormuz

Dubai

GULF OF OMAN

Abu Dhabi

OMAN

SCALE

1   50   100   200

CHAPTER ONE

SONOMA COUNTY, CALIFORNIA
DECEMBER, 1984

I have decided to put on paper an account of what really happened in 1979 – the year the world, as we knew it, fell apart.

I'm not sure anybody really cares any more, at least the people out here in California. They don't have to worry about starving or freezing to death like so many others. They have their horses, their vineyards, their church suppers. They would rather fish than think. Because they want to forget.

I cannot blame them. But I do not choose to forget. I liked the old days when we still had airplanes and television and dry martinis and pornography. I admit it. Sure, there are lots of Latter-Day Saints around these days who claim that it was hedonists like myself who were ultimately to blame for what happened; that it was we who brought the wrath of God down upon us – us being the world in general and America in particular – because we were so hell-bent upon the pursuit of pleasure and money.

Baloney! God had nothing to do with it. Men caused it, and a handful of men at that: the Shah of Iran and Prince Abdullah of Saudi Arabia, to name but two of the principal ones. But even those two Mideastern potentates would never have been able to wreak such havoc had it not been for the duplicity of the world's bankers, the selfish stupidity of the Europeans, the deception of the Russians (our new 'friends'), the greed of the Swiss, and the total incompetence of the last three men to occupy the White House, especially the fool who finished off our country by presiding over the Crash of '79.

Now don't draw the wrong conclusions. I am as religious as the next man. But that does not mean that I must agree to the propagation of myths where our immediate past is concerned. I happen to believe that we owe it to our children and grandchildren to tell them the truth. And the truth is that we, my generation, managed to ruin our world so completely that we have no legacy to leave them but poverty and disorder.

So it is for them that I am writing this – not, as some would have it, to exculpate myself.

I have spent two years researching the events of the late 1970's. I have talked to many people who were deeply involved, both in this country and abroad. But for the most part I have relied upon my own recollections. After all, I was there – right at the top – when it happened.

Where to start? And with whom? The autumn of 1978 seems as good a time as any.

That's when I went to work for the government. No, not the American government. The government of Saudi Arabia.

CHAPTER TWO

I'll be the first to admit that my appointment as chief financial adviser to the government of Saudi Arabia produced a few raised eyebrows at the time. Not because I was American – by 1978, Americans were all over Riyadh – but because I had been absent from the international financial scene for a number of years.

My absence was by choice – my choice. I had already decided as early as 1976 that things were bound to fall apart – by 'things' I mean *everything* – and I chose not to be part of the process. So I sold my banks, the one in the United States as well as those abroad, resigned all my board memberships, and settled down in northern California, where I proceeded to do precisely nothing. I was forty-four, and a free man.

A lot of people called me an eccentric. Brilliant international banker, they said : a pity he started to believe his own doomsday theories. How wrong they were! In retrospect the only pity is that I did not stick to my original convictions.

As so often, my mind was changed by a friend. In this instance, it was Reggie Hamilton. Not that I blame him. He meant well, for both myself and the Arabs. I had originally met Reggie way back in the 1950's, before I got into international banking. At the time I was employed by a think tank in Menlo Park, just down the peninsula from San Francisco. My field was international economics. Reggie's was energy. After a few years, I moved on while Reggie stayed. But we remained friends, probably because both of us became reasonably prominent men, each in his own way. My forte was making money. Reggie's was thinking about oil.

Which brings us directly to the Arabs. When they started taking over the properties of the international oil companies in the early 1970's, they did not know a hell of a lot about the business. They needed outside help, but hardly wanted to get it from the fellows at Standard Oil. Their talent hunt was soon focused on research institutes, especially those in California : research institutes because they had the expertise, for hire to the highest bidder; California because the Arabs, especially the Saudis, were at home there. To a very substantial degree, the young Saudi elite went to the West Coast for their higher education – Stanford, UCLA, Berkeley. In fact, I was told that one of Faisal's grandsons had flunked out of college, gone back to Riyadh and become a secondhand-car salesman with political ambitions.

In 1973 the Saudis were already on to Reggie, because his academic specialty was the calculation of price elasticities of demand for alternate sources of primary energy. In plain English, Reggie figured how much the price of crude oil, and its derivatives such as gasoline, could be increased within a given set of parameters (such as the price of coal) without wrecking the market for petroleum. In 1973 Reggie told them they could quadruple the price of Persian Gulf crude and not lose a customer.

They did, and Reggie was right. Under his continuing tutelage they had raised it to sixteen dollars a barrel by the fall of 1978 – and had still not lost a customer.

In a sense, Reggie had been instrumental in making those guys rich. And they knew it. So in the fall of 1978, when they were looking for a counterpart of Reggie in the financial field, one who would help them *stay* rich, they naturally sought his advice. Reggie nominated me.

When Reggie phoned, I was both intrigued and flattered. After all, he was suggesting that I take a crack at the largest hoard of money ever accumulated in the history of mankind. Furthermore, I was getting bored. So I agreed to at least discuss the idea with his Arab friends, or friend.

It was friend – in the person of Prince Abdul Aziz al-Kuraishi, the president of the Saudi Arabian Monetary Agency, that country's central bank. At my suggestion, we met at the Bohemian Club in San Francisco, one of my local watering holes. I thought the place would be especially

12

appropriate if my guest arrived in headdress, robes and scimitar. As it turned out, Reggie looked more like an Arab than he did. Prince al-Kuraishi's suit was strictly Savile Row, his accent Oxbridge with slight Stanford overtones, and he sported a Sandhurst clipped moustache.

We met in the bar, and when I offered al-Kuraishi a drink, he not only accepted but insisted that his dry martini be made with Tanqueray gin, very cold. An Arab who drinks very cold dry martinis cannot be all bad, and I told al-Kuraishi so. I was tempted to follow up by asking him if I could call him Al, but dropped the idea when Reggie arched me a warning eyebrow. So we went into the standard San Francisco opener about the city's gracious living being so obviously superior to anything New York, Paris or London had to offer. Both Reggie and I were professional Californians.

The prince by no means allowed me to dominate the conversation as I usually do, at least according to the opinion of my ex-wife. Nor did he stick to small talk. He moved from the economic situation in Italy to the outlook for the pound sterling to what I thought about the intentions of the Russians in Iraq. We traded opinions on some mutual acquaintances: the British chancellor of the exchequer (a fool); the chairman of the Swiss Bank Corporation (a peasant); the Shah of Iran (a nut). That is, I gave my opinion, and the prince nodded.

I obviously passed the test, because halfway through lunch al-Kuraishi abruptly changed the direction of the conversation – from me and my opinions to Saudi Arabia and its problems. According to the prince, they were all rooted in one common misconception: that the Saudis were just a bunch of dumb Arab nomads who had lucked it out. From this, the universal conclusion had been drawn that they should be treated more or less as children. Since children need guardians to protect them against their own immature follies, it was only natural that the civilized men of the West assumed that burden.

This attitude, al-Kuraishi pointed out, was the same everywhere: in Washington, Bonn, New York, and Tokyo.

13

Everywhere! And it had to stop. Not only was it insulting; it was costing Saudi Arabia incalculable income. Washington, for example, continued to offer only 8 percent interest on the special-issue Treasury bills it sold to Riyadh – in spite of the fact that Saudi Arabia had already lent the United States government almost $50 billion, and was, in fact, its second largest source of cash, topped only by the two hundred and twenty million American taxpayers. Surely 10 percent would be a more reasonable rate under such circumstances?

I agreed.

But it was not just governments, al-Kuraishi continued. Commercial banks throughout the world expected the Saudis to lend them money at rates a full two, sometimes three, percentage points below the prevailing market. Because, they said, the Saudis needed them more than they needed the Saudis' money. More insulting were the gangs of con men who kept flying into the country from all directions with harebrained investment schemes, ranging from gold mines in Denmark to hockey teams in Arizona.

Not only were the Americans and Europeans playing this game. The worst pests, al-Kuraishi continued, were the delegations from the dozens of destitute nations in Africa and Asia, plus a few from Latin America. Their reasoning was simple. They needed dollars. The Arabs had too many dollars. Both problems could be solved if the Saudis just handed over a billion or two. Never mind whether the money would ever be paid back.

Why had they put up with this sort of thing for so long? It had been the personal decision of King Khalid. He had wanted to demonstrate to all the world that in spite of the assassination of his predecessor, Faisal, his country's policies would remain the same. There would be no radicalization. Saudi Arabia would continue to be a patient, conservative, responsible, religious nation. But enough was enough!

Then came the pitch.

The Saudis had decided to start playing it tough in the financial field. They needed a top professional who knew the world money game to help them play. A Doctor No, as al-Kuraishi put it in a rare flash of humor. They had investigated me, at Reggie's suggestion. I fitted their bill. They realized that I was not for hire in the normal sense of the word. But they had concluded that I would be attracted by the challenge.

Their offer: the job of chief financial adviser to the kingdom of Saudi Arabia, with an annual rate of compensation of five hundred thousand dollars. I would be directly responsible to the Supreme Council, headed by King Khalid, and would report to it through al-Kuraishi. In practical terms, I would have full authority to commit funds on behalf of the Saudi Arabian Monetary Agency, subject to Khalid's veto, and subject to the guidelines approved by the Supreme Council. During the coming twelve months, the Agency expected to have around $250 billion at its disposal. I accepted the offer.

Twelve days later I took Pan Am to Beirut. After a good night's rest I caught the early-morning plane to Riyadh.

CHAPTER THREE

Three words suffice for Riyadh : flat, dry, hot. But the limo that was waiting for me at the airport was air-conditioned; so was the suite at the local Hilton. And so were the king's quarters.

My first duty, it seemed, was to make an appearance before Khalid. Al-Kuraishi made the introduction. The setting was businesslike. Khalid sat behind a desk, not on a throne. I had never met the king before, although quite a while back I had dealt with his brother, Fahd, who was now the crown prince. Nevertheless, Khalid immediately referred to this, and it was apparent that whatever Fahd had told him had been favorable. The king gave the impression of a tough, rather humorless man. Physically, his eyes left the most lasting impression : dark and piercing. Such words sound corny, I guess, but I definitely recall feeling highly uncomfortable when he gave me a 'fix' while his translator was speaking. The audience lasted perhaps five minutes. Nothing of significance was said.

On the way out I was approached by another member of the court, obviously one of the sons of former King Faisal from the shape of his nose and the arrogance of his bearing. He introduced himself as Prince Abdullah, and told me that he was the minister of desalination. He had heard about my coming to Riyadh, and just wanted to give his word of welcome. He explained that he had attended Menlo Park College in the early 1950's. He was sure we had many mutual acquaintances. He hoped I would be free to dine with him soon. After an exchange of perhaps fifty words, he gave the typical limp Arab handshake and disappeared down a corridor. For some reason, already during that first brief encounter he made me feel uneasy.

Al-Kuraishi had remained in the background during this interlude, and did not say a word about it on our way over to the Saudi Arabian Monetary Agency. I recall that it struck me as somewhat strange.

The first day on a new job is always difficult, even if you are starting at the top : dozens of introductions to people whose names you immediately forget; the grand tour of the premises which, where banks are concerned, invariably ends up with the vault. By noon I had it behind me, and finally found myself alone in my huge new office on the top floor. My name and title had already been posted on the door in both English and Arabic.

When in doubt, pick up the phone. After consulting the bank's internal directory, I did just that. The man who answered at the money desk obviously knew who I was. I asked him to bring up the bank's current position sheets, listing their foreign deposits and indicating the terms and due dates. Five minutes later they arrived.

After spending fifteen minutes scanning the IBM printouts, two things were clear : the amounts involved were absolutely staggering, and the Saudis were getting royally screwed. Al-Kuraishi had been right. What was done, was done, but it did not have to continue even one day longer. Saudi Arabia was the biggest single supplier of money to the Western banking system : it could demand, not request, fair treatment. I got al-Kuraishi on the line and told him what I intended to do. He said I should go right ahead.

I went back to the computer printouts and came up with the Bank of London and Manchester. They had a quarter of a billion of Saudi funds deposited with them on a ninety-day basis in pound sterling. Sterling being what it was, one of the riskiest currencies on earth, deposits in British banks normally provided a high rate of return, by international standards. The going rate at that time for three months was 16 percent. The Saudis were getting 14 percent. That deposit was due for renewal on November 2, 1978, the following day.

I got back to the bank's money desk. After a slight struggle, I determined that my man down there was called Jamjoom. Whether it was his first or last name I never did find out.

'Jamjoom,' I asked, 'has the Bank of London and Manchester called yet about renewing that big deposit you've got with them?'

He checked and answered no. It was logical, since due to the difference in time zones it was just nine thirty in London, the crack of dawn by City standards.

'Transfer the call to me when it comes in,' I said, and went back to the position sheets. An hour later London was on the line.

'Who's there?' I barked.

'Bank of London and Manchester, international office.'

'That I know. It's your name I want.'

'Ross.'

'Give me Gates.'

'I'm afraid we don't have a Mr. Gates in our department.'

'I mean George Gates. He's your boss.'

'Sir, I'm afraid Mr. Gates would not be available. Actually, I'm just calling in regard to the renewal of a deposit arrangement that comes due tomorrow. Routine matter.'

'No longer. I'd appreciate if you'd quit buggering around, Ross, and put Gates on the line. Tell him Bill Hitchcock would like to speak to him.'

'I can try, sir,' skeptically.

The line went silent for at least a full minute. Then a loud voice : 'Hitchcock, is that you?'

'That's right, George.'

'Where are you?' As if he didn't know.

'Riyadh.'

'Of course. We've heard about your appointment. Congratulations. We must have lunch next time you're in London.'

'Fine, George. But actually I didn't want to talk to you about lunch. It seems that we have a few deposits with you. Large ones.'

'That's right.'

'One's coming due tomorrow, a quarter of a billion ster-

18

ling and apparently your people would like to roll it over.'

'Bill, you know I don't concern myself . . .'

'Sorry. George, but you are going to have to concern yourself this time. Otherwise no renewal – on this one, or any of the others when they come due.'

'What exactly do you mean, Hitchcock?' The voice had gone very British.

'Exactly that. Your boys have been playing games with the Saudis, paying fourteen percent on ninety-day sterling deposits, for chrissake.'

'Those are the going rates, Hitchcock. You've been out of touch.'

'Crap, Gates.'

'Bill' – we had returned to first names, apparently – 'we are in a whole new inning. Bluntly put, if the Saudis want to use our deposit facilities, or those of anybody else in London, they are going to have to accept our rates. They might be able to blackmail us on oil. They can't do it on money.'

'So you're offering fourteen percent again.'

'That's right.'

'Sorry, George. Transfer that two hundred and fifty million to our account at Chase Manhattan tomorrow.'

I hung up.

Barclays, National Westminster, Bank of Hong Kong and Shanghai all came in within the next hour. All expected routine renewals from the Saudis on deposits coming due. In every case I refused. All in all, with four phone calls I had drained almost a billion pounds sterling from the British banking system.

It was one thirty. I ordered a lettuce-and-tomato sandwich and a glass of milk and went back to the IBM sheets.

Two hours later al-Kuraishi rang me. He said that the deputy governor of the Bank of England had called him and was waiting on the line.

'He has a problem?' I inquired.

19

'Apparently. Something about our creating a sterling crisis. He sounded a bit peeved. I'd greatly appreciate it if you would handle this. I'll put him on.'

A few clicks and I was back talking with London.

'Sir Robert,' I began, 'so nice to talk to you again.' We had met perhaps three or four times in the past.

'Dr. Hitchcock,' he said, 'my compliments on your new appointment.'

'Thank you.'

'Now as I just mentioned to Mr. al-Kuraishi, we have been told here at the Bank of England that, under your instructions, Saudi Arabia intends to make some rather substantial withdrawals from British banks tomorrow. The figure of nine hundred million was mentioned.'

'That's about right.'

'We would appreciate it very much if that could be reconsidered. As you perhaps appreciate, if this was misinterpreted there could be a major run on sterling. I'm afraid H.M. government would be greatly upset.'

'I understand. But all this was hardly necessary. If your banks pay fair rates, the funds will be kept with them. If not, we'll move into dollars.'

'Quite. What is your suggestion?'

'That they pay the going market rate of sixteen percent.'

'Yes. Well, let me have an hour or so, Hitchcock. I think we can resolve this. I'll make a few phone calls.'

I said nothing.

'And, Hitchcock, next time you're in London, do let's lunch together.'

'By all means.' English bankers were always very big on lunches.

'Good show.'

By five o'clock all £900 million had been renewed for ninety days – at 16 percent.

On a per annum basis, the difference in interest amounted to £18 million, or about $40 million. Not bad for a first day's work. The next day I would take on the Swiss and the Germans, and following that the banks in New York.

20

It was all starting to feel rather good, except for the nagging sentiment that something was very wrong indeed with our world if one man sitting in the Arabian desert could bring the British banking system to its knees with a half-dozen phone calls.

CHAPTER FOUR

That evening I had intended to just stay at the Hilton and go to bed early. But when I got back there was a message at the desk asking me to call Mr. Falk of the American Embassy. It was six o'clock, but I tried anyway. He was still there, and asked if we could get together for a drink that evening. He gave me his home address, an apartment building not far from the hotel. We agreed on seven thirty. He promised he'd also have something to eat.

Falk turned out to be a big guy, around forty, originally from Virginia. And he was Colonel Falk, one of the military attachés at the embassy, he explained. Which also explained the booze : they brought it in via military transport from Frankfurt. He'd be glad to supply me with anything I needed. Right then I needed a dry martini, and Falk came up with a good one. I have always claimed that the one thing American military men do well is drink.

'So what's your impression?' he asked, once we had settled down in the living room. He drank bourbon.

'Of what?'

'The situation.'

'I hadn't noticed any situation.'

'What did Khalid have to say?'

'Nothing, really.'

'Well, he probably was pretty damn friendly.'

'Friendly, but not excessively so. Should he have been?'

'Frankly, yes. He needs us badly, and he knows it.'

'By us you mean the United States, I assume. Or is it more specific?'

'Are you one of those?' he asked.

'What's that mean?' I countered.

'Hostile toward the American military.'

'Hell, no, as long as your wars don't involve me.'

'I'm glad to hear that. Yes, I do mean the American military support. Without us, he'd be a dead duck by now.'

'OK, you've got me interested. Who's the enemy?'

'Khalid has two : the Shah of Iran, who fully intends to make the Persian Gulf an Iranian lake.'

'I'll more or less buy that. And the other one – Israel?'

'No. There has never been any real trouble there – never a shot exchanged between an Israeli and a Saudi. No, Khalid's other problem is right here – in Riyadh. His nephew, Abdullah.'

'Explain that.'

'OK. When Faisal was assassinated it was his brother Khalid who became king – not Faisal's eldest son, Abdullah.'

'Abdullah resents it.'

'Yes, and so do his six brothers.'

'I guess I would have been pissed off myself. So Abdullah would like to dump Khalid and take over.'

'Exactly.'

'What makes you think he could pull it off? He would need a real power base. If I understood him correctly this morning, he's minister of desalination. That's hardly . . .'

'You've already met him?' asked Falk, surprised.

'Yes. Right after the audience with Khalid.'

'That son of a bitch doesn't miss a bet. What did he want?'

'Nothing. Just suggested that we get together for dinner sometime.'

'Well, don't.'

'Why not?'

'Look, Riyadh is a very small town. The government people will know every move you make. Prince Abdullah is bad news. That's why Khalid has parked him in that obscure ministry. If your name gets connected with his, then . . .' He waved a finger past his throat.

'I trust you mean that figuratively.'

'Right now, yes. Later, who knows?'

'All right, Falk. I'll keep it in mind. Now how come Abdullah is considered so dangerous?'

'He's got some of the top men in the Saudi army behind him. And unless things change, he'll soon have all of them.'

'What's the army's beef against Khalid?'

'Do you know the size of the Saudi Arabian military forces?'

'Frankly, no.'

'Thirty-six thousand men, for chrissake. Plus a local militia of about 25,000. It's pitiful. Iran's got 250,000 regulars, and another 300,000 reserves. Iraq can field over a quarter of a million men, given a couple of weeks' notice. Egypt has 300,000 regulars; Syria has 150,000. Even Jordan – Jordan, for God's sake – has a larger army than Saudi Arabia.' Falk was really disgusted.

'Why?'

'Because Khalid's clever. It's easy to keep a small army under control. So he keeps it small. And the brass does not like it.'

'And Abdullah has offered to let them off the leash. Provided they help him.'

'Exactly.'

'So why aren't you guys backing Abdullah? He seems like your type.'

'Now watch it, Hitchcock,' said Falk. Then, 'There is another element here. As I said, Khalid is no dummy. He knows that he needs a defense system. But instead of building it internally, he – like his predecessor Faisal – has been consistently contracting for his key military personnel abroad. Especially from the United States. Mercenaries are safe. They don't get involved in revolutions against the fellows who are paying their wages. American mercenaries are probably the safest of all. They are not free lances, like those you can hire almost anywhere in Europe these days. They are government-sponsored, and directly or indirectly controlled by the Pentagon.'

'How many are here?'

'Right now, there are just over four thousand regular American military personnel here. They come under the mutual-assistance pact between the U.S. and the Saudis – ostensibly to train the local army, but actually to occupy the key command posts. Then there are about fifteen hundred "irregulars" – old Vietnam professionals who are over here under the auspices of a Los Angeles outfit, Vinnel Corporation. They were originally contracted for back in 1975, again to "teach" the Saudi militia how to guard the Ghawar oil fields. They are still here. Then there are about twelve hundred technicians – mostly ex-air force – who man the air-defense system and keep this country's aircraft and missile system in shape. They are paid by McDonnell Douglas, Bell Helicopter, Litton Industries, Hughes Aircraft and a few other American defense contractors. If you add everybody up, it works out to a situation where there is one American involved in the defense organization here for every four Saudis in the regular army.'

'A bit like it used to be in Vietnam in the good old days,' I suggested.

Falk passed that one up and continued : 'So you see, we control the situation here in partnership with Khalid. As long as he stays we stay. As long as we stay, the Persian Gulf remains stable. But like I said, this whole situation irks the hell out of the local brass. They hate us just like the Egyptian high command hated the Russians when they controlled the military situation in that country. Of course, this is the fiddle Abdullah is playing on. If he manages to take over, we will be out on our asses within a month. Then look out !'

'Falk, how about another martini ?'

'Good idea.'

The colonel served it with an olive – the only local ingredient.

'So,' I asked, after we had settled down again, 'how do you fellows plan on keeping your pal Khalid and therefore ourselves in, and Abdullah out ?'

'By trying to get the king to give the military brass here what they want. Double the size of the army. And the air force. Get a real Saudi navy in the water. Equip the bastards to the hilt. That will calm them down so much they won't even notice us. They'd love Khalid, and forget Abdullah and his brothers. And we would have peace on the Gulf for a hell of a long time.'

'I see,' a bit skeptically.

'Why not?' asked Falk, getting excited. 'The king has got money coming out of his ears. Why should it just sit around in banks? It's stupid. Look at the Shah. He has the biggest and best damned army between Europe and China. He's been spending three or four billion dollars a year on them – just for new equipment, for God's sake. That's what Khalid must do.'

'Three or four billion a year, huh?'

'Sure,' said Falk. 'Maybe even a little bit more. All he'd have to do is push the button, and the Pentagon would take care of the rest. In a couple of years we'd have a real good operation here.'

'And where do I fit into all this?' I knew by now, but why not get it out into the open.

'Look, Dr. Hitchcock, we've heard about your new position. All we are suggesting is that you examine the situation here in the light of what I have told you. I'm sure you'll come to the conclusion that what Khalid needs is a crash military budget. Tell him so. His people will listen to you. You'll be doing both countries a favor.'

'Falk, I think maybe you fellows overrate my importance. I'm just a simple banker, hired to do a specific job.'

'I know. But nothing in this country is simple. Just remember what I've told you, and think it over. This place is ready to blow, one way or the other, very soon, unless big changes are made. Then you'll be working for either the Shah or Abdullah. *I* don't think you'd like that.'

Falk got up. 'Come on out into the kitchen, Hitchcock. I've got the biggest damned steak you've ever seen, right from the commissary of the Rhine-Main base in Germany. We can just keep drinking while I cook.'

We did. When I got back to the hotel around midnight I was slightly smashed. But not so far gone that I did not notice the little guy in the lobby tracking me as I weaved my way to the elevator. Maybe Colonel Falk knew what he was talking about.

CHAPTER FIVE

I found out later that Falk had also been right about the Shah of Iran. At precisely the same time – November of 1978 – the Shah was in the process of adding the final touches to his war machine, which, indeed, was one of the most powerful in the world. It was also a machine which the Shah fully intended to use. For Mohammed Riza Pahlavi, the King of Kings of Persia, was not the most stable of men. In fact, as far back as 1974, *Time* magazine quoted the then U.S. Secretary of the Treasury, William Simon, as describing the Shah as 'an irresponsible and reckless . . . nut.'

His hang-ups were, as is usually the case, rooted in his personal history. Despite the grandiose title, he was actually nothing more than the son of an obscure Iranian colonel –a man who was actually an illiterate until adulthood – who had lucked it out in a rebellion against the real Persian dynasty, the Qajars, in 1921. The colonel promptly crowned himself emperor, and, to give himself a bit of badly needed class, changed his name to Pahlavi, the word used to describe the ancient Persian language. As the new ruler of Iran, he did all right until World War II, when he bet on his fellow Aryan, Hitler, instead of Churchill. In August of 1941, British and Russian troops moved in, kicked the ex-colonel off his throne, and installed his twenty-three-year-old son, Mohammed, as their puppet.

Not exactly a glorious beginning for a King of Kings.

Eventually the foreign occupation ended, and Mohammed was on his own. But only for a short time. In 1952 along came Mossadegh as Prime Minister of Iran, a man with ideas well ahead of his time. Mossadegh's main program was to nationalize Iran's oil fields, and install himself as Iran's new strong man. The Shah, of course, did not like this, but since he lacked any popular support in his own country there was nothing he could do about it. However, there was another ruler who also did not like Mossadegh's ideas – the newly installed American President, General Eisenhower. What was bad for Standard Oil was obviously also bad for the United States. So Eisenhower sent in the CIA. They organized a military revolt that lasted three days. Mossadegh ended up in jail, and the Shah was once again secure on his throne, this time as a puppet of the Americans.

During the next decade, and beyond, the Shah remained a puppet of America. He did what the Americans told him, because it was only through American aid that Iran's economy was kept afloat.

So the King of Kings, probably out of frustration, took a fling at becoming the Playboy of the Eastern world. After dumping his first wife, the sister of King Farouk, he took on that dark-haired beauty from Germany, Soraya. For years during the 1950's they spent more time abroad than in Iran, hitting the party circuit, their usual round starting in Beirut, moving on to Rome, Cannes, Paris, and London, and ending up in New York. Then they would start over again. Come winter, the pair would set up house in St. Moritz, and break the monotony with occasional side trips to Gstaad, Zermatt and Klosters.

Soraya developed into the darling of the German *Hausfrau*. Her picture was on the cover of at least one mass circulation German illustrated every week for years – until 1959, when, to gasps of horror on the Rhine, the Shah divorced her. The reason : she had failed to bear him an heir. The Shah was approaching middle age and, if nothing else, he wanted to preserve the ancient Pahlavi lineage, which by then stretched back all of thirty-eight years.

So he married a twenty-one-year-old girl, scouted out for him by his friend Adahir Zahedi, then ambassador to France, later the Shah's envoy to the United States. She was a student at the Sorbonne at the time. Farah Diva, as she became known, was a smashing success in all respects. First, she bore children promptly and regularly – both

28

male and female. Second, she was lovely. And third, she was eminently presentable in the best of circles. So the Shah moved up to the jet set and beyond. In the early 1960's the Shah and his Diva were repeatedly entertained in the White House by the Kennedys; in the latter part of that decade by the Johnsons; by 1969 when Pat and Dick took over, the Shah, his medals, his uniforms, his caviar had become standard fare in Washington.

But nobody really took him seriously. Then came the 1973 bombshell. The Arabs put an embargo on oil exports to the West, and within months, in the most successful blackmail attempt in the history of the world, had forced through a quadrupling of the petroleum price. True to his past, the Shah contributed nothing to his coup. In fact, he despised the Arabs. But once the danger of possible Western military intervention subsided, he suddenly stepped front and center and became the self-appointed spokesman for OPEC, the Organization of Petroleum Exporting Countries, the oil cartel that emerged in 1974 on the heels of the Arab victory.

The Shah was now rich beyond belief. At the new price of over ten dollars a barrel, he was taking in $30 billion a year. He was a recognized leader of the world power elite of the future. He soon had Europe cringing at his feet. He was surrounded by delegations of bowing and scraping Japanese, desperate for Iran's petroleum. He was praised by Giscard D'Estaing, embraced by Harold Wilson, sumptuously entertained by Gerald Ford. His utterances were carefully documented by C. L. Sulzberger (with reserve), by William Hearst (with enthusiasm), by *Time* magazine (with pictures).

The King of Kings had arrived.

And the surfacing of his arrogance, born of his insecurity, followed almost immediately. When murmurs of his abuse of power started to arise, the real Shah could now speak back. 'Nobody,' he said, 'can wave a finger at us, because we will wave back.'

By the fall of 1978, the Shah was almost ready to wave. His aim : to establish Iran as a superpower. On November

5 of that year, he held a key meeting in his palace in Teheran that was to prove the key to his success or failure.

At stake were atomic weapons. Making atomic bombs is very simple, once you have the most deadly of known materials, plutonium. You need a hunk about the size of a baseball. The large atomic power reactors, built by Westinghouse or General Electric in the United States, or by Framatome in France, each produce such a baseball-sized quantity every three days. In 1974, France had contracted to build two such reactors for Iran, at a cost of $2 billion each. By the fall of 1978 both systems were working. By this November 5 of 1978, they had produced enough plutonium for about forty bombs – not big ones, but large enough to destroy the centers of New York and Moscow, or all of such small cities as Riyadh or Kuwait. A couple of them dropped at the right height could completely demolish any fleet that might seek to steam through the straits of Hormuz into the Persian Gulf.

The meeting was attended by three men in addition to the Shah. They were General Reza Barami, head of Iran's air force; Brigadier Shabanah, chief of the Iranian air-sea strike force on the Persian Gulf; and Professor Hadjevi Baraheni, head of the Iranian Atomic Energy Authority.

'But can you be sure they will work?'

This question was being put again to Baraheni. And the professor's answers were always hedged. 'I cannot be sure, Your Majesty. Nor can anyone. Unless we test at least one, preferably three.'

'Impossible,' answered the Shah. 'I have told you time and time again, that will be impossible.'

He turned to his chief military advisor, General Barami. 'Barami, you know my schedule.'

'Yes, Your Majesty.'

'Well then, think. Get an answer. Now!'

Barami was a strategist, not a scientist or even a weapons man. But he was shrewd. 'Well, first of all, Your Majesty, I think we should all agree that in this venture we cannot trust our own scientists. They are all second-rate.'

30

The professor was ready to protest, but one glance at the Shah put that thought out of his mind.

'Secondly,' continued Barami, 'we all know that building atomic weapons has become a relatively simple matter in the United States and Western Europe. I have heard that there are literally thousands of scientists – both physicists and chemists – who could do it with very little equipment, provided they had clean plutonium. Is that not so, Baraheni?'

The professor agreed, and added, 'We have at least a dozen men right here in Teheran, including myself, who could do the same.'

'Then,' interjected the Shah, 'why do you insist on testing?'

The professor chose not to answer.

'Your Majesty,' continued General Barami, 'I understand Professor Baraheni. He simply has not had the experience. We must get someone who has. Furthermore, as you know, we need more than crude atomic weapons. I have discussed my needs with you.'

The Shah nodded.

'I suggest,' said the general, 'that we get one of the very best men in either America or Europe – one whom we know has mastered this business. We pay him a monumental sum, lock him up for a month here in Teheran with some of Baraheni's men at the Institute, and we shall have bombs that work – without testing.'

'But that involves risk. What if the man talks?'

'Once he is in Teheran he won't be able to. SAVAK will insure that.'

'But beforehand? Before he agrees to come?' queried the Shah.

'Your Majesty, money can buy anything. You have had bankers, oil men, industrialists – the most powerful men from the West – fawning over you, making fools of themselves right here in this palace, for the sake of one thing : money. Scientists are no different. You have just not met any. Western people are all very greedy. All of them.'

31

'I know,' replied the Shah. 'It is one of their most disgusting traits. But who are the most greedy?'

Barami thought it over. 'The Americans and the Swiss,' he answered.

Now it was the Shah's turn to ponder. 'Barami, as usual you are right. But we cannot risk using an American. It must be a Swiss.' The Shah paused. 'Professor Baraheni, where do we find such a man in Switzerland?'

'I don't agree with . . .'

'You are not being asked to agree or disagree. Answer my question.'

'Yes, Your Majesty. I would suggest Roche-Bollinger Company. That is the heavy electric-equipment producer located just outside of Zurich in Baden. They make atomic reactors for power generation and export throughout the world. They also produce weapons. Conventional weapons.'

'Can you get some names?' asked the Shah.

'Well, I could . . .' hesitantly.

'I think we should turn that problem over to SAVAK,' said Brigadier Shabanah – his first words of the meeting.

SAVAK, run by Fawzi Tehrani, was the largest secret police *cum* espionage organization outside of the Soviet Union, controlled directly by the Shah. Brigadier Shabanah had spent ten years with that agency before taking over his military command on the Gulf.

'You are right. Get hold of Tehrani right away. I want him here within the hour. You may now leave.'

The three men went into a collective bow and backed out of the Shah's chambers in that position. Incredible in 1978, but true.

CHAPTER SIX

Had I known what was going on in Teheran that week, I would hardly have gone to Rome. In fact, I would have gone right back to California and gotten drunk.

But at that time, naively, my concern was not war, but money. Saudi Arabia's money. And in November of 1978, it looked like a lot of it was going down the drain. The Italian drain.

Just when my cleanup operation in Riyadh was starting to proceed nicely, I received a call from Herr Doktor Reichenberger, chairman of the Leipziger Bank in Frankfurt. His message was short. The Italians were going to default on their foreign loans – the whole monumental string of them – unless somebody once again bailed them out with yet more billions of dollars. Germany – that is, Germany's banks with the backing of their government – had done this three times before, out of solidarity with a Common Market partner. But they would not do so again, Reichenberger informed me. Italy was essentially a bankrupt nation. There was no sense in throwing more good money after bad. The West German cabinet had met that morning and told Reichenberger that the government would provide no new guarantees. That meant that the commercial banks in Germany would have to organize their own salvage operation. The Leipziger Bank was in deepest, so Reichenberger was the organizer. Why his call to me? Because Saudi Arabia, according to Reichenberger's estimate, had thus far put around $3.5 billion into Italian loans. The Saudi Arabian Monetary Agency was, therefore, after Germany, Italy's second-largest creditor. He then listed the groups of banks in other countries which had at least a billion plus at stake. A spokesman from each group was being invited to a meeting in Rome, to start at 10 A.M., Friday, November 12, at the German Embassy. A government spokesman from each country would also be present. Would Saudi Arabia wish to be represented?

Definitely, I stated. By either myself or the head of the Saudi Arabian Monetary Agency, Prince al-Kuraishi, or both.

Dr. Reichenberger hardly thought it necessary to suggest that the entire matter be kept from the press. Then he hung up.

Reichenberger was right about Saudi Arabia's exposure in Italy. It amounted to exactly $3.55 billion, according to the books in Riyadh. The debtors included the Italian Treasury; the cities of Rome, Milan, Turin, Florence, and Naples; IRI, the state industrial conglomerate, plus a string of IRI subsidiaries, including the company that operated the Italian Autostradas; Alfa Romeo, the automotive producers; FINSIDER, the combine that controlled most of the steel companies in Italy. All loans had one thing in common : they had been issued with the understanding that they were backed by the 'moral obligation' of the Italian state.

Starting in the mid-1960's, these Italian institutions had begun borrowing heavily in the Eurodollar market, that is, borrowing American dollars from European banking institutions. The banks almost fell over themselves trying to get into the loan syndicates. After all, what could be safer than loans to governmental or quasi-governmental agencies of a major Western European nation? Especially one that was in the midst of an economic miracle, its GNP growing at 10 percent plus each and every year, at least *almost* every year. Italy was the Japan of the West!

So in poured the billions, usually on a ten- to fifteen-year basis, at interest of around 8 percent. At first, the large merchant banks in London monopolized this business – until it outgrew even them. Then, increasingly, it was the so-called consortium banks in London, Paris, and Brussels which provided Italy with more and more billions. This type of institution was also a child of the mid-1960's. The idea was this : If a group of very large banks from different countries – say Chase Manhattan from New York, Deutsche

Bank from Frankfurt, Crédit Lyonnais from Paris, the Union Bank of Switzerland from Zurich – got together, and set up a joint subsidiary, this new type of 'daughter bank' would have almost unlimited credit, because of the immense power and resources of the parents. The concept became especially attractive when it was discovered that such banks could be founded with very little capital, and that even if the consortium bank took on huge deposits, and made huge loans – such as those to Italy – the European authorities did not insist that the parents keep feeding in more and more capital to keep pace with the growth of the bank. Terrific, everybody thought. Not exactly prudent, but very profitable. And they had very fancy names: Orion, Midland and International Banks Ltd. (MAIBL), Union de Banques Arabes et Françaises, Western American Bank (Europe), and so forth and so on. By the mid-1970's there were over thirty such institutions – many handling billions of dollars. All were predominantly backed not by paid-in capital, but by the capital and reputation of the parent banks back home. A highly sophisticated inverse pyramid device.

The problem was, if one of those consortium banks went under, who would bail them out? Not H.M. government, even though most were in London, because for the most part they were owned by non-British institutions. Not the Common Market, since the Common Market had no banking authority. Not the United States, even though many large American banks were involved – and heavily involved – in these inverse pyramid banks in Europe, because after all, they were in Europe.

No; ultimately if something went wrong, it would be the shareholders and depositors back in New York or Toronto or Zurich who would get stuck with the bill. And that was unthinkable. So, for the most part the managers of these multibillion-dollar consortium banks were given very strict guidelines. Stick to safe borrowers. And what could be safer than loans backed by the moral obligation of the government of one of Europe's largest countries? Especially, they reasoned, because under no circumstances would the

35

West ever let Italy go down the financial tube. There was also the matter of profit. The banks cleaned up on the Italians. On average, they took 3 percent of the face value of each loan, paid on the front end, to 'set up' the deal. That amounted to $30 million for each billion floated, their fee for what essentially amounted to a couple of weeks of paperwork, and a lot of phone calls to other banks in the issuing syndicate. Then, year after year, at least 8 percent interest – which was great, since for many years they were able to borrow or 'buy' the dollars at only 5 percent.

A sure and highly profitable thing. Until the middle of the 1970's. Then, one after another, those astute European bankers started asking themselves the same simple question: 'How are the Italians ever going to pay back all our loans?'

And nobody had an answer. So the spigot was turned off, at least by the commercial banks and their joint daughters, the consortium banks.

'Let the Common Market take care of Italy for a while,' was their attitude. And their prayer was that when the commercial loans started to come due – in 1979 – the Common Market would also supply Italy with enough dollars to start paying them back. The powerful bank lobby went to work, and the Common Market – actually, it was almost exclusively the government of West Germany – stepped in. Germany lent Italy the billions it needed for a few years. But not blindly. The Germans are the most prudent financiers in the world. They demanded collateral. First, part of Italy's gold reserves; later, all of them. Still Italy needed money to stay afloat : to buy oil, to buy wheat, to buy whiskey, Italy being the largest importer of Scotch in the world next to the United States. Then Saudi Arabia stepped in with its help.

Over lunch I discussed the entire matter with al-Kuraishi. He was highly disturbed. Saudi Arabia had lent that much money to Italy not out of greed – as had the London bankers. When Italy's oil bill had gone sky-high after the 1973 embargo – it bought its oil exclusively from the Middle East and Libya – the United States and Europe had strongly urged Saudi Arabia to help that country by recycling petrodollars back to Italy, that is, by taking a portion of the dollars Italy was paying the Saudis for petroleum and lending it back to Italian institutions. Saudi Arabia had cooperated to the tune of $3.5 billion in commercial loans. But with the quite definite understanding that both America and Europe would stand behind Italy's debt. Morally.

'So much for Western morals,' concluded the prince.

What could I do but agree? But maybe something could be salvaged.

Maybe, al-Kuraishi agreed. And maybe they would try to blackmail the Arabs into bailing everybody else out. He would not go to Rome under such conditions. I was to go alone.

My instructions were to commit myself to nothing, and preferably say nothing. I was to be a technical observer. I should also keep in touch.

I left for Rome on the 5 P.M. flight and got there just before midnight, after a stopover in Beirut. Italy was a relief after Riyadh. I did not even mind the ridiculous chaos at Fiumicino airport. After a week in Saudi Arabia, it was glorious to see women in public again, particularly Italian women with their hands, hair, and especially skirts, flying. It was even fun to see billboards advertising Cinzano and White Label Scotch instead of Phillips radios and Hondas.

In the cab on the long way into town, I decided on my order of priorities: first a drink, then a piece of ass.

The bar at the Hassler was still open, though barely, so I managed the drink. But – and believe me, it worried me – I decided that I was simply too tired to go to the trouble of getting laid. My ex-wife would have laughed herself silly at the very thought, the frigid old bitch.

I think her problems – by the way, her name was Anne – all stemmed from religion. She was Catholic. Not *a* Catholic, but *Catholic*. My father warned me. But when you are twenty-one, who believes that stuff? We met at Georgetown University. I was there because of their Foreign Service School; she was there because it was run

37

by the Jesuits. We got married in my senior year. That fall we went to London together. That winter I had my first extramarital affair. It was a marriage made in hell.

I made it to the embassy the next morning a few minutes before ten, rested and by now mildly horny. The mood inside matched that outside: Italy in November can be a very cold and depressing place. The conference room had been furnished at great expense, and with no elegance – strictly Knoll International from wall to wall. The seating arrangements reflected another feature of the modern German soul – respect for money. Herr Doktor Reichenberger had taken over the chair at the head. To his right were the Americans. To his left, Saudi Arabia, meaning me. On my left were the British (which shows how far that country had slipped); vis-à-vis the British were, of course, the French. Next tier down were Iran and the Japanese, something that obviously pissed off the two men from Teheran. Then the Dutch and Swiss; finally, Belgium and the Canadians.

There they were: the eleven countries that controlled the capital of the world. The bottom of the table had been given Italy – our Judas Iscariot!

There were two men in each delegation: one representing the respective government involved, usually a high official from either the treasury or the central bank; the other, the head of the 'lead' bank in the various countries, i.e., the commercial bank which had stuck its neck out farthest on Italy, either directly or via its participation in one of the consortium banks, or both. Saudi Arabia was the exception, since the government treasury, central bank, and commercial bank were synonymous, combined in that one institution which I represented, the Saudi Arabian Monetary Agency. Not a few men in the room gave me rather curious glances when the introductions were being made by the Herr Chairman. It ran through my mind that the Japanese were probably going crazy trying to figure out how an Arab had ended up with the name of Hitchcock.

By noon everybody but me (I had passed) and the

Italians had had their say. No promises of anything from anybody. So the head of the local delegation went into his pitch. All Italy needed was a couple of billion dollars. Otherwise it could not buy the food it needed in 1979 from America and Europe, nor the fuel it needed from the Arabs. In addition, it would not – could not – pay any further interest on any of the outstanding Eurodollar loans – all $16 billion of them. Nor, he continued, could it even consider repaying any of the commercial loans which were made in the 1960's and were now, unfortunately, coming due in 1979. About $2.6 billion of the latter, he believed.

'But,' interjected the treasury man from Bern, 'you need not only "a couple of billion" as you so lightly suggest. You need much more !'

Clever chaps, the Swiss. They can add very quickly, if their own money is on the line.

Well, answered the Italian, if the gentleman from the North insisted on being so precise, actually they could use maybe four billion. That should see them through 1979. Or at least most of it.

'*Vier Milliarden dollars!*' screamed Herr Doktor Reichenberger, lapsing from his role as the neutral chairman and lapsing into the use of his native tongue. '*Das ist unmöglich!*'

Ja, ja, nodded the Dutch and Swiss and one Belgian, who was Flemish. That was definitely *unmöglich*.

Now the fellows who were really upset were not the government representatives, the bureaucrats secure in their little lifetime niches, but the commercial bankers – the hotshot men in gray who had been doling out their unsuspecting depositors' money like candy for years, more interested in being royally entertained in Rome, Milan, and Florence – with wives, of course – than in realistically calculating whether they were lending or giving the bank's money. It was the future of their banks, no, worse – of their jobs running those banks – which might be at stake.

The same painful thoughts were obviously going through ten heads at the same time. By painful, it should not be inferred that any one of them was worried about whether the Italians froze and starved in 1979. No, their reasoning went like this (and I could not blame them – I used to be a commercial banker myself) : If Italy does not get a very large new loan from somebody, it will not be able to pay back those loans coming due. That means writing off $2.6 billion. Bad, but not impossible. However, if Italy also stops all interest payments on the remaining loans outstanding –$14-odd billion – then all those loans will be reclassified by the auditors. First, as 'non-income-producing,' then as 'dubious'; finally, for God's sake, as bad debts that had to be written off, immediately and in their entirety. Which would wipe out the bank's reserves and capital, plus some. Maybe Chase and First National City would survive, but even they would be seriously wounded. There would be absolute chaos in London. And out of the wreckage would come lawsuits, class actions accusing them of mismanagement, of fraud! Christ! Ruined for life just because of these fucking Italians!

One of the Canadians broke the silence that had suddenly enveloped the entire room. 'But,' he said, addressing the head of the Italian treasury, 'your government is morally obligated to pay back these loans.'

At first he just received a look of pity for such a display of naiveté. Then the words from the Italian government spokesman : 'With what?'

With what indeed! They had neither dollars nor gold. Maybe the Germans could take Venice, the Swiss Florence, and the Americans Sicily. Nobody, obviously, would want Naples.

'But,' continued the Italian, 'perhaps the American government, in its tradition of generosity, mindful of the strategic importance of Italy in NATO, and cognizant of the possibility that a financial panic might ensue if nothing is done, would guarantee such a loan of four billion dollars?' A rather long question. But perhaps a ray of light.

Until one of Harvard's best, the Undersecretary of the Treasury of the United States of America, spoke out : 'Congress would not stand for it.' So much for America's generosity.

'But,' hedged the American, 'perhaps they could be persuaded to contribute something, provided those countries with huge dollar surpluses would do their share.'

I could sense that all eyes were starting to drift in two directions : toward me and toward the men from Iran. After all, as everyone in the room knew, $4 billion amounted to not even a month's income for the two major oil powers on the Persian Gulf.

Fortunately for me, the head of the central bank of Iran sensed what was coming, and in a preemptive strike lashed out at the man from Harvard.

'You,' he said, pointing a finger, 'also have a moral obligation regarding the loans we have given your ally, Italy. Iran, and its brother nations on the Persian Gulf, will hold you to this obligation.'

A bluff, but a good one. The Undersecretary from Washington looked to his German ally for help. But the good Herr Doktor Reichenberger was hardly going to argue with the Iranians. Iran had billions of dollars on deposit – short-term deposit – with his bank back in Frankfurt. So did the 'brethren' on the Gulf : Kuwait, Abu Dhabi, Qatar, and of course, Saudi Arabia. His bank needed these petrodollars desperately – especially if a new financial crisis was brewing here in Rome. On the other hand, it was America's army in Germany that stood between Frankfurt and the Russians.

Hobson's choice for Herr Doktor Reichenberger. He looked at me. I shook my head. My instructions had been quite clear.

So he simply suggested that the meeting be adjourned until the following day, same time, same place. I left without saying a word to anyone.

When I got back to the Hassler, I immediately phoned al-Kuraishi in Riyadh and explained the situation. He took it calmly. He asked about Iran. I told him what their position had been. Somewhat less calmly, the prince told me that I must be very careful to avoid any identification whatsoever with the Iranian position. Was that clear? It was. Perhaps, al-Kuraishi suggested, I could come up with some interim solution.

I went down to the bar.

She was sitting at the end, alone. Dark hair, well built, early thirties, wearing a Pucci pants suit. Nice nose. So much for her profile. It was enough to interest a dirty old man fresh from the Arabian desert.

'Mind if I sit down?'

'Not at all.' She had an accent, one that I could not place.

'Are you French?'

'No, Swiss.'

'And what are you doing in Rome?' Hardly a new routine, but it is one that has worked the world over a million times.

'I'm with my father. He's attending a conference here.'

'Really. What does he do?'

'He's a physicist. Nuclear. With the Eidgenoessische Technische Hochschule. In Zurich.'

'Fascinating,' I lied. 'And you?'

'Do you mean what do I do?'

'Yes.'

'Nothing, really. Look after my father at home. Travel with him when he goes abroad. Do a little writing. Help out with some of my people's charities.'

'What people is that?'

'I'm Jewish,' rather defiantly. 'Or more precisely, half Jewish. My mother. She's dead.'

A solemn pause for the deceased. Then : 'What you said interests me. But please tell me if I am treading on something awkward.'

'Go ahead,' she said, looking straight at me in that direct manner which is so typically Swiss.

'But wait a minute,' I said. 'I haven't even ordered yet.'
I ordered a martini. The guy gave me a glass of warm vermouth. So we started again, and I ended up with a glass of warm gin with one tiny ice cube in it. The life of an expatriate is sometimes hell! 'Now where were we?' I asked.

'You were going to ask me something awkward.'

'Right.' Sipping my piss-warm martini and remembering just in time the new story line. 'Yes, what puzzled me is why you regard yourself as a Jew when your father is not a Jew.'

'You surprise me. You *look* like a fairly educated man.'

'Do I?'

'Don't you know anything about Judaism?'

'Of course. I've read the Bible. What the hell's the point?'

'The point is that it is the *mother* who determines whether the child is Jewish or not. The child of a Jewish mother and a non-Jewish father is Jewish, but the reverse is not true.'

'OK. I've learned something. So you were born a Jew.'

'It's not just the circumstances of my birth. I would be a Jew in any case.'

'Why?'

'Because I admire what Jews stand for. They feel they are God's chosen people, and they act accordingly. They are different from other people and proud of it. This world may corrupt almost anything, but it has not corrupted my people.'

She was coming on rather strong. And I really never give that much of a damn about religious stuff. But what she had just said was a bit much on top of a warm martini and a frustrating morning.

'Frankly,' I said, 'I find that rather hard to agree with. The Jews are like everybody else where money is concerned. In fact, more so. You can buy a Jew just like you can buy an Arab, an Italian, or an Eskimo.'

She looked at me with a rather annoying, supercilious smirk. 'What exactly do *you* do?' she asked.

'You obviously think that has something to do with what I have just said?'

'Yes.'

'Well, I'm a banker.'

Again the smirk, indicating rather clearly that I fitted

43

quite precisely her definition of a WASP money changer. 'In New York?' she queried further.

'No. Riyadh.'

For the first time, there was a real flicker of interest in her brown eyes. 'You mean you work with the Arabs?'

'No,' I replied. 'For them.'

'But you are American.'

'Yes.'

'Don't you sometimes wake up in the morning hating yourself?'

'No. Why should I?'

'First let me ask you this : Why are you working for the Arabs?'

'For money.' This was not precisely true, but so what?

'That I would term prostitution.'

'And?'

'What do you mean?'

'What's wrong with prostitution?'

'Now you're putting me on.'

'No. I'm serious.'

'Because it is debasing. Not that I blame the men. I just feel – and very strongly – that a woman should always maintain her pride in herself, starting with her body.'

'Under any and all circumstances,' I added.

'Yes. But I hardly expect you to understand that, since the people for whom you work treat their goats better than their women.' Now those brown eyes were really flashing !

'So to sum up what you've been telling me, you first believe that you cannot buy Jews with money. And secondly, that it is unthinkable for a person like you to sleep with a man for money.'

'I did not exactly say that. But OK. That's a fair statement of what I think.'

'Let me back up a bit. You said that you were interested in charities. Jewish charities.'

'Yes. Predominantly those organizations which support the emigration of Jews from Eastern Europe, especially Russia. But what has that got to do with what we have been discussing?'

44

'I'll get to it in a minute. Now, how much does it cost, on average, to liberate one Jew from the Communists?'

'I'm sure that has never been calculated.'

'Take a guess.'

'Starting with the initial organization, the cost of transportation, the expense of resettlement in Israel, I would say at least ten thousand dollars a person.'

'You strongly believe in that sort of mission?'

'I consider it,' she said, 'one of the most important aspects of my life.'

'How would you like to liberate two Jews tonight?'

'I don't understand.'

'OK, I will restate it. You can earn enough this evening to provide a new life for two fellow Israelites in Eastern Europe. At ten thousand dollars a head!'

'Don't be absurd!'

'I'm not.'

She was getting just a trifle excited. You could tell by the way her tongue moved nervously over her lips.

'How?'

'By spending one hour with me upstairs.'

'You are suggesting that you are willing to pay twenty thousand dollars just to sleep with me once?'

'I did not specify that it would only be once. I said . . .'

'That's disgusting!'

'I don't think so. Nor will those Jews. If one of them turns out to be female – and I hope it does – she would be willing to do a lot worse things than screwing an American in a Moscow hotel to get out of Russia.'

'You're sick!'

'No. I'm serious. And quite realistic about how this world goes round.'

She sat there for a full minute in silence, just looking at me.

'May I ask your name?' I finally ventured.

'I am hardly going to tell you after this conversation!'

'All right. Mine is Hitchcock. Bill Hitchcock.' I put out my hand.

And she took it, after more than a slight pause. 'I'm Ursula Hartmann.'

'Ursula. Very Swiss.'

'Yes. And I hate it.'

'I don't know. It's better than Heidi.'

'That is my second name.' And she said it with a grin.

Right then her father walked into the bar – the good Herr Professor Hartmann himself. Another man was with him : tall, blond, open shirt, around forty. He could have easily played the role of a British tank commander in a war film – not exactly the type you would expect to see hanging around Professor Hartmann, although where his daughter was concerned . . .

Both men sat on Ursula's right, and immediately the threesome started to converse in German. There was not the slightest movement indicating that she had any intention of introducing me. So after ten minutes I left, with the nagging feeling that I had made an ass of myself – hardly for the first time.

Back to work I went. Prince al-Kuraishi had suggested that I come up with something. OK, I would. Maybe nothing very permanent. But so what? Who has ever come up with something permanent?

My personal analysis, developed over the years, of Italy was this : Ever since World War II that country and its economy had resembled a man tied to a waterwheel. Up and around, and then a cold, wet dunking. But nothing fatal. All he had to do was hold his breath for a while. Then he was off once again into the giddy world of the illusion of eternal wealth. Until the next dunking.

So all we had to do was, once again, buy Italy some time. Maybe I should make a few calls – try to put together a new short-term facility, say a couple of billion – some payable now, the rest on standby. Perhaps for six months, with an option to renew for another six. Then there would be no defaults on the old loans. After all, that was why the Saudis had hired me – to help put out financial fires. I was sure that al-Kuraishi would agree to the Saudis' putting up a good piece of the action, say a half billion.

First I got on to Henri Duvillard, chairman of the Banque Nationale de Paris. He had kept very quiet at the meeting. It took about a half hour to find him with the help of the local French Embassy. Then it took less than two minutes, once I had him. He said *Non* three times, and that was it. The fucking French never could see beyond their long noses. So I rang the chairman of Barclays. He liked the idea, but his bank simply could not afford to put up the funds. I tried to get Reichenberger, but he was out, and his embassy had no idea where. I left messages all over the place and sat there in my hotel room getting frustrated. Finally he called back. Yes, he could get the large commercial banks in Germany to agree to one more big loan. Provided there was collateral. But the Italians had nothing to offer. They had explained that, I pointed out. Exactly, Reichenberger replied. But no collateral, no further loans. How about talking the government in Bonn into providing one more guarantee? No dice. His government had been quite firm on that. But, he concluded, if I came up with anything new – anything – he would be ready to discuss it. Anywhere.

Well, that was a start. And time for a bit of staff work. We – by that I mean the Saudis – had a small operation in Rome, to monitor the loans in Italy, and to keep a hand in with the Italian banking community. I called the head of the local office and made two requests : to compile a complete dossier on one of Italy's major corporations, and to arrange for the hand delivery of another item.

Then I called up the number two man at the American Embassy. He'd been there for at least fifteen years, watching various nitwit ambassadors come and go. And believe me, the United States has sent some dandies to Rome! Anyway, his wife was a cousin of my ex-wife, and like my former spouse, she had a lot of money and not much else. But that did not matter to him, since I think he liked boys. At least that was the impression I had gained when he and Priscilla (no kidding) had shown up at my old house in San Francisco now and then, mooching their way around the States during his periodic home leave. My ex loved it,

47

since she used to parade him around town as if he was a papist version of Henry Kissinger.

That part was all right, I guess. What was not all right were the hang-ups. Anne had dozens of them, and most related to the bedroom. They say that it is either money or sex which ultimately causes marriages to fall apart. In our case it was not money.

But so what? The point was that it was now my turn to get at least a little back. I invited him out to dinner, with very precise instructions not to bring Priscilla along. We ate in the rooftop restaurant of the Hassler. By ten o'clock I had learned all I needed to know about who was really running the finances of the country at that particular moment, and what their going rates were. Then I sent him packing.

When I returned to the room, both packages I had requested from the local Saudis were there.

So why not give it a try?

CHAPTER SEVEN

Her phone only rang twice before she picked it up. '*Ja?*' she answered.

'It's me. Bill Hitchcock.'

'And what do *you* want?'

'To continue our conversation.'

'That is out of the question.'

'What do you mean?'

'I have to wait for my father. He's not yet back from dinner.'

'Where did you eat?'

'In the room.'

'In Rome you eat in your room? Rather boring I would think.'

'A bit, yes.'

'Look, why don't you come on up and have a nightcap. I'm in 720–21.'

'I told you, Mr. Hitchcock . . .'

'Bill.'

'It is impossible, just as I said.'

'All right. But if you change your mind, just come on up and walk in. I plan on being up for a while. Reading.'

It was true. I had a one-hundred-page dossier to go through. I made it to page thirty when somebody knocked on the door. And when I opened it, there stood Ursula Hartmann. This time she was not wearing pants. She had on a rather starchy white blouse and a plain blue skirt. Looked like a goddam girl guide.

I had on a dressing gown – and nothing else. My Flash Gordon outfit.

'Welcome,' I said, shaking her hand in good Swiss style. 'Come on in and join the party of one.'

'My father called,' she said, entering, but not yet sitting down. 'He said he would not be back until quite late. So . . .'

49

'Sit down, for God's sake. What may I offer you? I've got gin, Scotch, and Campari.' Somehow Italy never seemed complete without a bottle of that red cough medicine.

She took gin and tonic – in fact, two of them within about fifteen minutes flat. We filled the time with small talk, especially about Daddy.

'Who was the Great White Hunter your father brought to the bar?' I asked.

'A colleague of his.'

'A colleague? You mean that guy can also *think*?'

'He is a brilliant scientist. From Israel.'

'So your father is also into the Jewish thing.'

For some reason she looked startled, but recovered almost instantaneously. 'By no means,' she said. 'Father has hundreds of friends in the scientific community throughout the world. Professor Ben-Levi is one of them. Period.'

There seemed to be no reason to press that one further, so I branched off into travel. She and her daddy had really gotten around. So she knew most of the good restaurants I had gotten to know and love, from Père Bise in Talloire to Charles and Maurice's little bistro in San Rafael – the latter having been added to her list during the time when Daddy was lecturing at U.C. Berkeley.

But food was not exactly what I had in mind, although my tastes in food somewhat parallel those in sex. By this I mean that during the past twenty years of my life, I had never – not once – just had steak for dinner. Anybody can eat steak. It's boring. You can also get bored with sex, especially if you are forty-four and have already done the entire circuit, starting with the teen-age hassles in the back seat of a secondhand Ford with the local parson's daughter, to laying a twit of an English lord's niece in the back seat of her uncle's Rolls on the way home from Ascot, as had happened to me just that summer. Screwing her, by the way, was like throwing a banana down Oxford Street. Be that as it may, the point is that one must move on to new frontiers. Challenge is what makes everything – business, sex, whatever – fun.

Now I am not modest enough to believe that I could not have scored with Ursula Hartmann after a long-drawn-out series of drinks, dinners, movies, theaters, and – as a clincher to prove true sincerity – the opera. But by forty-four I hated opera. So . . .

'Well, Ursula,' I said, 'it's time you and I got down to business.'

Again the tongue suddenly started moving nervously over her lips. And she crossed her legs under the neat blue skirt. 'What do you mean?'

I got up and walked into the bedroom and returned with the brown – yes, brown – envelope that my Saudi staff man had delivered earlier that evening.

I tossed it onto the table. She was sitting behind it on the sofa. I stood across, watching to see what would happen – thinking that Ursula Hartmann was a very attractive gal indeed. She had that rounded look that only comes to women after thirty. She took the envelope and then just sat there looking straight at me. I got out a cigarette. And she opened the envelope.

It contained twenty one-thousand-dollar bills, to the credit of my absent Saudi helper. Thousand-dollar bills are very difficult to round up in any number, even in the United States. How he had done it in Rome, in an afternoon, was beyond me, but it reinforced my earlier conclusion that one should never underestimate Arabs where money is concerned.

'You're mad,' she said, touching a few of the bills, but not actually taking them out of the brown envelope.

'No, just reasonably well off.' That twenty thou represented about one-half second of Saudi Arabia's inflow of oil money. All I was attempting to do was to recycle this minuscule portion of that vast fund of money, employing a truly innovative approach.

I reached across the coffee table, putting out my cigarette on the ashtray there along the way, grabbed her hand, and gave a slight tug. And . . . up she came!

The next stage in the operation was the most risky.

51

Would she take those fifteen-odd steps into the bedroom or bolt for the door? Well, it was touch and go for a second or two, but once she had passed through the mental crisis point she went over the threshold into my boudoir with a stride that would have stirred the heart of the best of Switzerland's Sunday hikers.

In the bedroom, efficiency and determination continued to prevail. First the crisp white blouse; then the white brassiere. Finally the skirt came whipping off in a blue blur. And there she was, in her white bikini panties, looking at me defiantly.

I, by this time, had shed my dressing gown and – not wanting to overdo the act – stepped forward and kissed her. At first it was like kissing a maiden aunt on the occasion of her eightieth birthday. But when she felt me stirring against her nylon, there was just the slightest hint of her tongue. Then a lot of it. My hand went to hers and brought it between us. She kept it there, while my hand proceeded on its own mission of mercy. She had a lot of pubic hair, and it was damp. So were her panties when I slid them off. That got me a bit worked up. I had not expected it.

Once onto the bed, an even bigger surprise occurred. Instead of just lying there limply, waiting for the worst to happen, she slithered down my body and took me swiftly and completely in her mouth. What then transpired can only be explained in terms of shock : I came no more than ten seconds later.

Two thousand bucks a second, for Christ's sake! I had been screwed!

Because that was it. Before I could recover, she was off the bed and back into her girl guide uniform. Then she just stood there, looking down at me as if I was some hunk of meat that the butcher had delivered to the bedroom by mistake.

'Mr. Hitchcock,' she said, 'let me suggest something to you.'

'Sure,' I said, by now struggling back into my gown.

'I think you might consider visiting a sex clinic. You can be helped, you know.'

And with that she was gone.

To cap it off, the next morning when I asked the concierge to check my box for messages, he handed me my brown envelope. When I opened it, all that was there was a single sheet of hotel stationery with the following words: 'I hereby acknowledge receipt of $20,000 for services rendered.' And her signature.

I felt it was in extremely bad taste.

Thinking, you cannot win them all, I decided to try to win at least one of them. So I went back to the German Embassy, intending to make a compromise proposal to the bankers, who had been scheduled to reassemble at nine. But by the time I arrived – late, but not that late – the meeting was in a shambles. The British were yelling at the French in bad French, and the Iranians were screaming at the Americans in worse English. The rest just sat there in the stupor of various degrees of hangover. This was the collective elite of the capitalistic world!

The German chairman finally broke it up by articulating what was obvious : This group would solve nothing. So he adjourned the meeting, suggesting that everybody go back home for consultations with their respective governments.

It was just as well, because it was obvious that if anything could be done to stave off the financial collapse of Italy, it had to be done by the few people who still had clout in our world of 1978. The Germans and the Arabs filled that bill; most of the rest of the clowns at that meeting did not. So I waited until the conference room had almost cleared, and then approached Dr. Reichenberger quietly. I wanted to chat privately with him on this matter, I said. I had an idea. The sooner the better, he replied. Over lunch? No, he had already scheduled himself on the one o'clock plane back to Germany. Then in Frankfurt the next day? We agreed on the Frankfurterhof at noon.

I spent the rest of the day in our offices in Rome, going over the dossier they had provided me with the previous

53

evening. The more I pored, the more I was convinced that the Germans would be the right partners. My plan involved the application of a bit of leverage, maybe even some good old brutality. Germans have always understood such things.

Thus I was fairly optimistic when I boarded the 7 P.M. Lufthansa flight to Frankfurt.

CHAPTER EIGHT

History records that Fawzi Tehrani – head of SAVAK, the Shah's personal Gestapo – also got on a plane that same evening in Teheran. And he also had a plan which involved the application of leverage, if necessary with brutality. But that was where all similarities ended. All I was attempting at the time was the lining up of some collateral for a loan. What Tehrani and his boss were after was symbolized by the name the Shah had chosen for his endeavor : Project 'Sassanid.' At stake was nothing less than the restoration of the ancient Sassanid empire (A.D. 226–651) when the borders of Iran had embraced the entire Persian Gulf, and when its power had been second to none on earth.

Tehrani traveled alone and under his own name. Why not? His face was on file in almost every airport on earth. He had the entire first-class section of the Pan Am 707 to himself. After all, it was an offer of the Shah's money that once kept that airline flying. The cabin crew – all American girls – did everything short of a striptease to keep him happy. The captain, from Cleveland, Ohio, came out every half hour to personally deliver his reports on the progress of the flight. Tehrani enjoyed having Americans bow and scrape. That's why he flew Pan Am instead of Iran Air.

When the turbines were shut down, and the front door opened at the docking site in Kloten airport, two Swiss entered the plane. They were Franz Ulrich, head of the Swiss secret police, and his assistant, who was also his chauffeur. Ulrich and Tehrani had known each other for years. Ulrich had been keeping an eye on the Iranians in Switzerland, especially the students, who tended to forget who was paying their way and who liked to shoot off their mouths periodically about the police state that existed back home. He kept Tehrani informed. In return, the Iranians had, to date, not really been able to reciprocate. But that's the way the Swiss liked to operate : build up credits where-ever possible. Some day it would prove useful.

Tehrani did not have to walk through the terminal. After leaving the plane, he was taken down some stairs directly to the car waiting on the tarmac. Then out the gates to the expressway leading into town. But they turned off after just a few kilometers and headed toward the Rhine. By ten that evening Tehrani was installed in a suite in the Adler Hotel, an inn on the outskirts of Baden, the small town ten kilometers north of Zurich. Baden was famous for two things; its ancient Roman baths, and the fact that it was the world headquarters of one of Switzerland's largest companies, Roche-Bollinger, a global leader in the manu-facture of turbines, generators, power plants – and nuclear equipment, especially large reactors. Tehrani said his prayers and went to bed.

The next day, Ulrich – who had spent the night in Zurich – picked up Tehrani once again, and they went directly to the twenty-story steel-and-glass building that dominated the center of town. The president of Roche-Bollinger, Dr. Hanspeter Suter, was waiting downstairs to greet them. Ulrich made the introductions and then left. He had done what protocol demanded.

Suter was not only head of Roche-Bollinger. He was also a colonel in the Swiss army, attached to the nuclear-de-fense planning unit. Switzerland has always had a citizens' army, with only a few thousand full-time military person-nel. Thus it was hardly peculiar for the top executive of a large corporation to have a dual function as businessman and officer. In fact, it would have been highly unusual if a man in Suter's position had not had a high military rank. This system greatly contributes to the fact that there has rarely been any discord on national policies in Switzerland: both the private and public sectors are essentially in the hands of the same Establishment. The rule of the military-industrial complex had already become an established fact in Switzerland as early as the 1930's. It had proven to be a highly effective form of 'government.' Switzerland had never been involved in any wars in the twentieth century, because the power elite in that nation saw no profit in it – quite the contrary. Thus Switzerland had emerged in 1978 as the second most prosperous nation on earth. Number one in per-capita income and wealth was, of course, Kuwait.

The secret of Switzerland's amazing record of non-involvement in the destructive conflicts of our century lay not in its declared policy of neutrality. Who cared? Rather, no one had invaded Switzerland because the power elite of that nation had always made sure that the country maintained a very effective military deterrent – combined with the willingness to 'do business' with both sides in any major conflict. In World War Two, for instance, the Swiss in effect told the Nazis : Invade us, and every Swiss male between seventeen and fifty will hole up in the Alps and fight an endless war of attrition, Tito-style. On the other hand, if you are smart enough not to invade us, we will be most happy to supply you with the best our highly developed industry can produce. Against cash, of course.

And that is exactly what happened. With the added touch that in return for cooperation, that is, providing Germany with anti-aircraft guns, power generators, aircraft parts, precision instruments, machines tools, plus allowing the Nazis to use the Swiss railroad system to transit weapons and troops to Italy to help out Mussolini against the Americans and British armies, the Swiss demanded additional reciprocity. Energy. Coal from the Ruhr. They worked out a very precise formula under which for every ton of military supplies sent through Switzerland to the Italian and German armies on the other side of the Alps, the Nazis sold Switzerland X tons of coal. This deal was absolutely essential for the survival of Switzerland during the five long years of conflict. For Switzerland has no coal or oil resources whatsoever – not one ton or one barrel. And they had already used up the country's entire hydro-electric potential.

It worked. The Germans kept their hands off Switzerland. And they provided the Swiss with enough energy to not only keep the country going, but to prosper when the rest of Europe was gradually falling into ruin.

Following World War Two, Switzerland, like all of Western Europe, found its new security in the United States. The American nuclear umbrella provided a deterrent for all. The commanding global economic hegemony of the United States insured that the material needs of its friends in Europe would always be met. America controlled everything, from wheat to timber to aircraft to bananas to oil. All a country had to do was stay on the right side of Uncle Sam, and all would be well.

This is exactly what the Swiss did, with one lamentable exception, and they continued to prosper as never before. But between 1973 and 1975 the entire foundation of this comfortable system began to crumble. The guardian of all, the United States, went into a sudden global tailspin. Militarily it went down like a whimpering, helpless giant in Vietnam. Politically it completely lost credibility as a world leader when the Presidential system all but collapsed in the aftermath of the downfall of Nixon. Economically the United States totally surrendered to the Arab oil blackmail abroad and went into a deep recession at home.

In the summer of 1975 the Swiss concluded that America could no longer be relied upon as the guardian of their own peace and prosperity.

So they did two things. First, they rapidly developed and then built their own atomic deterrent. In secret, of course, since Switzerland was a signatory of the nuclear nonproliferation agreement. Within a year they had well over a hundred nuclear devices, ranging from bombs to missile heads to mines. Second, they began to shift the direction of their economic ties – from New York and Chicago to places like Kuwait, Saudi Arabia, Iraq, and especially Iran. Coldly and logically they began wooing those countries that had the two most important things to offer, from the Swiss standpoint : rapid growing and highly profitable markets for the products of Swiss industry, and an almost inexhaustible supply of that most critical natural resource, oil.

The Shah of Iran knew the Swiss attitude and mentality

probably better than any governmental leader on earth. Ever since the late 1950's, he had spent at least a month of every year in Switzerland. To be sure, much of this time was spent relaxing, partying, and skiing in the Alpine resorts. But over the years, his contacts with that small group of men who ran Switzerland – the industrialists, the bankers, the politicians, and the military – became very deep, and in some cases quite intimate. The Swiss elite were regular guests at his chalet in St. Moritz; he was often seen in their country homes outside of Zurich, on Lake Geneva, in Locarno. The Shah of Iran regularly received the President of Switzerland – not vice versa, it should be noted – in his suite at the Dolder Grand Hotel in Zurich at the beginning of each annual visit. And in spite of the fact that the Shah always brought his own large security force with him, both the Swiss army and the national police force always provided further heavily armed personnel to guard the King of Kings from any possible annoyance while a guest in their country. At no charge whatsoever.

By the end of 1978, then, the relationship between the Shah and the Swiss was very cozy indeed.

Tehrani was there to make it even cozier. He had come as the personal representative of the Shah to offer a deal which would provide mutual advantage to Iran and Switzerland, a deal very reminiscent of the one the Swiss had made with the Nazis in 1940 : arms for energy.

To be more specific : atomic-weapons technology for cheap oil – *guaranteed* cheap oil.

But that subject was to come up last.

'Herr Doktor Suter,' Tehrani began, 'His Majesty has asked me to extend to you his personal regards.' He paused. 'And also to give you this token of his esteem.'

Tehrani produced a small package from the left pocket of his jacket and handed it to Suter.

Suter beamed. Beaming does not come easily to the Swiss, but to be given this singular honor by the King of Kings produced this quite extraordinary effect. But his expression sobered almost immediately. A decision had to be made :

59

to open or not to open. The Swiss are not too learned in matters of protocol where royalty is concerned. He opened.

It was stunning. A roundel of pure gold, depicting a lion head with gloriously spreading mane. Diameter : about six centimeters. Value?

As if reading his mind, Tehrani spoke again. 'It was found,' he said, 'in Hamadan, about twenty years ago. We believe it is from the seventh century.' He paused. 'B.C.'

At least twenty-five thousand dollars.

'I am most honored,' said Suter. 'Most honored. I do hope you will convey my many thanks to His Majesty.'

'I shall. But I am sure you will soon have the opportunity to do that in person. His Majesty will be coming to Switzerland again this winter, and no doubt would be highly pleased if you could be his guest – with your wife, of course – in St. Moritz.'

All this time they had been standing – something Tehrani did not like, since he was short, even shorter than Suter. So he sidled in the direction of the sofa. Suter normally – no, always – sat behind his desk when receiving visitors. But today he broke with tradition. With the result that when his secretary came in with the obligatory coffee and saw him sitting side by side with the foreigner behind the coffee table, she damn near dropped the cups right on the Persian rug. Suter's angry stare brought her back to normal. She would hear about her misconduct in detail on Friday night, when she received her obligatory weekend fuck at the Adler Hotel, Room 24, between 6 and 8 P.M.

After she left, Tehrani moved into phase two of the softening-up process. 'Dr. Suter,' he said, 'as you know, His Majesty holds Switzerland and your people in very high regard for your efficiency, your cleanliness, your honesty. And your great technical skills. He feels that the ties between Iran and your country must be strengthened.'

Suter's mind was still on the pending invitation to St. Moritz. How in the world could he possibly bring his wife to such a thing? She was not only fat and ugly, but could barely utter a word in any other language but the local Swiss dialect. She would disgrace him !

'His Majesty,' continued Tehrani, 'wants this new relationship to take on a concrete form, as part of a program which His Majesty feels is important for the very future of mankind. He is one of the few men on this earth who for years has recognized that petroleum is too precious a commodity to be simply burned – be it for the purpose of propelling automobiles or creating electricity. Its use as a raw material should be restricted to those areas where oil's unique properties can best serve the people of our planet – for the manufacture of pharmaceuticals, the production of fertilizers, and the like.'

Suter nodded, indicating his wholehearted recognition of the wisdom of the King of Kings.

'Therefore,' said Tehrani, 'His Majesty has developed a unique nuclear-power program which in time will serve as a model for all other nations. By 1985, he hopes that over fifty percent of Iran's electrical power needs will be met by nuclear-fueled plants. The only other nation which will come even close to matching this is your own country, Switzerland, as you full well know.'

Suter knew. Over 30 percent of Switzerland's electricity came from nuclear facilities – a ratio not even approached by any other country, including the so-called nuclear powers.

'Because,' Tehrani droned on, 'of the similarity of our two countries' energy policies, and the compatibility of our general political views, and because of the technology which has allowed your country to become the leading nation in the world in regard to the use of nuclear technology for peaceful purposes, I am instructed to inform you that His Majesty has decided to invite your company to be the prime contractors in the construction of two six-hundred-megawatt pressurized water-cooled nuclear reactors.'

When Suter grasped the meaning of that last long sentence, he actually choked on his coffee, much to Tehrani's inner amusement.

But while coughing, Suter was already beginning to calculate what all this would mean. Two such reactors would cost around $2.2 billion. Roche-Bollinger would net around 20 percent on such a contract, or just under a half billion, spread over around five years, which would mean around $100 million annually, or about 250 million Swiss francs, which would mean that average corporate earnings from 1979 through 1984 would be at least 50 percent higher than currently projected, which would mean that the shares of Roche-Bollinger, quoted on the Zurich exchange, would increase by at least that much, and probably more. If Suter started buying at the market now through his man at the Union Bank, using every bit of cash he could muster through mortgaging his houses and hypothecating everything else he owned, and then going on margin to the hilt, he could probably acquire 10,000 shares at an average price of 500 Swiss francs. When news of this deal became public, and the stock price went to 1000 or 1200, he would net around 5 million Swiss, or $2 million.

Again Tehrani seemed to have tracked his thoughts, for he added, 'We would appreciate it, Dr. Suter, if – for the moment – you would not unduly publicize this matter. Even in your own company, if I may suggest so. We would not like news of this to leak to our friends in France or the United States. They do not always understand that Iran's self-interest does not always coincide with their own.'

Tehrani was planning on buying a few shares of Roche-Bollinger himself, through his man at the Swiss Bank Corporation. And why not? If he knew his master – and he did – no doubt His Majesty's personal trust in Liechtenstein was already in the market for the Shah's own account.

'Now,' the Iranian said, 'we want a feasibility study started immediately. I have here' – and this time he reached into his right pocket – 'the authorization of His Majesty to instruct the Zurich office of the Bank Meli to pay you one hundred million dollars as advance payment on this project.'

He handed the paper to Suter. The authorization stated that the funds should be available for transfer on January 2, 1979. That gave Suter six weeks to acquire those 10,000 shares. There was obviously going to be quite a flurry of action in the stock of Roche-Bollinger on the Zurich exchange.

Suter handed the document back to Tehrani. Tehrani left it face up on the coffee table. He wanted the bait in sight when he moved on to discuss the next part of the package.

'We understand,' continued the Iranian, 'that you have a very fine nuclear physicist here. Professor Hartmann.'

'Yes and no. He is not an employee of our company. But he often serves as a consultant on various of our projects. He devotes most of his time to teaching at the Eidgenoessische Technische Hochschule in Zurich. That is our MIT, you know. However, his specialty is not that type of reactor you have referred to.'

'Yes, but His Majesty desires that the best possible man be assigned to this project, especially in the initial phases, where the feasibility study is concerned. We want both generalists and specialists.'

'Well, I am not sure of the availability of Professor Hartmann right now.'

'Dr. Suter, I must be candid with you. There are to be certain conditions attached to this contract. One of them is Professor Hartmann.' His eyes fixed on Suter's and Suter backed off immediately.

'But of course. I think you perhaps misunderstood me. Professor Hartmann will definitely be part of our team. I was only wondering out loud as to *when* he would be available, not *if*. Naturally we can – in fact, will – insist that he rearrange his schedule to accommodate our needs.'

So much for that.

'Now,' said Tehrani, 'I will address myself to the other condition. There are only these two. No more, I can assure you.'

Suter braced himself. This Iranian probably wanted a kickback. Foreigners always did. Well, why not? As long as it did not turn out to be too outrageous. The problem was the Americans. Before they had learned the art, such costs had remained under control. But like everything else, once they had caught on, they overdid things.

But no mention of money was made.

'We,' continued Tehrani, 'are going to ask that, in addition to his regular consultancy duties, you arrange that Professor Hartmann will also advise our government in the area of weapons technology.'

Now Suter squinted. 'What exactly do you mean?'

'We know that Professor Hartmann supervised the construction of your country's atomic weapons. We would like him to do the same for Iran.'

Suter belched. For Tehrani's words hit him like a blow to the stomach. Was this man insane? Suter abruptly rose from the sofa as if unconsciously he wanted to get as far away as possible from the Iranian. 'My dear Mr. Tehrani, I am afraid that you and your government are terribly misinformed. Switzerland is a signatory of the nuclear non-proliferation treaty. We are a neutral nation. We have never even conceived of . . .'

Tehrani once again reached into a pocket, this time the breast pocket of his gray suit. Then he also stood up. 'Here is a list of the atomic weapons your country has at its disposal, by type, yield, and current place of storage.'

Suter's demeanor was ice-cold as he accepted the paper. And even icier when his eyes ran down the list. 'Where . . . ?'

'Not directly, I can assure you. We do not spy on friends. We received this information from a third party. You realize, of course, that I cannot go into any further details.'

His source had been France. After France had pulled out of NATO and thus isolated itself militarily, for years it had repeatedly sought to establish a 'special relationship' with its neutral neighbor on its southern flank. This was not new. France and Switzerland had cooperated militarily – and secretly – before both World War One and World War Two. The 1939 plan was very similar to the one the two countries had agreed to in 1912. The idea was that the French army would sweep through Switzerland, and then into southern Germany together with the Swiss army – should the Germans attack both France and Switzerland simultaneously. As the Kaiser before him, Hitler attacked only France, so the contingency Franco-Swiss plan never became operational, and it was buried – though not forgotten. The renewal of the two countries' military joint planning had begun in 1975. This time it was not directed at a specific enemy – Germany – rather it grew out of the mutual conviction that the NATO shield, behind which both nations had felt reasonably safe, though neither contributed anything to it, would gradually disintegrate as the global military pullback of the United States progressed. The effects of the Vietnam disaster seemed never to end.

Inevitably, when such joint talks and planning take place, friendships are formed, political alliances are developed beyond normal national allegiances, and indiscretions follow. In this case, the adjutant to the chief of the strategic planning staff of the Swiss army, a Francophile from Geneva, became very chummy with his counterpart from Paris. After all, they shared a common language and culture, as well as sharing a common antipathy for the German language and culture – that of the majority of the Swiss population. He passed on the list in the belief that Switzerland's survival was inexorably linked to that of France. He wanted to demonstrate, in the ultimate concrete form, that he and many of his colleagues in Switzerland recognized this, and to prove that Switzerland would be a strong ally – one that could fight alongside France and win, even in a war where tactical nuclear weapons were employed. The rationale behind such a 'treasonous' act was that it was, if anything, merely premature. Both countries would at some point, have had to swap such information anyway, if their secret alliance was to be meaningful.

There was disagreement in Paris on the merits of the Swiss military link, as there is disagreement in Paris on just about everything. Just how the parties in question felt that leakage of the list of Swiss atomic weapons would injure the budding alliance has never become clear, but leaked it was. Discreetly. And strictly internally. By 1978, it had become rather stale material. So it became part of a trade mark between SAVAK and the Deuxième Bureau. In return Paris got a full and regular rundown from the Iranians

65

on the state of the military buildup in the entire region of the Persian Gulf. Not that they believed half the stuff they received – but it was an important input regarding a potentially explosive region, and one upon which France, like all of Europe, depended for its energy.

Dr. Hanspeter Suter, who had by now moved to the security of his desk, was not thinking about the source of Tehrani's list. It was the effect that had set his mind racing.

Finally he spoke. 'Mr. Tehrani, you are actually serious about this incredible proposition?'

Tehrani's answer came immediately. 'It is not I, Dr. Suter; I speak only as the personal envoy of His Majesty, the Shahanshah.'

'But you must realize that I could not possibly even discuss such a matter without the approval of my government.'

'Indeed we do.'

'Then I fear that for the moment . . .'

'Allow me to interrupt you. To make two points. First, I think you must realize that if we do not gain your co-operation in this matter – I should, of course, say Switzerland's – then we shall simply go elsewhere. For both our reactors and the additional technology we are currently seeking. I suspect that you could think of at least a half-dozen nations who would welcome being approached by us on this matter. Secondly, and I think you will find this important, His Majesty is willing to make a gentleman's agreement with your country to the effect that Switzerland would not be subject to any new oil embargo when – or rather, if – such an embargo is reimposed on the rest of the Western world. We would guarantee both the supply and transportation to your refineries.'

'Do you have the authority of His Majesty to make such a commitment?'

'I do. But he will give it in person early next year, to the appropriate representative delegated by your government – should we reach agreement on that other matter we have been discussing.'

Maybe, thought Suter, it could be done. If it was presented

66

just right. Which should not be that difficult. From Switzerland's standpoint, it was almost all pluses. And as this Iranian had just pointed out, his country could easily go elsewhere – to France, India, Japan, probably even the United Kingdom. The risk? That it would come out some day, just like that damnable list! But the Swiss government would not have to involve itself directly. It could, if necessary, totally disclaim any knowledge of any side deal that Roche-Bollinger might make with the Shah. And Roche-Bollinger – he, Suter – could disclaim any responsibility whatsoever for the behavior of some individuals they had sent to Iran on a project that was strictly commercial and civilian in nature.

Fawzi Tehrani just sat there watching Suter. And he knew – Suter was hooked. But could Suter, in turn, convince the men in Bern? If not, so what? He would go elsewhere. And get what he wanted a lot cheaper. In fact, if it had not been for the Shah's insistence, he would never have come to this dull country in the first place. But . . .

'Mr. Tehrani,' said Suter finally, 'I will do what I can. But it will take time.'

'We would not like it, Dr. Suter, if it took much time. His Majesty would like to have a decision as soon as possible. In fact, he has instructed me to determine the feasibility of our project one way or the other during my present visit.'

The Colonel in Suter thought of the enormous strategical value of his country becoming embargo-proof. The Herr Direktor in Suter was thinking of the $2.2 billion sale and the $500 million profit for his company. The Herr Doktor Suter could not avoid reflecting on those ten thousand shares of Roche-Bollinger he intended to acquire, and the resulting 5 million Swiss francs sure profit for himself. Altogether there was hardly a lack of motivation.

'I shall go to Bern this afternoon, Mr. Tehrani.'

'Excellent. I shall probably remain in that charming little inn until I hear further from you.'

'Could I arrange anything for you?'

'Not really. Although I could, perhaps, use a bit of assistance in doing some shopping.'

'But of course. My secretary would be more than happy to assist you.' Suter picked up the phone. 'Fraulein Schneider, would you please come in for a minute.'

Five minutes later, the Iranian left, accompanied by Trudi Schneider. Trudi was not aware of it, but this week she was going to get fucked twice in the line of business in the Adler Hotel. In the process, she would discover that Iranians have a great deal more imagination in bed than do the Swiss.

CHAPTER NINE

While Fawzi Tehrani was out buying a few dozen gold watches, including one for Trudi as a prelude to his later demonstration of the famous 'Persian position,' Dr. Hanspeter Suter was on the phone with the Swiss minister of defense, Jacques Dubois. They agreed to meet at six that evening in Bern. Dubois also agreed to insure that the other key members of the Swiss government were present.

Dubois was in the lobby of the Hirschen Hotel when Suter arrived. They went to a small conference room on the second floor. Already waiting for them were Franz Ulrich, head of the Swiss espionage *cum* counterespionage agency; Jacob Gerber, minister of finance and currently also the President of the Swiss Confederation – the presidency really not much more than a ceremonial function, the post being filled on a rotation basis from the ranks of the seven Federal Councillors who act as the collective executive branch of the Swiss government; and Enrico Rossi, the minister of foreign affairs. These men ran Switzerland's public affairs. They also fairly represented the diverse nature of the Swiss electorate : Gerber and Ulrich (the latter not elected, but as key to the system as was the head of the CIA to the American power structure) were both German Swiss; Dubois came from French-speaking Lausanne; Rossi was a native of Locarno, in the Italian-speaking canton.

The meeting was held at the Hirschen for one reason only : Suter had forewarned Dubois that everything must be off the record. The defense minister was not put off by this. Roche-Bollinger, the company Suter headed, was Switzerland's most important producer of sensitive military equipment – ranging from electronic counter-measure devices to rather simple anti-tank wire-guided missiles – for both domestic use and export. The export side was often conducted very unofficially, although with complete government approval. Since the Swiss were very touchy regarding their neutral status, custom had it that discussions of such matters were held on non-government property. The Swiss are very consistent in the practice of hypocrisy.

Dubois had arranged for two liters of Fendant plus five wineglasses, long-stemmed with a greenish tinge. Fendant was produced in Vaud, the home canton of Dubois, and thus he never drank anything else in public.

The industrialist, Suter, was in no way embarrassed by the presence of such an impressive array of government leaders. Switzerland is a very small country, and the elite stratum of Swiss society is paper-thin. Thus he had gone to school with Ulrich in Baden; he had done business with Dubois and his Defense Department for many years; Gerber had been on the Board of Directors of Roche-Bollinger before becoming finance minister; Rossi was his wife's sister's husband, related to the Martini and Rossi family of Italy, and was recognized by those who knew him well as one of the most steady consumers of the family product.

Therefore Suter was on a *du* basis with all of them. For in spite of their varying backgrounds, all spoke German at this little get-together. All could, of course, speak French or Italian as easily. But they spoke German in deference to the presence of the man who was currently President of Switzerland – Gerber – whose native tongue was German. It's a complicated country.

'*Meine Herren,*' began Suter, once everybody's glass was filled, '*Ich habe etwas enorm Wichtiges zu berichten!*'

And of all the enormously important matters to report, Suter had chosen to start off with the Shah's proposal to exempt Switzerland from any future oil embargo. It deeply impressed every man present, for Switzerland and its leaders were very touchy indeed on the subject of embargoes. In 1944–45 they had been damn near embargoed into starvation.

In December of 1944, six months after the Allied landing in Normandy, the American government had told Switzerland that she must immediately cease supporting the

Nazis with weapons and industrial equipment, or it would cut off the country's food supply indefinitely. This was aimed right at the jugular, since Switzerland always has had to import vast quantities of foodstuffs to survive. The war had meant that the country was cut off from its traditional suppliers in Western and Eastern Europe. But the Swiss had found an alternate source – Latin America, and especially Argentina, a neutral with a pro-Axis bent. At first it was rather simple. Neutral vessels, flying both the Swiss flag (yes, of the Swiss navy) and that of Argentina, sailed regularly through Gibraltar to the port of Genoa. Mussolini graciously allowed the Italian state railroad to transport their cargoes the rest of the way into Switzerland. Principally because of this, Mussolini's family was granted political asylum in Switzerland near the end of the war. He never made it, since he was caught just short of the Swiss border at Como and ended up hanging from his heels in front of the Cathedral in Milan. But once the Allies had made Italy a battleground, the Genoa route became impassable. So a new daisy chain was devised.

The origin remained the same. But now the ships were off-loaded in neutral Portugal, and from there transported by land through Franco-dominated Spain and German-dominated Vichy France, ending up in Geneva. In other words, as long as Germany and its 'neutral' friends on the Iberian peninsula held their own, Switzerland's food supply was guaranteed. But with the landing of the Americans in the south of France, the jig was up. As soon as control of that region was established in late 1944, the Americans were finally in a position to move against Switzerland. It came in the form of an ultimatum : either Switzerland must cease any further support of the Nazis, or the country's food supply would be cut off indefinitely. To the astonishment of the Americans, the Swiss refused to comply. So the food embargo was immediately imposed in December of 1944.

As a result, Christmas 1944 was not a very nice time to be in Switzerland. Every man around that table in the Hirschen almost thirty-four years later remembered it well. All of them had been in their late teens, or early twenties

71

– hungry young men. And as the weeks passed, their meals gradually started to consist of coarse black bread and barley soup. When the German counteroffensive in the Ardennes failed, it became painfully obvious to even the staunchest of Swiss neutrals that soon Switzerland would have the worst of all worlds, having neither food nor energy. For with Germany in the process of collapse in early 1945, it was obvious that the Nazis could no longer furnish Switzerland with coal for very long. And in January, the embargo against Switzerland was extended to all imports – including oil and coal. So the Swiss had no choice but to capitulate. Their ambassador in Washington was instructed to urgently request negotiations.

The American delegation, headed by Secretary of State Stettinius' personally delegated envoy, arrived in Bern on February 12, 1945. The Swiss tried to hard-line it. The envoy broke off negotiations, telling the Swiss that as far as he was concerned, he could wait for them to come to their senses. Months – or years, if necessary. He had to wait exactly ten days. On March 8, 1945 the Swiss signed an agreement signifying their complete diplomatic surrender. That same day the American total embargo was lifted, for they had gotten their price. Switzerland not only agreed to completely and immediately sever all economic ties with the Nazis, but was also forced to promise to give back to the Allies the hundreds of millions of dollars in gold bullion, plus a good amount of cash and securities, that the Nazis had been moving into Switzerland, both to pay for military shipments and to set up nest eggs for themselves under the cover of Swiss bank secrecy. The smart bigwigs had realized they would need it to start anew in some South American haven.

The gold was an especially sore point with the Americans, since almost all of it had been stolen, either from the mouths of Jews or from the central banks of Belgium, the Netherlands, and France. Up until then, the Swiss had firmly believed that money could never stink : that they could buy their way out of any situation. In 1945, the Americans taught them otherwise. Seldom has that nation been so devastatingly humiliated. And all because they had allowed themselves to be 'blackmailed' through an embargo.

To be sure, the whole affair had a somewhat happy ending. The Swiss eventually reneged on almost every commitment they had been forced to make. They just stalled, until the inauguration of the Cold War, when America's attention was diverted to much more pressing matters in Europe. But the Swiss had learned a lesson. Not that it was immoral to make deals with dictators. After all, as a neutral nation, if Switzerland did not defend its own interests, nobody else would either. No, what they had learned was that it was extremely important to calculate all the consequences of any such deals well in advance.

Jacob Gerber could calculate with the best of them. So it was he who put the first question to Suter. 'What does the Shah want in return?'

'I shall come to that,' was the industrialist's immediate response. 'But the Shah has offered us more – much more.'

The more was, of course, the contract for the $2-billion-plus power reactors. Suter explained that having such a contract would boost the prestige of the Swiss atomic industry right to the top of the international list. It would definitely lead to more export contracts, guaranteeing continuing high employment in that industry, and also giving Roche-Bollinger the opportunity to greatly expand its R & D – at the expense not of the Swiss government, which had been subsidizing Switzerland's atomic industry for decades, but of foreign customers. Finance Minister Gerber grasped that point immediately. And liked it.

In fact, the only man who maintained a highly skeptical look on his face during Suter's presentation was Franz Ulrich. Only he knew who the Shah's personal envoy was. Suter had glossed over that detail. And Ulrich knew full well that Fawzi Tehrani would never be party to any deal that did not involve something very dirty, and probably highly dangerous – for the other guy. But he let Suter ramble on for quite a while before he interrupted.

'You have left something out, Hanspeter.'

73

Suter intended to do things his way. 'Of course,' he replied, 'I am not through yet.'

'I don't mean that. I mean you failed to explain who your Mr. Tehrani is.'

At first Suter said nothing, thinking. Then came a well-measured response : 'Why don't you explain?'

Ulrich did, with pleasure, going into a long moralistic diatribe concerning the atrocities committed by SAVAK in general, and Tehrani in particular, over the years. They ranged from the indefinite imprisonment of hundreds of recalcitrant intellectuals from the urban centers of Iran to the mass murder of dissident tribes in the provinces.

Foreign Minister Rossi finally interrupted. 'Franz, most of this is hardly new to any of us. When you do business with Middle Eastern governments, you can hardly be choosy about whom you deal with, or how you deal.'

'I agree. But I did not make my point. It is this: Tehrani is a very crude man. This, perhaps, allows him to be very effective in enforcing the Shah's policies at home. But internationally – that is quite a different story. The man has no finesse. His organization is pitifully ineffective. My organization is one-twentieth the size of his, yet we are twenty times more effective. You see, I know this type of man. I know how to deal with them. It was, in my opinion, very foolish of Hanspeter to even start such talks without my being present. For this whole deal is simply too good to be true. Something stinks !'

'Yes,' replied Suter, this time harshly, 'and the stench can be traced directly back to you and your marvelous organization, you ass !' The word Suter actually used was *Arschloch*.

Ulrich had leaned back to light a cigar. Now he shot forward, leaving it smoldering. *'Was soll das heissen!'* he yelled.

'This,' replied Suter, reaching down into his briefcase and producing Tehrani's list.

Ulrich turned red when he saw its contents.

'Give me that,' ordered Rossi. He glanced at it and then said, 'This is incredible !'

74

The defense minister took his turn : 'And accurate.'

The finance minister was the last to get it. He did not appear overly surprised. 'So Tehrani brought both a carrot and a stick from the Shah. I wondered what it would turn out to be. What do they want from us, Sùter?'

Suter told them, repeating this part of his conversation with the Iranian almost verbatim.

The immediate response was silence.

'Tehrani is right,' commented Dubois finally. 'The Shah could get that technology from a dozen different countries.'

'And,' added the foreign minister, 'if he chose to be vindictive – and he is a very touchy man – he could at the same time put that list into circulation, and seriously damage our status as a neutral – perhaps permanently. Which leads me to ask this, Suter. Did he give no hint whatsoever concerning the source?'

'No,' replied Suter. 'Just that it was a "third party." '

'It could only have been the French,' said Ulrich.

Nobody disagreed. All were, of course, aware of the Franco-Swiss military talks which had been going on for years. However, nobody in that room wanted to upset the developing relationship with Paris. The alternatives would be the Germans, or even worse, the Americans. It was Rossi who put a damper on any further, possibly dangerous, speculation. 'Well,' he said, 'we can only hope that it has gone no further. Suter, did Tehrani give any hint in that direction?'

'No,' replied Suter. 'But he works for an extremely intelligent master obviously. The Shah would hardly try to use this list to pressure us if he had allowed any further dissemination of its contents whatsoever. My feeling, gentlemen, is that we must accept this leak as a fact, and go on from there.'

That made sense to everybody except Ulrich. 'Are you suggesting that we just let the guilty party, or parties, in our army get away with treason?' he asked.

'Hardly,' interjected Defense Minister Dubois, technically Ulrich's superior. 'However, I think neither you nor I want this error compounded by some clumsy investigation. So

75

the matter will be dropped for the time being. Do you agree, gentlemen?'

His two colleagues from the Federal Council were more than relieved to nod their agreement.

'At the proper time,' concluded Dubois, 'I will have a word with someone in Paris. In the meantime, I don't want any mention of this – not one word – to go beyond this room. Do you understand that, Ulrich?'

It was a well-known fact that the intelligence agencies are always made the scapegoats when something like this happens, thought Ulrich. But by keeping it silent, everybody else in this room was now on the line. That could prove useful. So Ulrich also nodded his agreement.

'Now,' said Defense Minister Dubois, 'let us get to the core of this matter. I frankly do not think we have a great deal of choice. But let us leave the blackmail aspect out of it entirely. We have an enormous amount to gain, and if handled properly, very little to lose. Our gain is very tangible : freedom from the possibly disastrous consequences of a future oil embargo, plus a major off-shore contract for our industry. The negatives? They can only arise if it becomes known that we provide nuclear-weapons technology to Iran, and that we have reneged on our commitment not to build atomic weapons ourselves. But in whose interests will it be to give the world that information? Not the Shah's, obviously. Not the French, for if they had chosen to do so they could have done it years ago. The list? An obvious forgery, leaked by some low-level bureaucrat, bent on creating mischief for some unknown reason. Impossible to verify.'

'But we must insure that the Shah enters into a binding agreement,' said Gerber.

'I shall draft it,' said Foreign Minister Rossi, 'and personally negotiate its final form with His Majesty upon the occasion of his next trip to our country. I would have met with him in any case.'

'And what is my position?' asked Suter.

'Tell Tehrani that his terms have been accepted. If he

76

desires that I verify this personally, call me. I shall arrange to meet with him.'

'They want us to send someone to Iran immediately,' continued Suter.

'Well, do so.'

'Even Professor Hartmann?'

'Yes.'

'That may be a problem.'

'Then solve it.'

The defense minister sent Ulrich out to get two more liters of Fendant and a deck of cards. No informal evening among men in Switzerland is complete without a game of jass – the national sport.

Jacob Gerber dealt the first hand. After all, he was the President of Switzerland.

CHAPTER TEN

That same week Tehrani had been doing his thing in Switzerland, I was a few hundred miles north in Germany working on the Italian deal, something that was really inconsequential, it later turned out, in the framework of events which were about to overtake the world in 1979. But it was the springboard which would eventually propel me to the front and center of the world's stage.

I, as usual, stayed at the Frankfurterhof. It is within walking distance of the large banks headquartered in that city – enough of them to make Frankfurt the financial capital of Germany, and thus to continental Europe. Herr Doktor Reichenberger, head of the Leipziger Bank, met me in the lobby at noon. We went into the small bar, just off to the left behind the reception area. He had a beer, with a Steinhaeger on the side. I had gin on the rocks, with a glass of water on the side.

'Bad idea, the meeting in Rome,' he began.

'I wouldn't say that. You have to begin somewhere,' I replied.

'Waste of time,' he continued. Then like a true German added, 'I hope you are not going to waste more of my time.'

'I told you on the phone, Hermann, that I may have something. *Mit Hand und Fuss.*' Nothing psychs out a German more than the unauthorized use of his first name. The added sacrilege of my speaking a few words of Goethe's mother tongue should have really gotten under his skin. But Reichenberger never blinked, and he stuck steadfastly to his guttural English.

'What is it?'

'We get a lien on a good piece of ENI – all its foreign properties, including exploration rights in the North Sea, off Nigeria, and in the Pacific.' ENI (Ente Nazionale Idrocaburi) was the state-owned Italian oil company.

'They must already be pledged.'

'Only a billion or so. The rest is free and clear.'

'It still cannot be done.'

'Why not?'

'Because it is politically impossible. The government there considers ENI a national asset. They'd block us out.'

'Not if we buy the right politicians.'

'Hitchcock – I thought you didn't do things that way.'

'Normally I don't. But these are not normal times.'

'What are ENI's external assets worth?'

'Enough to cover our risk. It is not exactly Exxon, but it is still one of the largest oil companies in Europe. It even surprised me a bit when I looked everything up. Hell, they employ over a hundred thousand people. It's by far the largest international corporation in the country.'

'What would Longo say?' Francesco Longo was the chairman of Ente Nazionale Idrocaburi.

'He'll go along with it. He doesn't give a happy damn about Italy's so-called national interests. He's an oil man. In fact, he would probably back any deal we offered to the hilt. He needs more working capital. So we would probably have to make a side deal with him. Nothing monumental. Probably a quarter of a billion would tide him over.'

'Do you know him?'

'Sure. Don't you remember? I put together a Eurodollar loan for him a number of years ago, when I still had my banks.'

'That's right. We were in it. Tell me, Hitchcock, why did you sell out?'

'For money.'

'But your banks were doing very well.'

'Of course. So were all banks, with the exception of a few like Franklin National. Or Herstatt.'

Reichenberger flinched. He, like all German bankers, did not like to hear about the collapse of the Herstatt bank, back in 1974. Just as American bankers preferred to avoid the subject of Franklin National. Both were billion-dollar institutions, and both had gone belly up. In late 1978, everybody in the business knew that such things could happen again. But on an unimaginably larger scale. And

Reichenberger knew full well that a financial collapse of Italy could act as the trigger.

'So you no longer wanted the responsibility,' he stated.

'No *personal* responsibility for other people's money.'

'Then why are you working for the Saudis?'

'Because I can walk away any time I want.'

'Still, in the meantime you are responsible for their money.'

'Yes, but it's not the same. There simply is nothing personal about two or three hundred billion dollars. Even if somebody gives me a billion to run – no sweat. A million? Well, there the problem already starts. A million is maybe a nice house and a nice boat. You lose that for a guy and you can visualize the consequences. But a billion is a thousand nice houses plus a thousand sixty-foot cabin cruisers. Then, who gives a fuck? Now three hundred billion . . .'

'I understand.' And I'm sure he did. Reichenberger's bank had assets of about fifty of those billions.

'Who do we have to buy in Italy?'

'Minoli – the finance minister. And Riccardo – Bank of Italy.'

'You are sure Longo wouldn't want something too?'

'Positive.'

'All right,' skeptically. 'Explain the mechanics.'

I had the balance sheet of ENI with me. The company's assets were stated at $8 billion. But it was an Italian company, and, for tax reasons, no Italian company ever tells the truth about its real worth. The rule of thumb is to add at least 50 percent. In other words, ENI was a $12 billion corporation.

Half its assets were in Italy and ranged from the AGIP service-station chain which blanketed the peninsula to their natural-gas properties in the Po Valley to subsidiaries active in the chemical, textile, engineering, and nuclear-power fields. So the company had about $6 billion worth of property available as collateral domestically. Against that, interestingly, there were 'only' $4 billion in loans from Italian banks. It meant that the local bankers were covered by hard corporate assets inside the country. They could not care less if somebody got a lien on the external assets. These properties owned abroad were again diversified. The AGIP chain had spread to Germany, Switzerland, Scandinavia, and Britain. There were refineries in northern Europe and the Caribbean. And there were many concessions which ENI had bought and was in the process of developing in some of the most important new oil fields in the world. I had done a quick double-check with Riyadh on the value all this represented, by Telex from the Rome office. They had their answer back within hours. Contrary to myth (or wishful thinking), some of the Saudis had become very savvy indeed in the oil business. They had learned their basic stuff at Harvard or Stanford, and then from Exxon in New York or Bechtel Corporation in San Francisco, where they were eagerly taken on as trainees. Back in Riyadh, they were now running one of the largest enterprises on earth, with eminent success. They knew value. They had come back with the same estimate I had come up with, over the thumb : ENI's properties outside of Italy were worth $6 billion at least.

Against that, Ente Nazionale Idrocaburi had only $1 billion outstanding in Eurodollar borrowings. That left 50 percent against that, we would have a damn good loan. Even if we lent 75 percent – or $3.75 billion – we would have an eminently acceptable one, even under the most normal of circumstances. But the current situation was exceptional, to say the least. By granting the loan to the Italians, we would merely be giving them enough cash to pay back their old loans which were coming due – to us. Which would take care of the present. But it would also take care of the future. If the Italians once again tried to renege, we would now have $5 billion of their assets, which we could spin off to the highest bidder and be home free twice in succession.

Nice. That, my friends, was what the Saudis were paying me a measly half-million dollars a year for. Talk about bargains !

Reichenberger was obviously impressed when I laid it

all out for him and was really strained to find a flaw in it – because there was none. But he tried.

'All well and good, Hitchcock. But what if, in the final analysis we are forced to take over those properties. Could we find a buyer with that kind of money?'

'I think,' I said, 'that I just might know one down in Riyadh.'

That was not just for the sake of upmanship either. If there was one industry which the Saudis would invest in with confidence, it was the oil industry. ENI's properties were especially interesting since they included a large number of retail outlets – the AGIP chain with its flamboyant symbol of the flying yellow dragon, plus a string of refineries in the major European markets, plus a reasonably large fleet of tankers registered in Liberia. With those properties the Saudis could become what the Exxons of old were – an integrated group that could move oil from the wellhead to the gas tanks of millions of consumers, and collect profits each step along the way.

Reichenberger decided to stop fighting it. 'How much would those Italian politicians cost?'

'They're not cheap. They've been badly spoiled over the years.'

'A million each?'

'No. After all, spoiled or not, they are just Italians. A half each should do it.' Priscilla's husband had thought a quarter each would do, but he always did think in terms of small change.

'Are you sure just those two can swing it?'

'Yes. I asked around.'

'Fine. Were you thinking in terms of us splitting the cost?'

'More or less.'

'Agreed.'

So much for the morals of Italians, Americans and Germans.

'Where and when? asked my pragmatic partner.

'Sure as hell not in Italy. Everything there is bugged three different ways. Furthermore, it never pays to negotiate on the other fellow's home ground, as you full well know, Hermann.'

'Where then?'

'Why not right here?'

Reichenberger agreed immediately. Maybe even a trifle too quickly. And I agreed to produce the Italians – within a couple of days. Reichenberger did not invite me to lunch, nor I him. He said he had to attend some crucial meeting, and I said that I had a lot of phone calls to make. When he disappeared, I ordered another drink. After all, I had just proven that in spite of my temporary retirement, I had hardly lost my touch with the Europeans.

About ten minutes later, a hand descended upon my shoulder from behind. I do not especially appreciate the laying on of hands, and swung around perhaps a trifle too abruptly.

'Christ, Hitchcock, it's only me.'

'Me' was Randolph Aldrich, president and chief executive officer of the First National Bank of America – the big daddy of the banking world, and I mean the whole world. I had known Randy professionally for years, in an arm's-length fashion. His arm, not mine. In fact, when I decided to sell my banks, Aldrich was the guy who bought them. For First National it was a small deal, and he had made that quite obvious at the time. He gave me all of twenty minutes in his office when we signed the closing papers. But I can be very thick-skinned where $32 million in cash is concerned, and that is exactly what First National paid me for my crappy little banking empire. It was in cash, by the way, and not in shares of the bank, because the big boys obviously did not want me to hold such a large block and perhaps try to bully my way onto their Board with it. Usually after a deal – any deal – somebody soon feels that he has been had, and that's the end of any personal relationship between the principals. Obviously that had not happened in this case, or else Aldrich would not have come up to me in Frankfurt. It was the first time we had seen each other since those twenty minutes in his office.

'Randy,' I said, feeling my oats, 'sit down. And then tell

me what you've got lined up for this evening, and whether she's got a girlfriend.'

This was pure bravado, since Aldrich and I belonged to two different worlds. I had maybe a net worth of $40 million. His must have been close to half a billion. I had inherited only part of my money. He had inherited all of his. But he was willing to humor me.

'Hitchcock,' he said, 'today I'm drinking, not fucking.' And he sat down, ordered a double Scotch – straight. No water, no soda, no ice. He downed half of it upon its arrival, the other half five seconds later, and then ordered another. That is real class.

'Hitchcock,' he continued, his complexion now just a shade pinker, 'what are you doing in Frankfurt?'

I thought I would be extremely devious, so I told him the truth. And when I was through, he said, 'You are dabbling, Hitchcock.'

'What was that word?' I asked.

'Dabbling. Who gives a damn about Italy? You are screwing away your time. When you have a couple of hundred billions to play with, you don't have to waste your time on some peanut rescue operation. What's your exposure there?'

'Three billion plus,' I answered – apologetically, for chrissake!

'One percent max of Saudi Arabia's cash float, and maybe only one tenth of that three billion is in any real current danger.'

The damn thing was – he was right.

'Then there's something else,' said Aldrich. 'If you insist on dabbling, why in hell are you doing it in partnership with the Germans?'

'Because they've got clout, that's why. And they are willing to use it.'

'Grow up, sonny,' he said, being all of ten years older, 'and don't let yourself be deceived by appearances. We still run the world from New York, and don't ever forget it. By comparison, these German bankers are bush leaguers. And so are the Swiss, and the French, and the Dutch and the

Belgians. Look, we could put together a package to solve that little Italian problem in three days flat. When I say "we" I mean my own organization. Three days! And we would hardly have to go around Europe begging. Five phone calls – local New York calls – would do it. Understand, Hitchcock?'

I just looked at him.

'And it's time that your new friends down in the Middle East finally figured that out too. Sure, they have the money – for the moment. But we are the only people in the world who know how to manage that kind of money. Understand? Hell, of course you understand, Hitchcock. What I'm suggesting is that you start doing something about it. Putting money into these European currencies and banks is foolish. Look at the trouble you've gotten yourself into in Italy. Do you know our exposure there? Nil. Nothing. Zero. Why? Because I never *did* trust the Italians, that's why! Now I'll tell you something else. It's good we ran into each other today. Your name has been coming up with regularity in New York. You are on to something big, Hitchcock. Provided you use your brains. And don't try bucking the system.'

The system? It did not exactly have an organizational chart, but it consisted of Randolph Aldrich and perhaps two dozen other men in the United States. They were sure that they had been running the world since 1945, and running it reasonably well. I had always been highly skeptical about any 'conspiracy' theories of history. You know, the stuff about the Rockefellers, the Rothschilds, the old boys at Morgan Stanley, First Boston, Lehman Brothers and a few other places like that being really in control of America, and thus the world, through their control of the world's only really big capital market, and their control of the puppet strings which such money provides – especially those extending a few hundred miles south from New York to Washington. But by the time I was middle-aged, I had become less skeptical. Not that I believed for one minute in any real conspiracy. But perhaps in something just this side of it – a something that was benign in intent, but rather

85

less than that in execution. A very closely knit old-boy net. There had simply been too many smooth transitions – back and forth and back – between the key spots in Washington and those on Wall Street. It really started in the 1930's, when Bernard Baruch acted as New York's liaison man with Roosevelt. John J. McCloy took over that function when Truman came in. First he ran the newly created World Bank. Then he took over the job of running West Germany from Lucius Clay. He was 'their' man, not Truman's, and he was slotted into these positions because both were key to keeping world safe for American capitalism in the postwar era. Clay, by the way, moved up to the board of Lehman Brothers. McCloy eventually returned to New York, where he became chairman of the Chase Manhattan Bank, and a director of at least a dozen of America's largest multinationals. Eisenhower had his Charlie Wilson, who put it right out into the open with his crack about what is good for General Motors being good for the United States. Kennedy's policies were shaped with the help of men like George Ball (another Lehman Brothers man) and George McBundy, who graduated from running American foreign policy strategy to running the Ford Foundation's megabucks. Johnson inherited MacNamara, the latter representing an almost classic example of how the 'system' works. He moved from running Ford Motor Company to running the Vietnam war from the Pentagon to running our old friend the World Bank. It might be said that Nixon was helped both into and out of the White House by the biggest bond lawyer in Wall Street annals, John Mitchell. And Jerry Ford was given little choice but to delegate half of his Presidency to the leading alumnus of the Rockefeller training camp, the good Herr Doktor Kissinger. Finally, the Coach himself, Nelson Rockefeller, took a leave of absence from the Big Apple to make sure Jerry did not screw up the other half.

By the end of the 1970's, the New York stranglehold on Washington, and therefore on global power, was, if anything, greater than ever. Because without the blessing of the New York financial community, the Federal Government could have become, as they say, inoperative – within a very short time. New York City had discovered that in 1975. The city had been chronically spending billions more than it had been taking in in taxes. The Mayor and everybody else naturally assumed that the New York banks would cheerfully arrange to lend the city the difference, indefinitely. Well, it did not work out that way. He was told by Wall Street to either run the place their way or they would let the city go bankrupt. What could he do? Thereafter Gracie Mansion was openly controlled not by Democrats or Republicans, but by the Wall Street gang. At the end of 1978, the Federal Government was in exactly the same position, except that the scale of its indebtedness, and thus exposure to the New York banking community, was immeasurably greater. Uncle Sam was in hock to the New York gang to the tune of well over one-half trillion dollars, and every week he had to borrow at least an additional billion to stay in business. For the 'Great Recession' of 1974–75, and the massive unemployment it had created, had not just gone away, like all other post-World War Two recessions. Unemployment did not return to a 'normal' 4 percent. No, it dropped back to 7.5 percent in 1976, and then started soaring again.

Thus the 'temporary measures' that had been initiated in mid-decade – tax rebates, extended unemployment benefits and welfare payments, food stamps, clothing stamps, federal support for state and local governments to assist them in their support of an increasingly idle population – all became permanent. So the 'temporary' federal budget deficits of $60 billion per annum had not only continued, but by 1978 had risen to more than $100 billion.

To increase taxes would have been the classical way to bring government financing back into equilibrium – in fact, the only way. But higher taxes would no doubt have brought slump and still higher unemployment. That was politically and socially impossible. So instead, like New York City a few years back, the men in Washington had merely borrowed and borrowed and borrowed to make up the difference between the country's income and its expenditures. And, at least until the end of 1978, the New York banks and their satellites around the nation had just lent and lent and lent. They really had no choice. The alternative would have been the collapse of government, and the end of the system which made Wall Street possible.

The problem was that the banks were starting to run out of money! And 'they' had concluded that this problem could only be alleviated in one of two ways. The easiest would have been simply to print money, through the mechanisms of the Federal Reserve System and the U.S. Treasury. But that would have led to runaway inflation, which in turn would most likely have also led to the demise of the system. The vastly superior solution was to tap a new source of savings – massively and quickly. And such a source existed in the Middle East, where the oil nations had accumulated a hoard of savings that was absolutely unique in the history of mankind – over half a trillion dollars, an amount almost equal to the value of all the shares of all the corporations listed on the New York Stock Exchange. This represented the wealth that had taken the United States two centuries to build up; the Arabs had taken less than a decade. Salvation for Wall Street could be found in Riyadh – and perhaps only in Riyadh.

And Aldrich knew it. But he did not know that I also knew it. That's why he tried to lay it on so heavy in Frankfurt. I am convinced that if we had not bumped into each other there, he would have shown up in Saudi Arabia within a few weeks at most. Things were getting very tight in New York. So he made his play.

'Hitchcock, let's go back to that Italian mess for a minute.'

'All right.'

'How much, exactly, are you trying to put together?'

'About three. Maybe three and a half.'

'How much are your Saudis going to kick in?'

'That's not yet established. But I was thinking of maybe a half billion.'

'OK, maybe I'll match it.'

'Why? I thought you didn't trust the Italians.'

'To help out, for chrissake. And let me tell you this. If the word gets out that we are joining the rescue team, every two-bit bank in the States will try to get a piece of the action. Our name on it means quality, and I don't have to tell you that quality is getting rather scarce in the capital market these days. Sure, money's tight back home. But if we join up on this, you will have to ration out the participations, Hitchcock.'

Again Aldrich was right. And who was I to fight a half-billion bucks? 'All right,' I said, 'You're in. Provided, of course, the fellows at the Leipziger Bank agree also.'

'Wait a minute, Hitchcock. I'm not sure you really understand me.'

'I thought it was all quite clear. But OK, tell me where I'm going wrong.'

'If we come in, the Germans stay out. And the Swiss, the French. Etcetera.'

'You want an all-American show.'

'Right Hitchcock.'

'Why? Look, there's risk in Italy. A lot of it. In fact, to repeat what you said once more . . .'

'I know exactly what I said. And I know risk. Putting up three billion against fifty percent of ENI's assets does not fall into that category. You're a lot smarter than you think, Hitchcock. This new loan is a beauty. It's the old ones that are crappy. And it's the Europeans that are stuck with them.'

'What about Saudi Arabia's three-billion-dollar exposure?'

'Look, if we put together this new package, one of the conditions will be an accelerated payback of your old loans.'

'The Europeans won't like that.'

'Fuck the Europeans.' Which described, quick bluntly, what Aldrich was trying to do.

'I don't get it,' I said.

'OK, then listen a moment. How much are you guys taking in right now?'

'I assume you mean the Saudis.'

89

'No, not just the Saudis. The whole gang down there on the Gulf.'

'If you include Iran, Kuwait, the Trucial States, I would say around one hundred twenty billion a year.'

'And how much are you spending?'

'About fifty billion.'

'Which leaves seventy billion cash left over.'

'About that,' I answered. 'But not for long. You know that every country on the Gulf has massive development programs under way. In a few years they will be spending almost as much as they take in. On steel plants, roads, fertilizer plants, chemical factories. The works.'

'And arms,' said Aldrich. 'Don't forget that.'

'All right. But what's the point?'

'The point is this : Where are they going to get most of the material and the technical capability to build all those goddam roads and factories and whatever? From the only place that's got all they need – the United States of America. And in the end, they are going to have to pay dollars for it, just like the Europeans did after World War Two. And the Japs. And everybody else.'

'Come off it, Aldrich. Look around you. This is not exactly 1945. Europe can supply anything America can.'

'Wrong. First, Europe is disintegrating. Portugal went a long time ago. Greece is a basket case. So is Italy. And let's not even talk about Britain. Point one. Point two is this, and listen carefully. All those factories and roads and whatever aren't going to help the Arabs one goddam bit unless they can defend themselves.'

'Who's the enemy?' I asked.

'Who isn't when you're sitting on half the oil on earth? But I can think of three right off. The Russians, who would really have all of us by the balls if they could control the Gulf. Ditto for the Shah of Iran. And don't forget the Israelis.'

'Come on now, Aldrich. The Israelis could hardly . . .'

'Israel, my friend, is still the only nuclear power in the Middle East. Hell, Saudi Arabia doesn't even have one ounce of plutonium. And not one reactor operating from which they could get some in the near future. They are exposed, man. Unless . . .'

'Unless what?'

'Unless the United States continues to extend its military umbrella – the whole umbrella, including nuclear – over that country. If things start to heat up militarily down there – and they will some day, as sure as we are sitting here – the Europeans will be useless to the Arabs as allies.'

'Now the real point, Aldrich.'

'I'll go right back to where I started. Saudi Arabia's future can only lie in a close alliance with the United States – militarily, politically, and economically. But alliances should be, and today must be, a partnership where both parties take and give. I can demonstrate what we can give in the economic realm right now. We'll solve your Italian problem for you. Immediately.'

'And the give on the other side?'

'That the Saudis redirect the return flow of their petrodollars.'

'Have you got any specifics in mind?'

'We're looking for a lot of dollars from the Middle East during the next six months in New York. About fifty billion to be precise.'

'You're nuts, Aldrich. The Saudis would never concentrate their deposits in one country and one currency to that degree.'

'Hear me out, Hitchcock,' he replied, and Scotch or no Scotch, it was the tough New York banker who said it, and meant it. 'Saudi Arabia is going to have to make a choice. It can continue to enjoy a "special relationship" with the United States, and continue to get everything from turnkey jobs on petrochemical plants to air-defense systems. It can continue to get the best engineering, management, and military talent we can provide. It can continue to enjoy the protection of the only great power in the West. Indefinitely. The price is dollars. Cash dollars. Dollars deposited in the American banking system. Now. Not in five years.'

'And the alternative?'

'Is there one?' Aldrich sounded exactly like my Colonel Falk back in Riyadh. Or, more likely, it was Falk that was echoing the concepts relayed from New York through Washington. 'Khalid should get out of his tent now and then and look around. We don't have to be so explicit about these things to some of the other people on the Gulf.'

'Like?'

'Like the Shah. He's smart, that Shah. He plays ball. And he smartened up a long time ago. Remember back in 1975? The banks in New York had a half billion dollars sunk in Pan Am, and not a hope in hell of ever getting it back. Those idiots in Congress could not have cared less if that airline went belly up – with our money. I personally went to Teheran on that one. He was willing to put up a quarter of a billion cash two weeks later, and another quarter of a billion in 1977. As it turned out, he did not have to. Pan Am came back on its own. But the Shah got himself a lot of friends at the time. And since then, a lot of action. Like three billion dollars a year in the best weapons our country can supply. Like two of the most advanced atomic reactors in the world. He names it, he gets it.'

'Provided he keeps his cash balance with you in New York.'

'Right, Hitchcock.'

Aldrich got up. 'So pass the word along to your friends in Riyadh. If they play ball we'll play ball. And right away. I'll get you guys out of that Italian mess, and any new ones that might come along. And believe me, they are coming. Provided those deposits roll in. And don't worry about the interest rates. We'll give you tops.'

'And what if they are not quite ready for all this good news?'

'I will leave that to your imagination. But for openers, don't expect to have an easy job packaging your Italian deal.' And he strode off, leaving me stuck with yet another bar bill. And stuck with the conclusion that the Americans, finally were going to start playing hardball with the Arabs.

But let them play, I thought. We had more money than they did.

How do you get the finance minister and the head of the Bank of Italy to drop everything and meet you in Germany on two days' notice? Easy, if you represent Saudi Arabia's money.

I don't want to go into sordid details about the bribery of these two gentlemen. After all, I assume they are still around somewhere. Let's just leave it at this: we gave them 25 percent down in cash and agreed to transfer the rest to their Swiss bank accounts in Lugano upon completion of the deal. Standard procedure.

That done, and having gotten rid of them, we put through a conference call to the head of ENI. After all, it was his company's assets which were going to be pledged to a group of foreign banks. Not that he could have really blocked the deal. ENI was state-owned, and we had just bought the state. But who wants waves? We promised him that quarter of a billion additional working capital. He wanted three-fifty. We settled on three hundred million. He wanted to pay 10 percent interest. We wanted 12 percent. We agreed on 11 percent. He wanted it for ten years. We wanted to lend for one year. We settled on three. He wanted all this in writing, immediately. We flatly refused. We compromised by agreeing to send him a letter of intent, cosigned by Reichenberger and myself, within two weeks.

So by December 2, 1978, we were ready to go.

Randolph Aldrich had claimed that it would take him five phone calls – all local – to package the three billion we were after. Reichenberger and I figured we would need nine, all long distance. We divided up the territory. I agreed to take care of the American, Canadian, British, and Japanese banks. Plus making a firm commitment myself for Saudi Arabia. Reichenberger took on the European continent, plus Iran. We worked out of his office in Frankfurt, just three blocks up the street from my hotel. His staff had everything lined up by this time. Most important was the summary of the conditions of the loan, starting with the term, interest rate, and repayment schedule, and ending with a meticulous listing of the collateral involved. A 'country quota' had been worked out, a deadline for agreement – twenty-four hours – and a penalty for nonperformance, following confirmed agreement by Telex within that twenty-four-hour period.

Reichenberger had added one further feature. The whole deal would be done in German marks, not American dollars. I went along with it. Why not? The mark was still the strongest currency on earth. My fellows back in Riyadh would love it.

This proposal went out simultaneously to the nine lead banks which were going to be invited in, from their nine respective countries. Needless to say, the First National Bank of America was not one of them. Each copy was addressed to the chairman, and each went to the special Telex number of the various banks reserved for highly sensitive material. They went out at midnight, meaning that they would be on top of the recipients' desks first thing the next morning.

The next morning we made those nine phone calls. All nine were successful. We had our three billion, plus the three hundred million on the side, all together by four o'clock that afternoon. That evening Reichenberger actually invited me to his home, along with about half of his Board of Directors, to celebrate the birth of the new German-Saudi financial alliance. Everybody got rather drunk except me. And thank God I didn't.

Because when I walked into the Leipziger Bank the next morning, it was obvious that overnight the whole damn deal had fallen apart. Reichenberger grimly told me what had happened. Already at seven thirty that morning, his assistant had received a call from the American lead bank, which means it must have been placed around midnight, New York time. The message : After a thorough review, the bank's executive committee had refused to approve their participation. Count them out. Permanently. At eight, the Canadians – same thing. The Japanese had not bothered to call. They had put it on a Telex : 'We herebye [sic] inform you that we have withdrawn from your Italian Euro-mark loan syndicate, signed Mitsubishi Bank.' The British had been last in, also backing out.

Reichenberger was howling mad. And I did not blame him. Every bank but one of those he had contacted – the Swiss, the Dutch, the French, the Belgians – had come through, and stuck to their decisions. The exception was Iran.

It was the exception which, in my mind, proved the rule, which was : Do not fight the Randolph Aldrich crowd and expect to win in the first round. The line was obviously about to be drawn between those who were going to be the leaders and those the followers in the new financial world that the oil revolution had brought into being : the battle was on between Wall Street, along with its financial satellites abroad, and the European hard-currency bloc. At stake were the Arab megabucks, and who, ultimately, was going to control their use.

The American group knew that by blowing the Italian deal, they were courting disaster. If Italy went down the financial drain, could New York be far behind? But if New York did not manage to get a very big piece of the Arab action, was not disaster inevitable anyway? The Americans were obviously willing to play chicken right to the edge of the abyss. And I, it suddenly dawned on me that morning in Frankfurt, was really the pivot man.

For instance, I thought, if I went back to Riyadh and told it exactly as it had happened – what then? The Saudis would not like my story one bit. They were extremely touchy people. Very nationalistic. Very touchy about money, especially losing it. What if they cut the Americans off? Not one more fucking penny, Aldrich! If the New York money market was tight as a drum in December of 1978, what would it be like in a couple of months? And while we were at it, we could do the same to the British and sterling as we were doing to the Americans and the dollar. The bloody island would sink in its own lethargy, and Aldrich and his friends could try to figure out how to solve that! I am not a vindictive person. Never have been. Nor has the ability to exercise power really influenced my judgment. It is just that Aldrich and his crowd might have badly underestimated William H. Hitchcock.

Not that I was exactly on the best of terms with Herr Doktor Reichenberger, and the crowd he represented either, that December morning in Frankfurt. Christ, he could have killed me. But, fortunately, he was too busy composing a new set of Telex messages, postponing the Italian Euromark deal 'temporarily.' When I think back, what was probably going through his mind was that I had set him up. Made him look like a fool, for whatever crude American or sly Middle Eastern reason. When you are Germany's largest bank and you blow a $3 billion loan syndication – where your name is right on the line, in bold type – the word gets around, to put it mildly. And people start to wonder about your touch. And, after all, it had been the Leipziger Bank's name which had been on the bottom of each and every Telex – at Reichenberger's insistence, not mine.

We take comfort in what we can. I decided that after this fiasco I needed more than just my thoughts to comfort me before I went back to Riyadh to regroup. A side trip, I decided, was definitely called for. To Zurich. To play a few games. But not with the gnomes.

CHAPTER ELEVEN

There were exactly fourteen Hartmanns listed in the Zurich phone book, but only one that had the occupation 'professor' noted after it. Furthermore, the full name was given as 'Hartmann-Seligmann.' The Swiss telephone company insists on adding not only the profession, but the maiden name of each male subscriber's wife. The Seligmann part also checked out. So I called.

And she answered. I said I would be coming to Zurich later that day. For one night. Would she . . .?'

Yes, she would. But not for long. She and her father were leaving for Teheran on December 6. They had a lot to do. But how about a drink at their place?

Their place was about four blocks from the university – up on the hill on the east side of the lake. I knew where, approximately. We agreed on seven.

What's in a coincidence? A lot. Because there is much more behind a coincidence than just pure chance. Take that trip at the end of 1978. First, I had met Ursula Hartmann. Then Randolph Aldrich. Neither planned nor expected. But the same thing has happened to me hundreds – no, perhaps a thousand times. And I will tell you why. Because what percentage of the earth's population stays at the likes of the Hassler in Rome, or the Frankfurterhof in Germany, or Claridge's in London, or the Beverly Hills Hotel in California? A minuscule proportion. The admittance ticket to all of these places has to be importance – in terms of money, fame, scholarship, political clout. The same thing holds true for the first-class section of a Tokyo– Los Angeles flight or a London–Joburg one. That's why you always meet friends, or friends of friends, or somebody vaguely connected with what you are doing in places or situations like that.

I throw this in because those two 'chance' meetings

turned out to be extremely important to the path of my life thereafter.

I will admit, however, that after that call to Zurich I started to wonder whether there had really been any element of chance whatsoever in my meeting Ursula Hartmann. Why the hell had she agreed – just like that – to meeting me again? Especially at her home, for God's sake. I mean, that Rome thing had been fun, but not the sort of happening that leads naturally to a Sunday evening with the folks.

But then again, I thought, maybe she was a bit . . . you know, kinky. Not really kinky, but slightly fucked up on fucking. In need of something different to really get turned on. Hell, we all have our problems. Right?

So I flew to Zurich, checked into the old standby, the Baur-au-Lac, took a shower, and then took a taxi up the hill. I arrived at seven on the dot, something quite out of character. Actually, I was enjoying myself because it had just started to snow. I like snow. It makes the world appear clean and fresh, especially at night when the stuff whirls in front of the headlights. Switzerland and snow always go together in my Californian mind. So I arrived at the Hartmann residence feeling quite at peace with the world in general, and the Swiss in particular.

But after I walked into the house, I was not so sure. First, it was the good professor. He greeted me at the door. It was one of those first-impression things. Sure, I had seen him briefly at the bar in Rome. But face to face, well, he did not look at you. He stared. He had long white hair and eyebrows to match. He also did not shake hands in the normal fashion. He just grabbed yours, gave one short tug, and that was it. He was at least six inches shorter than I was. And about twenty years older.

There was the house. It was dark and musty. Bookcases all over the place, absolutely stuffed to the limit.

Ursula was sitting on the sofa in the living room. The sofa, as well as the rest of the sitting group, was covered with a suffocating red plush velvet. Everything neat as could be – but stiff. She greeted me like a Swiss Jewish

98

princess. A bare touch of her fingers on my hand, and then a motion that I should be seated on her left. At least she did not have her girl guide uniform on. Instead it was a black cocktail dress – buttoned right up to her neck, of course. But let me tell you, she looked absolutely smashing.

'I told Father all about you,' she began, 'and we are both very pleased that you could visit us.'

The professor just kept staring at me.

'Papa,' she continued, 'I am sure Mr. Hitchcock would like a drink.' Then to me : 'We only have vermouth. Would that be all right?'

I hate the stuff. So I said, 'Certainly.'

The professor served it like it was golden nectar. It turned out to be not just vermouth, but very sweet vermouth at that.

Then we all just sat there.

'Mr. Hitchcock,' said the professor suddenly, 'my daughter tells me you now live in the Middle East.'

'Yes,' I replied, 'although to tell the truth, I have so far spent very little time there.'

'But you are stationed there permanently.'

'I guess you could say that, yes.'

'In Saudi Arabia, I believe.'

'Riyadh. Yes, sir.'

'How is the climate this time of year?'

'Cold. And dry.'

'Do you know Teheran?'

'Yes.'

'How is the climate there this time of year?'

'Cold. And dry.'

'And do you know Abadan?'

'Yes.'

I swear to God, he then said, 'How is the climate there this time of year?'

And I replied, 'Warm. And dry.' I tell you, you have not lived until you have spent an evening with the folks in Zurich !

'We are going to Iran,' he then stated. 'Tell me, Mr. Hitchcock, what do you think of Iran?'

'Fascinating place. You know, lots of ancient ruins and all that.'

'No, I do not mean that. What do you think of the regime in Iran?'

'Well, it is not exactly the most liberal on earth. But the Shah seems to know where he's going.'

'Do you know the Shah?'

'I have met him. Once. Briefly.' Which was true. In 1972, in London at a very large dinner party at the Savoy, given by Jocelyn Hambro, the merchant banker.

'What do you think of him?'

'Highly intelligent man.'

The professor nodded and then asked, 'Stable?'

'You mean mentally?'

'Yes.'

'I would think so. Why?'

'Father,' interrupted Ursula, 'I think Mr. Hitchcock needs something more to drink.'

Then the doorbell rang. The professor went into the hall. Ursula remained seated on the sofa.

'Is it awful for you?' she asked, in a voice that was for the first time not strained.

'No,' I lied, 'but to tell you the truth . . .'

'Where are you staying?' she asked quickly.

'At the Baur-au-Lac.' At which point Papa returned with the blond Errol Flynn type. From Israel, she had said.

'May I present,' said her father, 'my colleague, Professor Ben-Levi.'

'Bill Hitchcock,' I said. 'Pleased to meet you.'

'And I,' he said, with Oxford overtones, 'am absolutely delighted to meet you, Mr. Hitchcock. I am told that you are one of the richest men on earth. I love to meet rich men. I always have. Years back, when I was studying at the Sorbonne, I actually met a Rothschild. A real one. Delightful man. Now and then we have gotten together since. We both have a great interest in ancient Greece, and have done some digging there together. But I am boring you.'

100

'No, by no means,' I answered, and I meant it. This guy was a relief.

'You see, Ursula also has an interest in archeology. Don't you, my dear?'

'Yes,' answered Ursula quietly.

'I think it is just marvelous that she is going to Iran with her father. Persepolis, Pasargadae, Susa! Ah, how I envy you, Ursula. When I was an undergraduate at Oxford we used to dream of such things. But, Mr. Hitchcock,' he continued, his blue eyes darting back to me, 'I am sure you are more interested in the present world. And perhaps you can give me some advice. I have just bought some gold-mine shares in London. Kafirs, I believe they call them. Was that a good idea? You see, I am a simple physicist, like my good friend Hartmann. We know nothing about money. Now tell me, am I also going to become very rich with my gold shares?'

Ben-Levi was everything that Professor Hartmann was not: handsome, witty, congenial. About my age. Even in Zurich he was not wearing a tie. As I explained the facts of life on gold to him, his eyes kept darting about, shifting to Ursula a few more times than I personally would have thought necessary.

When we finished gold, he was off onto real estate. And after that, New York. He adored New York. He wanted to live there sometime. But he also adored California. He loved American movies. Did I know any of the really big stars? I did, and hammed it up a bit, for Ursula's sake as much as his.

Then : 'I hear you are working in Riyadh, Mr. Hitchcock. Or may I call you Bill?'

'Of course.'

'It must be a fascinating place.'

'Not really.'

'Well, of course I am not in a position to judge, never having been there. But still, for us it has a fascination, probably for the very reason that we *cannot* go there,' he said, and continued, 'Tell me, how long do you think this chap Khalid will last?'

101

'The king?'

'Yes.'

'I would say that he is completely in charge.'

'And what about some of those young Turks? I think I have heard vague things about a fellow named Abdullah. One of Faisal's sons.'

'Just talk, as far as I know.'

'So Khalid is there to stay. Do you think that is also true of the Shah of Iran?'

'Frankly, I don't know.' And at that time, I also did not particularly care.'

'Well, my guess is that he will be there for a long time,' said Ben-Levi. 'He's not that old, you know. And he has a very loyal army – and one that is extraordinarily well equipped. They even have some of the new F-5F's. Terrific aircraft. I hear that your country is going to supply them with another fifty this year. Is that right?'

'I wouldn't know,' I replied. 'But for a physicist, you seem to know quite a bit about military airplanes.'

'That is quite natural in our country. We are all involved with our military, one way or the other. They made me a pilot a long time ago. And they still let me take a spin over the desert now and then. Great fun. But I am more interested right now in your field : money. Tell me, how are your banks in America doing?'

'They have problems. But they will survive. They always have. Why do you ask?' Now this guy was starting to get on my nerves.

'Well, quite obviously my country has the greatest interest in your country's prosperity. At least that is the common wisdom. A lot of my fellow Israelis feel that without your dollars we would be in very deep trouble – that our very survival would be at stake.'

'My friend,' I said, hoping to shut him up, 'in that regard both you and your fellow Israelis can relax. The American commitment to Israel is total. Well, almost total.'

'Almost?'

'Yes. Because in spite of everything we have said and done in the past, ultimately, if our national survival is threatened, I am afraid that we Americans will have to think of ourselves. I am sure that you Israelis understand that.'

'Of course. But explain – in, shall we say, practical terms?'

'OK. Look, when you come right down to it there are really only two things that seem to matter in our world of today : money and oil. And of these two, oil is the more important. Without oil, our economy – and thus our money – goes down the drain. *That* no good American could even begin to contemplate. We are very materialistic, as you have no doubt heard.'

'In other words,' said Ben-Levi, 'if you Americans have to choose between no oil and no Israel, you will probably opt for no Israel.'

'Precisely.'

He kept silent, for a change. But not for long. 'Yes, I can see your point. But, you know, we Israelis must not make that sort of choice.'

'Come off it,' I said. 'You just stated that without American money your country would be dead. You need American dollars just like we need Arab oil.'

'No, my friend. You did not listen very carefully. I said that some of my fellow Israelis believe such things. Not I.'

'And what do you believe?'

Professor Hartmann had not said one word during the preceding five minutes, nor had his daughter. Both were literally sitting on the edges of their chairs, hanging on every word from Ben-Levi.

'What do I believe? I will tell you. My country is not built on money and oil. My country is built on a people, and on a religion. The Jews survived and prospered for thousands of years in Israel – without oil and without dollars. If necessary, we could do so again.'

I had heard enough Jews tell me that one before. And frankly, it bored me. So I looked at my watch. Professor Ben-Levi got the hint and looked at his. Then, abruptly, it was over. The Israeli got up, said goodbye, and out he went. I had really no choice but to follow his example.

Ursula called a cab. It arrived five minutes later. At eight thirty I was back in the hotel.

At ten she called. She wanted to come over. But it was simply impossible. Her father needed her. To pack and make sure the house was left in order. She was sorry, very sorry. But she hoped we could get together in the Middle East. She said she would leave her forwarding address with the Swiss Embassy in Teheran.

And that was all that happened in Zurich on December 5, 1978.

I went to sleep that night with the nagging feeling that somehow the whole evening had been deliberately rigged. That I was being set up. But by whom? And for what? By morning, that feeling was gone. After all, I reasoned, who could be more harmless than a couple of physicists?

CHAPTER TWELVE

The first time you go to Riyadh you somehow manage to kid yourself into believing that it is really an exotic place. The second time you realize that it is one of the world's most desolate dumps : built right in the middle of the desert, composed for the most part of hovels and dirt streets, and populated by lazy ex-nomads, plus their goats and dogs, which represent the city's only garbage-disposal system. Who in their right mind would return to such a hellhole?

Well, it was half past eleven on the morning of December 6, 1978, and I was returning to Riyadh. I had cabled Prince al-Kuraishi from Zurich, cryptically informing him that I was on my way back to Saudi Arabia for consultations. I had figured on spending the day meditating my future, which, after the Italian fiasco, would most probably unfold somewhere quite distant from the Riyadh airport – like about ten thousand miles distant, in San Francisco.

My string of consecutive miscalculations remained intact, however. From the moment I stepped out of the plane it was quite obvious that if the Saudis had a shit list, I was definitely not on it yet. Al-Kuraishi was not at the airport, but his limo and driver were – right on the tarmac. The note the driver handed me gave the reason : there was a meeting at noon at the Ministry of Planning, and I was to attend.

That ministry was about twenty minutes from the airport, in the center of the city, in a building a block long and two stories high. It was a study in the Arab mind as applied to functional architecture. The entire vast first floor was in pink marble – massive and stunning – and there was not a damned thing in it, except for wall decorations and a Knoll desk with a secretary – male, of course – behind it, way, way back at the foot of a sweeping marble staircase. The announcement of my name to said secretary produced a hand motion toward the staircase, and then up. So that is where I went.

On top was yet another reception area, smaller and with less marble, but as compensation, layered with at least twice the acreage of rugs. Semi-sunken in such was my prince. He spotted me right away, which was not that difficult, since there were not that many men up there. When I joined him, al-Kuraishi had been chatting with two Saudis. He introduced me to Sheik Ahmed Zaki Yamani, minister for petroleum; I had already met Crown Prince Fahd. That got the old adrenalin flowing. The occasion, al-Kuraishi quickly pointed out, was a special meeting of the Council of Twenty, the privy council of the Kingdom of Saudi Arabia. We had barely exchanged twenty words when the room fell silent. Khalid had arrived.

The king, boxed in by four armed bodyguards, swept right through the reception area into the adjacent conference room. We swept behind him. The places at the conference table were marked, mine beside al-Kuraishi, four down from the head, where Khalid stood until the massive doors to the room had been shut. No one spoke or made a move until Khalid was seated. Then, with a highly audible swish of robes, the nineteen other Arabs in the room, plus me, followed.

The king started it off, in Arabic. Now my Arabic is restricted to one sentence. *Yusharrifuni an uqabilikum,* which means, 'I am most pleased to make your acquaintance, sir.' It did not come up, either in the king's brief opening remarks or in those of the crown prince, which were less brief. After Fahd came Yamani. Then the minister of planning – another sheik whose name I have forgotten. Finally Prince al-Kuraishi. My boy was obviously not at the top of the Saudi big league. All this took about thirty minutes. Then the doors opened, and in came twenty-one servants, one for each person at the conference table. They bore tea. And produced a lull during which it was apparently quite in line with protocol to engage in small talk.

'What,' I quickly asked al-Kuraishi, 'is that all about?'

'The minister of planning is on the carpet.' I'm sure he intended no pun.

'The actions of his ministry,' al-Kuraishi continued, 'affect every sector of our country. Obviously. Thus the entire Council of Twenty is present. Our system, you see, is very democratic. At the top.'

'What's he done wrong?' I asked.

'Everything. The entire economic development of this country is in a total shambles.'

'But,' I interjected, 'with the enormous amount of funds at your disposal . . .'

'Exactly,' he interrupted. 'But our problem is not *obtaining* money. It is *spending* it. Quickly and effectively. So that we can become a diversified and self-sufficient nation. In that we have failed.'

'And why am I . . .?'

His hand stopped me. The room had suddenly quieted down once more. The crown prince, apparently at the suggestion of the king, had taken over the meeting. He must have pressed a button beneath the table, since the room was suddenly cleared of all servants; simultaneously, two aides moved into the conference room and behind Fahd – bearing dossiers, not tea. Fahd's hand moved, and one of the dossiers, already opened, was placed before him. He read from it, jabbing his finger repeatedly in the direction of the minister of planning – I wish I could remember his name – who sat directly opposite him. All in Arabic, of course. But even in that strange tongue, the meaning was quite clear.

Then Fahd's hand waved again. The doors opened, and two newcomers were ushered in – both in Western dress. They remained standing at the very bottom of the table, since no chairs were offered to them. Fahd immediately switched to English, perfect American English.

'Mr. Jones,' he began, 'you are president of the Multinational Research Institute. And you, Mr. Rogers, are head of Arthur D. Rand Associates.'

'Yes, sir,' they answered in unison. They represented two of the preeminent American think tanks, each having thousands of scientists, engineers and economists on their staffs : superconsultants to the super economic and political entities of the West, ranging from IBM to British Petroleum to the Pentagon. They wrote the scripts for the policy-makers.

'Your organizations were essentially responsible for the development of our five-year economic plan,' continued Fahd. 'Correct?'

Rogers answered : 'Not exactly. Our men were here in a purely advisory function. The *responsibility* . . .' Cut off. That line might work in Palo Alto, but not in Riyadh.

Fahd waved again. Again an aide produced a document, again open.

'This, and I am sure you recognize it, is the proposal you jointly submitted to us at the end of 1975. Shall I read some of it to you?'

'That will not be necessary,' answered Rogers.

'Yes it will. It says, on page thirty-six, at the top, under Summary, Point One, and I quote : "We shall formulate, monitor, and modify as necessary an economic plan for the Kingdom of Saudi Arabia, programming the expenditure of one hundred forty billion dollars during the five-year period 1976 through 1980, designed to . . ." '

This time it was the American, Jones, who cut the Saudi off. 'You will note, sir, that nothing is said about implementation. We can suggest what must be done. We cannot force your people to work.' Mr. Jones, still standing, was red-faced and furious.

Fahd never blinked an eye. 'Your plan,' he blithely continued, 'says that Saudi Arabia will invest one hundred forty billion dollars in the domestic development of our country, our cities, our industry, our schools, our agriculture. How much has actually been spent thus far?'

Jones : 'I am afraid that I don't know, in fact I doubt whether . . .'

Fahd : 'You don't know. Exactly. The planning minister does not know. But I know. Not half. Not even one fifth. And the first three years of your five-year plan are already up.'

'Mr. Hitchcock,' Fahd suddenly said, setting the old heart thumping, 'how would you rate a plan like this?' He once again held it up.

'Lousy,' I replied.

'You are an American, Mr. Hitchcock. This plan has cost us over one hundred million dollars. What would you do with the people who are responsible for it?'

'Fire them.'

'Exactly. And that is what I propose we do. Immediately.' He then looked back at my two compatriots, still standing rigidly at the end of the table. 'Take them out,' he commanded.

The think-tank men, both now ashen in appearance, were hustled out. Not one person in the room except myself bothered to even give them a further glance. They were just hired hands. Foreign labor.

Fahd then switched back to Arabic. After ten minutes, the minister of planning – now I remember his name, Hisham Nazer – rose abruptly and left the room. I must give him credit for doing so with much greater aplomb than had the Americans. A vote followed. It seemed to me that it was unanimous, except for one vote. The hand of Prince Abdullah, son of Faisal and minister of desalination, did not go up. He was sitting directly opposite me, studiously ignoring everybody else in the room, just as they were ignoring him.

That was it.

The king rose and left. So did almost everybody else. But al-Kuraishi motioned that I should remain. When the room had cleared, three other men also had remained behind : Fahd, Yamani, and a man with whom I was not familiar. Al-Kuraishi brought me over to him. He was Sultan Ibn Abdul Aziz, defense and air minister of Saudi Arabia. I started to use my one and only Arabic sentence when he interrupted in Sandhurst English.

'You are a very direct man, Mr. Hitchcock,' he said. 'So are we. I am looking forward to working with you.' Which left me more than slightly mystified.

Then Fahd came over. 'Excuse me,' he said, 'for injecting you into this affair. My reason was quite simple. We had to take immediate action on this matter. Yet in no way do we wish this to be construed as an affront to the United States. It was a business decision. Nothing more, nothing less. It should be clear to your government that we are not in any way changing our policies regarding the employment of American advisers. We are just changing our approach. I hope you will make this clear to your people.'

Sneaky, I thought, but what the hell. It would not exactly hurt my reputation when the word got out that Hitchcock was playing the role of hatchet man in Riyadh. On the other hand, maybe I would be next to go.

Fahd read every thought. 'It will be amply clear in a few minutes as to what our new policy is. It is one that would call for a somewhat expanded role of yourself as adviser to our government, Mr. Hitchcock, provided you choose to continue to work with us. We need men who know how to move quickly, for we must move quickly if –' and he paused briefly – 'we wish to avoid having to cope with unpleasantness, both domestically and perhaps from abroad.'

He looked around at the other men present. 'Why don't we all sit down?' he said.

This time Fahd took the head of the table – interesting, I thought – I sat to his right, al-Kuraishi to my right, and opposite us Sheik Ahmed Zaki Yamani and Sultan Ibn Abdul Aziz.

'I will come right to the point,' said Fahd, still addressing me. 'We, as you have just heard, are way behind in every domestic program. As a result, the younger people are getting impatient. Our policy of educating them abroad is proving to be a mixed blessing. There is increasing agitation in their circles for "progress," and one of the men who attended our meeting today – I believe you met him once, briefly – is unfortunately encouraging these attitudes. It is also, I am sure, no secret to you that we have a large number of Palestinians in our country. They needed work; we

110

have ample work that must be done. They are able people. But they are also radicals. What all this means is that we must – finally – stop planning and start doing, before it is too late.

'You might wonder,' he continued, 'why I confide these matters to you. You shouldn't. Your embassy is fully informed. This is of no consequence to us, because America is our friend. What is of serious consequence to us is that other nations are equally aware of our growing exposure. First among these is our very large neighbor to the north – Iran – and the man who rules that nation. The Shah is getting older; his ambitions have not been fulfilled. He is a dangerous man – for us, therefore also for you.' When Fahd decided to come to the point he obviously did so with a vengeance.

'I do not think that anyone in your country would want to see this nation fall victim to either domestic insurrection or subjection from the north. The economic consequences for the entire West would be disastrous. I hardly need expand further upon this. Now, to what must be done. First and foremost, we must accelerate – greatly and immediately – our weapons procurement from your country. This is of absolutely paramount importance. We also need many more technicians to help us with these weapons. Now! Not in a year or two.'

'Well,' I interjected, 'I would think that weapons procurement is a problem that is surmountable, if I know our people back home.'

'But you are wrong,' countered the crown prince. 'Explain, Abdul.'

The good Sultan Abdul Aziz did. 'It is a matter of delivery,' he said. 'For instance, we have one hundred and twenty F-16 interceptors on order with you. We placed that order five years ago. But the first planes will be delivered in 1981. This is impossible. We must have them next year. All of them.'

'Surely someone at the Pentagon can do something,' I ventured.

'I have spent the last three days with Pentagon officials. They are still here in Riyadh. They are more than willing to talk, but what they say is always the same thing : Their hands are tied. Production capacity is limited. Mr. Hitchcock, it is not just planes I am talking about. We need Hawk missiles, we need Pershing missiles, we need tanks, armored personnel carriers . . .'

'Yes,' interrupted Fahd, 'we can get to those details later. You still have not answered Mr. Hitchcock's question : Why such slow deliveries?'

'Because the Americans have also promised these same weapons to Iran, to Israel, to Jordan, to Turkey, to Korea,' said Aziz. 'The list goes on and on. They are getting deliveries. We must wait.'

'Were not these delivery dates made clear to you at the time you contracted for these weapons?' I asked, because it still did not quite make sense to me.

'They were,' answered the defense minister, 'but our situation was much different at that time. Also, we had assumed that there would be flexibility in such matters.'

The crown prince again interrupted : 'I promised to be quite clear in all these matters, and I will continue to be so, Mr. Hitchcock. What Sultan Aziz is referring to in regard to flexibility is that we were assured in the past that such matters as delivery schedules could be "arranged." These assurances came from those men – and I am sure you know those to whom I refer – who have traditionally acted as agents for our government in arranging for defense contracts throughout the world. They worked for – and with – commissions. Quite natural. They served us well, make no mistake about that. I do not criticize them. They were eminently successful until your Congress began to investigate such matters. You know the stories that surfaced in regard to Lockheed – but why go into names? As a result, your defense contractors in America are no longer flexible.'

'I understand.' And this time I finally did.

'The result,' said Fahd, 'is that we can no longer rely upon our agents. They have been discredited in your country. They are regarded as Mideastern confidence men,

112

people who do things with bribes, men not to be taken seriously. Yet we –' and his hand swept around to include not only himself, but Sheik Yamani and Sultan Ibn Abdul Aziz – 'cannot involve ourselves in bargaining with foreigners.'

These words could have been spoken by a member of the English aristocracy in the nineteenth century. Yet, it was obvious, they were said in Riyadh in 1978 with the greatest sincerity.

'Therefore,' said Fahd, 'we would like to ask you to act as both an adviser and perhaps at times as an intermediary, in regard to certain aspects of the new policy matters which I will come to. Do you agree?'

It had taken the Arab at least five minutes of almost continual palaver to come to the real point. But by Mideastern standards, I guess he had come very close to just blurting it out.

'I do,' I replied.

'Good.'

He reached into the one dossier he had apparently retained. 'This,' he said, 'outlines what we have in mind. It is a joint effort of Sheik Yamani and myself. It also has the blessing of our King Khalid. I want you to study it immediately and thoroughly. If you have any immediate questions, I will be available to answer them. I need hardly remind you that this document must be kept absolutely – absolutely – secret.' As he spoke the last six words, his eyes bore directly into mine. I got the message.

That was the end of the meeting. I shook hands with the crown prince, with Sheik Yamani, and with the defense minister, and left with al-Kuraishi.

When we left the Ministry of Planning, I was prepared to join the prince in his limousine. Instead, there were two spanking new Fleetwoods at the door – one his, and one, apparently, mine, the latter flanked by two men.

'Your driver's name is Abdul,' the prince said. 'The other man's name is Hamdan. They will be continuously at your disposal. Hamdan and some of his colleagues will

113

ensure your privacy at the hotel. You will have the entire top floor of the Intercontinental at your disposal.'

And then he shook hands and left me with Abdul, Hamdan, the crown prince's dossier, and the jubilant feeling that Hitchcock had finally come into his own.

CHAPTER THIRTEEN

At the Intercontinental I was greeted appropriately. The manager and a half-dozen lackeys almost carried me through the lobby to the elevator banks. Then Hamdan and his colleagues took over. The top floor was off limits – to everybody, it seemed.

I am sure that even Howard Hughes would have been satisfied. Privacy is great, but only if it can be enjoyed in luxury. To hell with monasteries. The top floor of the Riyadh Intercontinental was about as far removed from a monastery as a Bangkok whorehouse. That analogy, come to think of it, is misplaced : in Riyadh not even the maids are female. But everything else was there, except liquor. However, I had anticipated that.

I took a long shower, changed clothes, ordered lunch on the phone, got a bottle of Scotch out of a suitcase, and sat down to scan Fahd's supersensitive document.

It was not only sensitive – it was sensational. What was proposed was that Saudi Arabia opt out of the OPEC cartel. The oil-based alliance was to be replaced by a Saudi-American alliance. That simple. Saudi Arabia wanted to move totally and immediately under the American umbrella – politically, economically, and militarily. Especially militarily. The Saudis obviously realized that such a policy switch on their part would, at least initially, meet with a good measure of skepticism in Washington and New York. Especially New York. So their approach would be as American as the Making of the President 1972 : They would buy their way. Not with the crude purchase of politicians, however. As Fahd had pointed out earlier in the day, the Saudi ruling clique had concluded that the Lebanese approach to things no longer worked. No, the Saudis intended simply to overwhelm the American capitalists with capital. To show their goodwill. And to then demand reciprocity.

Why all this, all of a sudden? Fahd had given the reason, in vague terms, over at the Ministry of Planning: the planned economic and military buildup of the nation had failed, leaving the Khalid-Fahd-dominated government in a highly exposed position, both internally and externally.

This document was more precise. The Saudi economic-development plan had called for expenditure of exactly $140,997,910,000 between 1976 and 1980. The think-tank boys had estimated that the nation would earn $180 billion in oil revenues during the same period. So they would have a comfortable, though modest, surplus of $39 billion. When that new surplus was added to the cash accumulated prior to 1976 – about $50 billion – the Saudis would end up with a well-developed country, and 89 billion bucks in the bank. Right? Wrong. Because the development program was in shambles. By 1980, at most they would require an expenditure of $45 billion. And instead of earning $180 billion, Saudi Arabia would take in a quarter of a trillion, because both the quantities consumed by the West and the price of crude oil had gone up much faster than anyone had projected.

Result? Instead of ending up with just $89 billion cash in the kitty, the poor Saudis were faced with the dismal prospect of having more than $300 billion. Provided that the Shah of Iran or Prince Abdullah and his following of local revolutionaries did not raid the cookie jar first. The proposed new alliance with the United States, it seemed, was designed to prevent just such things from happening.

The Fahd plan, which for the remainder of the document dealt essentially with the disbursement of that $300 billion the Saudis were stuck with, put the greatest possible emphasis on the need for a crash military buildup of Saudi Arabia, to be based exclusively on American weapons, equipment, and personnel. The original five-year plan had called for the spending of $22 billion, to be spread fairly evenly over all five years. Fahd now wanted to spend $24 billion in 1979 alone! And almost all in the United States. Fahd wanted to do in one year what the Shah had done in a decade.

116

But, as the Saudi defense minister had pointed out earlier, allocating such expenditures, and even placing all the orders, by no means guaranteed deliveries unless American foreign-policy priorities could be radically altered in favor of Saudi Arabia. And there is where the Fahd plan really got interesting – to me personally. Because what the Saudis had in mind was a massive – and I mean massive – shift of funds from almost every major financial center in the world to New York. Heretofore the Saudis had – prudently, in my judgment – been very careful to spread their risks. Their liquid assets had been carefully dispersed among Zurich, London, Paris, Frankfurt, Brussels, Amsterdam, Singapore – the list was a long one. And the list of currencies involved was equally long : marks, pounds, francs, guilders and so forth. But come 1979, it was going to be New York and American dollars all the way. And it was obvious that I was going to be the guy in charge of the cookie jar.

The reasoning behind this maneuver was very clear : once these billions started to pour into New York – with the promise of many, many more billions to come – the happy recipients would collectively represent just what the Saudis needed : a highly influential, powerful pro-Arab lobby in Washington.

Which brought to mind my old buddy who ran the First National Bank of America, Randolph Aldrich. He would personally spearhead the Saudi cause both at the Pentagon and the State Department. In fact, if we lent New York City a few billion, half the Jewish politicians in that town would probably start to face Mecca when they prayed.

But the absolute clincher in the Fahd plan was the new oil policy. The Saudis were going to propose a three-year freeze on crude-oil prices to OPEC. If the other ten members did not go along, as seemed 100 percent certain, then Saudi Arabia would pull out of the cartel and enter into a long-term marketing agreement with the United States based upon just such a price freeze. Actually, it would be a price guarantee : the Saudis would agree that the price would not go up, but the Americans would have to agree

117

that it would not go down either. Not so dumb, from the Saudi standpoint. The American public would go ape over the Saudis when this was announced. And the Saudis would get all the military assistance they needed. Soonest.

By the time I had read the whole document and had reread quite a few parts, it was getting on five in the afternoon. Cocktail time. I was all ready to put on my jacket, and go down to the bar when the awful truth once again struck me : there was no bar within hundreds and hundreds of miles ! There were also no women. Gawd.

But Allah proved merciful. The phone rang.

'Hitchcock,' it squawked, 'is that you?'

'Yes,' hesitantly.

'It's me. Reggie Hamilton.' I hadn't seen or heard from him since that luncheon in San Francisco at the Bohemian Club – which had started this whole thing.

'Reggie, you don't know how happy I am to hear your voice. Where are you?'

'In town.'

'Doing what?'

'Same old consultancy job – advising the Saudis on oil.'

'Well, come on over. Boy, have I got things to tell you !'

'Look, Bill, I thought maybe you'd like to visit us.'

'Us?'

'Sure, my wife's here. We've got a house.'

'Hell, yes, if these guys will let me out.'

'What do you mean?' Reggie's voice had a slight edge of alarm.

'Well, it seems I've got protection.'

'Good or bad protection?'

'I guess good. Look, give me the address and I'll get my driver to bring me right out.'

'Bill, obviously you're still new in this town. There are no addresses. I'll pick you up. In about a half hour. OK?'

After I hung up, the relief at not having to spend the rest of the evening cooped up alone was just slightly diminished by the thought that this might turn out to be a somewhat less than completely social evening. Reggie Hamilton's outfit, the Multinational Research Institute, had just been given the ax that morning over at the Ministry of Planning, and I had been instrumental in cutting down Reggie's boss, the red-faced Mr. Jones.

When I left the suite, the man outside my door just continued sitting there, not saying anything or even moving. When I got out of the elevator on the lobby level, Hamdan, however, was there waiting, ready to be of service. I told him that a friend would be picking me up and that I planned on having dinner at his home. No problem. He and the driver would just follow us out to my friend's place with the limo and wait. Then I would have transportation back. After my assuring him three times that it was not necessary, I gave up. What the hell! If that was one of the rules of the new game, I could live with it.

Reggie drove a Mercedes 300. And he knew his way around Riyadh. His house was on the outskirts of the city – an American-style bungalow. The neighborhood it was in was composed completely of such houses. In theory, it could have resembled the outskirts of, say, Palm Springs. Or Phoenix. But the reality was quite different. The streets were made of dirt. The lawns were composed of sand with clumps of wild grass here and there.

'Reggie,' I said, as we pulled up in front of his house, which indeed had no number, since none of the houses had any address, 'you are really living in style.'

He grinned. 'Wait until you see the inside.'

His wife was outside the door waiting for us. We knew each other vaguely. Wives of people who work for research institutes are not the most interesting people on earth, and I have studiously avoided any unnecessary contact with them. That's why I like San Francisco. Women are still kept out of the good clubs there. And it was in one club or another that I usually got together with Reggie. Over the years it had become obvious that she regarded me as a bad influence on her husband. The wives who felt that way about me were legion in number around the Bay Area.

'Well, well,' I began, 'this is really something. How many years has it been, uh . . .?' I had forgotten her name.

'Pat,' she said, dryly.

'Pat! Of course. Pat!' Wives, you see, make me as nervous as I make them.

'Pat,' I went on, 'I couldn't find any flowers. But at least I brought this.' Triumphantly I held up a bottle of Chivas Regal. Pat winced. Reggie beamed.

'Thanks, Bill,' he said, grabbing it warmly since Pat just stood there with a dumb look on her face. 'Do you know what that stuff costs locally? One hundred and fifty dollars a fifth!' We were still on the doorstep.

'Who's that?' asked Pat, suddenly noticing the Cadillac that had pulled up behind Reggie's Merc.

'Abdul and Hamdan. Very devoted to me,' I replied.

Pat gave Reggie a look, no doubt confirming some opinion she had ventured about my person prior to this little exchange. Then we went in.

As Reggie had hinted, the inside was no great shakes either. It was a rather weird combination of Montgomery Ward and the bazaars of the mysterious East. Pat, it seemed, had become a connoisseur of thirty-nine-dollar antiques and one-hundred-and-seventy-nine-dollar rugs. Back home in Palo Alto, though, the kaffeeklatsch circle would, no doubt, Ooh and Ah no end when Pat put them on display.

'Gee, Pat, you sure have made something out of this,' I said.

Reggie didn't say a word. He had been married for twenty-four years. But he did disappear into the kitchen, soon to reappear with two stiff Scotches.

'Do you want the tour?' he asked, after Pat had taken her turn to disappear.

'Not really,' I replied.

'Then, do you mind if we talk shop for a minute?'

'No, go ahead.'

'OK. Look, Bill, this is a put-up job.'

'Because of what happened this morning over at the Planning Ministry?'

'Yes.'

'Are you in trouble too?'

'No. I never had anything to do with that screwed-up planning job. In fact, I told those guys years ago that they were so far off, it was mind-boggling. But you know how it is, Bill. That whole team was made up of a bunch of young geniuses who knew everything.'

'So you're staying on.'

'Yes. I work for Yamani at the Oil Ministry.'

'So you know what's going on?' I asked, carefully.

'Everything.'

Reggie walked across the room to his desk. And pulled out an exact replica of the Fahd plan.

'I should have known,' I said. 'How much of this was your idea?'

'Enough. But I've had these ideas for years. So did Yamani, for that matter. Remember, in every OPEC meeting since 1975 it has been Yamani who has been dragging his feet on increases in OPEC prices. The rest of the member countries hate him. The Iranians most of all. Although Libya is not far behind. About the only people who have sided with Yamani now and then have been the Kuwaitis.'

'Will Kuwait pull out of OPEC also?'

'Could be.'

'Crissake, Reggie. That would completely wreck the cartel!'

'Exactly.'

'And what would be the response of Iran and Iraq, and the rest of them?'

'I don't think they are going to be exactly overjoyed.'

Another automobile appeared to have pulled up in front of the house. Reggie read my mind. 'Don't worry. It's friend, not foe. I told you this was a put-up job.'

'Who is it?'

'You know him. General Falk, from the embassy.'

'He was Colonel Falk when I met him.'

'He's moved up in the world.'

'Is he in on all this?'

'Completely. Essentially, he's been my counterpart over at the Saudi Ministry of Defense. I'm Yamani's boy; he's the adviser of Sultan Abdul Aziz, the defense minister.'

'And I'm the front guy for all of you!'

'You've got it.'

'Like three fucking prostitutes!' I said.

Reggie shrugged.

'Was all this already in the works when you set me up for this job back in San Francisco?' I asked in a not-too-happy tone.

'It was being considered, yes,' Reggie replied.

Then the doorbell rang. Pat came out of the kitchen to answer it. I was rather pissed off at this point, but it was difficult to stay that way completely. For Falk, instead of flowers, had also brought a fifth of whiskey – bourbon, of course. This time she took it and fled back to her kitchen.

'Reggie,' he began, 'why in the fuck do you still live in this dump?' He expressed my views exactly. If Reggie was Yamani's number one boy, this was hardly the sort of place you would expect to find him in.

'Pat likes it,' Reggie replied. 'We've been in and out of this house starting back in 1972.'

Falk looked disgusted and then decided to drop it. 'Dr. Hitchcock,' he said, grabbing my hand in his paw, 'I hear you've just been promoted. Congratulations!'

'Congratulations yourself. Reggie tells me you're now a general.'

'That's right. And if this fucking thing works out, the Saudis will make me an admiral too. Right, Reggie?' He banged Reggie on the back and then headed straight toward the kitchen. Seconds later there was a high-pitched yelp, indicating, I hoped, that the good general had given Pat a nice slap on the ass. Hell, even her bony ass probably felt good by Riyadh standards. I grinned at Reggie, and to his credit he grinned also.

Falk was soon back, with his standard water glass full of Kentucky's best. 'All right, Hitchcock,' he then said. 'When do we start moving?'

I looked at Reggie for guidance. He nodded affirmatively.

'In January. I've got to set things up first over at the Monetary Agency.'

'Jesus,' he said, 'that means another month in this place.'

'What do you mean?'

'Strict instructions. No moves on our part – you know,

on the weapons-procurement side – until your go-ahead. So Sultan Aziz himself.' Falk was apparently holding the usage of verbs to a minimum today. He sounded like a Pentagon memo.

'Why?'

'Hell, didn't anybody tell you what I'm up against?' Falk did not wait for an answer. 'Look, I've been trying to convince those fuckers in the Pentagon for years now. Tell those Israelis, those Egyptians, those Iranians to go to hell. Here – here in Saudi Arabia – is where the action is. Give 'em what they want. Right away. But no. Those pissants – the whole bunch in Washington wouldn't listen. And why? Because they were all bought. Bought! I tell you, it's not been easy for an old soldier.'

I would have bet my wife's alimony – in other words, an amount that would have commanded respect even in Saudi Arabia – that Falk had millions stashed away in Zurich or Geneva. But what the hell? Why knock private enterprise?

'You want to know something?' he asked me, again rhetorically. 'I have been up against the most powerful lobbies in the history of the United States. The Shah has bought everyone, but everyone. He's spent millions of dollars! Christ, they wouldn't even ship World War Two surplus to us here unless they were sure that nobody in Teheran, Tel Aviv, or Cairo wanted the stuff first.'

'Can that be changed so quickly?'

'Hell, yes. Provided what Sultan Aziz tells me is correct. You lay it on them with money, Hitchcock, and you with oil, Reggie, and my job will be a cinch. We'll make this place look like Germany in 1939!'

The general sure knew how to put things in perspective. He would have made a perfect Secretary of State, if only Governor Wallace had won in 1976.

'Falk,' I said, 'last time we talked you told me that Prince Abdullah was trying to start something here. Has that suddenly heated up?'

'Sure. Just like I said. They're recruiting the Palestinians like crazy. Give them a year, and they will outman the Saudi army five to one.'

I looked to Reggie for verification.

'The general's right,' he said. 'And it's not just the Palestinians. The Yemenites are also involved.'

'Explain,' I said.

'Sure,' Reggie continued. 'You see, that's where everybody went wrong. Especially my colleagues from the Institute. To develop a country you need two things : capital *and* manpower. Saudi Arabia obviously has the capital. But no manpower. Half the population is out right to begin with : the women. So you've got maybe two point five million men available for the labor force. But they absolutely refuse to do menial labor – or what they consider to be menial labor. It's part of the Bedouin tradition. It's not that they are against the capitalistic system, or don't understand it. For instance, they make terrific traders. Every Saudi would love to have his own shop. But working on construction or in a chemical plant or on the docks – absolutely not. So the entire development of Saudi Arabia as an industrial nation had to be based upon the importation of labor. It's not a new concept. Germany, Switzerland, France – for years, their growth has been based upon the importations of Italians, Spaniards, Portuguese, Yugoslavs, even Turks. Same principle. Here they turned to two sources of manpower : the Palestinian refugees and the Yemenites. The Palestinians were the skilled workers – they are a very clever, ambitious, and educated people – and the Yemenites were brought in to do the shitwork. The whole five-year plan's success depended upon this.'

'So what went wrong?' I asked.

'I will tell you,' interrupted Falk. 'They are all a bunch of revolutionaries ! Just dying to do away with Khalid and Fahd and Yamani and Aziz – the whole clique – and establish a people's republic. And that Prince Abdullah – who is no dummy – thinks that with their help he is going to be for Saudi Arabia what Nasser was for Egypt. Right?' He looked at Reggie when he said that.

And Reggie agreed. 'That is the reason for the whole mess here. You stop the importation of foreign labor and

124

the whole industrialization plan is dead. You continue bringing them in, and you are just asking for revolution.'

'How many are here already?' I asked.

'About a million. The five-year plan called for another half million,' answered Reggie.

'And that is why it was scuttled this morning,' I said.

'Exactly. But that still leaves a million here.'

And the Shah of Iran to the north.

At which point, Pat came in bearing canapés. Mutton pâté, she explained, on unleavened bread. In my opinion, she deserved to be stoned!

The dinner that followed consisted of scorched lamb chops, soggy rice, and soggier canned peas. Even English-women could cook better than Pat.

After dinner we retired back to the living room.

'How's Anne?' asked Pat.

I just ignored her.

'Who?' asked General Falk.

'Dr. Hitchcock's wife,' Pat pointed out.

I still ignored her, but Falk, after his fifth bourbon, liked the idea. 'I didn't know you had a little woman,' he said. 'You should have brought her along.'

'I would have,' I replied, 'but she's ill. Mentally ill.'

Falk looked sympathetic, Reggie looked the other way, and Pat was simply disgusted.

'It started with severe symptoms of frigidity,' I continued, 'and ended with a classic case of greed.'

Falk obviously did not follow. 'And where is she now?'

'In a home in California. My home.'

'You haven't changed, have you?' suggested Mrs. Hamilton. 'All you have ever thought of was sex and money. And yourself.' She had left out alcohol.

'Let's drink to that, Reggie,' I said, after she had left once again.

He got three more whiskeys, all on the large side, his being perhaps the largest of all.

'Look,' I said, 'I've got to go soon. As long as we are all going to be part of this show, why don't we figure out some schedules right now?'

It took less than half an hour. Reggie had already figured out everything, and General Falk was not nearly so dumb as he sounded, once we got away from fascist philosophy and into military-hardware procurement. We all agreed that we needed at least another six or seven weeks of preparatory work before the first big move could take place. We also agreed that this was completely in keeping with the thinking of our respective masters : the oil minister, the defense minister, and the crown prince.

Pat came back as General Falk and I were in the process of leaving. She announced that New Year's Eve was only twenty-five days off, and invited us to spend the evening with them. I said I would think it over.

But three weeks later, after spending the interim time shuffling banks deposits, rearranging maturity dates, meeting with Fahd, with Yamani, with Aziz during the day, and spending my evenings more or less locked up at the Intercontinental, I accepted in the end. It was pathetic, but these people were the closest thing I had to 'family' on that New Year's Eve. If only Ursula had been there! But she wasn't. So I went.

I still remember the toast that Falk – who, it turned out, had been a tight end at West Point in the early 1950's – proposed at midnight : 'Gentlemen, here's to the Year of the Big Game – Seventy-nine or bust.'

At the time I figured that he was just a drunken general mixing metaphors.

1979

CHAPTER FOURTEEN

The Boeing 707 of the Royal Saudi Arabian Air Force took off from Riyadh around 11 A.M. on January 18, 1979, bound for Teheran. On board was the top negotiating team designated, or at least approved, by the King's Council, to begin implementation of the new Saudi foreign policy. It was jointly led by Crown Prince Fahd and the Saudi Arabian oil minister, Sheik Yamani. Of the trio now running Saudi Arabia, only Sultan Ibn Abdul Aziz was missing.

My new job was to serve as financial adviser to the three of them. Thus my inclusion in this mission. Reggie Hamilton – who, since 1972, had been serving as Yamani's one-man think tank – was, of course, also on board.

The purpose of the mission : to announce to the Shah of Iran, and his oil minister, Ali Dhermanagar, that Saudi Arabia was going to alter its oil policy drastically. The Saudis were going to go independent. The strategy of announcing the new policy – in suitably vague terms – to Iran in bilateral talks, rather than at the next meeting of all the OPEC countries, scheduled for April, had been Crown Prince Fahd's idea.

'Let it appear,' he had suggested in our final meeting the previous day in his palace, 'that Iran has broken up OPEC because it tried to impose its hard-line approach on us. If we call for a full OPEC meeting, in the end we may alienate every member. This way, who will ever really know the truth?'

It was a clever approach. The Shah had, in recent years, insisted that he, and he alone, spoke for OPEC. And his country, in contrast to Saudi Arabia, desperately needed as much oil income as possible to finance the Shah's grandiose schemes, even though an increasing number of oil-producing nations were having increasing doubts concerning how much more the Western economies could take. Fahd, however, did not want to take on the Shah, and his overbearing oil minister, Ali Dhermanagar, in a public forum for still another reason. He feared that the Shah, to save face, might overreact. Perhaps militarily. And the Saudis were not ready for that kind of showdown.

In the plane there was lots of room to move around. The interior was a carbon copy of that in U.S. Air Force One – all compliments of the Boeing Corporation at no extra cost – with no rows of seats, but rather a series of conference tables and lounging areas. The difference : no reporters hanging around drinking and playing foolish practical jokes.

Fahd kept to himself. But Yamani was in an expansive mood. I had met the man on at least a dozen occasions during the past month, during meeting after meeting, which had been held, often late into the night, for the purpose of working out the details of the Fahd/Yamani plan. He was, as Fahd's partner, one of the most powerful men in the Kingdom of Saudi Arabia, yet he was still only forty-nine. The man had class. His family was from Mecca, where his father had been a religious scholar as well as a judge in those peculiar Arabian courts where the rule of law is determined by the Islamic Code. Yamani had taken his B.A. at the University of Cairo and his graduate degrees from NYU and Harvard, studying law in his family's tradition – but Western law. As a result, he was an almost perfect blend of East and West. He could talk Mozart and existentialism; but he also went to the mosque every day, and rode a horse like a Bedouin. In London he was a living testimony to the skills of the Savile Row tailors. On that plane that day, however, he wore the *aba*, the traditional flowing black robe of the Arabs, with a *ghutra*, a white headdress, held in place by a circular black cord. Impeccable, impressive – and likable.

Shortly after takeoff he came over to the table where I had been sitting with Reggie. 'Dr. Hitchcock,' he asked, 'have you ever met the Shah?'

'Once,' I answered, 'briefly. At a dinner at the Savoy.'

'When?'

'1972, I think.'

130

'And Dhermanagar?'

'Never.'

'You have been fortunate. A very rude man. Likes to tell stupid jokes.' Then : 'You studied at Georgetown?'

'Yes. School of Foreign Service.'

'Why did you not enter your country's foreign service?'

'Because I decided to continue my studies. At the London School of Economics. Probably my father influenced me there. He was a banker, you know. Wanted me to take over our bank when he retired. Instead he died. After about ten years, I sold out.'

'Yes, I do know. Tell me, Dr. Hitchcock, what do you think of the future of the capitalistic system?' As I said, Yamani had a versatile mind.

'It is extremely precarious.'

'I agree. But tell me your reasons for thinking so.'

'Do you want it simple or complicated?'

Yamani grinned. He knew economists. 'Simple.'

'All right. I'll make it real simple. The whole system of capitalism is based upon economic growth. For only the promise of growth of capital gains attracts the investment capital that makes our system go round. If there is no such promise, and thus insufficient capital investment, then the government must step in. Otherwise the resulting unemployment will lead to revolution. A primitive recent case of that was what happened in Portugal a few years back. OK so far?'

Yamani nodded.

'The other way it can go has been demonstrated by England. When economic growth stopped there following World War Two, it first caused the demise of the pound sterling and ultimately a similar loss of faith not only in Britain's currency but in the whole future profit potential in the United Kingdom. So private investors – both foreign and domestic – either pulled out or simply refrained from pouring in more good money after bad. As private investment slowed, the government had to fill the gap by taking over industry after industry. And it did something else : it inflated the money supply in England, to create at least the

131

illusion of increasing wealth for an increasingly uneasy population. Result? Double-digit inflation, year after year. The masses, led by the militant labor unions in the U.K., saw through that illusion. They forced through wage increases which were even greater than the price increases. Something had to give. It was, of course, the middle class. The government had to increasingly tax them – the "rich" – to be able to meet the demands of the poor. So the middle class slowly gave up. Net result : Stagnation, inflation, and taxation have combined to sound the death knell of capitalism in England.'

Yamani was also a patient man. He listened to me without even once interrupting. 'And America?'

'A similar process, although hardly exactly the same. I'll repeat myself : Our whole system is based on growth. But our growth in America was based upon what? Cheap raw materials, abundant capital, low interest rates – and above all, cheap, plentiful energy. Well, we have run out of all of these things, Ergo, growth stops. Result : In ten years our population ends up either violently dumping the capitalistic system, as they did in Portugal, or our system just dies a slow, dull death, as it is doing in England.'

'Is this process not reversible? To be quite specific, are we not about to do something, in terms of both energy and capital, that will go a long way toward correcting the current malaise?'

'I certainly hope so.'

'And I,' he responded with visible fervor. 'It should be clear to you by now that we, the crown prince, the king, I – feel there is no alternative to the Western system. We dislike the Eastern system not only for its lack of freedom, its dullness, its inefficiency. It is especially the godless principles upon which it is based that are abhorrent to us. Communism is totally unacceptable for Saudi Arabians.' He sounded like an Arab William Buckley, Jr.

'I realize that,' I said, 'although most of my fellow Americans do not. However, if America goes down the tube, there will be nothing to stop the Russians in the Middle East. Except perhaps the Shah of Iran.'

132

That last sentence was a mistake. Yamani's eyes took on an uncomfortably harsh glint. 'Yes, exactly. That is what you Americans have believed for many years and still believe today. It is stupid. You believe that the Shah is the "great stabilizer" of the Middle East. That a strong Iran will keep the Russians out of the Middle East indefinitely. That the only viable countervailing force to the Soviets in the Middle East is an all-powerful Shah. It is something that goes back to John Foster Dulles, was fully endorsed by John Kennedy – and still is by all of his surviving relatives – and was a doctrine that fitted perfectly into Kissinger's neat little world. Do you know what can *really* happen?'

Yamani was mad. 'Look out that window!' he demanded.

I looked. We had just turned the corner after going east from Riyadh, and were now flying due north over the Persian Gulf, about five miles off its western coast.

'From here to the top of the Persian Gulf is about three hundred miles. Our major oil fields, those of Kuwait, of Iraq, of Iran, are all within a few dozen miles of that coastline. You control that coast and you control half – *half* – the petroleum on earth. If a dictator like Pahlavi would take such control – and make no mistake, he intends to – then your capitalism will be dead very soon! Do you understand that?' With emphasis.

'I do.'

'Then you must quickly convince your politicians at home of the same thing. Before it is too late. We are willing to make our contribution – to your system, and to our survival. If you are willing to do the same thing. But that will mean – with no reservations, Dr. Hitchcock – that the foolish illusions concerning the Shah of Iran be completely and absolutely abandoned in your country.'

He paused. 'You will see for yourself. We shall meet Pahlavi tomorrow. Then make your own judgment.' Abruptly he got up, and went to the aft part of the aircraft. Yamani had obviously articulated the principles behind this trip. He and the crown prince were playing for keeps, as they say.

Reggie, who had been sitting next to me the whole time, not saying a word, now spoke up. 'He's right, you know.'

'Maybe. But I'm by no means convinced that the Shah of Iran has everybody in Washington in his hip pocket.'

'Wait and see. We'll be there next week.'

I went back to the window. The coast was a flat, brown wasteland.

'Does Yamani really believe that the Shah is going to move militarily to take that over?' I asked Reggie.

'Yes. And say what you will, Bill, he is no fool.'

'I agree.'

I also thought it over. 'But,' I continued, 'can the Shah do it? He might be able to win a battle or two, but then we'd clobber him. And so would the Russians, probably.'

'That would depend,' answered Hamilton.

'On what?' I asked.

'On what kind of war develops.'

'What's that mean? For Christ's sake, Reggie, there's only one kind of war.'

'No,' he answered. 'Two. Conventional and nuclear.'

I just looked at him for a minute. 'Ah, get off it, Reggie. Where in hell would the Shah of Iran get nuclear weapons?'

Reggie ignored the question. But thirty minutes later we passed over Abadan. I could have looked straight down and actually *seen* the answer.

CHAPTER FIFTEEN

Abadan, the Iranian city at the northern tip of the Persian Gulf, is separated from Iraq on the west by the combined Tigris and Euphrates rivers as they enter the sea. To the north and east of Abadan are Iran's great oil fields. In Abadan proper was situated the largest oil-refinery complex in the world. It was originally built by the British, and later operated jointly by the Seven Sisters through the mechanism of the Iranian Oil Consortium. In 1979 it was, of course, 100 percent Iranian.

At the beginning of the decade, the Shah of Iran already had decided to make Abadan a major center of economic power – the site of the greatest concentration of heavy industry in the Middle East. He had been faced with a classic economic choice : to transport the vast excess of energy available in the Abadan region to the major centers of population in the north of Iran, or to build an industrial empire on top of the primary energy source in the tradition of Pittsburg or the Ruhr. He had chosen the latter. Thus, based upon the cheapest energy in the world, Abadan soon had a massive concentration of cement plants, steel mills, aluminum factories either already a reality or under construction, all designed to gulp up energy in the form of natural gas from wells just miles away, or oil from the refineries right in town, or electricity produced by the gas turbine generators, which converted into electricity that which had been formerly just burnt off in the desert. Abadan's location on the Gulf, with deep-water port facilities, was ideal for industrial development : the raw materials could be brought in by sea, converted through the application of energy, and either sent by railroad north to Teheran or exported, again by sea, to the world markets.

So much for economic trivia. What proved not so trivial later on was the fact that the Abadan region had also been chosen by the Shah as the site for the construction of Iran's largest nuclear-power reactors. This was ridiculous on the surface of it : the classic case of coals to Newcastle. But in the Shah's concept of history, it made very definite sense. For his theory was that already, before the twentieth century had ended, the entire world would recognize that petroleum was simply too precious a natural resource to be squandered as a source of energy. Its use would inevitably be limited to applications which took advantage of petroleum's unique properties – for the manufacture of fertilizers, of plastics, of pharmaceuticals, of pesticides. When that happened, Abadan would still have a surfeit of energy : but nuclear, not conventional.

The Shah's nuclear plans did not stop with Abadan. The whole country was to go atomic. Thus in the 1974–76 period, the Shah let contracts for a total of six nuclear facilities : two for Abadan, two for the Teheran region, one for Isfahan, and one to be built on the Caspian Sea – to bug the Russians. Invariably there developed a scramble for these contracts. The Americans fell all over themselves trying to get their foot in the Iranian nuclear door. So did the Germans, the British, and of course the French. Roche-Bollinger also joined in the bidding in 1974, but at that point the Shah did not need the Swiss. He needed the Western powers – all four of them.

So the Americans got the contracts for Teheran, the British got Isfahan, and the Germans the Caspian Sea – which doubly bugged the Russians. After all, they had invaded Iran in 1941 to kick the Germans out of Iran. The French got Abadan.

All nations agreed that the Shah was indeed a wise and farsighted ruler. After all he paid in cash. And there were more contracts to come, as Roche-Bollinger discovered to its delight at the end of 1978. Iran was the dream of that small club of Western corporations which had stuck their necks out with billions of dollars of research and development funds in the nuclear-power field. For while at home they were often completely bottled up in their efforts to sell nuclear plants as quickly and in as great a number as possible in order to recoup such massive investments, in

Iran there were no such problems. In Iran you did not have anticapitalistic agitators like Ralph Nader, or such commie organizations as the Redwood Club, talking their SLA type of nonsense about the dangers of nuclear reactors to the population. Had a nuclear reactor ever blown up? Ever? Even just one? Of course not. If Nader had shown up in Iran, the Shah would have had him before a firing squad within twenty-four hours. The Shah's was the type of national leadership that America so sadly lacked after its loss of Nixon.

Now the Shah, when letting these contracts on such a dispersed and benevolent basis, had more in mind than good public relations: what he coveted was membership in that *other* most important fraternity on earth (he already dominated the first, OPEC): His ultimate goal was elevation to that select group that had atomic bombs, and thus the key to world power.

Well, as every science major after Hiroshima knew, all you needed to make a bomb was plutonium. And they also knew that nuclear-power reactors produced plutonium – quite a bit of it. Knowledge of this eventually seeped up to the level of the statesmen of the world, especially to those statesmen who already had nuclear reactors running nicely and producing lots of the stuff needed to make those great bombs. Their conclusions: What was good for the United States, the Soviet Union, France, Britain, and China was obviously not so good for Sweden, South Africa, India, Brazil, Japan and the rest of them. Thus the nonproliferation treaty. And thus the most important feature of the treaty: the nuclear powers – i.e., those nations which were in a position to export nuclear technology for civilian use – all agreed that, yes, the reactors could be exported almost at will, but that the plants where the used fuel elements of these reactors would be reprocessed be strictly controlled by an international body. Why the latter? The answer necessitates more trivia. Let's use as a starting point the reactors which the French firm Framatome built for the Shah just outside of Abadan. They were pressurized water-cooled types, capable of producing six hundred megawatts each,

137

designed to be fueled with 20 percent enriched uranium fuel. This fuel was provided by enormous plants, situated in the United States, which took the raw uranium and, through a complicated and expensive process, brought it up to the level of concentration required for controlled nuclear fission. The enriched uranium was packaged in the form of long, thin fuel rods, which were really nothing more than metal tubes filled with hard black pellets of enriched uranium oxide, and sold to users throughout the world. The rods were inserted into the core of the power reactors, in carefully calculated arrays, immersed in water; then they produced, as a result of the fission process, enormous quantities of heat, which created steam, which ran the turbines which produced electrical power.

After months of immersion, these fuel rods lost their potency. In an extremely delicate process, heavy cranes removed the spent fuel rods, and – very carefully – transported them to a neighboring facility, a concrete storage basin filled with cooling water. These storage basins were quite spectacular affairs. For when the uranium oxide rods were immersed they emitted an intense sapphire-blue light. This light came from the radioactive decay of the accumulated products of nuclear fission, some of which, like cesium of strontium, remain lethal for tens of thousands of years. But the most important leftover was our old friend plutonium, which could be lethal either as it was, or as the key 'explosive' element in nuclear weapons.

But plutonium could also be extremely useful – as recycled fuel for the very nuclear reactor which created it. Enter the reprocessing plant. It was a combination of sewage plant and doomsday machine. Its function was to separate the radioactive garbage from that most valuable of human-made substances, the plutonium. The plant itself was a monstrosity – on the outside a blockhouse of super-massive concrete walls (to shield the innocent world around it from radioactive death); on the inside, a scene right out of science fiction : systems upon systems of mechanism, ranging from cranes to steel-clawed hands, all operated by remote control by men totally isolated from their tools by massive glass walls. The process that went on in such plants was not terribly complicated, however. All that the equipment was designed to do was to chop up the spent fuel after its removal from the storing basin, dissolve it in acid, and then chemically extract the plutonium from the resulting mess. What was left over was a soup that could, and still can, poison the earth for centuries. This residue was trucked off in equally monstrous vehicles, and eventually dumped into underground storage facilities where, one hopes, it will forever lie undisturbed.

The plutonium, however, stayed. After being suitably reprocessed in the fuel-conversion facility of the reprocessing plant, it was once again repackaged in oxide form in metal tubes, and these fuel rods were fed back into the power reactor, where the whole process started over again.

Which brings us to the crucial point. Once any nation has a reasonable quality of plutonium oxide, building its own nuclear weapons becomes a relatively simple affair. To acquire such plutonium oxide all that was needed was : (a) a nuclear power reactor, and (b) a nuclear-fuel reprocessing plant.

The original nuclear powers recognized this early, and – although they would permit export of nuclear reactors of almost any size, shape and tube to anybody who could pay for them – adamantly refused to allow the free export of nuclear-fuel reprocessing plants. They demanded that the spent fuel cells be brought back to the exporting nation – the United States, Britain, France, etc. – where the plutonium could be extracted and retained. As the number of nuclear reactors globally in operation expanded, this solution became impractical. So, in very few cases, the technology for the construction of reprocessing plants was exported and such plants were built on 'foreign' soil, but with the absolute condition that their functioning be completely and constantly monitored by inspectors of the International Atomic Energy Agency, an organization of the United Nations, headquarters in Vienna. Through a myriad of devices they controlled every step, to the extraction of the plutonium, to the replacement of the plutonium-filled rods

139

back into the reactor. The whole idea : to prevent any leakage of plutonium from the recycling process.

Iran, in 1976, was permitted to contract for the construction of such a nuclear-fuel reprocessing plant. After all, it was the biggest customer in the world for the atomic industries of the United States, Great Britain, France and West Germany. They all agreed that, with such a number of power reactors under construction in Iran, and – they hoped – with excellent prospects for additional orders for many more reactors, amounting to tens of billions of dollars' worth of business, an exception had to be made in the case of Iran.

In 1976, construction was started on such a facility in the 'nuclear park' north of Abadan. In the summer of 1978 it was completed. Together with the two Framatome six-hundred-megawatt power reactors already in operation on the same site, Iran now had the capability of producing fifteen pounds of plutonium each and every week – on its own soil. It takes just about that amount (six kilos) to make a reasonably effective atomic bomb. But of course, the inspectors of the International Atomic Energy Agency were there in force to prevent any such thing from happening.

On December 6, 1978, Professor Hartmann, head of the physics department of the Eidgenoessische Technische Hochschule in Zurich, technical adviser to Roche-Bollinger Company of Baden, and military adviser to the Swiss Military Department in Bern, had arrived in Abadan. With his daughter, Ursula.

They had come from Zurich on one of Air Iran's Concorde airliners, and then had switched to the feeder 737 to Abadan. No special attention had been given them along the way. But upon arrival on the Persian Gulf, that changed. Both General Reza Barami, head of Iran's air force, and Professor Hadjevi Baraheni, head of the Iranian Atomic Energy Authority, were there to greet them. So were four members of SAVAK. The Hartmanns had assumed that hotel accommodations in town had been arranged for. To their surprise, they never entered the city.

140

Instead, the two Mercedes – one for the bigwigs, the other for the SAVAK escort – whisked them out of the airport, and headed straight north along the river. Their destination proved to be Khorramshahr, about twenty miles away. In Khorramshahr a large villa awaited them. The villa was built very much along American ranch-style lines and had everything from a pool to air conditioning to a servants' wing, which, it turned out, housed a cook, a maid, and a man who took care of the heavy work and the garden. No chauffeur, though. SAVAK was in charge of transportation.

Thanks to the Concorde and an immediate connection in Teheran, it was only two in the afternoon when they were already installed. The cook had the usual light Iranian lunch ready : yoghurt, fruit, tea.

The Iranians, as they can be, were excessively polite to the professor and exceedingly gracious toward his daughter. It was suggested that the day was still young and that a brief tour could well be fitted in. By 'chance,' at two thirty the young wife of one of the inspectors of the International Atomic Energy Agency – an Austrian, like her husband – showed up. She offered to show Ursula the local sights and to keep her company for the afternoon. Ursula, delighted to have the companionship of another German-speaking woman, accepted. The men went their separate way, with a quite different type of scenery in mind.

Ursula saw the river, the palm trees and the local bazaar, while Daddy went to see the nuclear reactors and the separation plant.

At seven, they were once again alone – except for the servants inside, and SAVAK outside – in their new home in Khorramshahr.

'What do you think?' asked the professor, as he settled down to a sherry in the living room.

'Fabulous !' replied the daughter. Ursula was absolutely bubbling over with enthusiasm. Not only was the house ideal, but the town, the climate, the company of Frieda – everything. Gray, cold Zurich in December could hardly compete. 'And is everything here up to your expectations, Father?' she countered.

It was. Completely normal.

'Is this where you will now be working?'

'Yes,' the professor answered. 'The site is about five miles outside of town. Excellent location. It is also an excellent concept they have here. In essence, the Iranians are building the first futuristic "energy center" in the world. The French have already built two large reactors here. I am here to lay the groundwork for the two Roche-Bollinger power reactors. By the end of the next decade the plans call for a total of ten reactors on the same site. It is unique.'

'But why such a concentration? And why here?' For many years Ursula had been perfectly willing to replace her mother – not only as housekeeper back in Zurich, but also as listener in the evenings. There is much to be said for the way in which family duties are still discharged in central Europe. And there was no change in the Hartmann household, in spite of its being transplanted to Iran.

'The concentration is really for safety. If something happens, as it theoretically always can, no major population center will be involved. We are surrounded by desert here, and the prevailing winds blow into still more desert, which stretches, I am told, for a thousand miles.

'Why here?' Hartmann continued. 'Because, although this is a desert, still there is an almost inexhaustible supply of fresh water. The river. And that huge river here drains the entire fertile crescent of the Middle East. Eventually every drop will be necessary. For reactors use unbelievable quantities of water for cooling purposes. Reactors also generate a lot of heat and pollution. But again, here in the desert, who will care?'

'How long will we be here?'

'Hard to say. Perhaps as much as six months. Maybe longer, if the problem with the fuel cannot be solved.'

'Is that one reason why they asked you to come?'

'It would seem so,' replied her father. 'You see, in addition to the power reactors, they also have a nuclear-fuel reprocessing plant. It recycles the spent fuel rods, you know.' Ursula knew. You can't live all your life with a nuclear physicist and not know these things.

'Well,' he continued, 'obviously there is something faulty in the purification operation. After recycling, the new fuel rods with the plutonium elements are not up to performance. Their yield is at least twenty-five percent below normal.'

'Why?'

'There could be two causes. It might be a faulty design by the French. But I doubt that. More likely is simple sloppiness in the operations. Almost all the staff is now Iranian. The few Frenchmen that are left supervising things tell me that their quality is not the highest. Furthermore, for some reason, there has been an extremely high turnover of Iranian engineers at the plant, which I don't understand, really.'

'Well, Father, that's not so surprising to me. Frieda — the wife of the Austrian IAEA inspector, who took me around today, told me a little bit about how things work here. Her husband told her that, even if trained in Europe, the Iranian technicians are very unstable, professionally. Apparently some also developed radical political ideas when studying abroad. If they are found out, they are immediately fired and "removed" — that's the word she used — from this area. Father, you know what a reputation this country has as a police state.'

The professor chose to ignore this. He changed the subject back to Ursula's innocuous day at the local bazaar.

Heinz Gerhardt Hartmann had the reputation, both in Switzerland and among his colleagues abroad, as the epitome of the 'uninvolved' scientist: a man with a brilliant scientific mind, encased in a character that was bland, dull, and absolutely apolitical. In a word, Swiss.

He was not a young man. Born in Schaffhausen in 1916, he had attended the Mathematische Gymnasium as a youth, and, in the natural progression of things, went on to the Federal Institute of Technology in Zurich. It was logical, since his mathematical bent had led him to physics and the Eidgenoessische Technische Hochschule for further study — where Einstein had taught before his emigration to the United States. In his second year of graduate work, as was

143

usual for Swiss students, Hartmann had gone abroad, to Munich, where at twenty-one he was one of the youngest students of Dr. Werner Heisenberg at the Max Planck Institute. Heisenberg's research there had already proven the feasibility of atomic fission. As a result of Heisenberg's influence, nuclear physics became Hartmann's field for the rest of his professional life.

It was in Munich that he met his future wife, a German Jew – Leah Seligmann, of the Frankfurt Seligmanns, who was studying medicine at the University. He stayed for three semesters, from the fall of 1937 to the spring of 1939. His department was abrupt. It was triggered by the overnight disappearance of Leah. He returned to his studies in Zurich; she went to the horror of Dachau. In February of 1940 she crossed the German-Swiss border at Schaffhausen, and three days later they were married. Her case was unusual, but not that unusual. Quite simply, her family had bought her way out, as happened in thousands of similar cases. The Seligmann family was one of the oldest and most widespread banking families in the world. Their family network ranged from Frankfurt to Hamburg to Paris to London to New York and even San Francisco. There was also a minor branch in Switzerland. So she got out, where millions of others did not. In 1943, Hartmann became assistant to the head of the nuclear physics department of the ETH. In 1948, their only offspring, Ursula, was born. His full professorship came in 1956. In 1958 Leah died at the age of forty-two, a belated victim of her physical and mental maiming in that little village outside of Munich. Hartmann, from that point on, began a retreat from the academic world. Of course he retained his position and title as the Herr Doktor Professor at the ETH. But he never became head of its prestigious physics department. Instead he became a consultant, first to Roche-Bollinger in the nuclear-power field, and then to the Swiss Military Department in the nuclear-weapons field. In his latter activity, he developed computerized simulation techniques which allowed the Swiss government to develop nuclear weapons

144

without the necessity of testing them. If Hartmann's models 'exploded' in the simulation laboratory, there was no doubt that they would explode in an exactly similar fashion in the battlefield – if the need arose.

Thus, according to the current 'insider' opinions, Professor Hartmann, like many of his counterparts in the United States, France and Britain, had joined the ranks of amoral scientists. His attitude, it was thought, was really no different from that of the Swiss bankers, who were perfectly willing to handle the world's dirty money, since, they said, it was not their responsibility to police the world. Their loyalty was to Switzerland and its survival as a prosperous, independent nation, although devoid of natural resources, surrounded by jealous hostility. Their functions did not involve morality. They just did their job for their clients, and thus for their country. Meticulously. So also Hartmann. His client, the Swiss military, was synonymous with his country. His duty was to serve them meticulously. Period. And if they requested that, for whatever reasons of Swiss national interests, he serve as a weapons consultant to the Iranians, he would do it in the same fashion. Correctly. That was how the world – his colleagues at the Federal Institute of Technology, his superiors at Roche-Bollinger Company, and especially those at the Swiss Military Department – saw Professor Hartmann. Utterly professional and utterly reliable. The Iranians, after a thorough investigation by SAVAK of Hartmann and his background, were convinced of the same. Perhaps the only living exception to the universal view of Professor Hartmann as a sixty-two-year-old, slightly stooped, white-haired 'pure' scientist was that of his daughter. But she held her peace.

At nine the following day, as had been prearranged, Professor Baraheni and General Barami picked him up once again. Hartmann, at this point, was in a puzzled frame of mind. There had been a great deal of highly contrived wooing of his cooperation in Switzerland. The minister of defense had had him over to dinner, at his home in Bern – something that was totally without precedent. It was on that evening, in late November of the previous year, that the question had finally been put to him directly : Would he be willing to put his expertise in the nuclear-weapons field at the disposal of the Shah? His answer was immediate and without reservation : Yes, if that is what his government requested.

But, from what he had seen so far, the whole issue was moot, at least in a practical sense. To make nuclear weapons you needed fissionable material. From what he had seen yesterday, no plutonium produced at the Khorramshahr processing plant could possibly have escaped the control of the United Nations inspectors – unless something highly unusual had escaped his own notice at the nuclear park. He was looking forward to a more intensive survey of those operations, for they represented an interesting academic puzzle.

But that was not to be. Instead of traveling north to the reactor site, General Barami's Mercedes went due east. The road soon dead-ended at the entrance to a huge military installation. It was hardly anything secret. The place had been built by the United States in the 1950's under the mutual defense assistance program related to the formation of the SEATO alliance. In 1979 it was under full Iranian control. The American presence was, however, still highly visible in the form of equipment. The air base was the home of 220 of the Iranian air force's most sophisticated aircraft, all supplied by American corporations : 50 F-4 Phantom fighter bombers, compliments of McDonnell Douglas; another 50 variable-geometry F-14 interceptors, a product of Grumman Corporation; 120 Northrop F-5 fighters.

General Barami, as head of Iran's air force, pointed all this out with great pride.

The base's perimeter was guarded by two fifteen-foot-high fences patrolled by men with dogs, by guard towers every five hundred yards, and by the latest in day and night electronic surveillance equipment. Everything but the men and dogs had come from the United States, including the fence.

The general's car went through the checkpoints without

146

even slowing. It skirted, of course, the runways – two parallel east-west strips and one cutting diagonally on a southeast-to-northwest axis. There was a lot of activity.

'We have the best pilots and technicians in the Middle East,' Barami pointed out. 'Not even the Israelis can match us.'

'Where are they trained?' asked Professor Hartmann, who took a high interest in such matters, in his role as military adviser to the Swiss Military Department.

'Initially, in Texas,' was the answer. 'It's ideal. Flying conditions there are very similar to those here. But upon their return, the men are kept on essentially the same training programs. The United States air force has six hundred men on this base – purely in an advisory role, of course. How do you solve your training problems in Switzerland?'

'It is not easy,' replied Hartmann. 'We simply do not have sufficient air space. However, on occasion we use the French facilities in the Mediterranean. Off Corsica, you know.'

Of course Barami knew. 'But your equipment is hardly up to our standard,' the Iranian continued.

'No, I agree. We still rely basically upon the Mirage. But deliveries of F-16's are scheduled to start this year – if Northrop can meet its delivery schedules.'

Half the world, it seemed, relied upon the United States for its arsenal of weapons : the Saudis, the Iranians, the Egyptians, the Koreans, the Israelis, the Germans – even the neutral Swiss.

After ten minutes, they had passed the main body of hangers and barracks. But the general's car continued eastward into the desert. Its target, after a few minutes, became obvious – a huge windowless concrete building, topped by a stack that must have been five hundred feet high. Not exactly the sort of thing you expect to find in the vicinity of airstrips. It was surrounded by an even more elaborate security perimeter.

'That building is our destination?' asked Professor Hartmann finally.

'Yes.'

'What is it?'

'Officially, an incinerator.'

Before they had even stopped in front of it, the professor knew. Externally, at least, it was an exact – but exact – replica of the nuclear-fuel reprocessing plant in the Khorramshahr nuclear park.

Inside, it was the same thing – a 100 percent perfect reproduction of the 'visible' plant, which had been built by the French and was supervised by the Americans from the staff of the International Atomic Energy Agency. But here there was not a foreigner in sight. The entire staff was obviously Iranian. Which explained the mystery of the high rate of turnover and the 'disappearance' of the engineers and technicians from the other facility.

'How long has this been in operation?' was the first question Hartmann asked, after a swift survey of the installation.

'Six months,' answered Professor Baraheni.

'Where did you get the equipment?'

'Most of it on the open market. As you know, these same instruments find use in other applications. In some cases they had to be slightly modified.'

'And those that could not be found on the market?' The Swiss professor pointed at a panel of monitoring equipment.

The Iranian professor looked toward the general, who shrugged and chose to answer the question himself.

'From Israel. We supply them with their petroleum, you know.'

The Americans provided military hardware, the French, atomic technology, and the Israelis, sophisticated nuclear equipment. Now, obviously, the Swiss were going to be called upon to make their little contribution to the restoration of the Persian Empire. Professor Hartmann had lots of company.

'I assume your end product is plutonium oxide?' asked Hartmann.

'Of course. Exactly the same end product as is produced in the other facility.'

'And where . . .?' The Swiss professor chose not to finish the sentence.

Again his Iranian counterpart hesitated. But General Barami did not. 'It is very simple. Twenty-five percent of the spent fuel rods from the Framatome power reactors are brought here. Directly. They never go to the Khorramshahr storage basins, nor, naturally, to the separation plant there.'

'But how is that possible?' asked the Swiss.

'Quite simple. The IAEA inspectors do not concern themselves with the power reactors. Why should they? They concentrate on the separation plant, where the plutonium is extracted.'

'But surely they must realize that the quantities of recycled fuel produced by the separation plant are not what they should be? After all, it is an extremely easy calculation.'

'Ah,' answered the Iranian professor now, 'but the quantity being produced in Khorramshahr *is* correct. It is the *quality* which is, shall we say, not quite up to expectations.'

'Yes, of course. That was pointed out by the French technicians yesterday. What do you do?'

'Again, very simple. We replace the "missing" used fuel elements with dummy rods filled with ordinary uranium.'

And ordinary uranium was available from a dozen different sources.

'Which,' continued the Iranian, 'after the recycling process, results in perfectly functional fuel rods. They just function at only around seventy-five percent of "normal." '

'And the IAEA inspectors are still satisfied?'

'Of course. After all, it is predominantly "stupid" Iranians who are running the operation. What else could be expected? In time it is hoped that we will learn. And then, it is supposed, the reprocessed fuel rods will be up to optimum performance.'

'How much plutonium oxide have you produced here?'

'One hundred eighty pounds, as of the end of last week,' answered Baraheni.

'And how much end product do you have?'

The Iranians were puzzled. 'I already told you. That is our end product. We have done absolutely nothing more or less here than we do in Khorramshahr,' answered Baraheni.

The general did not like this turn in the conversation. 'What are you driving at?' he asked, his eyes now squinting.

'Well,' answered Hartmann, 'I was merely curious concerning the end use.'

The end use was as clear to the Swiss as it was to the two Iranians, and all three knew it.

'Mr. Tehrani, I am sure, satisfied that curiosity in Switzerland, Professor Hartmann,' stated General Barami. 'So please answer my question. What is wrong with plutonium oxide?'

'It is inefficient.'

'But,' interjected Baraheni, 'you misunderstand. We very definitely have weapons-grade plutonium oxide. You can test it yourself!'

'I do not doubt that. I did not say that you cannot build nuclear devices with the end product you have here. I am merely suggesting that they will be extremely inefficient in terms of yield.'

Now the general took on Baraheni. 'You idiot! It is exactly as I suspected.' In fact, it was General Barami who had convinced the Shah that an outside nuclear-weapons man had to be brought in. Thus Hartmann.

'Professor,' Barami continued, totally turning his back on Baraheni, 'what exactly do we need?'

'I am afraid I cannot answer that until I know exactly what your needs are, General. I only know from our own experiences – perhaps, I should say calculations – that a great deal more purification is probably called for. It will . . .' and now the Swiss professor, who was forced to use the English language in this situation, struggled for the right words, '. . . stretch, I believe is the right word, the amount of "bang" you can get out of your one hundred and eighty pounds of simple plutonium oxide.' The professor smiled at his little touch of idiomatic English.

'How many bombs can we build with the amount of substance we have available in its present form?' asked the general.

'Let's use a quite ordinary bomb as an example – the type dropped on Hiroshima. Their yield was fifteen kiloton. With plain oxide, you would need about fifteen pounds per bomb. You see, the rule of thumb is one pound for each kiloton. So, you could make twelve fifteen-kiloton bombs – an even dozen – with what you have available. But as I said, they would not be very efficient. Nor very versatile, I might add.'

That created a pause.

'What specific application did you foresee of these weapons?' continued Hartmann, blithely ignoring the sudden silence of the Iranian general.

The head of Iran's air force did not answer immediately. It seemed that he was in the process of doing a quick mental rundown of something. Probably a war game that had gone wrong. 'What do you use in Switzerland?' he finally asked.

'Metal.'

The general did not get that.

'No,' he said, 'what I meant is, what do you use in place of plutonium oxide for the core of the weapons?'

'As I said,' replied Hartmann, 'metal. Plutonium metal.'

'That is efficient?'

'Extremely. Our results with plutonium metal have been most gratifying.'

'How does one produce such metal?' Barami asked.

Professor Baraheni now attempted to interrupt. 'It is pure conjecture that . . .'

'Shut up.' This in Pharsee.

The three of them had been standing the entire while in front of the monitoring equipment overlooking, through the massive glass protective barrier, the key separation chamber of the purification plant. The technicians controlling them, who heretofore had studiously ignored the visiting brass, now visibly stirred, as the general's voice thundered out in their local language.

'Excuse me, Professor Hartmann,' continued Barami, 'but

151

what you are telling me I find highly disturbing. We have schedules – which we absolutely must meet. Now, I repeat, could you tell me what we must have in order to produce plutonium metal?'

'A highly sophisticated vacuum furnace that uses acetylene carbon black as the reducing agent.'

That meant absolutely nothing to the general, but generals are accustomed to hearing things they do not understand. 'Where can we get such a furnace?'

'That will not be easy. We, in Switzerland, constructed our own.'

'How long did it take?'

'A year, if I recall correctly.'

'A year! That is impossible!' exclaimed the general.

'But, of course, that included time for research and development.'

'Could you have one built in Switzerland now – more quickly?'

'Perhaps, perhaps not. And I am not sure that my government would be prepared to export such equipment.' Tracing the movement of physical equipment back to neutral Switzerland would be much easier than tracing the 'advice' given the Iranians by a visiting Swiss scientist.

'Yes, yes,' commented Barami, again deep in his thoughts. 'Perhaps we can come up with a solution. Professor, what we must have – immediately – are the exact specifications for such a . . .'

'Furnace. Vacuum furnace,' said Hartmann.

'We will give you the necessary office, staff, whatever you need here. Baraheni! See to it. Now!'

The general glanced at his watch. 'I must return to the air base. Professor Hartmann, this will now be your place of work. Of course, you will also want to spend time at the Khorramshahr facility. I shall remain in close contact. But in the meantime, Baraheni here will take care of what you need. I hardly need remind you that our discussions – in fact, the very existence of this place – must remain completely secret. But I am told you understand things.'

152

'Perfectly,' answered Hartmann, the father of the Swiss atomic bomb, and potential midwife to the Shah's.

He spent the next days on the specs for the vacuum furnace; the next few weeks sketching out a few new ideas he had been developing in the bomb field. On Christmas Eve, 1978, the vacuum furnace arrived in an Iranian air force Hercules transport, complete with the acetylene carbon black. The source? The markings on the crates made that clear immediately : they were in English – and Hebrew. By mid-January, after some technical problems, Professor Hartmann's furnace had already produced the first twenty pounds of plutonium metal. And construction on the first Iranian atomic bomb – a simple one, though extremely 'efficient' – was well under way. On January 15, Professor Hartmann gave General Barami his progress report. Barami personally flew up to Teheran that same day to give it to the Shah. He also took Ursula Hartmann along. She needed a change of scenery, her father had explained. A few days of shopping in Teheran, the general had suggested, would be just the thing.

CHAPTER SIXTEEN

I arrived in Teheran the afternoon of the following day. There was a total lack of pomp and ceremony at the airport. This was not a state visit. The Saudis had come to Teheran at their own insistence and not at the Shah's invitation. The treatment reflected this. The Saudi air force 707 was not directed to the passenger terminal after landing, but to a parking spot at least a kilometer distant, adjacent to the freight terminal. To be sure, the Saudi ambassador was there with his aides. So was the Iranian minister of petroleum, Ali Dhermanagar. But no Shah. Dhermanagar, a haughty man with craggy features, went through the motions on the tarmac as the Saudi delegation came down the stairs, but that was definitely all. If Crown Prince Fahd was in any way miffed at the low-key reception, he certainly did not show it.

The delegation then split up. Fahd and Yamani were to be housed at the Saudi Embassy, their aides somewhere that remained undefined. Reggie and I, it seemed, were being put up at the local Hilton, which was fine with Reggie, and very fine indeed with me. For I had tentatively made a date with Ursula Hartmann for that evening.

Making that date had not exactly been easy. Ursula had given me the Swiss Embassy in Teheran as her forwarding address, but it is not exactly my style to write letters asking young ladies for appointments. So I just phoned. Now 'just' is greatly understating it. Phoning anywhere from Riyadh was a chore; getting Teheran from Riyadh a major undertaking. And getting any information out of the Swiss Embassy was nigh on impossible. The Swiss have to be the most suspicious, closemouthed people on earth. The Red Chinese are warmhearted and loquacious by comparison. I got absolutely nowhere. By this time it was well into January. But by this time it had also been officially announced that I had been elevated to the position of personal financial adviser to Crown Prince Fahd. So I asked the Swiss Ambassador to Saudi Arabia – a Dr. Werner Vetterli – to come around, at his convenience. He showed up the next morning at eight fifteen, for Christ's sake. I hinted at a few billion that might be forthcoming for Switzerland – suitably vague in regard to the purpose, the timing, and the reason – and then suggested that he might perform a slight personal favor. By noon, he called with the address and phone number in Khorramshahr. By the next afternoon I was through to her. In retrospect, it seems a bit odd, considering the delicacy of her father's business in Iran, that I actually got through. But on the other hand, for a long time it was the simplest thing in the world to just telephone somebody in Moscow from London or Paris or San Franscisco and talk freely, provided you had the number. Until, years later, they caught on. Which, at least in my mind, proves that security agencies are probably the most overrated institutions of our century.

Anyway, she was glad I called. And she said she would try her utmost to make the rendezvous in Teheran. Where? She again said she would leave a message at the Swiss Embassy there. To which I, with great reluctance, agreed.

When Reggie and I had checked into the Teheran Hilton, the first thing I did was call that embassy. And miraculously, the message was there. She was staying at the Ambassador Hotel. And when I called the Ambassador, she was there – and wanted to see me right away.

The Ambassador was a nice little hotel with style, like the Algonquin in New York, or Brown's in London – the sort of place where women can stay alone in comfort, have tea in the lobby, or a drink in the bar, without the fear of being approached. Ursula was sitting in the lobby, looking very unapproachable in her winter coat, her black gloves, clutching her Hermès leather purse. She also had a marvelous tan to go with her black hair. Nice.

I don't know how it is possible to get worked up when touched with black leather gloves, but when she took both my hands in hers, I did.

'Bill,' she said. 'Oh, am I happy to see you!'

155

I hate displays of anything, but the fact that she had tears in her eyes did not bother me in the slightest, for some strange reason.

'Let's take a walk,' she said.

So, arm in arm, we went out into the dusk, which in January in Teheran arrives very early. The streets of that city are a mad place during rush hour, which apparently starts around four in the afternoon : an endless stream of cars and broken-down jitney-style taxis, all jammed to capacity, floods out of the downtown area to the sprawling suburbs beyond. The sidewalks are equally crowded, with bustling people – men, women and schoolchildren in their uniforms – all hurrying somewhere. There is the tingle of excitement in the air like that of New York on Fifth Avenue at five o'clock, or of central Madrid at seven, or of the Ginza in Tokyo still later on. Teheran, ugly as it was, had the same vibrations. After my many weeks in Riyadh and Ursula's stretch in Khorramshahr, it was exhilarating to us both. The cold, crisp atmosphere of Teheran in winter gave an illusion of Christmas in the air. Or maybe my memories of that evening have become slightly distorted over time. Perhaps it was just that Ursula was there, and Ursula had changed.

Like a kid, she insisted we go into a bakery and buy the Persian equivalent of a doughnut. Next stop was a toy store, where she got a doll. Then we checked out a few movie houses, trying to figure out from the billboards outside, all in Parsee, what on earth could be playing inside. We concluded that Doris Day and cowboy pictures were still big in Iran.

'Do you know that I've thought about you?' she suddenly said, as we continued our way through the crowd.

'Yeah?'

'In fact, I have thought about you every day since Zurich,' she stated.

'Um.'

'Does that bother you?'

'No, for God's sake.'

'Are you sure?'

'Of course I'm sure. Do you think that your pretty little face hasn't crossed my mind now and then?'

'Do you mean that?'

'Yes. I mean that. Very much.'

And the gloved hand tightened on my arm. 'How old are you?'

'Uh . . .' and I paused, because – and this is God's truth – I always forget how old I am. I have to go back to the year I was born and figure it out. This was January 1979, so : 'Almost forty-five.'

'I'm thirty-one. Is that too old?'

'Of course not. If anybody's too old, it's me.'

'Bill.'

'Yes.'

'What was your wife like?'

'A bitch.'

'How long were you married?'

'Is that important?'

'Do you mind?'

'Hell, no. Let's see – nineteen years.'

'No children?'

'No. Thank goodness.'

'Why? Don't you like children?'

'Of course. But not with Anne.'

'That was her name?'

'Yes.'

'I like children.'

'So do I, for God's sake.'

'Would you still like to have children?'

'Well, that depends.'

'On what?'

'On lots of things.'

'Would you like to have children with me?'

This was exactly the type of dumb talk that I never got involved in. It could lead to catastrophe. But that evening in Teheran . . .

She stopped abruptly. 'Bill, I must tell you something.' We stood face to face. She was serious.

'What?' with trepidation.

157

'That night in Rome. I don't know what got into me. I have never, never done such a crazy, stupid thing in my life. It was insane. Do you believe me?'

'Yes.' I did, and she knew I did. And she went up on her toes, put her arms around me, and kissed me. In the middle of at least ten thousand Iranians!

'Bill –' and we were walking again – 'do you believe in fate?'

'Sometimes, I guess.'

'I do,' she said.

'You've got something in mind?'

She giggled. 'You,' she answered.

'Why me?'

'Do you want to know the truth?'

'Of course.' And I wanted to.

'I think I have been waiting for you for thirty-one years. I know women are not supposed to say such things any more. Does it bother you?'

'No.'

'Do you . . .?'

'I think so, yes. Ursula?'

'Yes.'

'How come you never got married?'

'I really don't know. I never met anyone I wanted to marry, I guess.'

'Didn't you have any boyfriends, or whatever they call them these days?'

'Of course. I even lived with one for almost a year.'

'Yeah?'

'Yes. When I was at the University of Lausanne.'

'What happened?'

'Nothing happened. That was the problem. We went at each other in bed for a while, and nothing else happened. Does that bother you?'

'Hell, no.' Then : 'What did he do?'

'Bill – that was nine years ago. He was studying medicine. I have not seen him since.'

'And afterwards?'

'That was it.'

'Ah, come on.'

'It's true. Until Rome.'

'And why in Rome?'

'Because at first I hated you. And then I fell in love with you.'

'I'm . . . well, I guess I feel the same way.'

That was enough. Why say more? We both knew that something that had started by accident in Rome had 'happened' that evening in Teheran – by mutual design.

I looked at my watch, for no reason, really. But it startled Ursula.

'What's wrong?'

'Nothing. I just wondered what time it was.'

'You don't have to leave already?'

'No, no. But even if I did, it really wouldn't matter any more, would it?'

She beamed. 'No. Would it bother you if I called you darling?'

'Yes.'

'Do you know what we say in Switzerland?'

'No.'

'*Schatzi.* That's what my mother always called my father.'

'Say, I never even asked about your father. How is he?'

A mistake.

'What's wrong?' I asked. 'Is he sick?'

'No. Nothing like that.'

'Where is he? Back in the hotel?'

'No. In Khorramshahr.'

'Look,' I continued, 'if it's none of my business . . .'

Again both hands squeezed my arm. 'Bill, I want everything about me to be your business. If you . . .'

Two moves forward, then one back.

'Ursula –' and this time it was I who pulled both of us to a stop – 'I thought we got past that one?' It was now I who searched her eyes. And I who kissed her. Screw the Iranians!

'Bill,' she then said, 'I think I need you very badly.'

'Well, I think you've got me.'

159

And we walked still farther into downtown Teheran, for at least five minutes in full, satisfying silence.

'Now,' I finally said, 'what's gone wrong down there in Khorramshahr?'

'Nothing's gone wrong, in that sense. It's just that I have never seen my father this way.'

'What way?'

'Withdrawn. He doesn't talk to me any more. The first night or two, yes. But then less and less. He's either at the plant, working, or at home, sitting in a corner in the living room. With his pipe. Often late into the night. Alone.'

'Why don't you just ask him?'

'I tried. About two weeks ago. Shortly before you called.'

'And?'

'He told me that I would not understand. That perhaps my mother would have.'

'How old is he?'

'Sixty-two. But that is not it. He is not senile. Quite the opposite. He acts like a driven man.'

'What exactly is he doing here in Iran?'

'I don't know, exactly. He does not discuss it any more. I asked Uri when he was here. And – not very politely, I must say – he told me to leave my father, and his business here, alone.'

'Uri?'

'You know him, Bill. Professor Ben-Levi.'

Sure I knew him : the handsome, witty, hotshot Israeli in Zurich. That set a few wheels in motion. And Ursula felt the vibrations.

'Bill,' she said, 'don't be silly.'

'What do you mean, silly?'

'He means absolutely nothing to me.'

'Yeah?'

'Yes.'

'Well then, what in hell was he doing in Khorramshahr?'

'There was a problem with some of the equipment. Some kind of vacuum furnace. He came to fix it.'

'Why good old Uri? I thought he was an Israeli?'

160

'He is. There is no prejudice here against Jews. Swiss or Israeli.'

Christ, I thought, I hope we don't get back on *that* subject. 'I don't get it,' I said. 'What's the big secret down there?'

Which led to a few minutes of silence.

'Say,' I then went on, 'are you sure your father isn't mixed up in something very weird?'

I glanced at Ursula, but this time her eyes avoided mine.

'What,' I asked, 'is the official reason for his stay here?'

'He's a consultant. To Roche-Bollinger. They build nuclear reactors. He is here to prepare a feasibility study for the construction of two Swiss reactors for Iran.' Straightforward answer. But her voice was suddenly very flat.

'Has he got other consultancy arrangements back in Switzerland?'

'Of course. He is a very able physicist.'

'I realize that.'

'Well, what are you driving at?'

'OK. Quite bluntly : Does he also consult for the Swiss government?'

'Yes.'

'For the military?'

A long pause. 'Yes,' in a small voice. Then, 'No !'

'How can you be sure? Maybe that's what's bothering him.' I said.

'No. He is not a prisoner. We are under no coercion here.'

'I did not mean to suggest he was under any coercion.'

'It would not make sense, Bill. I know my father.'

'Maybe not as well as you think. What was that you said a few minutes ago about your mother?'

She repeated it.

'Does that make any sense to you?' I asked.

'Yes,' she answered, in an even smaller voice. 'Because of her, he violently hates the Germans. From the day they were married, he – and she, until her death – never set foot on German soil. Today he hates the Arabs even more.'

So there we had it. Obviously she had known. But to admit it to herself had been another thing.

'Has he been working on nuclear weapons for the Swiss?'

When I think back, by this point we had been walking for a full half hour. Downtown Teheran had come, and was already starting to go. In my whole life, I don't recall ever having such emotion packed into such a short time.

'Bill,' she replied, and now there was a pleading in her voice, 'please don't ask me to answer that.'

'OK.' And I put my arm around her shoulder. 'Look,' I continued, 'let's drop that subject for the time being. But —' immediately contradicting myself — 'at least I now understand one thing.'

'What?'

'The Israeli connection. Your friend, Professor Ben-Levi.'

'He is not my friend. He has, for years, had a very strong influence on my father. Much too strong. And not for good. Under that glib façade, Ben-Levi is a very violent man.'

'You have experienced something with him?'

'Yes. And I absolutely refuse to discuss it. Nothing happened, Bill.' And now the tears came in earnest.

'Ursula,' I said, 'let's go home.'

Miraculously, we not only got a taxi, but managed to direct it back to the Ambassador. It was completely dark by the time we got to her room. We never turned on the light.

When I turned up back at the Hilton the next morning around nine. Reggie was waiting, or should I say pacing, in the lobby. 'Bill, where the hell have you been? We're due at the embassy in an hour!'

'Not to worry, Reggie. Just an extended social call.'

I showered, shaved, and put on my banker's suit with vest. I was slightly tired. But, on the other hand, not having touched the stuff since arriving in Iran, I had not a trace of a hangover. Thus, on balance, I was in much better shape than most bankers are when abroad on business.

I was also somewhat nervous. When I'm nervous, I

smoke. I smoked a pack of Winstons before half that morning had gone by. Which was understandable. This was not going to be exactly a run-of-the-mill day in the life of William H. Hitchcock.

Reggie and I arrived at the Saudi Embassy at ten on the dot. Minutes later, Fahd and Yamani appeared – in full dress. The four of us fitted into the Mercedes 600 with ample room to spare. Fifteen minutes later we passed through the gates to the palace of the Shah of Iran. His chief of protocol was waiting at the bottom of the stairs to the main entrance. He took us immediately into the palace, through the entrance hall, and into a reception room ornately furnished in Louis XVI style. The Shah stood in the center of the room, flanked by his oil minister, Ali Dhermanagar, and two aides. The crown prince and the Shah shook hands. The chief of protocol made the formal round of introductions. Then he bowed to the Shah and backed out of the room. The Shah led us to a large sitting group, indicating that Fahd should sit in a chair to the left of his, leaving the rest of us to find our places on the three sofas which formed a U facing the two leaders. Yamani and Dhermanagar shared the one immediately to the Shah's right. Reggie and I took the sofa to Crown Prince Fahd's left. The two Iranian aides got stuck with the bottom of the seating order. It didn't matter. Neither of them spoke one word during the entire meeting. Nor did Reggie, for that matter.

'Your Majesty,' began Fahd – the proceedings were in English – 'we are deeply honoured to be received by you.'

'Your Highness,' replied the Shah of Iran, 'it is a privilege to receive you on Iranian soil. I would like you to extend my best wishes to His Majesty, King Khalid, upon your return.' Which put the rank of Pahlavi and Fahd in the correct perspective, namely that of a king addressing a mere crown prince.

'Your Majesty,' continued Fahd, 'if you agree, I would like to come immediately to the purpose of our visit, to which you so graciously consented.'

'Please,' answered Pahlavi. There was no doubt about

163

it : the man knew how to command respect. He sat with the ramrod posture of a British brigadier, spoke in perfectly articulated English, and his face was totally devoid of any sign of emotion whatsoever. A very tough customer.

'His Majesty, King Khalid, and the entire Royal Council of Ministers,' said Fahd, 'have delegated me to inform you that Saudi Arabia feels it necessary to pursue a revised policy in regard to the future pricing of crude petroleum.'

'I see,' replied Pahlavi. 'And that is the sole purpose of your visit?'

'Yes,' replied Fahd.

'Then I am afraid we really have nothing to talk about.'

Fahd said nothing in reply. Yamani said nothing. Dhermanagar said nothing. Nor did anybody move. This went on for at least a full minute. The Shah had fixed Fahd in a penetrating gaze, and he seemed intent on staring him down. He had met his equal, for finally it was the Shah who broke the silence, which had become so ominous that my hands had become not moist, but actually wet.

'I assume,' he said, 'that you have understood me.'

'Indeed I have, Your Majesty,' replied Fahd. But again, saying nothing further.

The Shah was not going to be trapped in the silence bit again. 'You are obviously receiving bad advice, if I may say so, from your Sheik Yamani – who certainly should know better – and the rest of them.' His hand waved airily in the direction of Reggie and myself. 'My views are quite well known. There is one forum and one forum only for the discussion of the pricing of crude petroleum. That is OPEC. If you wish to request a special meeting of the OPEC ministers, it is your privilege. I, however, will not be represented. For there is nothing to discuss. We have all agreed upon the formula for fixing our prices. It will rise at the same rate as prices in the West. That means fifteen percent this year. That is their rate of inflation. They, not we, make this continuing escalation necessary.'

'Your Majesty,' said Saudi Arabia's crown prince, 'I am afraid that you are badly mistaken if you feel that I am receiving poor advice. We have devoted a great deal of study and time to this matter, and have, I believe – with the help of these gentlemen – developed a new oil policy which will prove correct in the long run.'

'There is no policy outside of OPEC policy,' stated Pahlavi. And the OPEC policy has been set, and will not be revised.'

'Our new policy,' continued Fahd as if the Shah had never spoken, 'is based upon our belief that the Western economy is in an extremely fragile condition, and that it is in the interest of all oil producers to promote a correction of that situation.'

'Fragile!' exclaimed the Shah. 'Who tells you that nonsense? These two Americans? We have heard of them. Your Mr. Hamilton and your Mr. – excuse me – Dr. Hitchcock. Do you for one minute believe that they are capable of representing our interests? Their masters, their real masters, are quite obvious : Exxon, Shell, BP, Chase Manhattan, Bank of America, the Rothschilds.'

He looked at me, and I gave him an arched eyebrow back. The son of a bitch!

Fahd, to his eternal credit, completely ignored that outburst. 'Therefore,' the crown prince continued, 'Saudi Arabia intends to stabilize the price of its crude petroleum for at least two years, and more probably three. This means we will increase our output substantially.'

'That is madness,' interjected Dhermanagar. 'You will destroy everything we have built since 1973.'

'No,' said Yamani, also speaking for the first time. 'We shall do exactly the opposite. You have been leading all of us toward disaster, Dhermanagar. No more. The world needs a respite on energy cost. And we are going to provide that respite.'

Which, I thought, would have provoked a real tantrum from the Shahanshah. But no. Instead came a calm, measured question, worthy of the man who, in spite of all his faults, had still proved himself to be the world's greatest oil strategist.

'Tell me, Yamani,' said Riza Pahlavi, 'how do you plan on going about all this? By putting up your oil for tender?'

'No,' answered Yamani in his elegant English accent. 'Of course not. Our aim is not to create chaos in the world market. We shall, most probably, enter into direct long-term agreements with some of the major distributors.'

'The Americans?'

'Most probably.'

'I see. And on credit?'

'No,' answered Yamani. 'Strictly cash.'

'Dollars?'

'Yes.'

The Shah's fingers now started to drum on the arm of his chair. The royal calculator was humming at top speed. 'And,' he continued, 'with the economy so "fragile," as you put it – and I can only assume that by "economy" you are really talking about the United States – you will keep your receipts in dollars?'

'That is a fair assumption.'

'I see.' Then: 'Dr. Hitchcock – by the way, didn't we meet in London a few years back?'

'Yes. At the Savoy.'

'Yes, yes. I remember. Tell me, what will all this mean in the foreign-exchange markets?'

'Obviously a much stronger dollar, Your Majesty,' I replied.

'And sterling?'

'Hard to say.'

'The lira?'

I grinned and pointed a thumb up.

'Interesting,' he said. 'Dr. Hitchcock, where would you advise me to keep our funds this year?'

'Your Majesty, you also must have a friend at Chase Manhattan. Why don't you ask him?'

'Touché, Hitchcock,' he replied, and then leaned over toward Fahd. 'I was wrong. I think you have a good man here.'

Then he leaned back, raised his finger, for some reason, and said to Fahd, 'But I am puzzled. Why are you telling me all this?'

'Because of the long and traditional friendship between

166

our two nations, Your Majesty,' replied Fahd with a straight face. 'We have no desire to cause you or your country any difficulties. We admire the development of your nation under your leadership. We are convinced that our new oil policy will not disrupt your plans for its future development. Quite the contrary. We have come in peace, to demonstrate what value we place upon your friendship.'

'I thank you for those sentiments, Your Highness,' replied Pahlavi. 'You must understand, however, that your plans disturb me. Because of my people. My people and their king are so close that they and I feel as members of the same family. They have the respect for me that the children in a family used to have for their father. They expect me to help and protect them. I do not feel that your new policy will be to their benefit. But I respect the decision of your king and yourself and your family. I therefore thank you for your visit and shall pray to Allah that your homeward journey is a safe one.'

So help me God, those were the exact words he used.

With that, the Shahanshah of Iran rose, extended his hand to Fahd, and then to the rest of us in turn. To me he said, 'Dr. Hitchcock, please let my people know next time you are in Teheran. I would like to hear more of your views on the financial markets.'

What a charmer he could be. And let's face it : I liked being flattered by the Shah of Iran.

The crown prince requested that Reggie and I have lunch with Yamani and himself at the Saudi Embassy. And at the close of that meal came his summing up.

'Gentlemen, I believe this has been extremely valuable. We have thoroughly demonstrated our respect for him with our openness. He will now have no excuse for taking any retaliatory measures against us. And that is important, I believe. The Shah is a great believer in legitimacy. He has never taken any action unless he was sure he could demonstrate to the world that he had legitimate cause. We have given him no cause. We must now proceed with the greatest speed to insure that when he invents a cause – and I know the man; he will – we shall be militarily capable of with-

167

standing his pressure. You heard him at the beginning of that meeting. He was on the verge of committing an affront to my person, and thus my government, that could have led to an immediate and open break. Then he backed off. For what reason, we will perhaps never know. But at least we have bought time.'

An hour later, Fahd embarked on his return trip to Riyadh in the Royal Saudi Arabian Air Force 707. The domestic political situation was too touchy for him to stay abroad any longer than was necessary. Yamani, Reggie and I were scheduled on a commercial flight to London.

I called Ursula from the airport before departure. We agreed to meet as soon as my time allowed. But not in the Middle East. Instead, it would be St. Moritz, for skiing during the day and just the two of us alone during the night.

'Are you happy?' she then asked.

'Of course I'm happy. It will only be a couple of months.'

'I didn't mean that. I meant with your meetings today.'

'With the Shah?'

'Yes.'

'Yeah, I guess so. It is difficult to read that man. But it seemed to end up all right.'

'So, no trouble?'

'Trouble?'

'Here in the Middle East?'

'No. Not right now anyway.'

A slight pause. 'Bill, I talked on the phone with Father last night. He sounds better.'

'I'm glad to hear that.'

'Maybe it was because he was not alone. Uri Ben-Levi was there.'

'Did you talk to him too?'

'Yes. But very briefly. I had to, because of Father.'

'Right.'

'Bill?'

'Yes.'

'Will you write me?'

I said that I would not write to her but would definitely

telephone. Reggie tapped my shoulder and said that if I did not hang up and run, Yamani would be going to London alone. We ran, and made it.

I hated to leave Ursula, especially with Ben-Levi sniffing around at her again, but on the other hand I could hardly wait to get to London, and then New York, where I could start dropping some of the biggest financial bombshells of the century. But in the back of my mind, and not so far back either, there was the thought that some other bombshells might be in the works – the handicraft of my girlfriend's father, of all people.

I knew, and as somebody once said, knowledge is power.

CHAPTER SEVENTEEN

The special facilities at Heathrow were in full operation when we arrived, including a man from the Foreign Office, even though the Foreign Office had not been informed of the visit. That slightly annoyed Yamani.

The Rolls had us at Claridge's in twenty minutes. Mr. Lund Hansen, the tall Dane who had managed the hotel since 1949, was there to greet us. It was teatime and the Hungarian string quartet was quietly at work in the background as we were taken to the elevators. Yamani had been given one of the royal suites – Claridge's being, no doubt, the only hostelry on earth that truly needs more than one, since quite often royalty tends to descend upon it in numbers. Reggie and I were given simple apartments on a different floor.

At six, Reggie and I went down to The Causerie for a drink. Good old Mr. Robinson, who by that time had been mixing drinks there for exactly thirty years, remembered me. And thus it was a very dry martini, with a tiny twist and lots of ice, that he served up without asking. Reggie had, of all things, bourbon straight. We downed a couple and then went up to dinner, to Yamani's apartment on the top floor. It was cold and wet in London, as usual in January, yet the royal suite gave no hint of the surrounding gloom. Two large fireplaces were burning in the drawing room, casting a warm light on the pale-blue carpets and the dove-colored walls. Two servants – male, of course, since Claridge's knew their Arab guests' requirements – were there to provide the canapés and more drinks from the bar, which was situated discreetly at the far end of the living room. Sheik Yamani was clearly at home there and clearly satisfied with the progression of events thus far. At eight, the mahogany doors leading to the paneled dining room were opened and the three of us moved on to dinner. Candles had been set at the far end of the very long table, and it was around them that the three of us progressively worked our way through the Scottish salmon, the quail, and the cherries jubilee. Reggie and I were first given a white Burgundy and then a superb Bordeaux. I can identify the region in which almost any palatable wine grows, but – to my credit, I must say – I have never pretended to be able to determine with any accuracy the estate and year. Although sorely tempted, I did not ask to see any of the bottles. Yamani drank tea.

After dinner, Reggie, who had brought his bulging brief-case along, sat down beside Yamani on one of the divans in the drawing room and they settled down to a working session with the numbers. I just sat there and listened for the most part, with a cognac, or perhaps it was two cognacs. When the subject of Italy came up, I repeated the advice I had given Yamani earlier on that subject.

At nine the next morning, the Rolls was waiting outside. We headed immediately toward Western Avenue, and then took the M-40 to the Gerrards Cross exit. Within a short time after that we were in one of England's most delightful villages – Penn, home of probably the largest contingent on the original Mayflower passenger list. The driver stopped at the Boar's Head for directions. Ten minutes later we passed through the gates, which marked the place as simply 'The Oaks,' into a vast estate of rolling hills, lush green pastures, white fences, horses, all resting below hundreds of towering ancient oak trees. After a mile or so came the 'lodge,' which was really, at least from my point of view, an extremely large eighteenth-century country-estate mansion. The circular drive in front of it offered a rather unusual sight : four Silver Clouds – one black, like ours, two gray, and one pure white. Together, after our arrival, they represented over a quarter of a million dollars in transportation. We had barely alighted when our host appeared, rather appropriately dressed in a tweed jacket, and smoking a pipe. The illusion of country gentry was, however, immediately destroyed when he opened his mouth.

'Zaki,' he said to Yamani, pronouncing it 'Zaahki,' for

the man was pure West Texas, 'welcome to our little country place.'

The 'our' was not intended as a majestic plural, I immediately discovered. For The Oaks was one of the many hideaways belonging to the world's greatest corporation – Exxon, the successor to the world's most devious corporation, Standard Oil of New Jersey. And the man that greeted us was John Jay Murphy, chairman of the board of Exxon.

'Reggie,' he continued, 'glad you could make it.'

'J.J.,' replied Hamilton, in a startlingly familiar manner, at least from my point of view, 'nice to see you again.'

'And you're Hitchcock,' J.J. continued. 'I'll call you Bill.'

'Yes,' I answered, feeling a bit simple.

'Well, son, glad to have you aboard. Come on in.'

Inside it was a replay of the royal suite at Claridge's, except on a vaster and more opulent scale. Three men were inside waiting: George Simpson, the chairman and chief executive officer of Mobil Oil; Roger Smith, boss of Texaco; and Fred Grayson, the head of Standard Oil of California, or SoCal as it was generally known. Fred Grayson, of course, knew me since SoCal was headquartered in San Francisco, and we had done quite a bit of business together over the years. Everybody knew Zaki Yamani and Reggie Hamilton.

It was a get-together that was the absolute dream of the more simpleminded antitrust lawyers in the U.S. Justice Department : just one photograph of this clandestine meeting of these four men in the same room, and the result would be the trial of the century. For together, these four American oil companies controlled 40 percent of the entire world market for petroleum products. All were included in the most elite of corporate ranks – the top dozen in the world. Each one, singly, controlled more income than most nations on earth. Together, their income was matched by only a handful of the globe's largest countries. If these four men, and their corporations, acted jointly and in concert with Saudi Arabia on matters of oil, there was no power on earth that could stop or even mildly hinder them. Including the President of the United States or the Shah of Iran.

It was commonly believed for decades that the world oil markets were controlled by Seven, not Four, Sisters, the larger group including also Royal Dutch/Shell, British Petroleum, and Gulf. But that was an illusion. The key to the world petroleum situation, that of supply and thus price, lay with the country that had such immense reserves of immediately accessible oil that it could overwhelm the market any time it chose to – the Kingdom of Saudi Arabia. The people who had direct access to that key were, therefore, the potential masters of the world's energy destiny. It was Exxon, Mobil, Texaco and SoCal that had such access. For they were the co-owners of Aramco, and Aramco was the *exclusive* partner of Saudi Arabia.

'Zaki,' began J.J. Murphy, after the seven of us – the true Seven Sisters as one historian later described us – had taken our place in front of yet another fireplace, this one containing a huge roaring wood fire, 'I have some tea for you.'

Everybody roared, for this was obviously one of Aramco's little in-jokes. A man in a gray business suit brought it and served Yamani exclusively with the greatest possible deference.

'Now boys,' continued J.J. after he was satisfied that the Sheik had liked his tea, 'what will it be? Coffee or booze?'

It was five to one for booze, with Reggie being determined, I guess, to maintain a clear head for as long as possible. To some, I assume, it would have seemed peculiar that the top executives of the top American corporations would be drinking in the morning. But that would have ignored the backgrounds of the men who ran America's oil giants. They were not Harvard Business School or Princeton Law School types. Their backgrounds were not that of Wall Street or Pennsylvania Avenue. To a man, they were engineers. Their graduate schools were refineries in Louisiana and oil fields in Alaska or Venezuela. They were tough guys, and tough guys in America drink. So that January morning in Buckinghamshire, they drank. The

173

contrast to Yamani, urbane, immaculately dressed, sipping tea, could not have been greater.

'Well, Zaki,' said J.J., the obvious spokesman for the group, since he represented Exxon, and Exxon ran Aramco, 'what's on your mind?'

Zaki Yamani looked at all four oilmen in turn as they stirred the ice in their bourbon. I was the only one who took Scotch.

'I am worried,' Yamani finally said. 'My government is worried. And therefore you should be worried.'

From the looks on their faces, every one of the four oil tycoons was now definitely worried. During the past decade the Arabs had dropped enough bombshells on them. Yamani's words seemed to indicate definitely that another was about to be delivered.

'My worries concern the possibility of the onset of a worldwide depression. And they also arise from the fear that perhaps the integrity of Saudi Arabia may be endangered from within, from without, maybe from both.'

He paused. 'I and my government have concluded that all of you will surely agree that it is in our mutual interest to preclude either from becoming reality.'

'Zaki,' answered J.J., 'but of course we do. You know that we have steadfastly stood by you and your nation for many years.'

Actually, that statement was quite true. The major American oil companies had served as a direct instrument of OPEC, but particularly Saudi, power ever since the 1973 embargo. Saudi Arabia dictated who should be supplied with what quantity, at what price, and the Four Sisters obeyed. When the Saudis insisted that the Netherlands be totally embargoed, and France not, that was precisely what the Four Sisters did. When Yamani insisted that the American Sixth Fleet be cut off from its traditional fuel sources, the American oil companies cut it off, and the fleet had to turn to British Petroleum for its needs. On the surface, perhaps, it appeared as if the oil companies did not have to obey these commands of the Arabs. For, although they no longer controlled the supply of crude oil,

174

they still did control the tankers, the refineries, the gas stations making up the world distribution network for the Saudis' one and only product. In a sense, both needed each other. But the 1973 embargo proved that the Four Sisters needed the Saudis much more than vice versa. The Saudis could live without them. There were dozens of other oil companies on earth, ranging from Exxon's arch-rival, Royal Dutch/Shell, to little upstarts such as Occidental Petroleum or even the Compagnie Française de Petrol, which would gladly replace the original Aramco partners as the sole, exclusive vendor of the Saudi Arabian crude. The Four Sisters would, however, have faced financial catastrophe if the Saudis had ever cut them off. There was simply no alternative source of petroleum on earth that could even begin to match the quantities offered by Saudi Arabia.

Thus, though American-owned, American-based, and American-run, Exxon, Mobil, Texaco, and SoCal gave their true loyalties not to Washington but to Riyadh.

'J.J.,' continued Yamani, 'I realize that, and I would like to add that my government has asked me to express its thanks to all of you for your past loyalties.'

Well! That was a new tone! Within seconds, both Texaco and Mobil lighted Cuban cigars. SoCal ordered another bourbon. J.J. had both a cigar and another bourbon. Yessir, things were starting to look up.

'Now,' said Yamani, taking another cup of tea, all by himself over the protests of both J.J. and Texaco, 'I have come to you gentlemen today with a proposal. A very precise proposal. I can guarantee its immediate implementation, provided you can guarantee reciprocity in the form, and especially the time frame, which we shall require.'

That word 'reciprocity' put a slight damper on the collective mood of the American engineers, for oilmen have a very long and strong tradition of expecting to get something for nothing.

'But I will come to that later,' said Yamani, to their relief.

'Now, Reggie, let's start with a few numbers. How much

175

are we pumping right now?' Meaning how much crude oil was Saudi Arabia allowing to be pumped and sold to Aramco to supply the world market.

'Just under eleven million barrels a day.' A barrel was forty-two American gallons.

'And the average price to Aramco?'

'Sixteen dollars and four cents,' answered Reggie.

'Correct?' Yamani addressed the group.

J.J. decided to refer that one to the man from Mobil. 'They match our figures precisely,' he said.

'Good. Now, how many barrels a day is the United States currently importing to meet its domestic needs?'

'Six point nine million,' answered Mobil immediately.

Yamani looked toward Reggie.

'We have seven million even,' Reggie said.

'Close enough,' said Yamani with a wave of the hand. 'Next year?' he then asked.

'Same,' answered Mobil. 'Maybe even less, if you consider what kind of depression we seem to be getting into.'

'And in 1981?'

'Well, if some miracle happens in the economy, maybe ten percent more.'

It seemed that the oilmen's views of the current status and future potential of America's economy was at least as gloomy as those of Yamani and myself.

'Here, then, is my proposal,' stated Yamani abruptly, bringing everybody to the edges of their chairs. 'We, the Kingdom of Saudi Arabia, are prepared to increase our annual output to eighteen million barrels a day.'

First silence. Then a collective '*Jeezuz!*'

Finally, the inevitable initial response from J.J., the heir to the thinking of John D. Rockefeller. 'Christ, Zaki, that could wreck the price!'

There, outside, was the world on the edge of an economic catastrophe, starved for fuel at a price that the system could absorb, and J.J. was already envisioning a glut that could affect his company's profits which, in fiscal 1978, were only $3.7 billion!

'Hear me out, J.J.,' responded Yamani. 'I am not pro-

176

posing that this crude be dumped on the world market. I am proposing that the increment be used to meet America's import needs exclusively, and on a long-term fixed-price basis.'

Fixed price! Long term! Those were words which the American oilmen had not heard coming from an Arab in a decade.

'Zaki,' said J.J. in a hushed tone, 'are you serious?'

'Completely,' answered Yamani.

'What price?' countered J.J. immediately, thinking obviously that there had to be a hooker, and that the hooker must be price, and that if the price was way up there Exxon would get screwed.

'Thirteen dollars a barrel.'

That almost brought the house down. This was 20 percent below the current world-market price. It was hardly a price freeze that Yamani was talking about, that he had told the Shah of Iran about, that he had told me about. This was a major cutback in price, the first since 1961, that he was openly proposing to the heads of the world's largest oil companies. And they had not even asked, even dared hint at such a thing.

J.J. came closest to maintaining his cool, and, skeptical as ever, asked, 'That was thirteen you said? Not thirty?'

Even Yamani laughed at that one. 'J.J.,' he said, 'for once in your life you both heard me and understood me at the same time.'

'Yes,' countered J.J. Murphy, 'but what will be the posted price?'

A goddamned good question from the standpoint of the shareholders in Exxon Corporation. For its significance was twofold. On the one hand, the posted price was a fictitious price that served as the basis for the calculation of the royalties that Saudi Arabia would receive on each barrel of oil it sold to Exxon through Aramco. Presently this price was sixteen dollars. A reduction would, from J.J.'s standpoint, have been good. On the other hand, if the posted price remained the same, and the real price of thirteen dollars a barrel remained secret, there was no reason in

177

the world that Exxon and its sisters could not maintain their current prices for gasoline and fuel oil in the United States at the current levels and simply pocket the difference.

'Still sixteen dollars. But we will expect you to reduce your selling price in the United States by only fifteen percent on average.'

'George,' asked J.J. again turning to the chairman of the board of Mobil Oil, traditionally a very close ally of Exxon, 'what's that mean for the bottom line?'

George Simpson took out his slide rule, as do all engineers when confronted with any problem, including that of spelling. 'No change,' he said after ten seconds.

'Zaki,' said J.J. then, 'you've got . . .'

'Now wait a minute, J.J. There's more. And every element is part and parcel of the entire package.'

'Take it easy, J.J.,' interjected Fred Grayson, SoCal's boss, who obviously was irritated about the back seat he was forced into as a result of the presence of Exxon's boss. Heads of oil companies have a lot of self respect to maintain.

J.J. just glared at him.

'Reggie,' said Yamani then, 'tell them how we suggest they handle the new output.'

'Well,' said my old friend, 'it is like Sheik Yamani said. The new output is to go exclusively to the United States. And the new price of thirteen dollars a barrel applies exclusively to the United States. And only to the incremental five million barrels a day. The old price holds for the "old" crude – the seven million barrels we are already selling you. Nothing changes for the rest of the world. It means, however, that you may have to cut back on your purchases from Canada and Venezuela. And Iran, probably.'

'The Venezuelans won't like that,' said Texaco, which was very close to the President of that country.

'Nor will the Shah,' said Mobil, which had spent tens of millions bribing Iranians during the past few years.

'Nor,' contributed SoCal, 'will the Europeans and Japs. How come, they will ask, can we cut prices in the States, and not in their markets?'

178

Yamani heard them all out. 'Those problems, gentlemen, will be yours to solve. And I know that you will solve them.'

That ended that discussion.

'Zaki,' said J.J., getting things back on the track, 'what was that you said about long term?'

'Three years' guarantee of both quantity and price,' said Yamani.

'What does that mean exactly?' responded Exxon's pride.

'That means, J.J., that the Kingdom of Saudi Arabia will guarantee the United States, through Aramco, that it will supply the American market with an average of seven million barrels a day of Persian Gulf crude at a fixed price of thirteen dollars a barrel for three years, commencing right now, provided that the price condition of this arrangement be kept secret, and provided that other aspects of the overall understanding I am trying to reach today meet with the agreement of yourselves and your government.'

If Yamani had been chairman of Exxon, their 1978 profit would probably have been $10 billion. He outclassed the American engineers to a degree that was, for me at least, absolutely incredible. To think that the United States had, in essence, put the entire viability of their energy economy in the hands of such men for the past sixty years was difficult for me to fathom.

'OK,' said J.J., 'let's hear the rest of it.'

'First, the commercial aspects. We will want advance payment, in cash, on ninety days' supply of the American crude – by that I mean the additional seven million barrels per day – at the new market price.'

'How much is that, George?' asked J.J.

Once again the slide rule. 'Eight point two billion dollars.'

'Sounds all right,' said J.J.

It was a rather amusing response, I thought at the time, considering where we were – namely in the heart of what was once the world's most dominant power. If Yamani, or anybody, had asked Great Britain to come up with $8.2 billion, there was no way in the world they could have even come up with half! But here was one fellow, J.J. Murphy,

179

who could conjure up probably twice or three times that much without even a call to the bank. Well, maybe a few calls, since it was to banks that Yamani referred next.

'This is a minor item,' he continued, 'but important. We do not want you to draw against any of the big American banks for that cash.'

'What do you mean?' asked J.J.

'I mean that we want those funds taken from either your balances or against your lines of credit at non-American financial institutions. Not from Chase, for instance, but from the Swiss Bank Corporation or the Deutsche Bank or the Fugi.' Yamani had obviously learned a long time ago that you had to talk in simple language to J.J. in order to get through.

'Why? That won't be easy,' countered J.J.

Yamani ignored the 'Why.' 'What were your combined assets at the end of seventy-eight?' he asked.

'You mean all four of us?' asked J.J.

'Yes.'

'How should I know?'

Yamani looked toward the SoCal boss. He was known as a financial numbers man, in spite of his engineering background.

'Maybe eighty or ninety billion,' SoCal answered. 'But what does it matter? Of course we can handle it the way you suggest, Zaki.'

'No,' persisted Yamani. 'I want this on the record. Of that eighty or ninety, how much have you got spread around the world?'

Yamani knew his oil companies. They hedged every bet there was to hedge, including that of banks and currencies. But they also never talked about it.

'Enough,' broke in J.J. suddenly. 'All right Zaki, we agree. Now, what else is on your mind?'

'Italy,' was Yamani's answer. 'And Bill Hitchcock can tell you precisely what it is.'

For the first time, front and center.

Well, I explained the situation. First, that Saudi Arabia had $3.55 billion in outstanding loans to Italy. Second, that Italy owed the rest of the world around $16 billion, all in all, and that unless it could come up with a lot of money soon, it would default on both the interest and principal repayments scheduled for 1979. It was, I stated, felt that such default would not be in the interest of the world in general, Saudi Arabia in particular, and what was not in the interest of Saudi Arabia was obviously also not in the interest of Aramco, and thus, indirectly, also of Exxon, Texaco, Mobil, and SoCal. No one challenged the slightly dubious logic of all this, so I continued.

The answer to all of 'our' problems I then went on to point out, was a quick injection of a major amount of cash into Italy. But how? As they might have heard, an attempt had been made in December to put together a major international bank consortium for that purpose, but it had fallen apart at the last minute. OK. Saudi Arabia had a solution. It would be this: It would buy all of ENI's non-Italian assets from the Italian government for $6 billion. This would include its refineries, its tanker fleet, its petrochemical facilities outside of Italy, and, of course, its AGIP chain of service stations in Europe.

At this point, J.J. Murphy, whose eyes had been narrowing more and more the further I got into my presentation, suddenly broke in. 'Whose idea is this?'

'Mine,' I replied.

'What has all this got to do with Yamani's proposal?'

Yamani, coolly watching the exchange between J.J. and myself up to this point, broke in. 'Everything. As I said at the very beginning, I am offering you a package in which every element is essential.'

'Look, Zaki,' said J.J., 'this introduces something totally, entirely new. What that proposal of Hitchcock involves is your setting up the basis for a new integrated international operation.'

'Exactly,' replied Yamani. 'We have learned a great deal from you Americans. Now we intend to apply it.'

'You are just asking for trouble. What do you Saudis know about marketing? Nothing. That's why you've got us.'

'Correct, J.J. And we still need you. In fact, when the ENI deal is made — and it will be made, exactly along the lines that Bill just described — we are going to need more of your help.'

J.J. remained silent.

'We've done a complete rundown of ENI's European operations,' continued Yamani. 'Their retailing chain barely makes money because of the competition of the independents. Gelsenkirchen in Germany, Occidental in Scandinavia, Getty in other markets. We would like them to make more money. That means we would like a little less competition. So what we are suggesting is that there be a slight cutback in the amount of crude available to the independents in those markets.'

'Haven't you heard about antitrust laws, Zaki?' replied J.J.

'Probably more than you have, J.J. I also know how much attention you pay to them. One more thing. We will need more refining capacity in West Germany. We would like to buy two more refineries there. I think Exxon probably has a surplus capacity there at the moment. We'll be glad to consider any offers.'

Well, there it was — right out in the open. The next logical step which the Four Sisters had been fearing all along. Heretofore it had been monopoly dealing with monopoly: the Arabs controlled the production of crude oil, but the Four Sisters controlled the marketing of petroleum products. Now the marketing monopoly would be breached. And once breached, the power of the international oil companies would inevitably begin a decline that probably could never be stopped.

'Zaki,' said J.J., now speaking in a soft voice, 'do you know that we could kill you in those markets? Remember what happened to Mattei?'

Among other things, the Italian oilman Mattei, who in the 1960's had tried to break the monopolistic control of the European petroleum markets by the Seven Sisters, had been killed in a mysterious airplane accident. But that was obviously not what J.J. meant. What he was driving at

182

was that when Mattei made his challenge, the big companies had organized a price war that brought the ENI empire to the verge of collapse.

'J.J., you try that . . .'

Yamani did not have to finish his sentence. George Simpson of Mobil Oil cut him off. 'Zaki,' he said, 'I suggest a short adjournment.' He immediately rose from his chair.

J.J. glared at Simpson, glared at me, glared at Yamani, and finally got up. The four American oilmen left the room without a further word.

'Bill,' said Yamani, as if nothing had happened, 'how do you propose to structure that deal?'

'Through a Liechtenstein holding company. We'll get a group of bankers on the Board – American and Swiss – capitalize it at around a half-billion dollars and put the rest in long-term loans. The whole ownership will be in terms of bearer shares held by nominees, and the loans will be made indirectly, probably through New York banks. There is no advantage in making Saudi ownership of the ENI properties public knowledge. You might point that out to the gentlemen when they return, without necessarily going into any details.'

'Right,' said Yamani, and then got up and walked across the room to the windows overlooking the estate. He stood there for the next ten minutes. Then the Aramco crowd returned. Everybody assumed their places in front of the fireplaces.

'Zaki,' said J.J., the spokesman, as always, for the group, since he represented Exxon, 'we agree. With one proviso.'

'And that is?'

'You said that you intended to freeze the market price on crude for the United States – you know, that seven million barrels a day – for three years.'

'Exactly.'

'We want a freeze on the posted price for *all* the crude we take during the same period.'

Not dumb. For the eleven million barrels a day that would go to the rest of the world had been left completely out of the discussion by Yamani. The posted price – on which the royalties which Aramco had to pay the Saudis were based – could be changed at any time, at Yamani's discretion, and cost Aramco and their owners a bundle.

'Done,' said Yamani – just like that. 'And as Bill had just reminded me, we consider it understood that all of these arrangements remain off the record.' Christ, that guy was a negotiator. He obviously intended to freeze the posted price in any case.

J.J., surprised, to put it mildly, looked at his three colleagues. Then nodded. That was that.

'Now,' said Yamani, 'the crucial item.'

Let me tell you, engineers or not, those oilmen knew how to maintain their poise. For logically, after the ENI coup, only worse could come. But not an eyelash blinked.

'Let me assure you at the very outset,' Yamani continued, 'that what I am about to discuss has nothing whatsoever to do with either Aramco or any of your corporations directly. What I really mean, J.J., is that it won't cost you a nickel.'

J.J. chuckled. He liked that. 'In that case, Zaki, I'm going to go get me another bourbon.' He did, and so did the rest, including me – Scotch, not bourbon – and even Reggie.

Then Zaki Yamani made his pitch. The room was hushed. and remained hushed, when he explained the increasingly perilous situation in Riyadh. Rebellion was in the air. There was leadership for insurrection right in the royal family. The large number of Palestinians who, unfortunately, had been given so many key positions in the Saudi economic system, represented a potentially elite revolutionary corps; the laborers – from Iran, from Yemen, from Pakistan – who numbered close to a million, the potential foot soldiers. All directed against the ruling elite. How were they being financed? At this point Yamani threw his hands in the air. Where else? From Qaddafi. The American oilmen all nodded solemnly at this juncture. They knew that Libyan maniac. He had really been the first to break their stranglehold on production, and thus prices, in the world. He was the nut who had actually commissioned a submarine to torpedo the QE2 in the Mediterranean in the 1973 conflict. He was the man who had promoted and financed the massacre in Lebanon in 1975. He was the Arab revolutionary who with his money enabled the IRA to continue endlessly their slaughter in Northern Ireland. Qaddafi. A name that struck terror equally among Christians, Arabs, and Jews.

'But,' said Yamani, noticing that his audience was getting unusually perturbed, 'there is no reason for panic. We still have things under control. We have stationed the entire national guard in and around Riyadh. One Bedouin is a match of any ten Palestinians, as Hussein has proved in Jordan. But the situation is still urgent, in fact, grave.'

Then, with a remarkable frankness, Yamani moved on to the subject of the Shah of Iran. The man was no Qaddafi, he said. And the American oilmen nodded. They all knew the Shah. They all disliked him. They all knew he was inherently unstable. But he was no nut! Nevertheless, continued the sheik from Riyadh, he had greatly overcommitted himself in every respect. The grandiose military schemes, industrialization plans, absurdly expensive projects for the almost complete reconstruction of Teheran to include the world's largest plaza, in honor of himself of course, and the world's most luxurious subway system – all goals publicly announced. But how could all this be financed? Only through continuing and rapid increase in the OPEC price of petroleum. For with Iran time was really of the essence. Their reserves were down already to forty billion barrels, by common consensus. The Saudis had calculated that, in truth, the reserves were far smaller. By 1985, Yamani said, the Shah was going to start running out of crude oil. And then?

So there lay the other danger. If the Shah had his way within OPEC, Persian oil crude would be twenty-five dollars a barrel within two years. And that, said Yamani, would beyond any doubt break the backs of the Western economies; they would collapse. By increasing its output to eighteen million barrels a day, Saudi Arabia was, in fact, putting a lid on any immediate price increases. That, however, would put the Saudis directly at odds with the Shah of Iran. His reaction? Again Yamani threw his hands in the air. Who knows?

'But,' he then said, 'I think all of us realize that the man controls the largest and most highly equipped military establishment between Europe and China. We, in Saudi Arabia, have the world's largest reserves of crude oil. And no effective counterforce.'

He paused at this point and stroked his beard pensively.

'Gentlemen,' he then said to his completely American audience of six, 'we need American support. Military support. Immediately and massively. On a scale that would approach that given to Israel in the fall of 1973. As simple as that. Otherwise we, and thus you, and thus your nation, will find ourselves in the greatest possible peril. For years we have tried everything in our power to convince your Administration, your Congress, the Pentagon, of the urgency of our needs. We have gotten nowhere. Now we must have your immediate and total support in this effort. You must help us mobilize the necessary forces in the United States. We are willing, as you have heard today, to make that task easy. We shall guarantee the United States its old supply. We shall guarantee that the price of oil in America will go down, not up. And this guarantee shall hold, irrespective of what the rest of OPEC chooses to do. If necessary, we can increase our output immediately to twenty million barrels a day. And one thing more – very important. We are prepared to make available a very large proportion of our monetary reserves to the American money and capital markets. We are willing to supply America with both enough oil and money to aid your industry and government in avoiding a very serious economic decline in your nation during the next years. Bill Hitchcock, who has made all the preparations in the monetary field, can give you all the details later. But – and then I will have no more to say on this subject – everything – I stress everything – depends upon our getting an immediate response to our request for total American support in the military sphere. If we do not get that, you get neither our oil nor our money. We shall go elsewhere.'

J.J. Murphy took it upon himself to speak on behalf of the Four Sisters. 'Zaki,' he said, and his voice was husky, 'we'll get action, I promise you. Otherwise, and I guarantee you this, that dumb son of a bitch in the White House won't get one goddamned dime from anybody ever again. He won't even get a job after he's thrown out of office.'

Not the most diplomatic of responses to Yamani's elegant plea, but one that at least indicated J.J.'s intimate knowledge of how the great American republic was run.

The meeting broke up for lunch, and after lunch it seemed naturally to break up into committees. Reggie, who had come prepared with almost every possible detail on the oil side, sat down with Texaco and Mobil. The agreement, he pointed out, would have to have approval of the Justice Department. To get approval a certain proportion of the cheap new Saudi crude would have to be allocated to the other major oil companies – Gulf in particular – plus the independents. Reggie thought it could be done along the lines worked out and approved by the Justice Department in 1955, when the same problem had cropped up in regard to the sharing of cheap Iranian oil, negotiated by the Iranian Oil Consortium at that time. This, plus a lot of really tedious stuff concerning how the Canadian, Venezuelan, Nigerian, Libyan, Iranian crude would be shunted around the world, to make place for the new Saudi crude in the American market, without anybody – meaning the Canadians, Venezuelans, Nigerians, Libyans, and especially the Shah of Iran – even hearing the details. The oil companies were old hands at this, of course, but Reggie insisted that the logistics be worked out immediately. I could see why Yamani always traveled with Reggie at his side. Reggie also had very specific ideas on how to put the squeeze on the independents in Europe – the key to my ENI takeover plan. I sat down with J.J. Murphy, who was, to put it mildly, very close to the New York bankers, and with Fred Grayson, chairman of Standard Oil of California, who knew them all in California. I laid out my game plan for the dispersal of Saudi Arabia's megabucks in the American financial community. They liked it. In fact, they suggested that it would represent the clincher. Washington could not possibly stand up against a pro-Saudi alliance which included the oil industry, the banking industry – and the defense industry, for my plans included dropping a few bucks in their treasuries also.

Exxon's J.J. Murphy had made arrangements that everybody spent the night at The Oaks, and it was good that he had. The meeting lasted all through the next day.

It was not until noon of Monday, January 22, that we all embarked for New York on the Aramco 707 that had been standing by the entire time.

I remember thinking, as we all boarded that luxury liner of the skies, that we really had the world by the balls.

CHAPTER EIGHTEEN

There was, unfortunately, another man who at approximately the same time had had exactly the same idea, namely Mohammed Riza Pahlavi, the Shahanshah of Iran. While we had been laying the groundwork for a power play against OPEC and the Shah in London, he had been laying the groundwork for an end play around all of us in Khorramshahr.

Two days after Yamani, Reggie, and I had left Teheran for England, the Shah had flown down to the Persian Gulf to get a firsthand look at the stage of development of his latest toy. Lots of grown men like toys: electric trains, motorboats, model airplanes, tin soldiers. So also the Shah. But he played with full-sized models: F-16 fighter-bombers, Chieftain tanks, armored personnel carriers. He loved to drive and fly them. A sportsman in the royal tradition. The toys he went to Khorramshahr to play with were different. They were not ones that could be driven, or flown. They had to be dropped, or tossed, so to say: atomic bombs.

As Ursula later told me, he had arrived at their home in Khorramshahr the morning of January 23. His arrival was completely unannounced. Their doorbell rang at nine, exactly the time it usually was rung by the SAVAK man who chauffeured her father to the separation plant on the near-by airbase each morning. She opened it – and there stood His Majesty. She recognized him immediately. It was impossible not to; his picture hung on every other wall in Iran.

'My dear,' were his first words, 'you must be the daughter of Professor Hartmann. I am most delighted to meet you.'

Give the guy credit: he knew a good-looking gal when he saw one, and he also knew how to charm the pants off them – quite often literally. Ursula, thank God, had her mental defenses up. From the look in his eyes at the front door that morning, she later told me, if she had given even the slightest hint of interest, there was no doubt in her mind that before the day was done she would have been on the receiving end of her first royal fuck. Ursula normally does not talk that way, but when she told me about what had happened that day, we were in St. Moritz, and we had just had our first big fight. But that occurred a few months later. Anyway – at least that's her story – she put on such a demure act that the Shah, though not totally discouraged – that was not part of his makeup – was at least temporarily deterred from direct action.

In fact, she did not have to say a word, since her father had come to the door just seconds after she opened it.

'My dear Professor Hartmann,' said the King of Kings, 'this is indeed a pleasure. I do hope my sudden visit will not inconvenience you.'

'Not at all, Your Majesty,' said Hartmann in his guttural English. 'May I invite you in?'

The Shah was not alone. Behind him were both the head of Iran's air force, General Barami, whom the Swiss professor knew very well, and a second military man, Brigadier Shabanah, chief of the Iranian air-sea strike force on the Persian Gulf, who very quickly introduced himself to the professor and then shyly to Ursula.

Ursula scurried to the kitchen to mobilize the staff for tea. For that much she had learned in Iran : you can serve tea to anybody, any place, and at any time. When, after about ten minutes, she returned with the tray for the guests, they were all sitting around the dining-room table, watching her father, as he made a simple sketch on a pad of yellow paper.

The sketch, which she somehow managed to retain, and actually told me about that evening in St. Moritz when she decided to tell all, was this :

It was an atomic bomb, in all its beauty and simplicity. While she poured, her father explained.

'This is, of course, greatly oversimplified. It merely demonstrates the principle, not the detail. And it shows only one dimension – a front view, really. You see only six sections of the bomb, but you must imagine it in spherical

190

form, containing twenty-four sections in all. The sections are conic-shaped, and all exactly equal in size. Together, as I said, they must form a sphere – an absolutely perfect sphere. But, Your Majesty, surely I am boring you.'

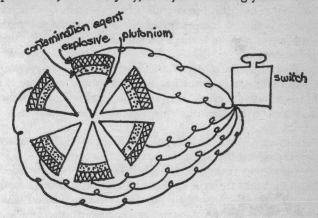

'No, no,' said the Shah. 'This is fascinating. Fascinating! Go on.'

'Well,' continued the professor, 'each of these pieces –' and his finger went to the sketch – 'is triggered by an individual nitrostarch-based explosive charge that produces a detonating velocity of twenty thousand feet per second.'

'Twenty thousand, you say?' interjected His Majesty.

'Yes, sir. It is highly important that the velocity be precisely that,' said Hartmann. 'Now, between the chemical blasting agent here –' again his finger pointed – 'and the plutonium metal are these sections of materials that produce the radioactive contamination.'

'And what type of material is that?' asked the Shah.

'That depends, of course, on what exactly you have in mind,' answered the Swiss physicist.

'Yes, I see,' replied the Shah in a pensive tone.

'Now,' continued Hartmann, 'how does it work? Very simply. You trigger the explosive charge – you can use a variety of switches to perform that function – and the explosive charge simultaneously brings all the sections together. The momentum generated, you see, would prevent them from being forced apart in the first microseconds of reaction. The critical mass thus achieved causes the nuclear chain reaction to increase exponentially until the enormous force of the nuclear bomb is generated.'

He stopped.

'There is nothing more?' asked the Shah in awe.

'Nothing. Of course, what I have sketched out here is a very primitive device. It would be terribly cumbersome. But it does, I hope, illustrate the principles with which I work.'

'Perfectly, perfectly,' replied the Shah, who then paused before probing the professor further.

'Something that you said fascinates me,' he continued. 'You said that the type of material here –' and this time it was the Shah's finger that pointed – 'depends upon what one has in mind. Am I repeating your words correctly?'

'Yes.'

'Well,' said the Shah, 'could you expand on that just slightly.'

'But of course. However, perhaps it would be better if I could demonstrate some of these matters on a real model.'

'You have some available?' responded the Shah with visible excitement.

'Not here, of course. But over at the plant. Perhaps we could proceed further there.'

The Shah was so worked up that he did not even bother to say goodbye to Ursula. No one had even touched the tea, either.

They took the Shah's Mercedes 600 – he loved all things German, including their women – and, escorted by four military jeeps, two fore, two aft, made it to the air base in ten minutes, to the nuclear separation plant in another ten. The Shah had obviously told the driver to step on it.

Inside, they went directly to Professor Hartmann's laboratory. There on the workbench in the center of the room was a gleaming metal sphere about four feet in diameter.

192

'Is that . . .?' asked the Shah.

'Yes, Your Majesty,' replied the professor.

'May I . . . touch it?'

'But of course.'

All eyes were on His Majesty as he approached the object and then, carefully, caressingly, put a finger, then a hand, then both hands on the atomic bomb.

'It feels so cold,' he said, with his hands still upon it, 'but it has a magnificent beauty.'

Finally he stepped back. The gleaming metal was dulled with perspiration where his hands had touched it.

'Is it – functional?' he then asked.

'Yes, Your Majesty,' replied the professor. 'But it is really nothing special. Its yield is only fifteen kilotons. I must apologize for that, but you see, for this first model we were terribly restricted by the amount of plutonium we had available here.'

'No, no, my dear Professor. No apologies, please. One must start somewhere,' said the Shah. 'You said fifteen kilotons. How much is that exactly?'

'Nothing. Really nothing. Hiroshima size. That's all. But of course our next ones will – if you want – be much more productive. But, as I said before, it really depends upon what you want.'

'Exactly,' said the Shah. 'But now I would very much appreciate your explaining what . . . what varieties might be available.'

'You can have them in almost any flavor,' replied the professor, who then let out a rather loud cackle. Which produced a chuckle from the Shah and a loud hee-haw from General Barami. Brigadier Shabanah, whose English was somewhat limited, failed to get it.

'For instance,' continued the professor, walking over to another workbench, 'I would highly recommend you consider using this.'

'This' was a white powder. He shook a little out of a bottle.

The Shah looked at it, but this time refrained from touching. 'What is it?'

'Lithium fluoride.'

'I see. And what can it do?'

'It's one of the substances I use for special effects.'

'Explain, my dear man.'

'Certainly. Let's take a situation where you might want to kill all the inhabitants of an area without causing extensive damage to the area itself.'

'How big an area?'

'Oh, let's say Teheran.'

'Could it be a bit bigger?'

'Teheran?'

'No, the area.'

'But of course. No problem. How big an area do you have in mind?'

'Oh, say fifty square miles. Like an oil field.'

'No problem. Could give you more.'

'Good, good. Now how would that work?'

'Well, we would simply pack some of this lithium fluoride around the external surfaces of the bomb segments. A layer of, say, a couple of inches. We could use a very simple bomb – even the one over there. Now, what you would have to do is be very precise in how you drop it. My suggestion for the size of area you have in mind would be about a thousand feet – no more – and about five miles upwind from the area you have under consideration.'

'Yes, and then?'

'Well, when the bomb detonates, it will do no damage to the target area. It is just a small bomb.'

'But how are the people in the target area killed?'

'With fluorine eighteen. Deadly stuff. Works fast, very efficiently.'

'Fluorine eighteen?'

'Yes. You see the nuclear explosion would partially convert the fluorine salt into fluorine eighteen. Fluorine eighteen is an isotope with a half-life of only two hours. But it kills humans, simply upon exposure, within minutes. The whole population in your area would be dead before they even began to realize what was happening to them. In fact, they would probably die rather happy, thinking that somebody had tried to drop a bomb on them and missed.'

Again the cackle. And when the Swiss professor laughed, his head and the mass of white hair flowing from it bobbed up and down.

'Wonderful,' remarked the Shah. 'And all you would need is that' – pointing at the substance still in the professor's hand.

'Yes. Simple fluorine salt.'

'But,' said the Shah, his brow now wrinkled in worry, 'but what about our people?'

'What people?'

'Our people.'

An obvious impasse. General Barami broke in. 'What His Majesty is, I think, referring to, is what about the troops that would seek to then occupy the target area?'

'Ah. I see. But that is no problem. None at all. In fact, that is the beauty of this substance' – again pointing to the white powder. 'As I said, it has a half-life of only two hours. Your troops could move in within a day!'

The general looked at the Shah. Both nodded.

'I'd like to order one just like that,' said the Shah. 'No, come to think of it – two.'

'Certainly,' replied the professor, carefully putting the salt back in the bottle and making a note on a pad beside it.

'General Barami,' continued the Shah, 'perhaps you have something in mind that the professor might be able to help you with.'

'I do. But it is perhaps asking too much.'

'Please,' said Professor Hartmann, 'just ask. If it is not possible, I will tell you.'

'Well,' said Barami, 'let me give you a theoretical situation. Purely theoretical.'

'Of course,' replied the Swiss.

'Let's take a city like Mecca. Purely theoretically, of course.'

'Of course.'

'Let's say we wanted to do something along the lines you

195

have been describing – you know, not in any way damaging the holy place, but, contrary to what your powder will do, also not killing anybody immediately. In other words, forcing them to evacuate the city by letting them know that if they stay, they will die from the fallout. Do you get what I mean, Professor?'

'I do. This problem is not new. It has been solved. Not by myself, however. It was the Israelis who came up with the solution.'

'Can you develop such a weapon?'

'Of course. With this.' Another bottle, this one containing a grayish metallic powder.

Both the general and the Shah went over to look at it.

'Magnesium,' said the professor. 'Simple magnesium. And we use exactly the same system. Pack a layer of it around the bomb. When it goes off, the product is sodium twenty-four. Has a half-life of fifteen hours. If we drop the bomb upwind, say three miles from the city, at an altitude of, say a few hundred feet, it would do the trick perfectly. With its peculiar contamination properties, the population would have ample time to get out before the contamination agent started to take effect.'

'And once it started taking effect, how long would it last?'

'A week. Maybe two, if one wanted to stay on the safe side.'

'Then our troops could move in?'

'Yes.'

'Remarkable,' commented the Shah, now picking up the bottle containing the magnesium powder. 'I think we should have a couple of these, too. What do you think, Barami?'

'Definitely.'

The professor wrote it down. That made two lithium fluorides and two magnesiums.

'Now,' said the Shah, 'I've got something else in mind. Let's say, Professor, that we wanted to totally obliterate an area the size of, say . . .

The conversation went on for the rest of the day. The

Shah ordered a total of twelve bombs – that was all that could be made with the amount of plutonium that would be available between then and March 28. And it was on that date – March 28, 1979 – that the Shah wanted delivery.

CHAPTER NINETEEN

While the Shah was playing with his new toys in Khor-ramshahr, I was flying the Atlantic in the Aramco luxury liner, complete with sleeping berths. It was just like the old Stratocruisers in the 1950's. If you had a gal along in those days, it was one of the only ways to go. Pullman cars were the other. I was in college then, and such things had left a deep impression. In fact, the airlines' and railroads' sudden abandonment of these accommodations for fucking at high speeds in comfort was, in my judgment, one of the reasons behind the current decline of western civilization.

I expressed this opinion to Reggie, who – and I stress this – was not sharing a bunk with me, but was standing beside me at the bar, also provided courtesy of Aramco, at the rear of the plane. Reggie disagreed. The real turning point – no, points, plural – were the inventions of the dry martini and vaginal deodorants.

I pondered that, and finally had to admit to Reggie that he was probably closer to the mark, but only because he had much more time to think these things through, in solitude in the Arabian desert, while I had been out there in the real world.

About five hours later – in my bunk, alone – I woke up with more than a slight headache. The whole plane was still dark inside, since all the shutters had been closed when the flight began. But when I opened mine, the sun was high in the sky. Nights are not long when you fly east–west. In two hours we would be landing at Kennedy. And then the action would really start. It was juvenile to stay up drinking half the night when so much was at stake. But what the hell? I thought. What's really that important?

I thought of Ursula. That was important. I'd try to call her from New York right away. Then there was Ursula's father. There seemed to be little doubt that the mad old bastard was actually fooling around with nuclear weapons down there. But what the hell? Which country wasn't fooling around with them? The point was – would anybody dare use them? I'd met the Shah – twice now. And although he was an arrogant son of a bitch, no doubt about that, was he nuts enough to actually use them? No. At least not now.

OK, so that left us with the real immediate problem: not war, but money. Not Iran, but the United States of America. I thought, how could it have happened so fast? Within just one decade, just ten years out of more than two hundred. Sure, it was not yet visible. America still stood like a beautiful edifice built upon a foundation that was just about to crumble. That foundation? Look, nobody could ever kid me about that. America has always had one foundation and one foundation only: money. Enough money, wealth, whatever you want to call it, to spread around in sufficient quantities to keep everybody happy. *That* is what attracted the English in the eighteenth century, the Germans, the Italians, the Eastern European Jews in the nineteenth century, the Puerto Ricans and Mexicans and Cubans in the twentieth. Not the Constitution nor Abraham Lincoln, nor freedom of religion. It was the freedom to make a pile of money – and to keep it – that was always American's magnet. Cynical? Maybe. But also correct.

But what would happen when the gold mine ran out? How would the two hundred and twenty million Americans react when they began to realize that it was running out? There, in my judgment, lay the real, immediate problem. Because they still didn't know. They had been lulled, pacified, deceived, lied to so consistently and so effectively, for so long, that the majority were still convinced that the economic troubles of the 1970's were just a passing phenomenon, that the good old days would return, and very soon. They did not want to know the truth, I guess, when you come right down to it. In 1973–74, the country came damn close to an economic breakdown, when the oil embargo was on. If the Arabs had kept the spigot closed for just a few more months . . . Then in 1975, the New

York City thing. Sure, everybody said that if it had gone bankrupt, somehow everything would have been worked out anyway. But the big guys, led by Nelson Rockefeller — they knew. They knew already back then – that the American economy was in such a shaky position that a New York default could have set off a chain reaction in the financial markets that would have led . . . where? Nobody wanted to know. In 1978, when Chrysler Corporation looked like going broke – that was a close one. Sure, it had happened before. Penn Central had gone belly up, and Wall Street had survived – some said just barely. But another close one. Highly dangerous. Why? Because the American people were nervous. Ready to panic.

In 1979 it was not Penn Central, nor Lockheed, nor Chrysler, nor New York City that was on the brink. This time it was the banks. Not *a* bank, nor *all* the banks. But *the* banks. In the United States, that meant twelve, maybe fifteen banking groups at most. They were where all the money and credit in the United States came together. They were the linchpin in the system. Yank it and that's it : total shambles.

For contrary to the almost universally accepted myth, it is not the Federal Government that 'insures' banks; it is other banks – the other big banks – that 'insure' banks. All the FDIC does is provide insurance to small depositors – up to $40,000. Period. Of course, nobody says *when* they have to pay off on that insurance. In a simple case, right away. In a case of massive failure? Who knows?

We bankers all knew that, every single one of us. I remember a guy in Switzerland who ran a bank there who once put it right on the line. Every banker, he said, has one foot in jail. In his case, he ended up with both feet there, the simple bastard. But only because in his instance, the 'insurance' system was not put into effect. He hadn't played by their rules, so the big banks just let him dangle. The risk of the game, he said later. And he was right. Because if a bank does go broke, and if the big boys don't step in, let me tell you – the guy who ran that bank doesn't have a chance. Because everybody hates bankers. And every banker knows that. That's why they have to stick together. They know that if they don't protect each other from the wolves outside, nobody else will. Especially the goddam agencies in Washington and the simpleminded bureaucrats who run them.

A fucking useless rat race. That's why I sold out. My father would never have understood why. He thought of himself as a real pillar of the community – in the same class as the judge, the minister, the doctor. He thought, when everybody kissed his ass, that they did it because they loved him. Hell. They did it because they never knew when they might need him. Period. My ex-wife was the same. She loved being the banker's wife. When she sent out invitations to dinner, she always got 100 percent acceptance. Never a no show. She thought it was because of her looks and charm. Hah! Well, I got rid of both her and the bank. And I thought I'd never go back to anything resembling either. And now, there I was, juggling the Saudi billions around and hooked on Ursula Hartmann.

And flying right back into the biggest damned mess in American banking history. It was not a mess that was created overnight – messes never are. It had taken my fellow American bankers a full decade to get to the point they had reached in 1979. And it was the top fifteen banks – those that 'insured' everybody else – that were in the most trouble. Their problem lay in both sides of the balance sheet. On the asset side, where the loans and investments of a bank are listed, their situation was bad enough to give an honest bank examiner a case of cardiac arrest, even though it is generally considered extremely bad form to drop dead in a bank. For at least 25 percent – one quarter – of the assets of the top fifteen banks in the United States were worthless. They were carried on the books at full value, of course. But they were simply not there. They represented loans and investments that had gone down the drain, totally and irrevocably.

To realize how bad the situation was at the beginning of 1979, one must go back to numbers – not detailed statistics, just ball-park numbers. By that time, the total assets owned by all the commercial banks in the United States were about $1 trillion, *i.e.*, $1,000,000,000,000. The 'big' banks, my top fifteen, controlled about 25 percent of that – or about $250 billion. OK? Their annual reports indicated that most of this $250 billion was safely invested in such marvelously safe things as government bonds, especially municipal bonds (what could be safer than a municipal government?), in real estate (what could be safer than land and buildings?), in loans to America's largest corporations (those great companies that make America rich), in tankers (tangible wealth if there ever was any), and loans to foreign governments (doubly safe, since not only was government again involved as the safest possible debtor, but the banks had diversified their foreign governmental loans among dozens of different nations).

It was extremely important that everybody should believe that all these loans were as solid as the Rocky Mountains, for after all, the loans had all been made with the money of depositors. If the loans were not repaid, the depositors would never get their money back. If word got around that such a possibility – no, probability – existed, and everybody showed up at the same time one fine day at the withdrawal window, no power on earth could prevent the panic of the century. So the truth was not – could not – be told.

What was the truth? Well, let's start with real estate. Back in the 1960's the banks started to get very hungry for profits. If everybody else was making a bundle, why not banks, and why not – then – also bank executives? Everybody knew that really big bucks were being made in real estate – but not by the banks. By the developers and by the middlemen who financed the developers. Banks got only 8 percent on their money. If they went into the real-estate-development business, they could get 15 percent! So they went into real estate in a very big way. The medium was a new creation of their – the REIT, or Real Estate Investment Trust. They all put up one or two or three captive corporations and then lent their new babies all the money they needed. The REITs, in turn, started to finance everything in sight – condominiums in Florida, shopping centers in Arizona, resorts in California, commercial buildings in Manhattan. At 12 percent, 14 percent, 16 percent. Marvelous! The REITs managed to lend about $21 billion that way, and the banks made parallel loans directly to such construction projects totaling another $10 billion. Also at 14 percent on average. Well, something happened. The great American boom, which had started after World War Two and went on and on and on, suddenly came to an end. People could not afford condominiums in Florida or high-rent offices in New York. So the REITs and the banks got stuck with half-completed projects spread the length and breadth of the United States. They just 'parked' them, waiting for the next boom to come along. They waited and waited and waited – while the half-finished buildings crumbled into decay. But not the loans on the banks' books. They did not crumble in the slightest. All $31 billion was listed as good money, while at least half of it – $15 billion – was irrevocably lost. Which meant $15 billion of depositors' money was irrevocably lost. That was the optimistic view. Pessimists said the losses were at least $20 billion.

Then take tankers. Again the malaise dated back to the late 1960's. At the time every large American bank – my top fifteen again – decided to go abroad in a big way. Why? Because foreign banking operations were essentially unregulated. It was hard to make a buck in the States with the government regulating everything in sight. And there were taxes. Uncle Sam demanded much too much. But if you went abroad with your banking operations – no regulations to speak of, and no taxes. And what taxes you paid abroad could be used to reduce – dollar for dollar – the taxes you paid in the United States. The result was that by the mid-1970's over 50 percent of the profits of the top fifteen banks in the United States were being earned abroad. Another result was that taxes paid by the large banks to the American government were not merely small, but infinitesimal. In some years they paid no taxes at all! But – and as they found out, there was a big 'but' – when the American banks decided to go big abroad, they discovered that there was competition out there. Especially for good loans. Good big loans, since big banks are predominantly interested in big loans, since they think big. And after all, a loan for $100 million essentially requires no more, or not much more, than one for a measly million.

Well, tankers – no, supertankers – were an ideal answer. First, they were more than big – they were huge. Second, everybody in the world was building them like crazy, since the demand for petroleum and petroleum products was zooming at 10 percent to 15 percent per annum, and would obviously continue to do so for the next thirty years. And third, because there was a good number of banks – Swiss, German, Belgian – who were not competing for these loans, since they thought them to be high-risk, the idiots. So in stepped the Americans, through their branch operations in London. They fed about $15 billion into the tanker market – in Scandinavia, in Japan, in Greece, in Germany, in Britain and Ireland and Norway.

Then came the 1973 oil embargo. Oil consumption dived worldwide. Tanker rates sank to historical lows. Nobody could employ the old tankers, much less the new ones that were being constructed with the money of the American banks. So, like the real-estate projects in the United States, the American banks were stuck with tankers that were half-built, three-quarters built, or completely built, but simply sitting idle for years and years in some remote Norwegian fjord. Result: At least half the $15 billion in loans would never be repaid.

About the same time the big American banks discovered tankers, they discovered another market, much bigger, and more exotic: lending to foreign governments. Italy, of course, was one of their earliest discoveries. Well, we know what happened there, not just to the American bankers, but the rest of us as well. Not that they had not been warned. Way back in 1974 the U.S. Comptroller of the Currency warned all American banks against lending one more dime to Italy. That did not stop them. But Italy was nothing compared to the so-called LDC's – the Less-Developed Countries. All told, by 1979, American banks – again, almost exclusively the top fifteen – had lent them $33 billion. All this from savings of little old ladies in upper New York State, or Sacramento, California, who thought that their deposits in the local bank were being lent to the local butcher to buy meat. Uh, uh. Their money was going to places like Zaire, Uruguay, Egypt, Burma, Sri Lanka, to enable these countries to stay alive, to enable them to buy oil from the Arabs at exorbitant prices, and manufactured goods from Europe, Japan, and America at equally exorbitant prices. Sure, they were all backed by governmental guarantees, but these guarantees were worth even less than those given by New York City. For the only source of income for most of these nations – income with which to pay interest on their loans, and eventually pay them back – was the sale of raw materials and foodstuffs in the world market. But, with the world in a depressed economic state for most of the 1970's, the prices they were getting on cacao, coffee, copper, zinc, cotton, etc., etc., had been going nowhere, certainly not up. Result : As high as 40 percent of their total earnings, as countries, was necessary just to *service* the outstanding debt to American banks, in the cases of Uruguay, Egypt, Zambia, Mexico. In the cases of Burma, Nicaragua, Algeria, Bolivia, the Congo, Sudan, Sri Lanka, the ratio was 30 percent – just to pay the interest. Then came Morocco, Argentina, Israel, Chile – the list went on and on. A few more years, and the funds needed just to service their debts would begin to approach the *total* income of such countries.

In other words, these loans were not just bad, they were lousy. Of the $33 billion, no more than 25 percent could be considered good. The rest – $25 billion – would have to be written off.

On top of all that, these linchpin banks in the system also had their share of the entire banking industry's woes : billions of dollars of bad loans to essentially illiquid American corporations – led by the airlines and railroads. Then there were the billions upon billions of dollars that the banks had invested in suspect municipal bonds – New York, Detroit, Cleveland, the State of Massachusetts – the list went on and on in 1979.

Net result : Of the $250 billion in assets shown by the top fifteen banks in the United States, at least $50 billion was worthless. And their combined net worth, that is, their capital that could not be withdrawn, was only $25 billion. In other words, they were broke twice over.

Yet they were all still operating, all intact, their presidents, vice-presidents, cashiers, and assistant cashiers all cheerful and prosperous. Because everybody, starting with them and ending with their auditors and the bank examiners from Washington, kept their heads firmly stuck in the sand. Because the official rules said that a bank in the United States did not have to call a spade a spade, as in any other business. It did not have to call a bad debt a bad debt, at least openly. For banks operate by rules of their own. Loan losses must not be declared as such immediately, but can be 'written off' at the leisure of the banks' executives. Bad loans could be converted into good loans by merely lending the bad debtor some more money – so that he could at least pay the interest on the bad loan, thus making it unnecessary for the bank to declare the loan as bad. Crazy, but true.

Now all this was sad enough – the asset side of the large American banks' balance sheets – but when combined with the status of the liabilities side, the situation was nothing less than criminal.

For you can have all the bad loans in the world, as a bank : as long as nobody knows it, they will keep putting money in your bank. And you can cover up forever. If someone wants his money back, the bank does not have to recall some loans to secure the funds, since the debtor could not repay in any case; no – he just finances the withdrawals by getting new deposits.

This system was key to the survival of the banking system. As any banker can tell you, no bank ever went belly up because of bad loans on its books. What kills banks is a shortage of liquidity – ready cash – to pay off doubters when they appear at the door. The classic way of avoiding such a fix is to lend short and borrow long. In other words, the cautious banker will make one-year loans and accept two-year deposits. That is the Golden Rule of Banking. Nothing can happen then. In America, for years, just the opposite had been going on. Banks were giving fifteen-year loans to the Congo and financing them with ninety-day certificates of deposit in the United States, or thirty-day call money from the Eurodollar market. They were not, however, just borrowing short and lending long, they were also breaking that other cardinal rule of banking : Spread your deposits among the largest possible number of depositors. If ten depositors control 25 percent of your total deposits, you are highly exposed. Half of these depositors might show up on the same day and want their money back – which you, as a bank, might not have. But if you have your deposits spread among hundreds of thousands of depositors, and if no given ten of these control more than a few percent of the total, such a 'coincidence' cannot happen. The law of averages protects you. Clear. However, the large New York banks in the 1970's did not have a choice. They *needed* fresh money. Their loans were *not* being repaid. They had to continue to make new loans to save old ones, and to save face. So they were willing to bend the traditional banking rules and get more and more of their money from fewer and fewer depositors, and accept shorter and shorter maturities.

The risk of illiquidity was thus ever present. The risk was perhaps at its highest in early 1979, because the money and capital markets in the United States were drying up. The U.S. government was getting almost all the new savings. It had to – to finance the federal budgetary deficit which, by fiscal year 1979, had reached $136 billion. Result : there simply was not enough left over for the large banks to enable them to paper over their monumental bad debts, as well as supply their still viable customers with their usual lines of credit.

So you can imagine what would happen when Yamani and I stepped in with the Saudis' billions. Joy would reign on Wall Street, for another reprieve had miraculously been granted by an ever-forgiving God – be He called Jaweh, Allah, or whatever. The point being. He supplied Cash.

When the Aramco jet landed at JFK that cold January day, I must say I was happy. I liked New York. It was the best city on earth. No other place even came close. You could feel the vibrations even before you touched down on the runway there.

My feelings about that town were once more confirmed after we got inside the terminal. I put a half dollar into the machine and got the early edition of the *New York Daily News*. They had obviously been tipped off. The headline read : WELCOME SHEIK : WE'RE UP THE CREEK ! I showed it to Yamani and he laughed. To his credit, the guy found New York as heady as I always have.

Exxon was there waiting in the style of old. With both J.J. and Yamani arriving on the same Aramco flight, the guys in New York must have gone out of their minds making sure that everything was right : no less than six of the longest goddam limos mankind had ever devised, and a contingent of at least fifteen of the biggest goddamned bodyguards I had ever seen. They all looked like linebackers from the Pittsburg Steelers. And they made us move. We were through the airport and out onto the expressway in less than five minutes. Our destination was Sixth Avenue and Fifty-fourth Street, site of the global headquarters of Exxon.

The entire bank of elevators going to the top floors of the building had been blocked off, pending our arrival. J.J. and his pals went all the way up to the fifty-first floor, a world of luxurious office suites the equal of which could not be found anywhere. We – meaning Yamani, Reggie, and I – got off a few floors below, at the headquarters of Aramco, situated so conveniently in the same Exxon Building.

It was quite a setup. The first thing that hit you was a huge portrait of King Khalid, then banks of Arab engravings, finally the stark photographs of pipelines in the desert. When American oilmen and Arab sheiks got together, their contribution to interior decorating was uniquely absurd. But what the office decor lacked in terms of art was more than made up for by the deep feeling of awe it inspired : the place absolutely reeked of money.

Yamani and Reggie were completely at home there. Reggie made a feeble attempt at introducing me to the young Saudis who populated the place, but he soon gave up after I told him that all Arabs looked alike to me. J.J. had wanted us to come to the fifty-first floor and have lunch with his fellow Exxon directors. Yamani had declined, thank God. Instead we went to work.

I had been assigned an office of immense proportions, including a full staff of secretaries, female, thank goodness, and a carte blanche from Yamani to start pushing my buttons, while he took a suite of offices at the other end, where he intended to start pressing his.

My first call was to the man who by universal recognition now was at the top of the American financial heap : Mr. Randolph Aldrich, Chairman of the Board, President, and Chief Executive Officer of the First National Bank of America. My Aramco gal had him on the line in five seconds. In the old days it used to take me five days to get through.

'Hitchcock,' he almost shouted, 'where are you?'

'In town, Randolph. How are you?'

He would have none of that stuff. 'Where in town?'

'The Exxon Building.'

'Look, let's get together right away.'

'Sure, Randolph. That's why I called.'

'Your place or mine?' I'll bet that was the first time Randolph Aldrich had said that for a decade, including the times when the President of the United States had wanted to see him.

'Mine,' I answered promptly. 'Which means, more specifically, the Aramco offices here.'

'I know where they are. When?'

'Say an hour.'

'Done. Who else will be there?'

'Nobody.'

He liked that. 'Bill, let's keep it that way for the time being.'

'Sure, Randy.'

I didn't say goodbye because Aldrich never ever said goodbye. He just hung up when he was done talking. I must say I admire those little things.

Sixty-one minutes later Randolph Aldrich was in my new Aramco office suite.

'Every time I come here,' he said, dispensing with any type of greeting, 'I wonder what the Jews across the street think when they look out the window.'

Across the street were the three American TV network headquarters.

I decided not to comment on that for two reasons : first, it was a very old joke; second, my new girlfriend was of the same faith. And third, come to think of it, I liked Jews a lot more than I liked Aldriches.

Aldrich took the chair opposite my desk. 'OK, Hitchcock, let's get to it. We've heard.'

Of course they had heard. Hell, that ultrasecret discussion in the English countryside was already twenty-four hours old. In another twenty-four it could well be printed word for word on the broad tape.

'How's the market?' I asked.

'Up sixteen points. What would you expect?'

Exactly that. The banks' trust departments were loading up before the really big action started. Yet not showing their hand by overdoing it. It was not a nice world.

'Well, before we get to "it," Randolph, could you tell me what exactly you have heard?'

'That the Saudis are finally going to play ball. Just like I told you they would have to in Frankfurt. Remember?'

'I remember.'

'But with how much?' he wanted to know.

'We'll get to that, piece by piece. But before we do, I'd like to suggest something.'

'Go ahead.'

'I want you to put together a little meeting. For tomorrow afternoon. At three fifteen. Here.'

'All right. Who do you want to come?'

I told him. Sixteen men in all. I had written their names out by hand.

I gave him the list. He scanned it.

'All right. I can probably get everybody, except Larsen.' Larsen was the chairman of General Dynamics.

'What's with Larsen?' I asked. 'Out of the country?'

'No. He died last night. I'll get his number two.' He crossed Larsen off the list and wrote in somebody else. The end of Mr. Larsen.

'Let me use your phone.'

I pushed it across the desk to him. He called his bank, dialing the number himself. 'Marjory,' he said, addressing his fifty-nine-year-old secretary whom I had been forced to go through on various occasions in the past, which was like going through Mont Blanc without a tunnel. 'I want some guys over here at the Aramco offices tomorrow at three.' Not three fifteen, as I had suggested. He read the list and hung up. There was no doubt in either his or my mind that everybody would show.

He handed me back my list. You never know about pieces of paper. 'All right,' he said, 'let's hear it.'

'First, I've got eight point two billion available for you right now.' I referred to the prepayment for ninety days of crude oil, as arranged with J.J. in England. The funds were already available.

'What terms?' asked Aldrich.

'Hold on, for Christ's sake. I'm just starting. This is something special. I want to get it out of the way first.'

'OK. What is it?'

'Remember that Italian deal that you torpedoed?'

'Me?'

'You.'

'I remember.'

'Well, it's on again. Only this time with a little twist. We – and by that I mean . . .'

'I know who you mean, for God's sake.'

'All right. We are going to buy out all the foreign assets of ENI. For six billion dollars. We've got a holding company

211

in Liechtenstein which will act as the purchaser. It's ready to go. Since yesterday it's been capitalized at a half-billion dollars. All paid in. The rest will come in in five-year loans. We want you to put together a consortium to make the loans. As I said, we'll provide you with the money.'

'For five years?'

'Christ, no. On the usual basis.'

'No deal.'

'Look, Aldrich. This is part of the package.'

He thought that over. 'Why don't you do it directly? Why do you need us?'

'One reason : the Saudis want it that way. They like to lend their money short term. You ought to know that by this time, Aldrich. They want their banks to lend long term or medium term or whatever. You know their reasoning. That's what banks are there for. If the banks want their money, then . . .'

'Look, I've heard that enough times to make me sick.'

'All right. Then why the fuss? In any case, all of the ENI assets will be pledged as collateral. What more do you want? That's as sweet a deal as you'll ever get. You act as the lead bank on this and you'll net fifty million dollars, front end, without flexing a muscle. I'm giving you the whole works – the deal, the funds, the collateral – on a platter, Aldrich.'

'But can you guarantee that the Saudis will renew their short-term deposits until that five-year loan matures?'

'Sure. So will Yamani. And Fahd, if you insist.'

'What's the spread?'

'Pretty good. We want eight percent on our deposits. You can ask ten percent on the loan. Two-point spread. Nice, huh?'

'Look, we've got a risk.'

'Sure.'

'All right. Anything else?'

'Yes. We would like you to come on the Board of Directors of the Liechtenstein holding company. The Saudis won't want to advertise the fact that this is completely their deal. You know how it is. Maybe you could get somebody

212

from Chemical and Chase to come on too. The directors' fees will be, shall we say, ample.'

'All right. Who will be chairman?'

'Dr. Willi.'

Dr. Willi was one of the smartest, crookedest, and thus richest lawyers in Vaduz. Thus Aldrich knew him well.

'Willi is arriving tomorrow morning with the documents. He's already fixed the Italian end of the deal.'

'I'll bet he has,' replied Aldrich, with a grin. Then : 'You said the funds were available. Where?'

'Europe,' I answered. 'All eight point two billion will come from European banks. Eurodollars.'

'Hell ! They'll be screaming !'

'Wait until you hear the rest.'

The rest was that an additional $20 billion would be made available to American banks during the next few weeks.

'Why twenty?' asked Aldrich – a damn stupid question, really.

'Because I say so.' Which was an equally stupid answer. But he let it ride.

'Where will it come from?'

'All over. Germany, Switzerland, Japan, France – the works.'

'Again out of Eurodollars?'

'No. Most of it from local currencies.'

'Those guys over there will *really* scream !'

'Yeah. It's tough.'

'What do I have to do?'

'Line up the takers on this side.'

'Who have you got in mind?'

The top ten banks in the United States. Who else? The Saudis never – and I mean never – deal with any bank that was not included in the list of the top fifty largest in the world. Period.

'And who gets how much?'

'I thought that it should probably be based on the Marxist principle of each according to his need.'

213

Aldrich liked that. 'All right,' he said, 'I think I'm getting the picture. Now. What about the terms?'

Aldrich and that question shall always go together in my mind.

'Good terms. We are going to give you these funds at five percent.'

'Five?' he asked, puzzled for the first time.

'Five.'

'But federal funds are going for eight.'

'I know. But not for long.'

'You're right. Good thinking, Hitchcock.'

The point was that the cheapest money available to banks in the United States were so-called federal funds. These were funds lent from one bank to another on very short term, out of excess reserves held with the Federal Reserve System. As a result of the continuing insanity of the people who ran the Fed, in spite of the fundamental economic difficulties in the country they insisted on maintaining a tight money posture – starving the banks for money because some professor in Chicago had told them that this approach was the one and only way to hold down the rate of inflation. Sure, it was *one* way. But hardly the one and only. Nevertheless, it was a simpleminded theory – thus one that appealed to many politicians, and most financial journalists. It was also one that actually predated the Chicago professor by a hundred years, and it had not worked then either. But no matter. The people in Washington were true believers. But their power to enforce their faith was restricted to the United States. There was no way they could block the massive inflow of Arab funds. And once the Saudi billions started flooding the American banking system, of course interest rates would plummet – the short-term rates probably back to around 5 percent.

Aldrich figured that out in a flash. 'So you are also coming in short term with these funds,' he said, in a voice that did not reflect total joy.

'Of course. Thirty days, maximum. But for God's sake, Aldrich, you can't have it both ways.'

'I know,' sulking.

'And remember whom you are dealing with. I know the Saudis by now. They are as responsible as any governmental leaders on this globe. They are coming to the United States with their money for keeps. The rollovers will be automatic.'

'I guess you're right, Hitchcock. It's like I said in Frankfurt : Without us they will soon be up shit creek. OK. I don't like it. But we really don't have much choice right now, do we?' He knew that I knew what shape his bank, and the rest of them in New York, were in.

'I guess not. But think of it this way, Randy. What would have happened if we hadn't come along?'

He ignored that one. 'Now who is going to tell my competitors and colleagues the good news?'

'I think it ought to be you, Randy. This will finally put you in the big leagues.' I don't know why I say these things.

'How will the transfers be managed?' he asked.

I explained. The mechanics would be the same in every case. The funds would be placed with the London branch of each borrowing institution on a thirty-day fixed basis. The branches would pass the funds through to headquarters back in the States. Headquarters would have to explicitly guarantee the deposits on behalf of their offshore branches. The transfers could start within three days, and would then come in, staggered, until the full twenty billion had been placed. All I needed was a listing of which banks wanted in, and how much they could accommodate.

'Can you sort that out this afternoon?' I asked.

'Probably. How late will you be here?'

'Until six, at least.'

'I'll call. Now about that meeting tomorrow.'

'Yes?'

'You're trying to put together a Saudi lobby, I assume.'

'Right.'

'Fair enough. You know I back the concept. Who's going to chair the meeting?'

'I thought you might, Randy.'

'With pleasure. You know, Hitchcock, I like doing business with you.'

'It's mutual, Randy.'

He called back at five. He had gotten commitments for all of the twenty billion. The New York banks, including Aldrich's, took most of it. They needed it more than the fellows out West, he explained.

I spent the next few hours sending out Telexes all over the world, telling dozens of banks that the short-term deposits that the Monetary Agency of the Kingdom of Saudi Arabia held with them would not be renewed, that further instructions would follow.

Zaki Yamani came into my office around seven. He was pleased when he heard what had already been accomplished. He also suggested I knock it off for the day. He had scheduled a meeting for nine the next morning, and he wanted me to be there. It would be on the fifty-first floor. J.J. was going to preside, and he thought I would enjoy the show.

CHAPTER TWENTY

That evening I was alone in New York for the first time in a long time. I stayed at the Plaza, a much overrated place, but it was only a few blocks from the Exxon Building.

I left the Aramco offices shortly after seven, walked over to the hotel, had a few drinks at the bar standing up, which is the only way to drink, a fact recognized by only two cities in America, San Francisco and New York, and was ready, For what? I knew exactly for what, but does one do that when one has a murderous schedule the next day?

One shouldn't, but one does. So I consulted my little book and dialed a number. After two rings, I hung up. Why act so goddamned stupid? I was dead tired, going on fifty, worried – yes, worried, in spite of how everything was going – and there I was, about to take some twenty-seven-year-old twit out to a wildly expensive restaurant, where I would not feel like eating anyway, then on for a drink somewhere, where I would have at least a Scotch too many, and finally her apartment, where I would have to spend the rest of the night, since it was no longer good form to just fuck and run like in the good old days, to wake up the next morning an aged, hung-over miserable, tired wreck.

To hell with it, I concluded. What I did was get the operator, and ask her to put a call through to Ursula in Iran. Five minutes later she called back, and said there would be at least a twelve-hour delay. So I told her to forget it. Then I said, 'Shit,' took a shower, and went to sleep.

Twelve hours later I woke up. Another shower, and I felt like a million bucks, and looked it too. Funny how a little bit of fatigue can confuse you.

At eight forty-five I walked out of the Plaza, raring to go.

When I got to the fifty-first floor of the Exxon Building, J.J. was standing in the corridor, outside the boardroom, talking to Yamani. When he saw me he came right over.

'How did you and Aldrich get along yesterday?' he asked.

'Fine.'

'How much money are you fellows going to be moving over here?'

'Didn't Yamani tell you?'

'No. I didn't ask him. I'm asking you.'

J.J., when ensconced in the trappings of power on the fifty-first floor, came on a bit heavy. He probably was trying to figure a little private play in the market. But fuck him. He had enough money.

'J.J.,' I replied, 'if it was any of your business, I would have invited you. It is not, and so I did not.'

J.J. plowed on as if I had not spoken a word. 'That ENI deal involved?'

'Might have been.'

'So you fellows are actually going to try to go through with that crazy idea?' J.J. had obviously thought it over, and was already prepared to weasel out.

'J.J.,' I said, 'I know what you've got in mind. But let me tell you : If you try to renege on just one goddam thing we all agreed to in London, Yamani will have your ass.'

The guy turned purple. He also decided to end the conversation.

But I hadn't. 'By the way,' I said, 'we are expecting your offer of those two German refineries. I would appreciate something in writing within the next day or two.'

'Look, Hitchcock. Don't get too big for your britches. That is a matter between Yamani and myself.'

'Wrong, J.J. I'm handling it. Dr. Willi is over here to do the paperwork. I'll have him call you later today.'

'Willi? That crook?'

'That crook. I try to get the best, J.J.'

He stalked off. That, I thought, would teach him not to lean on William H. Hitchcock. Altogether, a good beginning to the day.

Yamani, who was surrounded by Texaco, Mobil, and

SoCal, had been watching the exchange. When it was over, he winked at me.

Only minutes later, the three men from Washington arrived : the head of the Federal Energy Authority, the Assistant Secretary of State for Economic Affairs, and the Undersecretary of the Treasury. All were nervous. They were, after all, second-rate. They were too young and inexperienced for their jobs. They were also too accustomed to being surrounded by hundreds of pandering bureaucrats, of very limited capabilities. New York, the Exxon Building, the Exxon boardroom, the heads of America's four largest oil companies, Sheik Yamani, *me* – they simply did not belong and they knew it. But, if anything, it made them even more aggressive. Especially the fellow who ran the Federal Energy Authority. He was thirty-four years old, a lawyer, and, of all things, a Southerner. Three strikes against him, as they say, before he even opened his mouth that day. Which did not prevent him from opening it right away.

'Gentlemen,' he said in a very loud drawl, 'I can only give you an hour. I would think that we should get right down to business.'

J.J. looked at him as if he were some kind of rodent that, beyond rational explanation, had crawled into his boardroom on the fifty-first floor.

'Young man,' said J.J., which immediately produced a flush in Weatherspoon's face – that name didn't help him either – 'most happy to oblige.'

The old bastard, when he wanted to, could out-drawl anybody, and on this occasion he gave his best West Texas imitation of a Georgia cracker. 'Why don't you come over here first? I would like you to meet some people.'

The people were Yamani, Reggie, and myself. Although he had been in office only two months, Weatherspoon already knew all the American oilmen. When he shook my hand, his was sweaty, which figured. The men from State and Treasury duly followed.

'I am most obliged,' he said, obviously liking that word, 'that you very busy gentlemen could come up from

219

Washington on such short notice. I think, however, you will find it has been very worthwhile, after you hear what we have to say today.'

The emphasis was on the 'we.' His words did not seem in any way to diminish the skepticism of the Washington contingent. After all, it included Aramco and the Arabs, that unholy alliance that had gotten America into the energy mess in the first place.

J.J. then called the meeting to order, turned it over to Yamani, and Yamani began his pitch. Seven million barrels a day guaranteed to the United States, through Aramco. Thirteen dollars a barrel. A three-year guarantee on both price and quantity. Plus the reasons why : Saudi Arabia recognized that its future economic interests and those of the United States were essentially the same. Thus, he wanted to end the era of confrontation and introduce an era of Saudi-American cooperation.

His presentation was precise, elegant, and totally convincing. I thought. Until the reactions were voiced.

'This is, of course, highly interesting,' began Weatherspoon. 'It represents a major shift, of course. It will require study, a great deal of study. Because the ramifications – positive and negative – are obviously manifold.'

Which meant absolutely nothing. Incredible !

But Weatherspoon was in a bind. He was – also incredibly – committed to maintaining the highest possible price for crude petroleum to encourage domestic exploration and development. Ten dollars a barrel was more than enough incentive for such, and everybody in the room knew it. But sixteen dollars a barrel had been Weatherspoon's publicly announced 'solution' to the energy crisis when he had assumed office a few months prior.

Then the Assistant Secretary of State spoke up : 'I agree with my colleague. First, it would be highly dangerous, from our national security standpoint, to develop a sole reliance upon one nation for our oil-import needs. Secondly, any such program would, by definition, raise serious and complex questions in regard to our relationships with a

220

number of our best friends abroad, who have traditionally stood by the United States.'

Meant here were Venezuela, Canada, Nigeria – and of course Iran – who were the chief external suppliers of crude oil to the United States. These 'friends' had stood by us in our hour of need – at twenty dollars a barrel! And given a chance, they would put it up to thirty, just like that.

The only guy who made sense was the Undersecretary of the Treasury. He had put his pencil to paper during the meeting and come up with the only thing that mattered to him.

'I don't see anything complex nor anything that requires any study whatsoever. This offer will save this country three dollars a barrel on each and every barrel it imports. That means twenty-one million dollars a day. Seven point six billion a year. Simple as that.'

Weatherspoon and the State Department looked disgusted. Nothing is simple.

'What are the formal arrangements that are proposed?' asked the man from State.

'A long-term contract between the government of Saudi Arabia and Aramco,' Yamani replied. 'Nothing further. I believe, however, that a public endorsement of this arrangement by both your government and ours would serve the interests of all parties involved.'

Weatherspoon did not like that at all. For it meant that the Federal Energy Authority would be recognized for what it was – useless. The State Department did not like it either, since it had vowed never again to let foreign energy policy slip back into the control of the oil companies. Two major bureaucratic empires were in dire danger. Only the Undersecretary of the Treasury looked as though he liked it. In fact, he had been planning for months to find a way to quit Washington. Now the way was clear. If he got on the Aramco bandwagon immediately and completely, there was no doubt in his mind that a very cushy job indeed would be available in New York in this very building when he needed it.

Weatherspoon, looking for an out, immediately came up with the antitrust considerations of such an exclusive Aramco deal. Reggie, seconded by the chairman of SoCal, had an immediate response. When a similar arrangement had been made in the past with the Iranian Oil Consortium, the Justice Department had given it an explicit waiver. There was no reason why the same could not apply now. State then came up with the sacredness of contracts with his old friends the Canadians, the Venezuelans, the Nigerians, *et al*. J.J. said that would be no problem. The oil they had contracted for there would simply be diverted to other world markets – although the price might become negotiable. Which prompted State to suggest that if a two-tier pricing system evolved – low prices for America and high for the rest of the world – a crisis in our relationships with our NATO allies could well result, an unthinkable thing.

To which J.J. had the perfect response. 'But my dear man,' he said, 'Exxon's only interest has always been to serve the American consumer. We feel it is high time you men in Washington started to do the same.'

Finally, State came up with his last-ditch ploy. 'And what about Israel?' he asked.

'The hell with Israel,' J.J. said. That seemed quite adequately to formulate the consensus of every oilman in the room. Israel was a bore. At stake here was a more important matter : the survival of the Four Sisters !

Yamani just sat there passively for almost a full hour. Then, deliberately, he looked at his watch. 'Gentlemen,' he interrupted, 'I believe you said at the outset that you only had an hour. I am afraid we have already kept you longer.'

He withdrew three identical documents from the dossier in front of him. 'Here,' he said, 'is our proposal in triplicate. I would appreciate it if you could duly inform the President of its contents, and I respectfully request that he let me know if he finds it of interest.'

Then he rose, and that was the end of the meeting. The Washington boys had no choice. The three messenger boys came to the head of the table to shake hands with Yamani and J.J., and then left. It was 10:30.

Frankly, I thought the entire show had been mishandled. Why fool around with these second-rate guys? Why had Yamani and J.J. not gone directly to the White House? When we got back down to the Aramco offices, I put it exactly so to Yamani.

He had a ready reply. 'Bill,' he said, 'it is a matter of matching the approach to the man. I know your President. Not well, but I know him. A likable man. Yet a man with a very limited knowledge of economic matters and a limited attention span where oral presentations are involved. He must have matters explained to him in writing, simply and repeatedly, in order to be able to grasp them. He will now receive my message in exactly that way – in three different written versions, from three different sources, with three different conclusions. That will enable him to *A:* understand, and *B:* come up with a fourth conclusion, which will be his alone, allowing him to demonstrate once again his singular powers of leadership.'

Great theory, but it did not work out that way. The three men returned to Washington on the next shuttle and were in the President's office by three that afternoon. The President barely glanced at the written material. For his mind immediately grabbed onto one significant item, and one only. This was 1979. 1980 was an election year. The Saudi offer would allow for a ten-cent-a-gallon reduction in the price of gasoline in the United States. Therefore, he would not only endorse the Aramco-Saudi agreement; he would do so publicly, bombastically, and immediately.

He personally called Yamani at four that afternoon to tell him just that. He suggested that he come down to Washington the next day to prepare a joint announcement. Yamani suggested a twenty-four-hour delay. The President agreed.

Yamani relayed this information immediately in a note delivered to me in the Aramco boardroom, where I was co-chairing the second big meeting of the day. The chairman was Randolph Aldrich. And he was loving every moment of it.

'Gentlemen,' he had begun, 'I think we are out of the

223

woods – thanks to my old friend, Bill Hitchcock here, and his friends in Saudi Arabia.'

The audience was composed of the chairman of the six other multinational banking giants and nine of their biggest corporate clients, so big that all of the bankers were involved one way or the other with all of them. The names of the companies: General Motors, General Dynamics, Lockheed, Litton Industries, McDonnell Douglas, Raytheon, Northrop, General Electric, and Colt Industries. All had one thing in common: in addition to being among the largest corporations in the world, they ranked number 1 through 9 in the list of the suppliers of military hardware in the United States in terms of annual dollar sales. They were the producer end of the military-industrial complex of the United States of America. They had only two masters: the Pentagon and the banks. One of these was present – the banks, led by the financial-establishments chairman, Randolph Aldrich. So everybody had shown up.

Aldrich explained the purpose of the get-together. Twenty billion bucks was on the way. From the Arabs. The days of tight money were over. The guys at the Federal Reserve, who had almost brought the country to ruin, were finished. He knew how strapped for cash everybody was – except General Motors, of course. Well, no more.

'We are ready to talk now, boys,' Aldrich told them. 'We've finally got the cash to get this country moving again.'

And, he went on, it would not be 10 percent money either. He figured that they could drop the prime rate by two points within two weeks. That would bring every interest rate in the country down – short term, medium term, and even long term.

'That,' he continued, 'will insure, as you full well know, that the Dow-Jones will take off for the first time in three years. My guess is that it will pick up two hundred points during the next six weeks. And you know what that will mean for us all.'

They knew only too well. Their shareholders had been

at their heels for years, yapping from some action in their stocks.

'All right,' continued Aldrich. 'I don't think it's necessary for me to go any further. We all know the impact this will have. But, and this is the real point of this meeting, what you have heard today is only the beginning. A lot more money is on the way, and at even better rates.' That was purely extemporaneous. But what the hell!

'Now,' said Aldrich, 'we all know that nobody gets something for nothing. What, you are asking yourselves, do the Saudis want in return? I'll tell you. Complete, total, and immediate support for their military program. They want aircraft' – his finger pointed at Northrop and Lockheed – 'tanks' – the finger pointed toward General Motors – 'your fire support systems' – this directed at Raytheon and Westinghouse – 'your ships' – that at Litton – 'everything down to small arms' – which meant Colt Industries. 'I know, you know, that you've had the orders in hand for years now. What the Saudis now want is something very simple : delivery! They get delivery, you get yet more orders. With substantial cash-down payments – made through us – on each and every one.'

'Look, Randy,' said Litton Industries, 'it's not simple. The Saudis have three missile destroyers on order with us. You know that. Everybody knows that. But Iran has four on order. Our navy has six. The South Koreans have two. They are all ahead of the Saudis.'

'That's the point,' I interrupted. 'We want that changed.'

'Well, tell that to the Pentagon,' said Litton.

'We're going to. What we want is that *you* tell that to the Pentagon. All of you. Now. And tell it to the White House, too,' I said. I looked to Aldrich for support.

'That is the exact point,' he said. 'Now Hank—' (that was Litton) 'and Abe—' (the fellow from General Dynamics who had replaced that dead guy) 'and Jim—' (that was Mr. Big, General Motors). 'I think we all ought to go down to the White House this week and lay it right on the line.'

General Motors did not like that. He really didn't need anybody's money. But who could tell about the future?

These days anything was possible. At least that was what I surmised was going through his mind, from the painful expression on his face.

'All right,' he said. 'But don't expect miracles. And for God's sake, let's keep all this to ourselves. If the Senator from Iran or the one from Israel hears about this, all hell will break loose. Understood?'

Even Aldrich nodded.

But then Abe spoke up – his name was Abraham Silberschmidt. 'Hold on,' he said, 'we can't just ignore Israel, as you suggest.'

'Why not?' asked General Motors.

'Because all this means a diversion, or at least a potential diversion, of military equipment from Israel to the Arabs.'

'So what?' asked General Motors.

'Well, what if they are used against Israel?'

'They are not going to be used against Israel,' was the response. 'I don't think you understand what is happening here, Abe. What is being proposed is *good* for Israel. Don't you get it?'

'No How?'

'Because what is good for Saudi Arabia is now good for the United States, and what is good for the United States is good for Israel. Get it?'

Abe still did not get it. But nobody really cared. For right then was when I got the note from Yamani. Since it nowhere indicated that the information was confidential, I told the meeting of its contents.

'Hitchcock,' said General Motors, 'I have heard about you. But, by God, this is really something you've pulled off.'

'Randy,' he continued, 'get me a phone.'

Randy did. And in less than two minutes, General Motors had the President on the line. He wanted to see him tomorrow. A matter of urgency. They agreed on three o'clock.

Ten-cents-a-gallon decrease in the American price of gasoline would mean five hundred thousand additional General Motors cars sold per year.

The Arab lobby had been born.

CHAPTER TWENTY-ONE

The next two months produced a kaleidoscope of activity that was unique in my lifetime. The ego trip began, appropriately, at the White House, where the President put on a little lunch for Yamani and entourage – me, Reggie and J.J. – prior to their afternoon news conference. The whole affair was presented as a triumph of the Administration, a tribute to their tough negotiating skills, and a turning point in history. The questions that followed from the Washington press corps were, of course, dumb, concentrating mostly on how this would affect the Administration's attitude toward Israel. Yamani, with his usual patience, tried his level best to explain that Israel had nothing whatsoever to do with it.

That evening, J.J. and Exxon put on the party of parties for the friends of big oil in Congress. They were numerous. Especially now, when the oil cartel appeared to be back in the driver's seat.

The next morning, I joined Yamani for breakfast in his suite at the Hay-Adams to review with him the press reaction. *The New York Times* gave the event full coverage. The front page lead headline was factual : SAUDI ARABIA AGREES TO LONG-TERM OIL CONTRACT WITH U.S. The editorial page headline provided the interpretation : THE END OF OPEC? The editorial itself left little doubt that the question mark would soon be superfluous. With Saudi Arabia going its own way, it could only be a matter of months, at most, until the OPEC cartel collapsed. With the world in an ever deepening recession, the resulting competition for markets in the West could very well lead to a worldwide petroleum glut and a collapse in the price of oil. It was gratifying to see that patience and restraint in regard to the Middle East, not the militancy advocated by some, had produced this result. The editor of the *Times*, harping on a theme that had become his favourite over the years, summed up the money side : 'For years,' his article stated, 'the prophets of gloom and doom have propagated a great myth : that the OPEC nations were going to accumulate hundreds of billions of surplus dollars and thus endanger the entire stability of the world money system. The situation today shows how wrong they were. Venezuela, Nigeria, Algeria – all have become net *borrowers* of funds in the world capital markets, as their import needs overtook their oil income. With the collapse of OPEC imminent, their situation will only deteriorate further. So much for that subject.

'True,' it went on, 'there has been, and still is, an exception : Saudi Arabia. Due to its unique situation, with its enormous oil income and its limited population, that Arab country has not been able to spend its petroleum income as quickly as other OPEC nations. As a result, that country still has a fairly large reserve of so-called surplus funds, perhaps well over one hundred billion, although no one knows exactly. In any case, the amount is insignificant relative to the total money supply of the West, and thus hardly represents a potentially disruptive element in the world financial markets. In fact, the Saudis have apparently discovered that it is no longer easy to find either a market for their crude oil or a safe haven for their rather limited hoard of dollars. Wall Street, acording to rumor, is being flooded with Saudi Arabian funds this week.

'It is gratifying that the men in Riyadh have come to their senses. It is to be hoped that the local prophets of impending doom will now do the same.'

The *Wall Street Journal* contributed its wisdom on such matters under the headline : ARAB MONEY : IS IT DANGEROUS? The headline writers in New York were fairly big on question marks that day. The editorial stated the following: 'As everybody must know by now, the Saudis are giving us both oil and money. The oil we can use. But what about their money? It is a well-known fact that the Arabs have a propensity for investing their surplus funds for very short terms, usually funneling them into the American banking system through the Eurodollar market. What, the worriers ask, will happen if, all of a sudden, they started to yank it out again?

'There are two answers to this. First, the funds involved are not that great : twenty, maybe thirty billion dollars, at most. By New York standards, not really all that much. Certainly a sudden withdrawal could create problems, but hardly the end of the world. Secondly, where could the Arabs go with their funds? The Mexican peso? The Brazilian cruzeiro? Hardly. The Arabs have finally discovered that the dollar is indispensable, and that the American banking system is the only one large and viable enough to absorb their funds safely and profitably. Our only question is why it took them so long to find this out.'

Splendid, I thought. Perhaps uninformed, naïve, stupid. But nevertheless, splendid.

'Well, Bill,' said Yamani, after I had put all the papers back on the floor, 'what is your judgment?'

'You've done it,' I replied.

He nodded. 'Now,' he said, 'it is up to Sultan Aziz to do his stuff.'

Sultan Ibn Abdul Aziz, defense minister of the Kingdom of Saudi Arabia, had arrived quietly the prior evening. In fact, very quietly. His plane had sneaked into Andrews Air Base at midnight, and he had stayed the night at the Saudi Embassy to keep his name and presence out of the Washington hotels.

I went over there with Yamani around noon.

'Mr. Hitchcock,' said Sultan Aziz when he saw me, 'your friend here tells me that you have made things much easier for us.'

My friend was General Falk, military attaché at the U.S. Embassy in Saudi Arabia and old drinking pal. He was standing next to Sultan Aziz, grinning. 'You son of a bitch,' he said. 'We were over at the Pentagon this morning, and you've got the fuckers there mad as hell.'

'Why's that?' And I did not ask it with any feigned innocence.

'That end run through the White House. I don't know who you all got to pressure the President, but whoever they were, it sure worked. The Secretary of Defense is so worked up I'm told he is threatening to quit.'

'Why?' I again asked.

'Because the President called him on the carpet last night, and told him to get off his ass with deliveries to the Saudis. And this morning, about twenty guys from Congress did the same.'

'What's he got against the Saudis?'

'Nothing, really. It's that he has always had the hots for Iran. The Pentagon theory is that the Shah of Iran is the Great Stabilizer of the Middle East. So he gets arms, while the Saudis get promises. But no more. You must have sent some pretty heavy guys into town on this one, Hitchcock.'

I guess you could call General Motors and Exxon and Lockheed and Litton pretty heavy.

That afternoon, Sultan Aziz, Yamani, and General Falk were personally invited to the White House to get the good news directly from the Commander in Chief. The Secretary of Defense was also there. He was instructed to remain after the Saudi visitors left.

'Now,' said the President, 'do you still have problems?'

'No, Mr. President. I fully agree with your decision. But there is, perhaps, one small matter which you may have overlooked.'

'What?'

'Israel. And I have a suggestion in that regard, sir. I think it would be highly appropriate if you would get the Israeli Prime Minister on the line and explain. Tactfully, of course.'

'Explain what?'

'That the weapons shipments we are diverting to Saudi Arabia will in no way pose a threat to Israel. That their purpose is for defense only, and that . . .'

'Look, I am going to do no such thing. Those Israelis get on my nerves, slowly.'

'I agree, sir. I mean about the Israelis. But you are really making my point. They are so touchy. They think there is always an ulterior motive behind everything. Like some women.'

'I have no time for stuff like that. They have to finally learn that we owe them no explanations for anything. They toe the line – our line. Period.'

Within a week, a freighter left one of the Gulf ports, carrying twenty-four spanking new F-4 fighter-bombers, bound for the Saudi port of Jedda. One left a Great Lakes port shortly thereafter, with one hundred M-113 armoured personnel carriers. Yet another, from the same port, sailed a few days later, also bound for Jedda, carrying seventy-five M-60 battle tanks. Five Hercules transports flew from Los Angeles to the Jedda international airport during this same period, loaded with three different types of surface-to-air missiles.

Arms shipments from the United States to Iran, Israel, Egypt, Turkey, South Korea were all, inexplicably, cut back at the same time.

That really pissed off the Iranian Ambassador to the United States, Ardeshir Zahedi. His measured response came in the form of the biggest cocktail cum dinner party of the year. He got half the Senate, one-quarter of the House, and all but one of the senior Washington press corps. Of course, the Secretary of Defense was also there. At midnight he disappeared into Zahedi's library with the ambassador for a little private chat. After the party was over, Zahedi sent the Shah a long coded message.

I left Washington for New York the day after Sultan Aziz arrived. After all, as Yamani had said, now Aziz had to do his stuff on his own. The green light had been turned on in Washington. Now he had to follow through with the defense contractors.

I had enough work waiting for me in New York to keep me busy twenty-four hours a day. First and most tedious was the job of moving funds from Europe to the United States. Mechanically it was relatively simple. During December of the previous year, in anticipation of all of these events, and acting under the instructions of Crown

231

Prince Fahd and Yamani, I had carefully concentrated the maturities of our Eurocurrency deposits in the final weeks of January and early February of 1979. Thus, for example, the Monetary Agency of the Kingdom of Saudi Arabia had DM 500 million coming due on January 25, at the Deutsche Bank, Frankfurt. On the 24th, the Deutsche Bank received cable advice from Riyadh – duplicating the message I had sent to Riyadh via the Aramco communications network from the Exxon Building on Sixth Avenue and Fifty-fourth Street – instructing them to transfer the principal and accumulated interest to our DM account with the First National City's London branch upon maturity the following day. Simultaneously we instructed First National City in London to deliver those DM 500 million, which they would receive from the Deutsche Bank, Frankfurt, to the London branch of the Dresdner Bank, against payment in dollars. I had already presold these DM back in 1978 at an extremely good rate. In fact, I recall that on that one small deal alone I had made well over $2 million profit on the foreign exchange differential. Anyway, First National City in London was then further instructed to just hold on to the dollar receipts of the DM sale until further notice. Next step was to call up Chase Manhattan's head office in New York and ask them what they would offer on the $192 million that was now sitting in London for thirty days. Sure, in theory I had promised these funds for around 5 percent. But what the hell! Chase offered $5\frac{1}{2}$ percent and put it on a Telex to Riyadh. Simultaneously I Telexed Riyadh, telling them to accept the offer and to instruct First National City Bank in London to transfer the $192 million they were holding to Chase's branch in London. That branch, upon receipt of the funds, immediately had the amount – in a purely bookkeeping transaction – transferred to the books of the New York parent bank. The following day, the $192 million, plus $8 million more to make it an even $200 million, left Chase, drawn by the treasurer of United Airlines against their revolving line of credit, and was transferred to the account of McDonnell Douglas at Security Pacific Bank, Los Angeles, in payment for aircraft, the delivery of which had taken place months ago, but which United Airlines could not pay for since both they and their banks had been too strapped for cash to do so.

Repeat this process a hundred times and you will describe exactly what I was doing in New York in the period between January 29 and February 15, 1979. A banker's life is not all fun, you see.

Now despite what The *Wall Street Journal* and The *New York Times* had claimed, when you move money into New York as I was moving it those weeks in early 1979, it has an impact. One hell of an impact.

Obviously, the first thing that happened was that the cost of federal funds plummeted. Then the New York banks dropped their prime rate a full percent within a week. The interest rates on Treasury bills, bankers' acceptances, and commercial paper fell by the same amount. Within days, as the downtrend continued, the effect slopped over into the longer-term fixed-interest securities markets. Industrial bonds, municipal bonds, Treasury bonds – all took off in price. And the stock market – yes, the stock market, which had been the loser of all losers during most of the 1970's, finally started to move : straight up. The Dow-Jones industrial average was 798 the day Yamani and I had arrived in New York. Two weeks later it was 995. Volume, which had been averaging 40 million shares a day, was now up to 66 million – the all-time record. The market leaders were the aerospace companies, the airlines (now saved from collapse), the oil companies, naturally, and the automotive stocks, just as naturally. And of course the banks, especially the big banks, the multinational banks, above all, those headquartered in New York : Because with the specter of bank failure banished as a result of the massive infusion of Arab dollars, everybody could hardly wait to get a piece of those greatest of all money machines – the big banks.

Hitchcock was the darling of Wall Street, let me tell you. But the damnedest thing was, I literally had no time to enjoy it. I say that with regret, and with some advice to people who have followed my career : Take the accolades when they come and relish them to the hilt, because when they stop – and stop they did in my case, as in all cases – they are lost and gone forever. But I had gotten caught up in the same euphoria as everybody else. With cheap oil and cheap money back, what could possibly stop me and America? I would have plenty of time to enjoy my fame and fortune.

To be sure, joy was by no means universal. The Europeans were so mad it was almost comical. Not, peculiarly enough, at the Saudis, but naturally at the Americans. They had been double-crossed. They, who had so staunchly stood by America for so long, were being bled of the two chief components of their life blood : money and oil. It had all been engineered by the goddamned Americans, who, down on their luck during the entire 1970's, were now trying to get back on top by screwing everybody else in the world. Europe, which by so nobly accepting Marshall aid after World War Two and thus making America what it was today, was being stabbed in the back by an Arab dagger, guided by a Yankee hand.

There is nothing to unite Europe like a common enemy. So it was not only the French who were foaming at the mouth : the Germans, the British, even the Italians – whom we had bailed out of their financial mess with our six billion dollars – were in there bitching with the best of them. In fact, the Italians now claimed that the Americans had deliberately pushed Italy to the brink of bankruptcy in order to be able to steal half of their ENI for a pittance.

Whereas America was getting a sound hammering from its friends in Europe, the Saudis were getting their fair share from their friends around the rest of the Arab world. After the news of the Saudi-American oil deal was announced, Colonel Muammar el-Qaddafi, ruler of Libya, had moved front and center as the self-appointed new spokesman of OPEC. He had called a special meeting in Tripoli. Of course the Saudis did not attend. Interestingly, neither did the Iranians. So Qaddafi filled the vacuum. The Saudis, he said, were now nothing more than a satellite of the United States. Not that the Saudi people wanted such a thing. No, it was being forced upon them by the fascist ruling clique of Khalid-Fahd-Yamani-Aziz, who had become lackeys of the American imperialists.

The United States, Qaddafi continued, had obviously declared war on the rest of OPEC. They would learn the hard way that this was a war which they could not possibly win. Imperialism in all its forms was doomed. That had been proven in Lebanon, in Northern Ireland, in Portugal, in Malta *(Malta?)* where the people had defeated the Americans and their front men. The Saudi ruling clique would be the next to learn this lesson. They had betrayed the holy Arab cause.

Iraq and Algeria endorsed Qaddafi's position without qualification.

When all this came through on the wire service, I asked Yamani what he thought about it. He shrugged. 'It just proves our point,' he said. 'Unless our efforts here prove successful, unless we are able to stabilize the Middle East with American support, that area will end up as the Balkans of our generation. And if it explodes . . .' His voice trailed off.

Personally, I regarded the Qaddafi communiqué as just his usual mad crap. But what was not so unusual, and I thought rather worrisome, was the fact that Qaddafi visited Paris shortly thereafter, and then Bonn. It seemed that he was warmly welcomed in both capitals. It seemed that two rather unholy alliances were developing : the United States and Saudi Arabia on the one hand, and the rest of OPEC and Europe on the other. Strangely, Iran was staying very quiet.

Iran. Ursula. Her father. The bomb.

You know, it had been a week – no, more like ten days – since I had been with Ursula in Teheran. And except for the night I tried to call her from New York after arriving from London, I frankly had not thought much about her. I guess women find this hard to fathom. But, goddammit, I'll bet most men do not. Because they know : When you get caught up in the chase, as I was, it takes you over. It

235

has nothing to do with thinking about or not thinking about somebody. It is just so.

But on the other hand, if things started to heat up in the Middle East, Khorramshahr would not exactly have been my choice as the ideal place to ride it out.

So I went over to Reggie's office.

'Reggie, you know your way around this place one hell of a lot better than I do.'

'OK. What do you want?'

'To telephone somebody in Iran. But I don't want to wait ten hours to get through. Can your pals here at Aramco speed it up for me somehow?'

'It depends,' said Reggie. 'Is this call business or social?'

'Get it down, Reggie.'

I had Ursula on the line three minutes later.

'Hello?' Very faintly.

'Ursula! It's me!' Very loudly.

'Bill! Where are you?'

'New York. I tried to call you last week, Ursula, but couldn't get through.'

'It doesn't matter, Bill. Are you coming to Iran?'

'No. But look, we'll see each other soon in St. Moritz.'

'I know. But I wish it was not so long off.'

'That's what I'm calling about. Ursula, why don't you get out of there sooner? I'm tied up here in the States. But there's no reason why you can't go back to Switzerland earlier. Then I'll join you.'

'It's not so bad here, Bill. I mean, I miss you terribly. And I hate the way this country is run. You would not believe how scared everybody is of the government and the police and the army.'

'Then why stay?'

'Because I am so busy I don't really have to think about it much.'

'Busy with what?'

'Bill, every day I get taken up to Susa. It's only about an hour north. The government has given me – through father, of course – permission to dig there. Nothing big, but I do have three local men helping me. Father is paying them.

We have already found dozens of pottery fragments which are probably from the early part of the second century B.C. – the proto-Elamite era. Some of them have inscriptions in a very early cuneiform. I have written to my professor in Lausanne, and he has verified that in his opinion they can probably be dated around nineteen hundred B.C., to the period when the Elamites were constantly at war with the Sumerians – that's when the people of Susa were first exposed to the cuneiform script. I am starting to photograph everything, and . . .'

'Ursula, I know how important that sort of thing is to you,' I said, although it was beyond me why. 'But you will have the rest of your life to dig around if you want to. I'm just suggesting you postpone it for a while and get the hell out of Iran.'

'No, Bill. I can't.'

'Why not?'

'I must take care of Father. And anyway, we are expecting a visitor.'

'Yeah? Who?'

'You know him. Uri Ben-Levi.'

'What the hell does he always want down there?'

'He's doing something with Father.'

'With or to?'

'Pardon?'

'Forget it. When's he coming?'

'On the fourth of March.'

'Well, let him come. What's he got to do with you?'

'Bill, I told you before. Nothing.'

'Well then, why stay?'

'Because Father needs me.'

'Is he still fooling around with those little toys?'

'Bill, let's not talk about that now.'

'Ursula, I saw that man in Teheran your father is working for. You know who I mean?'

'Yes.'

'The man is dangerous. For all of us.'

'I know, Bill.'

'Well, talk to your father, for God's sake. And then get out of there.'

'Let me do things my way. Trust me. Do you?'

'Yes.'

'Are you sure?'

'Yes.'

'And we will see each other in St. Moritz on March eighteenth?'

'Yes. I'll call you once more before then. Just to make sure everything is OK.'

'Bill?'

'Yes.'

'Do you still love me?'

'Yes.'

'I love you very much.'

But when I hung up I was something less than overjoyed. That fucking Ben-Levi – sniffing around Ursula, and doing God knows what to her father. The son of a bitch.

The next day I stopped thinking about it. Because I was busy – very busy, wrapping up the peripheral details of the Italian takeover deal. We had obtained the ENI properties, and Italy had received its $6 billion. The last aspect of the entire transaction had been the purchase of those two German refineries from Exxon. The Saudis had insisted that they get the German market – or at least a large hunk of it, as part of the overall deal. J.J. had come through. His asking price was at least 25 percent too high, but Yamani approved it anyway. So we paid up. The other part of that end of things was the arrangement of a slight slowdown in the supply of crude oil to the independents operating in Western Germany. J.J. also arranged that. How, I do not know, nor did anyone ask. But within a week it started to happen. In a sense, I guess, we Americans were selling the Germans down the drain. But what the hell – it was strictly a business decision. Nothing against the Germans. It could just as well have been the French.

And a few days after that, I got a call from my old German friend, Herr Doktor Hermann Reichenberger, chairman of the Leipziger Bank. He was in New York and suggested lunch. So I met him at Le Madrigal, which was an easy walk from the Exxon Building, but not exactly a banker's hangout, since the noon crowd was almost exclusively made up of publishers putting on liquid lunches for visiting authors in the hope that they would be so grateful that they would agree to almost anything. I took a table way in the rear overlooking what in New York passes for a garden. Hermann had to walk all the way back to find me, his displeasure growing with every step as he surveyed the decadence of the crowd.

After he was seated, his first question was : 'What kind of a place is this, Hitchcock?'

'It is where the Goethes and Schillers of the New World gather,' I replied. 'See that fellow over there?' I pointed to the publisher of *New York* magazine.

'*Ja*,' he answered.

'He,' I said, 'is the Hermann Hesse of Second Avenue.'

'*Ja, ja. Sehr interessant.*'

My Hermann was impressed. Literature is something that Germans respect almost as much as the D mark. And he could obviously now sense that greatness which surrounded him. 'Are you active in this field?' he wanted to know.

'You mean literature?' I asked.

'Yes.'

'Not any more. But I used to be.'

'What exactly?'

'Fiction. But I gave it up.'

'What kind of fiction?'

'I used to publish the balance sheets of my banks.'

That got a wheeze out of old Hermann.

'*Ach*, Hitchcock, it is funny, but not so funny any more. Could we talk seriously for a moment?'

'Of course.'

'I will come to the point immediately. It is not clever what you are doing.'

'What do you mean?'

'You have gotten everybody in Europe extremely angry.'

'Like who?'

239

'Our bank. The other banks in Germany. The French banks, the Swiss banks, even the English banks.'

'Why?'

'You know why. You have seriously drained deposits from all of us. We – remember – had a consortium to float that Italian loan. You have now done it completely through American banks. And with Arab money, taken from Europe. You do not make friends that way, Hitchcock. Especially since you put in that proviso that the Saudi loans to Italy will be repaid immediately, while the rest of us will have to wait it out.'

'Hermann,' I answered, 'I have done nothing – nothing whatsoever – that you would not have done in the same circumstances.'

'That is not correct. We must live together. Stick together, we Europeans and you Americans. Otherwise we are lost.'

'Look, I am merely carrying out decisions made in Riyadh. The Saudis make the policies, and I carry them out.'

'Could you not at least slow things down?'

'Look, Hermann. If I thought you or any of your big banks in Europe were really getting into liquidity problems – we would. But you're not. You might be hurting, but look – you've been sucking funds out of the United States for decades. And the banks here were hurt. Now you're getting a bit of your own medicine. You'll just have to live with it.'

'I don't think my government would agree with you. We have serious unemployment in Germany. Even the Swiss are having problems. No one trusts you Americans any more.'

'Come off it, Hermann. Nobody in Europe ever did.'

And then we ordered. And talked about nothing in particular. Over coffee came the real subject of the meeting.

'Dr. Hitchcock,' said Dr. Reichenberger, 'you probably know that our bank is a major shareholder in Gelsenberg.'

240

'Yes. Last week, it suddenly started to experience diffi-company.

'Something peculiar has been happening with that company.'

'Oh?'

'Yes. Last week, it suddenly started to experience difficulties in obtaining crude oil.'

'Oh?'

'Yes. Would you by any chance be able to help us with an explanation?'

'I'm afraid . . .'

'I will tell you why I hope you might be able to help. You see we Germans have always been very cooperative with your oil companies – Exxon, Gulf, Mobil – all of them. They essentially control our market, and we Germans have never complained. Now I do not feel that it is in anybody's interest that this close, and tolerant, relationship be upset.'

'I'm afraid . . .'

'I think you must have heard about the visit of Colonel Qaddafi in Bonn. He has convinced some of our governmental people that it would be in Germany's interest to enter into a special relationship with his country, very similar to that just achieved between yourselves and Saudi Arabia. This would, in my judgment, be very unhealthy. Economically, politically, and perhaps . . .'

'Militarily' is one word Germans never use in mixed company.

'We suspect that the major international oil companies are putting a squeeze on Gelsenberg, and . . .'

Again I tried to interrupt, but to no avail.

'And we think that there is a relationship between this event and the takeover of ENI's German retail system by the Saudis.'

'The Saudis did not take it over. As far as I know,' I said, 'it was an American-Swiss consortium.'

'It was the Saudis,' declared Reichenberger.

I shrugged. 'And what exactly are you driving at?'

'Call it off. It's stupid.'

241

'Look,' I said, 'I told you right at the outset – I'm just a messenger boy. My hands are tied on such matters, Hermann.'

'Fine,' he said. 'But you might, by chance, be able to talk to somebody who is not just a messenger boy, as you put it. My advice is that you do so before these things go beyond the point of no return.'

'I'll see what I can do, Hermann,' I said.

An hour later I did. I talked to Yamani.

'No,' he said, with more anger than I had ever seen in the man. 'They want to play games with Qaddafi, let them. We shall see who is stronger in the end.'

What happened was that the squeeze on Gelsenberg was, if anything, intensified. So much for my letting my good intentions get the better of me.

The big news later that day was the resignation of Mr. Weatherspoon as head of the Federal Energy Authority. He was replaced by a Mr. Sisler, an extremely qualified man. For twenty years he had been a senior vice-president of Exxon. Rumor had it that the chairman of the Federal Reserve System also threatened to resign. He claimed that the White House was sabotaging his tight money program by irresponsibly allowing foreign funds to flood American money markets. Rumor further had it that the President had told him to take a flying fuck. Well, he did not take that advice, and he also did not resign. His term expired in 1986, when he would be ninety-one years old, and he intended to serve his country to the full extent allowed by the recent advances in geriatric medicine.

Wall Street responded enthusiastically. For the first time in years, the Dow-Jones industrial average went well above 1000. *Barrons* ran – actually it was just a rerun of the same article they published biannually – an editorial head-lined : WHERE WILL THIS MADNESS END? It pointed out that every business cycle discovered by mankind, starting with the short-term Kitchin cycle, and ending with the long-term Kondratieff cycle, was headed down. That the world was entering a period of acute danger, and that the recent surge of wild speculation merely confirmed what the economic theoreticians had already calculated.

The first day of March I went to Texas to give a speech at the Houston Club. The chairman of LTV had set the show up. The theme of my speech was 'The New Energy Alliance,' and the text was pure propaganda for the Saudis. Not that I did not have an enthusiastic audience down there. Houston is an oil-cum-defense-industry town. Sultan Abdul Aziz came along to add a bit of native color, and also to take a look at some of the military hardware coming off the LTV production lines. General Falk was, naturally, at his side – always – showing the flag of the pro-Saudi clique in the Pentagon, and insuring that if LTV ever needed a general as a consultant, following honorable retirement, of course, that his name would be right up there on top of the list.

Well, the whole affair was quite innocuous until we returned to the Hyatt Regency, where we were staying. I remember the scene only too goddamn well. We had walked back from the Houston Club, admiring the architecture of the city, which even by night is spectacular.

'Sultan,' I had said to the Saudi defense minister, 'this is the most interesting city in the United States, no doubt about it. And if I were you Saudis, I would spend a lot of time here.'

'Why?' he had asked.

'Because in my opinion Houston is the model for the future of your cities. It is spread over what used to be a wasteland – impossibly hot and remote, just like your desert. Houston was just a little dump twenty years ago. But with the advent of air conditioning, look what happened. It is already the fifth largest city in the United States. My bet is that in another ten or fifteen years it will be number three – after New York and Los Angeles. And the whole place is built on oil and money and air conditioning. See what I mean?'

General Falk, who had been walking on the other side of Sultan Aziz, immediately saw an opening. 'You know,

Hitchcock, you've got something there. What is really needed is a study commission. Maybe a little consultancy company for city planning. By God, you know even I might be tempted to retire and take on a job like that. I've got a lot of friends here. It would only take a couple of million seed money to get it going, and . . .'

At this point we had barely entered into the atrium area of the huge 'outside is inside' building, when some dumb son of a bitch opened up with a submachine gun. He had it mounted on the railing of the tenth floor, overlooking the court below. He was a piss-poor shot; the only guy that got hit was a Houston policeman, and not very seriously at that. But that turned on the Houston cops like nothing else could have. Within seconds, they went after that bastard in droves. The gunman's way out was simple. He just dived off the railing, gun and all, and splattered all over the tile flooring below. From what was left of him, there was no doubt in anybody's mind that he had been an Arab. But that's as far as anybody got.

General Falk turned out to be the hero of the evening. At the first crackle he had jumped on top of the sultan and stayed there until it was over. Nobody gave a happy damn about me, giving me some food for thought later on in the hotel room. Sure, there were two cops outside the door and about a thousand of them spread around the hotel that night. But still, stuff like that gives you a rather tight feeling in the gut. Falk and Sultan Aziz did not hang around. The air force flew both out a couple of hours after the incident.

That was the last time I saw either.

That was also when I decided to drop out of sight for a while. Not that I was chicken, but goddamm it, I never did trust those fucking Arabs.

I spent most of that night trying to get a connection to Khorramshahr. At dawn I got it. It was a horrible connection, but I got my message through. I wanted, badly, that Ursula come to St. Moritz earlier than we had planned. This time she relented, because I promised that I too could be there ahead of schedule. I suggested March 4. She said

March 5. So March 5 it was. Where and what time? Five o'clock at the train station. She thought that was a bit peculiar, but left it that way.

It was 7 A.M. when I finally got to sleep. I had a police escort to the airport at noon. And on the flight to Los Angeles I had four martinis.

The trip to L.A. was ostensibly to work out some big deposit arrangements with Security Pacific – by this time over $32 billion in short-term Saudi funds had already come to the States, and they were still moving in at the now reduced rate of a couple of billion a week. But actually I had just wanted a little respite from the heavy types in the East. New York is fine, but six weeks in a row there is a bit much for a California boy, not to mention being shot at in Houston.

I went directly from the airport to the Beverly Hills Hotel, and after checking in, my first stop was the bar of the Polo Lounge. Gus was there, beaming, and ready to fill me in on the latest in-jokes making the rounds. I had been standing there about fifteen minutes when two dark types came in and took a table in the area behind. I gave them a quick scan, and let me tell you, I did not like what I saw.

'Hey, Gus,' I said in a very low voice.

'What was that, Dr. Hitchcock?' he answered, in what seemed to me a bellow.

'Not so loud, Gus,' I whispered.

Now Gus had known me for a long time, and he was accustomed to strange behavior in general, so he played along.

'What's up?' he inquired, also in a whisper.

'Those two guys.'

'What two guys?'

I jerked my head back, as one is taught to do by the movies.

'Those Arabs. You know them?'

Gus looked at them, looked at me, and laughed. 'Arabs? Look, I don't know what your problem is, but the guy on the left is Mr. Levi, and he is president of the Beverly Hills

245

Synagogue. His friend is an American rug merchant — Faghali, I think his name is. They come in here all the time.'

'OK. Forget it, Gus. Just gimme another one of those.'

When I left the bar a little later to take the elevator up to my room on the third floor, somebody else was waiting. Alone. To be sure, he was blond, and very L.A. in his dress. But shit, I thought, why take a chance? I kind of wandered around until he went up. Even then, I decided to take the stairs. After all, it was only three stories.

That evening I went to a friend's house for dinner. He knew a lot of the young ladies around town. A few of them were there, but I still went back to the hotel at midnight. A call message was waiting for me. It was Falk, wanting to know if I was all right. Hell, yes, I told him, I hadn't given the matter another thought since Houston.

The following morning I flew up to San Francisco and then drove up to my ranch in Sonoma Country. It's just a little place with a few thousand cattle and some horses, but it's got a fair-sized lake full of trout. That day it was too wet to ride or fish, so I just sat around most of the day bullshitting with Manuel, my Mexican-American friend who runs it for me. Around five I was back in town, and went to the Bohemian Club looking for company. I found it immediately in the person of the boss of Standard Oil of California, Fred Grayson. Word had spread of Hitchcock's billions, so we were soon surrounded by the money establishment West. Actually, the Bohemian Club had been created in the nineteenth century as a meeting place for artists and writers. That evening, over dinner, our group of eight included two bankers (Wells Fargo and myself), two oilmen (SoCal and Texaco), two pipeline men (both from Bechtel), and two lawyers (one antitrust and one tax). The only artist in the lot was the Mexican waiter who served us. The world was indeed ours.

After dinner I leaned on Grayson to do me a favor. I needed the aid of his communications system. No problem. He personally took me up to the eighteenth floor, where the communications room was humming, as it did in the headquarters of all the major international oil companies, twenty-four hours a day. After all, they had not just a company or country to run, but the entire world.

Anyway, they put me through to Aramco in New York, who put me through to Aramco in Saudi Arabia, which had Yamani on the line perhaps three minutes later. Fahd had not been available. I told Yamani that I was going to take a couple of weeks off. I figured that since everything was moving along on schedule, al-Kuraishi could take care of the technical side of things for a while. I gave Yamani my address and phone number in St. Moritz in case somebody needed me. Yamani took it down and then asked, 'That Houston affair upset you, Bill?'

'Hell, no. I'm just getting a bit fatigued.'

He understood.

'And how are things back there, Zaki?' I asked.

'Fair,' he replied. And then the line faded out.

Grayson and I had a nightcap in his office and parted company.

The next day I took the Pan Am polar flight to London, Swissair to Zurich, the Swiss railroad to Chur, and the Rhaetische Bahn to St. Moritz.

That evening Ursula Hartmann was in Khorramshahr, packing, and also expecting a visitor – his second visit since she had moved there with her father : Professor Ben-Levi of Tel Aviv. It was complicated flying from Israel to Abadan, but that did not deter Ben-Levi. Her father had gone to the airport to meet him, chauffeured as usual by a SAVAK man.

At seven they arrived, joking and laughing together in the highest of spirits – something completely out of character where her father was concerned, at least since his arrival in Iran – a country which, after being there more than three months, Ursula had learned to hate with a fury.

'My dear,' said Ben-Levi, barely inside the door, 'I have never seen you more beautiful. Come.'

He held out his arms, and Ursula had no choice. But

247

when he tried to kiss her on the mouth, she turned her head. He got a cheek, and a slight-shove back.

'Still the same Ursula,' said Ben-Levi, the eternal smile slightly diminished.

'Yes. And I intend to stay that way.'

'Ursula,' interjected her father, 'please take Uri inside, and get him something to drink. He has had a long journey. I must get some papers from the study.'

She did as told.

'How is your banker friend, Ursula?' Ben-Levi asked as she handed him his sherry.

'Fine.'

'Your father said that you met him in Teheran a while back.'

'Yes.'

'I believe that he works for the Arabs.'

'Yes.'

'Is that clever?'

'Is what clever?'

'Your associating with him.'

'I think that it is a lot more clever than my father associating with you.'

Her father joined them at that precise moment. 'Ursula! What is this? How dare you say that to our old friend?'

'Friend? Friend of whom? He is not my friend. His friends are some crazy generals, or politicians in Israel. Or the Shah or Iran. Those are his friends. Not us, Father.'

'Ursula!'

'Father, you can no longer shut me up. I know what you are doing here. And I know that Uri Ben-Levi is responsible for your staying here and doing his dirty work for him.'

'You know full well that I am here of my own free will. And with the agreement of our country.'

'Yes. But still with the agreement of your conscience?'

'What do you mean?'

'You are building nuclear weapons for Iran. For the Shah of Iran. I have known this for months. But since then I have also seen what is going on around me in this country. This is not Switzerland, Father. The ruler of this country

248

does not need those weapons for defense, as our country does. He intends to use them. To suppress and murder other people, deliberately. Just as he has been using every weapon at his disposal thus far to deliberately suppress and murder – his own people. Haven't you seen what goes on in this country? It is as bad as Spain under Franco, or Chile under the generals. It is almost as bad as Nazi Germany. And they killed my mother.'

'This is totally absurd,' said Ben-Levi. 'Don't you realize, you spoiled little fool, that in 1973, when the whole world turned its back on us, it was only the United States and Holland and Iran, yes, the Shah of Iran, who stood by us?'

'So what? You sound like so many American Jews a long time ago. They did not care what Nixon was doing to their country then, as long as he supported Israel. They were willing to accept a man who was prepared to undermine the entire fabric of their country – their own country – just because he was supposedly a friend of Israel. But for how long would he have remained a friend? He was probably insane. And so is the man who runs Iran. And so are people like Uri Ben-Levi who want to help the Shah of Iran.'

'Ursula,' said her father softly, 'you must understand. We are not helping the Shah of Iran. We are merely providing him with some tools that may save Israel.'

'By killing hundreds of thousands of Arabs? Murdering them?'

'It is not necessary that we murder them,' answered her father.

Now Ben-Levi turned to the Swiss professor. 'You are wrong, old friend. There is only one way. They must be destroyed.'

'You see, Father,' screamed Ursula. 'This man is insane. If the Israeli government knew what he was trying to do here, they would lock him up.'

'I still say,' said her father in the same quiet voice, 'that there will be no killing. We can accomplish what we want without that.'

'I disagree,' said Ben-Levi.

'Who are you two,' said Ursula, 'to determine such things? I know what the Shah wants. He wants to take over the entire Persian Gulf. It is now so obvious, Father, have you not noticed the military movements around Khorramshahr, around Abadan, and to the north? They are now moving in tens of thousands of troops every day.'

No response.

'You give him those weapons and you give him the Persian Gulf. And then, with all the military power he is massing, plus your bombs, do you think he will be satisfied with just that? If you do, you are both crazier than I thought. He will want all of the Middle East. All. Including Israel. And nobody will be able to stop him.'

'Ursula,' replied her father, 'the die is cast. I assure you, my bombs will kill no one.'

'How is that possible?'

'Because none will be dropped on any Arabs. They will be dropped over empty desert, if they are dropped at all. And whoever is in the vicinity will be able to escape before the radioactivity can kill them.'

'And then?'

'Then, my dear, they will no longer possess the oil fields. And will no longer be a threat to Israel.'

'You are wrong, my friend,' said Ben-Levi. 'They will always be a threat. Your way is not good enough. They must die. And your bombs must be designed accordingly.'

'You are disgusting. And stupid,' said Ursula. 'And I will not tolerate your staying in this house, ever again.'

'Ursula!'

'I mean that, Father. I am going away tomorrow. I want to go away at peace with you. This man will not stay here. I am going to my bedroom.'

She did.

The two men remained talking until midnight, and then the front door opened and closed behind Ben-Levi, who was to spend the night at a hotel in Abadan.

The house was quiet for the following half hour. Then there was a knock on Ursula's door. 'Are you still awake, Ursula?' asked her father.

'Yes.'

'Then come out. We must talk.'

'I will.'

In a minute she was out and into her father's arms.

'I am sorry I had to say all those things,' she said, 'but I had no choice. And I have no regrets.'

'But you are wrong. I now know how you feel about this country. But there is no other way. Unless the Arabs are defeated now, it will be too late.'

'But, Father, you are naïve. You are giving an evil dictator immense power. In the end you will only help destroy Israel. Forever.'

'But how do you know, Ursula?'

'Father, you have never involved yourself with politics. You have been isolated in Switzerland, and now you have been isolated here in Khorramshahr for almost four months. You must change. You must talk to people other than scientists and military men. To free people. To people who know about these things. They will tell you what I am telling you.'

'I cannot leave now.'

'Father, I am leaving tomorrow. Will you promise me something?'

'Yes.'

'Think about what I have said. There must be another solution. For Israel, and for all of us. There must be a third way. I will call you from Switzerland. I also will think about this. And I will talk to people.'

'Your friend Dr. Hitchcock?'

'Yes. But I will also read. And listen. And then I will telephone.'

'Yes. Now go to sleep, Ursula. You have a long journey tomorrow.'

She left by air at 7 A.M. She arrived in St. Moritz ahead of me.

CHAPTER TWENTY-TWO

My train pulled into the station in St. Moritz Bad at five minutes past five that March 5, on time to the second. That ski train was enough to lift the spirits of anyone, even the possible object of lurking Arab hit men. You've got people from all over the world, all in ski clothes, and all having one hell of a good time. The cocktail area was the dining car – at least fifty years old, with wood paneling, and an honest-to-God stove at one end to heat it. The major type of sustenance served was wine – white from the Lake of Geneva area and red from the Valais. At least for the foreigners. The local Swiss hot dogs lapped that up too, but garnished it with an occasional Kirschwasser, which became less and less occasional the nearer we got to our destination.

At first I was an object of scorn, dressed as I was in a dark-blue suit, dark-blue vest, dark-blue tie, and shoes. Shoes! But when I explained to the train wit that I was on my way to the funeral of a friend who had died from too much fucking at high altitude, they started to forgive my strange appearance. The result was that I arrived in a slightly boisterous mood.

Ursula was sitting inside the station alone, and huddled in the middle of a pile of suitcases. When I weaved in at her, it was touch and go for a moment.

'Bill,' she asked after the preliminaries were over, 'where are we staying? I checked, and every place is full. And none,' she added, 'has a reservation in either your or my name.'

Practical, those Swiss girls.

'Not to worry,' I said, and sat down beside her, after the porter had deposited my luggage – one small overnight bag and one large briefcase. Ursula took a quick glance at that but said nothing, although the next few minutes were a bit strained.

Then Hans arrived.

'*Gruetzi, Herr Doktor,*' he said.

'*Salü, Hans,*' I replied. '*Isch alles bereit?*'

Ursula gazed at me in wonder. And gaze she well might, because it was in that mysterious tongue of the Swiss – Schwyzertütsch – that I was speaking, without any aid from the Holy Ghost.

'Bill,' she exclaimed, 'where did you learn that?'

'Boarding school, my dear. In Gstaad.' Which was true. Ages fourteen through seventeen had been wasted in Switzerland, except for one minor and one major achievement. The minor one was mastering, more or less, German and French, plus the local dialect. The major one was learning how to ski – really ski.

'Hans,' I asked, 'is Gertrude here?'

'*Jawohl, Herr Doktor.* She can hardly wait to see you.'

'Gertrude?' from Ursula.

'I hope you don't mind,' I said. 'But Gertrude and I always spend some time together when I'm here.'

Hans commandeered a couple of porters, and out we went. Gertrude was waiting. And when she started to nuzzle me, Ursula clapped her hands with happiness. Because Gertrude was a horse. And behind Gertrude was a sleigh, piled high with blankets, and a big fur comforter.

Hans loaded the luggage and Ursula and I got under the blankets. Within five minutes we were up the hill to the town, and then heading west. It was one of those evenings that make up for all the other defects of our world. The temperature was already down well below zero; the air had not a particle of moisture in it; the stars, a billion of them, were as bright as the average man ever sees them; the bells on our sleigh, the warmth of Ursula, and the exhilaration of being alive – that's the St. Moritz I shall never forget.

After a while, Hans and Gertrude left the main road at the Suvretta House – and then began the climb up the long, winding path.

'Where are we headed?' asked Ursula, as all signs of civilization started to disappear.

'Wait and see, and in the meantime keep your hand exactly where it is.'

I decided to move mine slightly.

'Bill!' she exclaimed. 'What about Hans?'

'Well, if you want. But I personally would prefer if Hans would stay up front driving.'

A half hour later we were on a plateau – the Chantarella. On that plateau are two structures, the Chantarella Hotel and the chalet – the Villa Chantarella – which I had leased from the hotel each winter since 1968. Hans, the chief concierge of the hotel, kept an eye on it during the months I was not there, and that was most months each winter. But when I cabled him, the place was ready for occupancy within twenty-four hours, complete with Theresa, the housekeeper, cook, keeper of my St. Moritz wardrobe, and the worst giggler I have ever known.

She must have heard the bells, because she was out in front waiting.

'Theresa,' I shouted, 'I'm coming!'

'Not now!' exclaimed Ursula.

'Halt!' said Hans, but not to me, to Gertrude.

And Theresa, watching me trying to extricate myself from Ursula and the bear rug, started giggling, of course.

I finally made it out onto the snow, and promptly gave Theresa a hug which, according to our tradition, ended with a firm pat on the fanny.

'Herr Doktor,' she shrieked, and then started giggling even worse.

'Theresa,' I said, 'I would like you to meet my fiancée, Fraulein Ursula Hartmann.'

Theresa, upon hearing the fiancée bit, stopped giggling for a very brief moment and curtsied in front of Ursula. Then she was all business, grabbing the two heaviest suitcases herself, and giving orders to Hans in her shrill voice at the same time. Neither I nor of course, God forbid, Fraulein Ursula, could touch a thing.

Inside it was just as I wanted it. Warm, the fire burning, the candles lit, and the cognac ready. Ursula just stood there for a few minutes, taking it in. Then: 'Bill,' in a very serious voice, 'How many girls have you had up here?'

'Ursula,' I began, 'I swear to God, this is the . . .'

She came over and kissed me and had the good sense to say, 'I don't want to know. All I want you to promise is that I will be the last one.'

'Let's drink to that,' I said, and hurried to fill up two cognac glasses.

'To us,' I toasted.

'*Zu uns zwei*,' she replied, and then started to cry, for God's sake. 'No, no,' she said, looking at my face, 'it's nothing bad. It is just that I have never been so happy. Ever!'

Nevertheless, Theresa came in the room at exactly that time and, noticing Ursula's tears, gave me a dirty look that defined description. But the message was clear: If I was in any way causing trouble to that nice *Swiss* girl, my punishment would be eternal damnation. Theresa was very Catholic. But Ursula saved me from that by intervening.

'Don't worry, Theresa,' she said, going over and patting her hand. 'I think your Dr. Hitchcock is the nicest man in the whole world.'

That 'your' Dr. Hitchcock sealed her loyalty to Ursula for life, and ended – almost the threat of domestic insurrection. For Theresa gave me one more look which said in no uncertain terms that I had better behave in a manner fully worthy of such words. Then she took Ursula in hand, showing her where everything was, helping her unpack, telling her how pretty she looked, asking her what her favorite meals were, when she liked to eat, what wine she liked to drink – in other words, ingratiating herself with Ursula in a thoroughly disgusting manner, while I was left alone in the living room to ponder past and possible future sins.

But dinner proved where Theresa's heart really was. She made the best lasagne in the universe. I loved it, and she knew it. So that is what we had. Plus two bottles of barbera.

That night we went to bed at eight thirty. And the next morning when Theresa knocked on the door and came in bearing hot croissants and coffee, she was beaming.

She approved.

There is no better place and no better time to ski than St. Moritz in March. Period. I have skied the entire American West and every place in the Alps, and, believe me, no place else even comes close. Because the snow is perfect at that time of year – powder, from two thousand meters up; the temperature soars in the sun; the ambiance is neither completely phoney, as in Gstaad, nor completely athletic, as in places like Jackson Hole, but a healthy, invigorating combination of both. It is where the world that counts gathers in March.

We started out in the morning by lugging our skis over to the funicular station just a few hundred meters from my villa, on the Chantarella plateau, taking it to the top and then switching to the gondola that takes you to the Piz Nair. Twenty minutes from our villa to the peak. I let Ursula shove off first. You know, just to see. Well, I saw. She took off like a bat out of hell and didn't stop or look back once until mid-station. I did the same, with the minor interlude of falling and damn near breaking my neck on the third turn. When I finally pulled up beside her, and when she noticed the white stuff around my collar, she grinned and asked, 'Fall?'

'New bindings,' I said, which was more or less true since I had only acquired them three years ago.

'Another run?'

'Of course.'

So we traversed and took the gondola back up. This time we skied together, and I won't say she took it easier, but at least she did take account of the fact that it was quite natural for somebody to require a bit of time to get used to new bindings. Four more runs, and I suggested we might pull in and have a slight refreshment. There was a great little restaurant about halfway down from the Piz Nair with a huge outdoor terrace, and that's where we went.

My boots were also fairly new, so the first thing I did was to take them off, and plunked me down on a lying chair. It was sunny and hot. Ursula went inside to get the refreshments. She came back with bread, cheese and a bottle of Aigle.

256

'Bill,' she asked after a while, 'how long can we stay?'

'A couple of weeks.'

'And then?'

'Well, I'll probably either go down to Riyadh or back to New York. It depends. Let's worry about that later. I'm here to forget about all that stuff for a . . .'

'Dr. Hitchcock!' came a voice from behind. 'What a pleasant surprise!'

I looked up and into an obviously Middle Eastern face, but no one I could place. There was a slight recurrence of the Houston syndrome – like a mild internal panic – until I figured him.

'Yes,' I said, not getting up, 'we met in Iran.'

'Of course. And His Majesty has spoken of you since.'

'How nice. Yes. Well, what brings you here?'

'Not just vacation, I can assure you,' he said.

'Oh?'

'But you must surely know. His Majesty will be arriving tomorrow. He always comes to St. Moritz in March.'

'Of course.' And I did remember, although our paths had never crossed in St. Moritz before.

'Well,' I continued, 'I hope you and His Majesty have a good time.' A rather dumb sort of remark, but it got rid of him.

'Who was that?' asked Ursula, after he had disappeared into the crowd.

'Just some guy that works for the Shah.'

'Oh.'

'Say, how about a bit more of that wine?'

We took another four runs that afternoon, then decided that we had had it. So we skied on down to the Chantarella and packed it in for the day. Theresa had a platter of *Bündnerfleisch* and Salzis waiting, plus hot chocolate, which she claimed was the world's only healthy drink.

'You want to go out to dinner?' I asked a bit later.

'No,' answered Ursula. 'I want to stay home all alone with you.'

So that's what we did. Very domestic. To the extent of

my even watching the news on TV and shooing Theresa out of the house so that Ursula could cook.

'Bill,' she said, a little after midnight, at which time she happened to be lying on top of me, 'can anything happen to ever change this?'

'What do you mean, "this"?' I asked.

'Everything. You. Me. This life. Everything.'

'Well, hell, nothing just stays the same.'

'I don't mean that. Aren't you afraid?'

'Of what?'

'That something very serious could go wrong.'

'You mean with money? Or war? That sort of thing?'

'Yes.'

'I'll tell you. A few months ago I would probably have said yes. But now – no. I think the world is in better shape today than it has been for years. So stop worrying.'

'You're sure?'

'I'm sure.'

That conversation took place a few minutes into the morning hours of March 7, 1979. Incredible when I think of it now.

Later that morning the phone rang, the first time it had done so since we arrived. It was the Iranian chap we had bumped into the previous afternoon on the slopes. The Shahanshah was arriving, he told me, and was giving a small buffet party that evening at the Suvretta House. I was invited. Would I come? Sure, I told him, and hung up.

'Hey, Ursula,' I yelled, since she was still in the bathroom, 'your daddy's boss wants us to come to a party tonight.'

She came flying out of the bathroom. 'My daddy's boss? Bill, what are you talking about?'

'Mohammed.'

'Mohammed who?'

Now that was an opening that could have led to almost anything, since I have always had a penchant for the old knock-knock jokes. But I realized that they had probably

258

never been very big in Zurich. Furthermore, 'Mohammed' was very difficult material to work with.

So : 'Mohammed Riza Pahlavi.'

'Oh, him.'

'What do you mean, "Oh, him"? He's the fucking Shah of Iran!'

'Did you accept?'

'Of course. Why not?'

'I really have nothing to wear. Why don't you go alone?'

Christ! 'Come on. It'll be fun. Is it because of your father?' We had not exchanged one word on that subject since we had arrived in St. Moritz.

'No, of course not,' she answered quickly. 'All right. What time?'

'I forgot to ask. So we'll go at eight.'

She went back into the bathroom and I picked up the phone again. I had deliberately not been in contact with the bank in Riyadh for days, but there was no use carrying the vacation bit too far.

'Operator,' I said to the local girl, 'give me the overseas operator in Bern.'

A few clicks and Bern was there. 'Fraulein,' I said, 'I want a line to Saudi Arabia. Riyadh. The number there is . . .'

'I'm sorry, sir,' she cut in.

'About what?'

'We cannot get you Riyadh.'

'Look,' I said, 'I know about the delays. Just book the call and . . .'

'I cannot book any calls for Riyadh, sir.'

'For Christ's sake, why not?' Telephone operators the world over can be the most frustrating people.

'No lines are available.'

'Look,' I said, 'they never are. Just book the call, and then when you get a line, call me back.'

'You misunderstand me, sir. All communications with Saudi Arabia have been cut. We can book no calls until they are restored.'

'When did that happen?'

'Yesterday.'

'Oh,' I replied. And hung up.

Ursula was back out of the bathroom, this time fully dressed. 'Who was that, Bill?'

'Nobody. I was just trying to make an overseas call, and as usual the phone companies are all screwed up.'

We decided to try another ski area that day. We took the funicular down into town, and transferred to the bus that ran to Pontresina, and then to the Diavolezza, a terrific mountain to ski on, though a bit tough. We had a slight delay in getting there : the police pulled our bus over to the side to allow a motorcade to pass, apparently on its way from the local airport at Samedan. It consisted of four Mercedes seven-passenger 600's and ten police motorcycles. The curtains in the limos were all drawn.

'Guess who?' I said to Ursula.

It was, of course, the King of Kings and the royal entourage. But nobody in the bus seemed to particularly care. All sorts of peculiar people come to St. Moritz in March.

We had a good day on the Diavolezza and got back to the chalet around five, which gave us time for a bit of fooling around, plus a hot toddy in a hot bath ...

At seven thirty Hans and Gertrude were outside ready to go, so off we went, down the mountain to the Suvretta House. It was the best hotel in town. Sure, the Palace was better known but that was where the *nouveaux riches* stayed. Those who inherited wealth or title, or succeeded to both through marriage, stayed at the Suvretta. It had been a hangout of the Shah for many years. While he was still married to Soraya in the 1950's he had learned to love skiing in the Swiss Alps and also to appreciate this particular Swiss hotel, with its pine forests and the towering Piz Nair beyond. But he especially enjoyed the solitude provided by the hotel's huge grounds, where he was beyond the rude stares of German tourists, with knapsacks full of *Leberwurst* sandwiches and *sauer Gurken*. Around 1968 or 1969 the Shah had purchased a villa on the grounds of the Suvretta. It was perhaps half a mile west of my place on the Chantarella, but farther down the mountain. We passed it on our way to the hotel that evening and I pointed it out to Ursula, who did not seem terribly impressed.

The hotel was lit up for the gala evening and the parking lot was full of limousines and uniformed police. Our arrival by sleigh created no sensation at all. One does not notice such things at the Suvretta House. We were barely into the reception hall when we were approached by two security men, who asked to see our invitation. Not having one, I could hardly oblige. They did not like that at all. So before a hassle got under way, I asked for Rolf Mueller, the manager. He appeared almost immediately.

'Herr Doktor,' he said while still approaching us, 'I am so sorry. You see, we must be extremely careful, what with His Majesty in the hotel this evening.'

I have always put up guests at his hotel over the years, so we knew each other.

'You have come to dine?'

'Actually not, no. I was invited to the party, but unfortunately I have no invitation. One of His Majesty's people just telephoned this morning.'

He looked slightly skeptical, which rather pissed me off. Swiss hotel managers could be goddam uppity at times.

'Let me check,' he said, letting us just stand there.

Ursula, watching me develop a slow burn, had herself developed a rather supercilious grin.

'Shocking,' she said. 'Imagine, *the* Herr Doktor Hitchcock arrives, and . . .'

'OK, Ursula. Cut it out.'

The security guys had backed off but stood in the distance keeping their eyes on us. Obviously two more Swiss.

'Herr Doktor,' said Herr Mueller, this time coming back at a full trot, with yesterday's Iranian right behind him, 'please excuse me. Mr. Khamesi has told me that, of course . . .'

'Dr. Hitchcock,' interrupted the Iranian – apparently Khamesi – 'I am sorry if you have been inconvenienced. Please come with me.'

This time we left Mueller standing there. Ursula gave me a slight nudge in the ribs, indicating her pleasure at this small but satisfying victory. We went into the west wing, checked our coats, and were ushered into the large ballroom area. When the Shah put on a party, he did it in style. We were obviously late, since the reception line was no longer there. But we were not to remain wallflowers for long. Almost immediately a rather, shall we say, fat, Swiss woman came right at us.

'Ursula,' she screamed in the local dialect, *'was machst du hier? Das ist ja eine Ueberraschung!'* She grabbed Ursula's hand and gave it the old Swiss shake : three times, and firm. Boy, I thought, if this is the type of crowd the Shah invites to his parties, thank God I had been spared them thus far. Then she whirled and yelled at somebody in the crowd, 'Hanspeter!' Then again, louder, 'Hanspeter!'

Hanspeter lost no time in getting over to us, and was he mad ! 'Shhh,' he said to the fat gal, 'you are making fools of us !' Then to Ursula, 'My dear, what are *you* doing here? Surely, your father . . .'

'No,' she said, he is still in Iran. I merely came here for a bit of vacation.'

She finally made introductions all around and cleared up the mystery. Hanspeter was Dr. Hanspeter Suter, General-direktor of Roche-Bollinger, the company for which her father worked as a consultant. The fat one was his wife. I was introduced as an American banker. Period.

'Have you met him?' Frau Suter then asked Ursula.

'Who?'

'His Majesty,' she whispered loudly.

Ursula did not have to answer, because His Majesty suddenly was there at her right shoulder.

'My dear,' he said, 'what a totally unexpected pleasure to see you again !' After which he proceeded to kiss her none too delicately on both cheeks. 'I am told you are doing some very interesting archeological work in Susa,' he continued. 'I do hope we will have an opportunity soon to talk about it. In private.'

Well, I don't know who was more surprised : Hanspeter,

Frau Suter, or me. Maybe it was Ursula, since she was in full blush when she stepped back from the royal embrace.

Then the Shah turned to me. 'Dr. Hitchcock. How good of you to come. Under the circumstances. We heard about that affair in Houston. Dreadful. Thank goodness no one was killed by that madman.'

'These things happen,' I replied. Circumstances?

'What things?' asked Ursula.

'Didn't he tell you?' answered the Shah. 'They tried to murder Dr. Hitchcock. And a few of his friends. At least he is now safe here. But I wonder about the friends.'

No one said a word, so he continued. 'Hitchcock,' he said, 'why don't you drop by for a talk one of these days? We are practically neighbors, I hear. And bring along your charming lady friend.' At which point he once again gave Ursula the royal smile, as well as a royal look down her decolletage. Talk about dirty old men!

Then he turned to the Suters and even took the fat Frau's arm. 'Come,' he said, 'I want you to meet somebody.' And off went the Swiss pair with the Shah.

'What's that all about?' I asked.

'What?'

'You and Mohammed.'

'Don't be silly.'

'When – and where – did you two get so friendly? I won't ask how.'

'I think we should go.'

'No, no, I haven't eaten.' Whereupon I grabbed her arm and steered her through the crowd in the direction of the buffet.

It was different. As far as the eye reached, caviar. Both black and red, to break the monotony.

'I think,' I said, 'that I might have caviar.'

'Me too,' she said, as if there were any choice.

'I would have thought that by now he must have sent you enough of the stuff,' I said.

'Bill,' she answered, 'if you insist upon making a perfect ass of yourself, when I have already told you that . . .'

'Doktor Hitchcock,' a voice said, 'back in town, I see.'

The voice belonged to Werner Meier, manager of the local branch of the Swiss Bank Corporation.

'Herr Meier,' I said, 'I want you to meet a compatriot of yours – Fraulein Ursula Hartmann. A very close friend of His Majesty. Good person for a fellow like you to know.'

Herr Meier bowed and clicked. And Ursula could have killed me.

Meier suggested I drop by his bank when I had time. For a little exchange of views. He had heard about my recent activities. Quite impressive, he thought. I said I would, and he went.

'Bill,' said Ursula, 'if you prefer, I can go by myself. In any case, I am not going to stay around here for any more of your stupid remarks.'

'Don't get touchy.'

'Touchy? Me?'

'All right, we'll go.' We had been there all of twenty minutes.

Outside the sleigh was waiting.

'Bill,' she said, after a couple of minutes of riding silently through the snow, 'I want to tell you exactly how and when I...'

'Frankly,' I said, 'I don't particularly care any longer.'

'I do!' she screamed, for God's sake. Even Gertrude jumped. 'Because I love you, and I hate that man back there. He is evil. And he is destroying my father.'

So she told what had happened in January to Khorramshahr: the Shah's visit to their home there, the drawing she had found on the dining room table after they had left, and, finally, what had transpired a few days ago between Ben-Levi, her father, and herself.

'That's why I am afraid,' she concluded. And she clung to me. Frankly, I clung back.

'Can't you do something?' she then asked.

'What can I do?'

'I don't know. But Bill, you must.' The usual feminine logic.

'OK, Ursula,' I said. 'But first I have to find out what the hell is going on. Some of those remarks back there were

264

puzzling, to put it mildly. Obviously the Shah knows a lot more than I do.'

Then: 'Bill!' She could get somewhat shrill at times.

'Christ, Ursula. What now?'

'Did somebody try to kill you as he said?'

'Yes. Well, at least he took a few shots at a group of us. I doubt whether I was the target.'

'Who?'

'An Arab.'

'Why didn't you tell me?'

'I didn't want to bother you.'

'Bill,' she said, 'now we will stop that. Now we will tell each other everything. Yes?' She was slipping back into Swiss English.

'Yes,' I replied.

'We need each other,' she continued. 'Otherwise we are alone.'

'Yes,' I said.

And neither of us said another word until we were back home. She went directly to the bedroom. I said I would be right with her — but would first make a nightcap for both of us in the kitchen. I did, and I also made a quick call to the overseas operator in Bern. The lines to Saudi Arabia were still out, she told me.

I did not sleep well that night.

I do not think that Ursula did either, because already at seven she was up and around, well before Theresa arrived, puttering in the kitchen, getting the ski clothes ready, and making enough noise at it to get me out of bed by eight.

The first thing I did when I made it into the breakfast room was to turn on the radio – Beromuenster, the German-language national radio station of Switzerland. It had yodelers on. So I tried the French-language channel – Sottens. The Swiss don't give their radio stations call letters; they give them the names of the places where the transmitters are located. Interesting, but not very. Anyway, Sottens had on Mozart or some damn thing. Everything but news.

'You're rather fidgety this morning,' Ursula finally said, bringing me a cup of coffee.

'I am never fidgety,' I replied.

'Well,' she said, 'where shall we go today? Back to the Diavolezza?'

'I've got a better idea,' I replied. 'Why don't you go shopping?'

'At eight o'clock in the morning?'

'Well, then, ice skating. It looks like another terrific day. And the ice on the lake must just about be perfect.'

'I don't have any skates with me.'

'I will rent you some.'

'And you?'

'I've got a few things to do in town. Nothing important. we can go down to St. Moritz together. And then meet for lunch. At Hanselmann's. I'll reserve a table.'

Before we left, I tried Bern again. Still no lines to Riyadh. In town I got her some skates at the sporting-goods shop next to the Palace Hotel, and then walked with her down to the lake. The music was on and the fresh-air freaks were out there twirling around. Ursula, like a good Swiss girl, joined them.

I went to the local branch of the Swiss Bank Corporation to see Herr Meier. Swiss banks open at eight, so when I arrived at nine thirty Herr Meier was ready for his mid-morning coffee and asked me to join him in his office in the rear. It was nothing sumptuous. Swiss banks feel that luxury corrupts. But although the furniture was twenty years old, the communications equipment in the place would have made an astronaut feel at home. The St. Moritz winter clientele needed to know what was going on at home – and home included everywhere from Tokyo to Johannesburg to Los Angeles. The Swiss Bank Corporation stood ready to serve – in any language, in any currency, and in any-sized deal, even a very small one. Switzerland is a democracy.

'So, so, Herr Doktor,' began Meier, 'did you enjoy the party last night?'

'Terrific. What's on the Reuters this morning?'

'Not very good news. You want to see?'

I wanted. He handed me a stack of sheets which had been ripped off the Telex machine and carefully stacked on his desk. I searched out the latest roundup. Saudi Arabia was the focal point of attention. Communications into the country were still down, but some were apparently coming out. Unconfirmed rumors had it that there had been serious armed clashes between the National Guard and the Saudi army both in and around Riyadh. Rumor further had it that violently anti-Zionist forces had gained the upper hand. Three American senators had already demanded that a total arms embargo be imposed on Saudi Arabia and that all U.S. military advisers in that country be withdrawn forthwith. That was U.S. time, late last evening. Now it was 10 A.M. in Switzerland, which meant 5 A.M. in New York and Washington, where everybody was asleep: Zionists, anti-Zionists, senators, bankers, *et al*.

So . . . 'Herr Meier,' I said, 'what's going on in the foreign-exchange market?'

'The spread on the forwards has widened a bit,' he said.

'In what direction?' innocently.

'Against the dollar.'

'Oh? Why's that?'

'I guess nervousness, as they say. Because of that stuff about Saudi Arabia. Not logical, but then speculators never do act very logically, do they, Herr Doktor?' I chuckled along with him.

'Probably somebody big selling,' I ventured.

He just shrugged. There was always 'somebody big' either buying or selling. At least according to that most quotable of sources, 'rumor.'

'How about the spot market?' I asked.

'No major movement.'

'Say,' I said, 'would you bankroll me for twenty-four hours on something?'

Swiss bankers definitely do not like that bankroll type of terminology, and to finance anything for as long as twenty-four hours is definitely a high-risk venture, but . . . 'Herr

267

Doktor. For you that is no problem.' Fame and fortune have certain advantages.

'Just a million dollars. U.S. For twenty-four hours.'

Eyebrows up.

'Not cash,' I hurried to add. 'Face value on a few foreign-exchange contracts.'

Eyebrows down. 'Of course.'

'OK. Buy $250,000 equivalent of Swiss, Norwegian, Venezuelan, and Canadian. A quarter of a million each.'

'Against?'

'U.S. dollars.'

'Delivery?'

'Spot.'

Eyebrows up.

'I'll have the U.S. cash equivalent cabled here within twenty-four hours. But if you need some collateral . . .'

'No, no. *Selbstverständlich, Herr Doktor.*' This time the eyebrows remained at half mast. But he gave me an order form. I filled it out and signed. He went out and executed.

He came back, with the confirmations. 'More coffee?' he asked.

'Yes. Black,' I answered. 'Herr Meier,' I said, 'would you call up your Geneva branch and check on my balance there? The account number is 435 9392.' That is my private phone number in California, minus six on the last digit. No fool, me.

He picked up the phone and got Geneva.

The balance was 1,374,565 Swiss francs. 'What's gold?' I asked.

'$150.25 an ounce,' he said, just like that.

'OK, buy ten thousand ounces. Use the balance in Geneva as margin.' I signed a new order slip. Good man that he was, he once again marched out of his crappy little office. He was back thirty seconds later. 'It's now $152.35.'

'Buy,' I said.

One minute later he was back with the Telex confirmation. 'Where do you want it held?'

'Here. In my safe-deposit box. I want those currencies put there also.'

'Number?'

'Nineteen forty-eight.' That was the year I had scored for the first time. The IRS could only catch me with a Freudian hypnotist.

Meier looked a bit happier now. He had made a few commissions on the foreign-exchange deals, and now the gold. The coffee he offered me had not been wasted.

A young man now came in with another broad tape. Meier handed it to me after he had read it. Zaire, it said, had announced a moratorium on all of its foreign debt. Zaire owed the rest of the world about $7 billion. Half to the World Bank and half to the commercial banks in New York. Between the Arabs and the Africans, they were really starting to pour it on.

'Herr Meier,' I said, after pondering this and that for a few seconds, 'could I possibly impose upon you for a little help in the communications department?'

'What was that?'

'I'd like to use your Telex,' I said.

'Certainly. For another message to Geneva?'

'No. New York.'

Shit.

'Clock it. I'll pay. Cash.'

'Certainly,' said Herr Meier.

I helped myself to a pad of paper from Herr Meier's desk and wrote the following: 'Goldman Sachs New York Attention Robert Kelly Sell my entire portfolio of stocks and bonds at opening today transfer proceeds immediately to my account Bank of America San Francisco Telex confirmation of all transactions to myself care of Werner Meier Swiss Bank Corporation St. Moritz Switzerland signed William Hitchcock.'

Meier took it, read it, and went out to send it. It would pile up on the machine in the Goldman Sachs office, waiting for my investment banker's arrival in the morning.

'Herr Meier,' I said, when my local banker had returned once again, 'knowing Kelly as I do, he will come back to you requesting confirmation from you that I actually sent that Telex, using the usual codes. I would appreciate your immediately giving that confirmation.'

'But of course, Dr. Hitchcock.'

'Now those confirmations should start coming in later this afternoon. I would like to see them. Would anybody be around here by any chance?'

'We are preparing for the annual audit this week. Everybody will be in the bank until ten this evening, including myself. You will be more than welcome. Just ring the buzzer.'

In America we buzz buzzers, but what the hell. I got up, shook Meier's hand, and left, happy with myself. For I had personally followed another of Hitchcock's rules for survival of the richest: He who hesitates to act on inside information is lost. Not that I had any inside information in the classic sense. But if the signs and portents that had been piling up during the past twenty-four hours pointed in the direction I thought they did, then I knew what the economic consequences would be – probably better than anybody else, anywhere. And there was no sense in being a masochist.

It was a lovely day in St. Moritz. The town was jammed as usual with cars and pedestrians and skiers and dogs, pushing their way either up or down the town's one and only main drag, but all in good spirits. After all, it was a world full of peace and prosperity. I stopped at the kiosk to get the *Herald Tribune, Time* magazine, the *Neue Zurcher Zeitung*, the *Journal de Génève*, the *Economist*, and *New York* magazine. Then I went to Hanselmann's, nabbed a table on the terrace that was sunny and quiet, ordered a Campari and soda, and read.

At noon, Ursula Hartmann, her cheeks red, her black hair flying, arrived on schedule. 'Here,' she said, handing me a small package.

'What's all this?'

'Just something.'

I opened it. Inside was a box, and in the box were a pair of cuff links. They were made from two chervontsi, the Russian 10-ruble gold coin.

270

'God, Ursula, they're terrific. But what's the occasion?'

'None. I just wanted to.'

'Thanks. In fact, thanks a lot.'

You know, that was the first sincere present I had received from anyone in I don't know how many years. Funny.

'Hey,' she said, watching me, 'they're only cuff links.'

'Right,' I said. 'Now, how was the skating?'

We hung around Hanselmann's until three, then transferred to the Chesa Veglia for a pre-pre-dinner drink, which turned into about three such.

Around five thirty we finally made it back to the chalet. I could hear the phone ringing long before we made it inside. But it didn't matter. It just kept right on ringing.

It was New York, the First National Bank of America. In fact, the chairman of the board of the First National Bank of America.

'Hitchcock,' bellowed Aldrich, 'what are you *doing*, you son of a bitch?'

'Easy, friend,' I replied.

'Cut out that "friend" stuff. What are you trying to pull, Hitchcock?'

'Look, Aldrich, I don't know what in the hell you're talking about, so get to the point.'

'You promised that those Saudi deposits would be rolled over every thirty days. Right?'

'Right.'

'Well, four billion – *four billion* – were due for renewal this morning, and they were not.'

'Look,' I said, 'don't get so excited. You know that something's going on down in Saudi Arabia. Probably nothing big. But communications are down. They didn't renew because the lines are still down.'

'Oh yeah? Look Hitchcock, our branch in London received specific instructions on those funds. On maturity – that means today – they are to be transferred to the Leipziger Bank, Frankfurt.'

'Who gave those instructions?'

'Prince al-Kuraishi, Managing Director of the Monetary Agency of the Kingdom of Saudi Arabia, that's who.'

'Shit.'

'What was that?' squawked Aldrich.

'Shit!' I yelled.

'Hitchcock' – and now the voice was strained – 'there's more. They also gave notice to us, and all the other banks in town, that there are going to be no rollovers of any deposits for the time being. Today, tomorrow, next week.'

'Look, Aldrich, I have not had one goddamn thing to do with all this, I swear to God. I've been completely out of touch for five days. I can't get through to Riyadh. I don't know what's happening in Riyadh any more than you do. I . . .'

'I believe you,' said Aldrich, now in a very quiet tone.

'But don't worry. I'm going to keep trying. As far as I know, I'm still working for the Saudis. If I get through, I'm sure they'll listen to me. Hell, it's not in their interest to create this kind of financial trouble.'

'Sure,' said Aldrich.

'Has this gotten out?' I then asked.

'Of course not,' said Aldrich, 'but you know how these things are.'

'What does the Fed say?'

'Those dumb bastards. They said we should never have accepted those Saudi funds in the first place. We made our bed, now we should sleep in it. Incredible.'

'Yeah. OK, Randy. I'll be in touch.'

'You got my home phone, Bill?'

'No.'

He gave it to me. Christ, I thought after I had hung up, he must really be psyched out to go so far. I tried the overseas operator in Bern immediately. Same answer as before. No lines. I called up Swissair. All flights to Saudi Arabia from everywhere had been suspended. They would not even make any tentative bookings.

'Trouble?' asked Ursula, who had been sitting quietly across the room the whole while.

'Yes.'

'You must leave?'

'Yes. And no. I must leave. But, for Christ's sake, I can't. It is absolutely ridiculous.'

'What is happening in Saudi Arabia?'

'I don't know. That is what is so goddamn frustrating. But whatever it is, it's not good.'

'What are you going to do?'

'Nothing. Look, why don't we go out for dinner?'

We changed and were back down in St. Moritz an hour later. It was cold and snowing hard. The night sky seemed to have closed right in on us.

'Ursula,' I said as we walked down the street from the funicular station toward the Palace Hotel, 'mind if I stop in at the bank for a few minutes?'

'Of course not.'

I buzzed, and Herr Meier personally answered the door. He was somewhat surprised to see Ursula there. After all, money in Switzerland is strictly men's business. But at least he let her in.

He had a whole stack of Telex confirmations from Goldman Sachs. I had just dumped $13 million worth of securities. Even Meier was impressed. Ursula never said one word the whole time we were in the bank.

'You were extremely clever,' commented Meier.

'Oh, why?'

'You sold at the opening. Since then the market has gone straight down.'

'How far?'

'Thirty-seven points on the Dow-Jones.'

'Volume?'

'Seventy-eight million.'

'Jeezuz. Gold?'

'One hundred sixty-six dollars an ounce in the afternoon fixing.'

'The dollar?'

'Down five percent, on average, from this morning.'

'What's new on the Reuters?'

'Ford Motor Company withdrew a bond issue scheduled for tomorrow. One billion dollars, as you know.'

273

'Anything else?'

'French wire service says King Khalid and Yamani are dead.'

'What do the French know?'

He just shrugged.

'Herr Meier, could you send a few more Telexes for me?'

'Certainly.' My $13 million sale in New York put me in the big leagues, even by St. Moritz standards.

This one went to Dean Witter, my investment banker in San Francisco. It was simple : 'Purchase San Joaquin valley property immediately. Asking price of $10 million acceptable. Insist that escrow be closed within 48 hours. Cash funds available my personal account Bank of America. Am currently sending instructions to them for transfer of funds to you. William Hitchcock.'

The second Telex went to Bank of America instructing them to send $10 million to Dean Witter, one million to Swiss Bank Corporation, St. Moritz, and to take the other two and put it into my safety-deposit box in hundreds.

'Herr Meier,' I said finally, 'couldn't we buy you a drink or something?'

'Yes,' he said, totally unexpectedly, 'I would like that.'

So the three of us walked down the street to the Palace. We took a table in the bar.

'Dr. Hitchcock,' he said after the booze had arrived, 'I must confess something to you.'

'Yes, go ahead.'

'Our head office is aware of your various transactions today.'

'Yes.' With a bit less warmth this time.

'They have also asked me to inform you of a few matters that have occurred today.'

'Yes?'

'Your ambassador came to St. Moritz today. At noon. For one hour. Then he returned to Bern. He visited the Shah.'

'I see.'

'The ambassador of the Soviet Union was here for forty-five minutes. He left around four this afternoon. The chancellor of West Germany, who is vacationing in Pontresina, made a courtesy call at the same place around five. And the French, I'm told, are with the Shah right now.'

'Why have you been told to tell me all this?'

'Our management in Zurich feels you may be of some aid to them in interpreting all these events.'

'Why me?'

'Because of your intimate knowledge of circumstances in the Middle East.'

'Meier,' I said, while Ursula was watching, her face pinched, and her hands tightly folded, 'I frankly do not like to be approached in such a manner. I also do not at all appreciate your management tracking me and my personal financial matters. But that's part of the system, isn't it?'

Meier said nothing.

'All right. What does all this mean? It could mean war. And it could mean a financial disaster. And it could mean both.'

'That is why you have been selling in New York?'

'Maybe.'

'Do you think we should sell?'

'Maybe. Maybe not.'

'Are the Israelis behind this trouble as usual?' asked Meier.

'Israel? Don't be stupid. In this game Israel does not even have the status of a pawn. It's completely out of it.'

'And the United States?'

'Yes, Herr Meier. Now you are getting closer. Which way will Uncle Sam jump in the Middle East? Right?'

He chose to answer with a question. 'Do you feel that the Arabs are going to transfer their funds completely out of the United States and into Europe?'

There we had the real question he had been asked to put.

'I think that if you Swiss, and the Germans, and the French are stupid enough to encourage the Arabs in their madness, and the Shah of Iran in his – yes, you will get all the money you ever dreamed of. And more. You will get the biggest trouble Europe has ever seen since 1939. Now get out of here.'

He began apologizing profusely, but when he was ignored, he gave up and left.

'Bill,' said Ursula, 'it is not his fault.'

'I know, I know. I'll send him flowers in the morning.'

'Did you mean all that?'

'Yes.'

'But what will we do?'

'I don't know.'

'What about Father?'

'Ursula,' I answered, 'I am afraid that your father is beyond help.'

'If something happens to him,' she said, 'you will be surprised what's going to happen to everybody else – including the Shah.'

CHAPTER TWENTY-THREE

The man Ursula Hartmann had referréd to – the King of Kings of Iran, the Shahanshah of Persia – had by no means been acting in a manner befitting an evil man. In fact, ever since his arrival in Switzerland a few days earlier, quite the opposite had been true.

On March 4, 1979, the Shah had arrived quietly in Zurich. As usual, he had moved into the Dolder Grand Hotel. It was close to the clinic where he always had his annual medical checkup. His entourage was not large : his young wife, Farah Diva, their children, her lady-in-waiting, his aide-de-camp, and about twenty security men. Few people took notice of them. It was, after all, the Shah's fifteenth consecutive winter visit to Switzerland.

On March 7, apparently in good health, the Shah had briefly attended to some business of state. That morning he received the foreign minister of Switzerland, Enrico Rossi. Rossi had brought with him the final draft of the proposed agreement between Switzerland and Iran, in French and Pharsee. Under its terms, Iran committed itself to exempt Switzerland from any possible future embargo imposed by OPEC for the next ten years, and further, in the event of such an embargo by the other OPEC producers, Iran committed itself to supply Switzerland with crude oil, on a monthly basis, for the duration of such an embargo in an amount equal to approximately 75 percent of the normal consumption of Switzerland at a price no higher than 25 percent above the f.o.b. price, Abadan, which had prevailed, on average, during the three months preceding the imposition of the new embargo. It would, however, be the responsibility of the Swiss Confederation to arrange for the transportation of the crude oil from the port of Abadan to the Swiss refineries. All in all, a splendidly precise document.

Nevertheless, the Shah frowned when he read it. For

indeed, through his emissary, Fawzi Tehrani, he had promised to exempt Switzerland from any future embargo, for the *quid pro quo* to which neither party had ever again alluded. But those details on amounts and price had been embellishments of a strictly Swiss origin. The Shah pointed this out to Rossi. Rossi squirmed, mumbled about an apparent misunderstanding, apologized about the apparent misunderstanding, suggested that the apparent misunderstanding was perhaps magnified in the Pharsee translation, that the French text should be regarded as superior, that . . . And all the while the Shah watched the little man, amused. Without saying a word to the Swiss, he finally called for two pens from his aide-de-camp. They were gold pens, of course. After they signed, the Shah let Rossi keep both of them. Mohammed Riza Pahlavi had once again demonstrated that not only was *he* a man of his word, but a generous, flexible, benevolent ruler and guardian of one of mankind's most precious resources.

After lunch, he and his family left by private jet for St. Moritz. Just before takeoff, two men who had arrived at Kloten airport from Teheran just an hour earlier joined the flight. The Shah was at the controls of the jet most of the way, but turned the plane over to the Swiss pilot before landing. The Shah knew the small airport at Samedan : it was squeezed between the mountains behind Pontresina to the south and those of St. Moritz to the north, and it averaged 1.6 fatal crashes a year. Most of the security men had gone on ahead the day before, in four Mercedes 600's. All four had been on the tarmac when the Lear's engines were turned off. Also the Swiss police escort.

Ursula and I had witnessed their passage through town, and had renewed our acquaintanceships with His Majesty that evening. All of which had led to Ursula bad-mouthing the Shah the following day. But even on the morning of that day, while I was rearranging my finances via the Swiss Bank Corporation's communications network, the Shah had continued to behave in a quite impeccable manner. In spite of the rigors of the party the evening before, Pahlavi had risen at eight and was out on the slopes by nine. Kings

278

do not ski alone, of course. With him were his empress, their children, and a good dozen security men. Wise father that he was, Pahlavi had insisted that the family begin their first day on the small practice slope on the grounds of the Suvretta House, situated about seventy-five meters from his chalet. Herr Mueller had naturally arranged that the royal family have exclusive use of the tow lift for the morning – or for as long as His Majesty wished to use it. Two veteran ski guides were there to assist. The children, of course, protested the need for spending any warm-up time on what the Swiss term an 'idiot hill'; they preferred to move right up to the main slopes of the Piz Nair. But Papa remained firm. At least until eleven, when the icy patches had disappeared. Then he relented. He kissed his wife, patted the heads of his children, sent them up the mountain, and returned to his chalet alone.

The Shah was happy. It had been the perfect start to a perfect day, set against the perfect background – tranquil, neutral, clean, moral Switzerland. It was the perfect place to plan a war.

And that was what the Shah had scheduled for the afternoon. The chalet had been appropriately organized for this. The south wing of the structure had been declared off-limits to the family. It had been taken over by those two passengers that had joined the Shah's flight from Zurich at the last moment: General Reza Barami, head of Iran's air force, and Brigadier Shabanah, the Iranian air-sea strike chief for the Persian Gulf. As military men are prone to do, one of their first acts upon settling into their St. Moritz billet the prior day had been to pin a huge map to the wall. Its dimensions were illuminating, stretching from India in the east to the Mediterranean in the west, from the southern perimeters of Russia to the north to as far south as Yemen and the Sudan.

When the Shah joined them that day, both the general and the brigadier had the appearance of happy men. And why not? They controlled the biggest and best-trained army in the Middle East; the largest and most sophisticated air force; a flexible, modern navy.

In addition, Iran possessed the world's most extensive operational military Hovercraft fleet (British-built SRN-6's and BH-7's) and an awesome arsenal of missiles, ranging from the U.S.-built Hawk to the British Rapier to the French Crotale. Even the new American Phoenixes had been fully integrated into the Iranian air 'defense' system. To man all this equipment, Iran had an army of 460,000 men (including reserves), reputed to be the most efficient fighting force in the Middle East (with the exception of the Israelis), thanks in part to the training provided by over one thousand American military personnel who had been stationed in Iran during the entire decade of the 1970's for that express purpose.

'Have you prepared it? was the Shah's first words to his military men when he entered their quarters.

'Yes,' answered General Barami.

And pinned to the wall was what the Shah had demanded : a chart, with a complete listing of the combat-ready hardware of Iran, updated to March 10, 1979. It made impressive reading :

Iran had 486 combat aircraft, ready to go. They included 80 F-14's, the world's most advanced military aircraft, supplied by Grumman; 170 F-4 Phantoms, next to the F-14 America's best missile-armed combat aircraft, with nuclear capability as a long-range, all-weather fighter-bomber, built by McDonnell Douglas; 221 F-5's, built by Northrop, with an ordnance capability of 3.5 tons. Helicopters? The Shah had 739 of them, ranging from 287 UH-1H214A's – the principal attack helicopter used in Vietnam – to 202 AH-1J's, the deadly 'Sea-Cobra,' which first started to come off the American assembly lines in 1974. Iran had more of these machines combat ready in early 1979 than did the U.S. Army!

The tank count came to 1,660 : the list included 400 M-47's and 460 M-60's, the best the United States could offer. The backbone of the Iranian panzer force consisted, however, of 800 British-built Chieftains, the world's most modern battle tank. Its 120-mm. gun could hit and destroy an enemy tank within 2,000 meters. With its snorkel, the

Chieftain could wade up to 16 feet. Besides the tanks, the Shah also had 2,000 armored personnel carriers, most of them Soviet-built BTR-60's and BTR-50's. Both models were equipped with rocket launchers.

The Iranian navy was not large – only thirty-nine vessels – but it included seven very deadly ships : the two aircraft carriers, the *Kitty Hawk* and the *Constellation*, on lease from the United States, both 1,062 meters long, and both capable of carrying 90 Phantom fighter-bombers, plus five of the world's most sophisticated attack ships – Spruance class destroyers, supplied to Iran by Litton Industries of Pascagoula, Mississippi.

It was an awesome list.

The Shah went down the chart, item by item, with Barami, and, apparently satisfied, left the room to change from his ski clothes to something more appropriate for the afternoon.

At noon a gray Cadillac pulled into the ground of the Suvretta House. Inside was Mr. Stanton Sinclair, the United States Ambassador to Switzerland. Sinclair was a career man. He had served as number two in the Embassy in Teheran in the early 1970's, and then had managed America's affairs in Athens, Chile, and Turkey before receiving the quiet and cushy job in Bern. But despite his more recent posting, he regarded himself as a Middle East specialist. He had spent a total of almost seven years, off and on, in the territory, and he knew most of the men who still ruled it, including the Shah. Thus he had not balked at being summoned to St. Moritz by the Persian potentate on very short notice.

Since they had met before, there was little need for introductory small talk. The Shah took a chair beside the fireplace, not yet lit, and suggested that Sinclair take one to his left.

'Mr. Sinclair,' began Pahlavi, 'I must assume that your government is following the events in Saudi Arabia with great interest.'

'Naturally,' replied Sinclair.

'And I must further assume that you share my acute alarm.'

'I am not in a position to speak on behalf of my government on that issue, Your Majesty,' replied Sinclair.

'Of course. But Mr. Sinclair, a man of your background must certainly have reached certain conclusions, considering what is going on in a country of such paramount importance to your country's national interests.'

'What is going on, exactly, if I may ask?' countered Sinclair.

'My sources – and I have superb sources in Saudi Arabia, and direct communications with them – have definite, I repeat, definite, information that your friends in Saudi Arabia are out. Not only out, but in the case of the principal ones – Sultan Abdul Aziz, Yamani, and most important, Fahd – they are dead. Killed. Two days ago.'

'By whom?'

'Prince Abdullah and his supporters.'

'How?'

'Kidnapped and then shot through the head.'

'And the king?'

'He is alive. But he is no longer in charge. Abdullah is.'

'How can you be sure of all this?'

The Shah waved his hand impatiently. 'Do you think, my dear Mr. Sinclair, that I would request that you come here to listen to some rumors?'

'Hardly.'

'Exactly.'

'You desire that I communicate this information to my government?'

'Yes.'

'You said that you view these events with acute alarm, Your Majesty,' continued Sinclair.

'Yes.'

'Why?'

'Do you know Abdullah?'

'No.'

'Abdullah's support comes from Qaddafi. He completely

282

shares Qaddafi's views of the world. He is violently anti-Semitic, violently anti-American.'

The Shah of Iran paused. 'And also an enemy of my country. And myself.'

'Why?'

'Because he seeks to control the Persian Gulf, and all the power that would come with it. I am the only man who stands in his way. Thus he considers me his most important enemy.'

'And America? What about the recent commitments which his country has made in regard to supplying the United States with petroleum? Will he honor them?'

The Shah laughed aloud. 'Mr. Sinclair! Of course not.'

'And what will he do with the oil?'

'What does Qaddafi do? Libya's production is one third, one quarter of what it used to be. One sixth of what it could be today if he had not kicked out Occidental and everybody else. Abdullah will do exactly what Qaddafi has already done. Sit on his oil.'

'That would be madness.'

'Of course. Do you think Qaddafi is sane?'

'And what about the population of Saudi Arabia? The country's development program?'

'Abdullah will tell them to read the Koran and tend their goats. As they did before. Or get shot.'

'The army goes with Abdullah?'

'Of course. It represents his principal support. And my greatest threat.'

'Threat?'

'Yes. They have been chafing at the bit for years. Ready to have a go at me – with your weapons, I might add. Well, Abdullah is going to give them their chance.'

For the first time Sinclair's face expressed pronounced skepticism. 'How?' he asked. 'They have a pitifully small army.'

'Perhaps. But that small army is – thanks to your country – perhaps the most superbly equipped in the world. However, that is not the point. The Saudis will not – do not have to – act alone. Iraq is more than eager to help them. Iraq can field an army of three hundred and fifty thousand men against us. And Iraq has been our enemy for generations. Mr. Sinclair, you of all people should realize that.'

Mr. Sinclair nodded. He did know. He also knew that the Shah of Iran harbored an extremely deep hatred for the Iraqis. For Iraq was the only nation which the Shah had attempted to take on militarily during his entire reign – and the Shah had lost. It had not been a direct confrontation. Rather, in the early 1970's the Shah had sought to engineer a collapse of the regime in Baghdad through the back door, by promoting a domestic military insurrection in Iraq. His client mercenaries were the Kurds, that tribe living in the north of Iraq which had always rejected domination by the Baghdad government. For years it had been a standoff between the Kurds and the Iraqis. But in 1972, the Iraq army finally had their enemy on the run. In a desperate move to reverse the trend, the Shah had personally appealed to President Nixon for support – support of the Kurds. But there was a problem. If modern American weapons showed up in Iraq in the hands of the Kurds, the Russians might well step in on the other side – something that neither the Shah nor Nixon wanted. But Nixon and Pahlavi – perhaps the two most devious statesmen of our generation – came up with a brilliant solution. They would supply the Kurds with Russian weapons!

The source for such weapons? Israel. They had captured an enormous amount of Soviet military hardware from Egypt in the 1967 war. The Israelis, when faced with the American-Iranian request, could hardly refuse: Nixon was the man who guaranteed their political survival through the supply of American arms, and the Shah of Iran guaranteed their economic survival by supplying them with oil. So the Soviet weapons were purchased, and the U.S. number two at that time in Teheran, Sinclair, supervised their delivery.

The only problem was – it didn't work. The Kurds were smashed, forced to flee to Iran, and the Shah was forced to eat crow. In the tradition of dictators of the twentieth century, in 1975 he had signed a treaty of eternal friend-ship with the government in Iraq. Now, four years later, revenge was at hand. For both sides, thought Sinclair.

'What do you expect to happen?' he asked the Shah.

'They will attack us. Jointly. And soon.'

'Do you have any proof of this?'

'Yes. Wait.'

The Shah left the room, went to the south wing, and was back within a very few minutes.

'Here,' he said, handing Sinclair a set of aerial photo-graphs. 'This,' he continued, taking the first photograph and pointing at the river forming the borders between Iraq and Iran where the two countries meet at the northern tip of the Persian Gulf, 'is the Shatt al-Arab River. You know it well, of course. Now note that incredible concentration of artillery emplacements here, and the missile-launching sites there – opposite Abadan, and vis-à-vis Khorramshahr.'

He took up a second photograph. 'Now this,' he said, 'is the territory immediately to the north – the narrow plain between the Tigris River and the Iranian border. You can see quite clearly the armor. Here, ready to move on Ahvaz. There, poised at Dezful. The idea, obviously, is to sweep east and then south to secure Abadan and its surrounding oil fields.

'All told,' the Shah went on, 'we have counted about seventeen hundred tanks in that corridor east of the Tigris – eight hundred T-55's, four hundred and fifty M-60's, and around five hundred BTR-152's. They represent ninety percent of the total tank force Iraq possesses. They have been threatening our southern flank for twenty years, but we have never seen such a concentration before.'

'Oh?' countered Sinclair. 'I definitely recall that in 1969, in 1971 and 1972, there were very similar buildups. It was the standard Iraqi winter military exercise. As I further recall, those maneuvers always were in March. Each time, the Iraqis used to lob a few shells across the river at you. And you at them. And that was it.'

'Ah, yes, perhaps,' said the Shah, 'but this is completely

285

different. The Iraqi weakness has always been air cover. You know that.'

Sinclair nodded. The Iraqi air force though large in numbers – a total of 285 aircraft according to the latest report he had seen – was composed for the most part of antiquated Soviet and British equipment: MiG-21's, Su-7's. MiG-17's, and even a few squadrons of British Hunters, dating back to the 1950's.

'No more. They now have seventy-five American F-5's, twenty-five Mirage 111's, and thirty F-15's. Combat ready, south of Baghdad.'

'Ah,' answered Sinclair, in total disbelief, 'where could they possibly have gotten that type of equipment?'

'From Saudi Arabia,' answered the Shah with a frozen smile. 'Your noble ally.'

'Do you have any proof of this?'

'Yes.' Now the third photograph, this time taken on the ground. And a fourth and fifth. 'You see them? There – Phantoms. There – F-15's.' His finger jabbed.

Sinclair saw. And he knew a Phantom or an F-15 when he saw one. His schooling had been quite complete. He also say that the markings on the planes were those of the Kingdom of Saudi Arabia.

'These photographs. Where were they taken?'

'I told you,' replied the Shah. 'At military fields just south of Baghdad.'

'When?'

'Two days ago.'

'How did they get here so fast?'

'Two aides of mine brought them. Yesterday. Directly from Iran.'

'But the trouble in Saudi Arabia only started three or four days ago.'

'Exactly. This whole thing has been extremely well prepared: the gradual buildup in Iraq, then the coup in Riyadh, the transfer of aircraft from Saudi Arabia to Baghdad. Qaddafi, Abdullah – and I am sure also Boumedienne of Algeria – have been working on this for months. Probably years. Here –' again he waved the photographs about – 'you see what they are really after. Total control of the Persian Gulf, and all the oil around it.

'And,' continued the Shah, 'it is in some ways understandable. Fahd, Yamani, Sultan Aziz – they have been acting as foolish as the Qaddafi crowd. Yamani, playing his games with the American oil companies. Fahd, putting all of his nation's funds at the disposal of American banks. And Sultan Aziz, parading around the United States with American generals. It was total madness. And now I – my country – must suffer from the inevitable reaction. Listen, Sinclair. The Arab nationalists want you, America, out of the Middle East. Along with all of your friends. I, and only I, stand in their way now.'

He stood up. 'Tell that to your government.'

'I will, Your Majesty. And I thank you,' replied Sinclair.

The ambassador left in a hurry. He was barely inside his Cadillac when he picked up the mobile phone. The people in the 'basement' of the embassy in Bern were instructed to be there – all of them – when he returned, which would be in about three hours. He also wanted Washington to be immediately alerted to the fact that there would soon be some extremely important incoming mail arriving from Switzerland. When he hung up, he told his driver to step on it.

The Shah had lunch, alone, after the American left. There was not a sound in the chalet except for an occasional humming – the Shah, humming a rather aimless tune, maybe from a Persian folk song, perhaps from a Beethoven sonata. In any case, he was happy.

At two – not shortly after three, as Herr Meier of the Swiss Bank Corporation mistakenly reported to me later that day in the bar of the Palace Hotel – the Russians arrived. There were three of them, in a Bentley: the driver, the Soviet Ambassador to Switzerland, and his military attaché. Their names were Pyotor Shelest, Yuri Voronov, and Andrei Andropov respectively. Pyotor Shelest's only appearance that day was to step out of the car to open the door for

287

Voronov and Andropov. They were greeted by General Barami, who knew Andropov from the days when the Russian had been military attaché in Teheran, about the same time as the American, Sinclair, had served as first secretary in the U.S. Embassy there.

The Shah was standing in front of the fireplace – now lit – when they entered. He extended a hand to each Russian and indicated that they be seated on the sofa behind the massive coffee table. He himself chose an armchair on the opposite side. Barami remained standing, to the Shah's rear.

'We shall speak English,' were the Shah's first words. Ambassador Voronov nodded his agreement, after first checking with Andropov, so the Shahanshah continued. 'I do appreciate your coming here on such short notice.'

'We fully understand, Your Majesty,' replied Voronov.

'The subject I wish to discuss is the . . . Arabs.' The way he voiced that final word gave his visitors to understand that he, the Shah, held the ignorant, backward, unstable Arab people in at least as much contempt as they, the Russians, did. 'It is not the first time these people are causing us difficulties.' An enigmatic statement, but Russians are quite accustomed to enigmatic statements. Thus silence from the sofa.

'If it were just the Arabs,' continued the Shah, 'I would hardly have inconvenienced you to the degree of asking you to come to St. Moritz in the middle of the winter. But of course, you are used to winter, are you not?'

The Russians were not sure whether the latter question was rhetorical or whether it demanded an answer. Again both opted for continuing silence.

'But it is not just the Arabs,' continued the Shah. 'It is now the Arabs *and* the . . . Chinese.'

That did it. 'What are you talking about?' asked Andropov, not exhibiting the greatest of finesse, but getting rather directly to the point.

'I am talking, my dear man, about Saudi Arabia,' came the tart reply.

288

'And what on earth have the Chinese got to do with Saudi Arabia?' A rather sound question.

'Where have you been the past few days?'

'Your Majesty,' said Andropov, 'we did not come here to waste our time.' The Russians had occupied Iran during World War Two and had kept the Shah penned up in his Teheran residence the entire time. They were not impressed by his new act.

The Shah studied Andropov's arrogant expression and decided that a brief show of regal humility was in order. 'My dear Mr. Andropov, I assure you that I am not in any way wasting your time. I regard myself as a friend of the Soviet Union. I have asked you here as one good neighbor invites another when they both are in peril.'

Both Russians just sat on the sofa.

'All right, I shall explain. You, of course, realize that the ruling clique in Saudi Arabia has been overthrown. You must also know that the new man in power there is Prince Abdullah.'

The Russians did not know. So: 'Yes, of course,' was Voronov's response.

'Now, what you may not know is who has made Abdullah's success possible.'

Of course they didn't know. 'We have heard various rumors,' said Andropov.

'Well, I do not have to rely on rumor,' said the Shah, making a slight comeback now in the King of Kings department. 'I have the facts.'

'Yes?' said Andropov, now dropping the mask of disinterest.

'The Yemenites. There are almost a half million of them in Saudi Arabia. They did the dirty work for the Saudis. They have also done the dirty work for Abdullah.'

'I find that difficult to believe,' said Andropov. 'The Yemenites simply do not have the organization, or the funds, to make such a thing possible.'

'You are right. They do not. The organization and the funds and the necessary weapons all came from China. Would you believe that?'

The Russians did not totally disbelieve. Southern Yemen had been infiltrated by the Chinese as far back as 1970. The Yemen regime had developed into one of the most radical of any on earth in the subsequent years. But the Russians had done nothing about it. After all, Yemen – that desert hovel of a nation at the southernmost tip of the Arabian peninsula – could hardly be developed into a power base of any consequence. But if the Chinese had used the Yemenites to gain control of the man who ruled Saudi Arabia – that was something quite different. If there was anything the Russians did not need, it was to have the Chinese creeping up on them from the southern flank.

'Your Majesty,' said Andropov, the man obviously in charge, 'you must understand that if what you say is true, this is an extremely serious matter for my country. We would view such a development with the gravest of concern. You understand that?'

'Of course.'

'Good. Because I want to be sure that you understand,' continued Andropov. Then sharply : 'Where did you get these facts?'

'From one of Prince Abdullah's lieutenants. His name is Abdullah El Fahte. He has been in my employ for the past ten years.'

'What about the Americans?' asked the Russian.

'What about them?' countered the Shah.

'Saudi Arabia is their responsibility. They have a large number of military advisers in that country. Why have they not stopped this?'

'Ah,' said the Shah, 'because they did not know. They first found out the truth of what is happening a few hours ago. From me.'

'And what will they now do?'

The Shah shrugged. 'They are in a delicate position,' he said finally. 'If they move against Saudi Arabia, they will eventually have to confront the entire Arab world. It is delicate.

'Then there is the problem with Iraq,' continued the Shah.

'What about Iraq?' said Andropov. The Shah had struck another nerve. Iraq had been a semi-client of the Soviet Union for many years.

'They apparently intend to take advantage of the developing turmoil around the Persian Gulf. By attacking me. I strongly suspect that their actions are being closely coordinated with the events in Saudi Arabia. I think you must realize better than perhaps anyone how unreliable the Iraqi leaders are.'

In spite of himself, Andropov nodded.

'Do you have proof of the actual presence of Chinese in Riyadh?' asked Voronov, whose mind, obviously had been wandering a bit.

'Of course. From my man there.'

'I mean physical evidence. Photographs, for example.'

'Not yet. But I have physical evidence of something which verifies every word I have told you.'

The Shah turned around to Barami, who had been standing behind him the entire time, and whispered. Barami immediately left the room, returning with – what else? – the same set of aerial photographs that the Shah had shown the American ambassador a few hours earlier.

The Shah's routine was exactly the same. 'This,' he said, taking the first photograph and pointing at the river forming the borders between Iraq and Iran where the two countries meet at the northern tip of the Persian Gulf, 'is the Shatt al-Arab River. Now note that incredible concentration of artillery emplacements here, and the missile . . .'

And so forth. The repeat performance ended with the mysterious presence of American-built Saudi Arabian military aircraft on the ground in Iraq, as further documented from the Shah's photo album. But for this Russian presentation the summing up was in marked contrast to the one employed for the American one.

'Now,' he said, after Barami had retrieved the pictures once again, 'what lies ahead?' He paused. 'I will tell you. Abdullah, with the blessing of his friends in Yemen and those in Peking, and further, with the cooperation of the other madmen in the Arab world – those in Iraq, Qaddafi in Libya, Boumedienne in Algeria – intends to take over the entire Persian Gulf. That would mean that both of our nations – I stress both Iran and the Soviet Union – will have to then cope with a powerful and violently radical Arab leadership, being steered from Peking, right at our doorstep. Not only that, although even such a development is totally unacceptable. No, much worse. He who controls the oil of the Persian Gulf controls the most important source of global power there is. Can you imagine what it could mean if the Chinese, ultimately, were in a position to exercise such control?'

The Shah's performance was masterful. Absolutely magnificent. For although the Russians knew him, as a result of their long occupation of his country, he also knew them. Intimately. Perhaps better than any other ruler on earth. And he knew that there were absolutely no bounds whatsoever to Soviet paranoia where China was concerned. In Asia, they saw a Chinese behind every tree, every bush; the vision of one, now, behind every oil rig was a bit much.

'This is impossible!' exclaimed Andropov.

'Exactly,' replied the Shah. 'And I shall insure that it remains impossible.'

'How?' asked the Russians simultaneously.

'Very simple. At great sacrifice to my country, but for the good of both of our great nations, I shall make a preemptive strike. I shall destroy the Iraqi attack force. And simultaneously I shall neutralize Kuwait, Bahrain, Qatar, Abu Dhabi, Dubai as well as the northern tip of Oman. We shall have the Saudis half encircled before they even know what is happening. If Abdullah and his friends do not then remove themselves and allow a restoration of legitimacy, then we shall also destroy them.'

'And afterwards? 'asked Andropov.

'I have also given that great thought. And I have the answer. You see, I am a realist. I realize that one should never attempt to act in any manner which is contrary to natural geopolitical forces. What I mean is this : There are three great powers which have an enormous interest in achieving and maintaining peace and stability in the Middle East. They are Iran, the Soviet Union, and the United States. I shall propose that a tripartite arrangement be established to achieve that end in those Arab territories on the Persian Gulf. Will it work? I am convinced it will. And I will tell you why. Just such an arrangement was established in my country in 1942, as you know. The Soviet Union, the United States, and Great Britain occupied, ruled, and eventually left my country to its legitimate ruler – myself. It worked to everyone's advantage – then, and ever since then, to this day, as our meeting here once again proves. The only difference in what I am now proposing is that Britain will, of course, no longer be involved. It is no longer a world power.'

'And what do you want from us now?' asked Andropov.

'Nothing. Only that you do not intervene.'

'And if the Americans intervene?'

'They won't,' said the Shah flatly.

'How soon do you need our answer?'

'Within three days.'

Three minutes later the Russians had left.

The French began arriving one hour later, in black Citroëns. In contrast to the two prior meetings, this one had, at least partially, been scheduled well in advance. Its purpose was designed to be of both short-term and long-term importance – for both Iran and France.

The first group was from the Dassault-Breguet Aviation Company, the largest French aircraft producer. The subject which had been under discussion with them for many months : the Mirage F-1's. In fact, 120 of them. In addition to the aircraft, the package Dassault hoped to sell included 1,500 Matra R.530 missiles (some with radar, and others with infrared homing heads), as well as 500 of the new French laser-guided weapon, its characteristics being very similar to the hottest new item in the American missile arsenal, the Phoenix. It had tested out with a better than 95 percent hit rate even on targets as small as single armored vehicles or parked aircraft. The French asking price? $5.1 billion. They had proposed that 50 percent be paid on signing, the other half on delivery.

They had brought all the documents with them with the idea of at least having something on paper to start with. They had no illusions of any quick action. The French had dealt with the Middle East for generations. So the Dassault-Breguet men just sat back, completely at ease, while the Shah and his two military aides went slowly through their proposal.

Finally, the Iranians put the documents aside. The Shah fixed his penetrating gaze at the president of Dassault. And then said, 'We accept.'

The Dassault men waited with his response – he knew these people – and was again proven correct, for the Shah immediately followed up with the inevitable 'Provided a few conditions are met, and a number of minor alterations to the financial arrangements can be worked out.'

'Your Majesty,' said the Frenchman, 'we are highly flexible, as you know.' Of course they were flexible. Iran was the largest single customer for weapons in the entire world. The United States had dominated that market. Now, perhaps, the French could take it over.

'First,' said the Shah, 'on the matter of delivery. We want fifty of the F-1's flown to Teheran within three days, and we want a thousand of the Matras within the same time frame.'

'That is flatly impossible,' responded the Dassault man.

'No, it is not,' said the Shah. 'Your air force has a very ample supply of both. We are only asking that they reduce their inventories slightly, in our favor.'

'That, however, is a purely governmental decision. Those aircraft are no longer ours to dispose of.'

'I know that, my good man,' said Pahlavi. 'But you will agree if the people in Paris do.'

'Naturally.'

'That is all I wish to know.'

'And the price?'

'Perfectly acceptable.'

The Frenchmen squinted. All of them. There *had* to be something wrong.

'I believe,' said the Shah, 'that your other party should be arriving shortly. May I request that you wait in the hotel until after I have seen them?'

'Yes, Your Majesty.' Stunned, the Dassault men left.

Fifteen minutes later the second group of Citroëns pulled up in front of the chalet. In contrast to the first, two of the three cars were packed with French security men. The two passengers in the middle vehicle were the prime minister and the finance minister of the Republic of France. Also, in contrast to the Dassault visitors, they had been summoned on very short notice. But like the Americans and Russians, they had responded immediately, though on a much higher level. The sale of $5.1 billion in weapons was a matter of the highest priority for the French government, and thus demanded attention at the highest level.

The Shah greeted both French ministers with the greatest possible deference when they entered his home. The Shah was highly adept in the French language and French manners : he loved to demonstrate this.

'First, my dear sir,' he said, addressing the elegant and highly intelligent premier, 'I should like to address myself to matters concerning our two nations, before discussing the much broader – and extremely grave – international crisis which is facing us.'

'But of course,' was the premier's response.

'I am prepared to sign the contract with Dassault-Breguet Aviation. Today.'

In spite of himself, the premier's eyebrows rose.

'Yes,' continued the Shah. 'I realize this surprises you somewhat. But you will shortly realize that it is not in the interest of either of our nations to haggle on a commercial transaction of such limited proportions.

'But,' he said, 'there are two conditions. The first is that you deliver fifty of the aircraft and one thousand of the missiles immediately. They must be flown to Teheran with your personnel.'

'But why the . . .?' interrupted the French premier.

'Wait,' said the Shah. 'The second condition is that there be an adjustment in the financing. I propose that the initial payment of fifty percent be financed with a loan, to be provided by your banks, backed by the guarantee of my government. At the normal bank rates. I propose that the other fifty percent be paid for through your purchase of Iranian crude oil. We are prepared to supply you with the equivalent amount during the next year at –' he paused – 'twelve dollars a barrel. In fact, we are prepared to immediately inaugurate conversations concerning the sale of much larger quantities of our crude to France, over the next three years. At the same fixed price.

'Furthermore,' the Shah continued, 'we are prepared to extend such conversations to other members of the European Common Market, specifically Germany and Italy. I would appreciate it if you could inform them of this at your convenience.'

'This is totally unexpected,' said the Frenchman.

'I understand that. Are you prepared to accept my conditions?'

'Yes. Completely.'

'There is, perhaps, one further detail that I should mention. Should we reach agreement on long-term crude-oil deliveries with Europe, we would expect some advance payments. They may range as high as ten billion dollars. Perhaps a bit more.'

The premier looked at his finance minister.

'That would certainly be possible, Your Highness,' said the French money man. 'Especially in view of very recent developments. As you may know, our commercial banks throughout Europe are becoming extremely liquid, as a result of the massive transfer of funds from the United States.'

'Yes,' said the Shah, smiling generously at both Frenchmen, 'I am aware of that development. So we are essentially in agreement?'

'Yes,' they both said.

'Now,' continued Pahlavi, carefully watching his two guests, 'I wish to discuss the crisis in the Middle East.'

'The developments in Saudi Arabia?' asked the premier.

'Yes. As you may or may not know, the ruling clique in Riyadh has been overthrown. Fahd, Yamani, Sultan Aziz have been killed.'

Both Frenchmen winced. They were just as exposed to the madmen of the increasingly ungovernable world.

'Yes,' said the Shah, 'our burden is very heavy. But I, for one, do not shirk from it. Now the problem, as always, is with the United States. Just a few hours ago I received the American Ambassador to Switzerland. He informed me that his country is extremely upset about the developments there. As you know, the United States very recently entered into some extremely favorable arrangements with the Saudi regime, regarding both oil and the recycling of the Saudis' petrodollars. Both are now in peril.'

'Has the Saudi oil been cut off?' asked the premier.

'I don't know,' answered the Shah. That, after all, could be checked out. 'But you know what is happening in regard to the Saudi deposits with American banks.'

'Yes,' answered the finance minister.

'The new clique in Riyadh has cut their money off. Oil will not be far behind.'

'And what did the American intimate?'

'They will intervene. Naturally. I believe the Seventh Fleet is already under way.'

'The Seventh?'

'Yes. It is currently off Formosa.'

'It is a long way.'

'Exactly. Thus there is no doubt in my mind that the Americans will have no choice but to activate their NATO forces against the Saudis. And perhaps the rest of the Arabs, since I am convinced that neither Qaddafi nor Boumedienne, nor of course the Iraqis or the Syrians, would allow an American occupation of one square foot of Arab territory.'

'But that . . .'

The Shah interrupted. 'Exactly. That would place Europe squarely on the side of America. If the air base in Frankfurt, the paratroopers from outside Munich, the naval

297

base in Naples are activated against the Arabs, you are through. Either way. If the Americans take over the Gulf, they will be able to squeeze Europe to death. If not, the Arabs will squeeze all of you.'

'What about the Israelis?'

'Forget them,' answered the Shah, with an impatient wave of the hand. 'In this affair, Israel is about as important as Liechtenstein. The issue is how to react to the Americans.'

'And what do you suggest?' asked the premier.

'That we both – Europe and Iran – stand aloof from the machinations of the Americans. Make any intervention from European bases impossible – under any circumstance. You saw how Europe paid for the 1973 American-Israeli war against the Arabs. The price you will have to pay in 1979 could be fatal.'

'But are you sure that the new men in Riyadh intend to precipitate such a crisis?'

'I am. I am further convinced that it will be compounded by an Iraqi move against us. They have been waiting for an excuse for years.'

'But I fail to understand that,' said the French premier. 'What is the connection between the happenings in Riyadh and Iraq?'

'You see, you know the Middle East – but not like I do. Once the Americans intentions become known, Iraq will attack us because they will claim that we are an ally of the United States. Nonsense, of course. But that is what they will claim.'

'And what does your nation intend to do?'

'Remain completely neutral. Our natural ally is Europe, not America. Our conversation today should have removed any doubts whatsoever on this issue. We are turning to France, and its friends in Europe, for our needs : industrial, financial, and military. In return, we shall guarantee you energy.'

'But if Iraq attacks?'

'We shall reply with a measured and limited response. I repeat : measured and limited. We would appreciate your

298

support to insure that no damage is done to our oil fields and refineries in southern Iran. After all, they may soon represent your lifeblood as well as ours.'

'Please excuse us for a few minutes,' said the premier.

'Of course.' The Shah motioned to his two aides to leave the room. He followed them.

'Is he telling the truth?' was the first question the premier put to his most trusted cabinet member.

'I can only judge from my perspective,' said the minister of finance. 'And everything that has been happening during the past forty-eight hours confirms it. Our estimate is that during that period eight billion dollars has already left the United States for Europe. All Saudi funds. The Fahd-Yamani clique must be out. No doubt dead, as he said.'

'Yes,' replied the premier. 'What amount of funds do we currently hold with the United States government?'

'Around four billion dollars. In their Treasury bills.'

'If the Shah's scenario proves correct, and we, with our German and Italian friends, arrange to preclude European military involvement through American use of our bases in this affair, could sequestership possibly become an issue?'

'If the drain picks up momentum, with the Americans anything is possible.'

'Sell, Fouquet.'

'Now?' incredulously.

'Right now,' came the reply.

Finance Minister Fouquet left the chalet and trotted over to the hotel, where he commandeered a room with a telephone. Inside of ten minutes, he was back in the Shah's living room. Pahlavi himself appeared a few minutes later, bearing a new set of documents.

He put copies before the two Frenchmen. 'These are agreements, in principle, on the proposed crude oil arrangements between our nations, as well as the bank financing of the initial two-and-a-half-billion financing of the weapons purchase. We thought, by the way, that if the French government would also guarantee those loans, it would ease their placement with the European banks. Thus we have included that.'

The premier of France looked at his finance minister. The latter just shrugged. Both then read.

'I believe that, in principle, this is acceptable,' said the premier. 'We would be prepared to initial these agreements. Final signatures would have to await some minor refinements, for which we will need further time.'

'Well, then . . .' began the Shah.

'Of course,' said the Frenchman, 'it would probably be appropriate if the contracts governing the weapons purchases were signed by you first.'

'But of course. I assume you will be able to amend that agreement by assuring your government's agreement to the immediate transfer of the initial shipments, from government inventories.'

'Certainly.'

General Barami was sent over to the hotel to retrieve the Dassault-Breguet delegation. Then they all sat down to read once again, then revise, then revise again, and finally, one by one, either to sign or initial the contracts. The French did not leave until nine that evening, in the longest convoy of black Citroëns ever seen in St. Moritz.

Once again my local bank manager's intelligence had proven faulty. According to his earlier version, the French had been joined by the chancellor of West Germany after a few hours at the Shah's chalet. Not so. The chancellor was indeed in St. Moritz at this time. He was vacationing there. He had a twenty-three-year-old Japanese masseuse along, from Düsseldorf. They had been holed up in a small chalet on the outskirts of St. Moritz, just a mile up the road from the grounds of the Suvretta. Both were exhausted – not from skiing, since neither had gone near the slopes. No, the chancellor had been relieving himself of the enormous tensions that inevitably build up in a leader of state, while the little Oriental had been providing assistance in this task, which sometimes proved strenuous where the somewhat elderly and dissipated statesman was concerned. So both agreed that a temporary diversion was in order. They decided to risk a walk down to the Suvretta House and a few drinks at the bar there. They were seen there together, naturally. But all later accusations against the man were completely and totally false. It was not the Shah who had set him up with that Japanese fluff in return for a slight political favor. No, it was strictly one of those unfortunate coincidences. It was the *French* who later convinced the Germans to screw the Americans. The Japanese had nothing to do with it.

By nine thirty that evening, things were extremely quiet on the grounds of the Suvretta House, and inside the Shah's chalet. Empress Farah Diva appeared from her quarters at this time, but the Shah sent her back with an impatient wave of the hand.

'Barami,' he said, 'get those tapes.'

The tapes were, naturally, of the conversation between the two French leaders which had taken place during the Iranians' absence from the Shah's bugged living room.

Barami got the tapes and played them back on a simple Sony machine that belonged to one of the Shah's kids. The Shah listened for a minute or so and then said, 'Stop it right there.'

Barami stopped it.

The recorder then replayed : '. . . in this affair, could sequestership possibly become an issue?'

'If the drain picks up momentum,' the replay continued in the voice of M. Fouquet, the French minister of finance, 'with the Americans anything is possible.'

'Sell Fouquet,' was the French premier's reply.

'Stop it,' said the Shah to Barami. Barami stopped the recorder.

'What were they talking about?' he asked his general.

'Money,' answered Barami.

'Of course, you idiot. But what is this "sequestership" business?'

Barami had no idea. He did not even know what the word meant. Neither did the Shah. He sent Barami looking for a dictionary. There was none in the chalet. He sent Barami to the hotel. There was none there.

'Sequestership?' the Shah said, time and again.

But Barami was not interested in little financial puzzles. His war was now ready to go. And the most important aspect of it had not yet been resolved. 'Your Majesty,' he said, 'I must return to Iran tomorrow.'

'Yes,' said the Shah, 'I know that.'

'We have still left unresolved the issue of . . . the nuclear devices.' He approached the subject carefully, since he had been instructed never – never – to discuss the matter on foreign soil. But now he had no choice.

'I told you, Barami,' came the inevitable harsh response, 'to never . . .'

'But I must know. How many Phantoms do we equip with nuclear-bomb racks?'

'One.'

'Just one?'

'Just one. We only need one. We are going to set off that bomb over the desert, for demonstration purposes only. That needs just one plane with one nuclear bomb.'

'But, Your Majesty . . .'

'That is all, Barami.'

It was a very disappointed general who was sent to his quarters in the south wing of the Shah's chalet.

'Sequestership?' the Shah still puzzled after Barami had left him alone in the living room, in front of the fire.

He picked up the phone that connected him with the main desk of the Suvretta House. 'Get me Mr. Khamesi.' Some of his aides were put up there.

'Your Majesty wants me?'

'What does "sequestership" mean?'

'I think it means to seize or take over or something like that.'

'Seize?'

'Yes. I believe it is usually used in a financial context. I am not expert in that area, Your Majesty. I am extremely sorry, and . . .'

'Yes, Khamesi. Say, do you have the phone number of that American banker?'

'American . . .?'

'Hitchcock.'

'Yes, sir.'

'Give it to me.' He got it, and hung up without another word. Then he dialed it.

After my Swiss banking friend had left the bar of the Palace, Ursula and I went on to dinner alone in the dining room. It was all right, as usual, but neither Ursula nor I felt like eating a thing. We got back to the chalet at nine, and again the phone was ringing. It was Herr Meier from the Swiss Bank Corporation.

'Dr. Hitchcock, I want to again apologize. I certainly understand why you were so upset a few hours ago, and . . .'

'Forget it, Meier. It is I who should apologize. Let's both consider it forgotten.'

'I greatly appreciate that, sir. By the way, there is something I feel you should know.'

'Yes?'

'New York is in great turmoil. Or at least it was an hour ago, when the market closed there.'

'What happened?'

'Somebody has begun selling an enormous quantity of United States government Treasury bills. It is unbelievable how they fell in price during the last two hours of trading. And the dollar. It fell another two percent in two hours this afternoon. The biggest plunge was against the French franc. I will tell you one more thing. We are getting out too. I hope that makes up for our problem.'

He was ready to hang up.

'Wait a minute, Werner. What does that mean – you're getting out?'

'We are advising our Swiss clients to liquidate their holdings in the United States.'

'But that's crazy! Look, it never pays to liquidate in a panic. When the Middle East settles down, prices will go right back to where they started a few days ago.'

'Perhaps. But we feel that a more fundamental problem may arise. We remember what your country did to us in 1941. We cannot afford to risk that again.'

'I understand.' Then lamely, 'Thanks, Werner.'

We both hung up.

Ursula saw my face. 'What's wrong?' she asked.

'The Swiss have memories that are too goddamn long. And the United States has painted itself into a goddamn corner. And there's not a goddamn thing anybody can do about it. Unless the Swiss have the right idea.'

'Is it money?' she asked.

'Of course.'

She looked relieved. It was just money. Nothing to do with her father. She went and got a book. I got a beer. And thought. It was like 1914, for Christ's sake. Everybody moving into collision course with everybody else, and nobody knowing exactly why, or how it had started.

At ten the phone rang again. Ursula took it. A few seconds later, her face white, she handed it to me without a word.

'Dr. Hitchcock, it is Pahlavi. I am sorry to disturb you at this hour. But I would greatly appreciate it if you could drop down to my chalet for a drink and a brief chat.'

'Now?'

'Yes. As I said, I do regret any inconvenience it might entail. But I have something on my mind. And please, by all means bring along Miss Hartmann. I insist.' And he hung up.

'Would you believe?'

She said nothing.

'Well, might as well find out what's on his Aryan mind. Let's get the coats and boots. It's too late to get the sleigh.'

'Oh, no. Not me.'

'Ursula! Don't be an ass. You can't help your father by hiding your head in the ... snow. Come on.'

'No!' But she did.

It was a half-hour's walk. The moon was full, and it was not very cold, so in any other circumstances it would have been a wonderful evening stroll in the Alps. But the circumstances were not such. The only noise either of us made came from our boots, crunching in the snow.

The security men had obviously been informed. They asked for identification but were immediately satisfied when

304

I showed them my passport – which I always carry with me abroad, even when in ski clothes.

The Shah personally came to the door – he was obviously alone – and fretted over Ursula until she was settled in a huge armchair by the fire. Her tightly pressed lips showed the pressure she was under. But that was all.

'Now,' said the Shah, 'what shall we drink?'

'I would very much like a hot toddy. With rum,' replied Ursula. So she was going to behave.

'I will have the same.'

'Good. My servants have been dismissed. I am afraid you will have to wait a few minutes. But very few. I will have the drinks sent over from the hotel.' He picked up his phone, and that was taken care of.

'Now, Dr. Hitchcock,' he began.

'Call me Bill.'

'Certainly. And you are Ursula, are you not, my dear,' he said to my house guest.

'Yes,' she answered.

'You have a marvelous tan, Ursula. You look very lovely, if I may say so.'

'I tan easily.'

'Yes. So do I. Now Doctor – Bill, I would appreciate it if you could explain something to me. What is going on in the financial markets right now? I have heard that some very dramatic happenings have occurred.'

I explained. The Saudis had recently come into New York with a tremendous amount of short-term funds. Now they were pulling them out. When they went in, the dollar and the New York markets went up. Now that they were going out, the dollar and the markets were going down. Very simple.

'But do you know the reason for this sudden shift? After all, I thought you were the Saudis' chief financial adviser?'

A low blow, but . . .

'I was. Maybe still am. The point is, I have not been consulted now for five days. I am sure you know that it is impossible to communicate with Riyadh. So . . .'

'Yes, I understand your feelings. Well, Bill, I do know what is happening. And I shall tell you.'

He told me. Fahd, Yamani, etc., were dead. Abdullah was master.

'So obviously I am out.'

'I would say so,' he replied dryly. 'But I hardly think you needed the job in the first place.'

I let that pass.

'But it is not just the Saudis, is it?' he went on.

'What do you mean?'

'I mean that other people appear to be fleeing from America with their money.'

'That's a fair conclusion. You know how it is. When a bandwagon starts, everybody gets on it. At least for a while.'

'Like?'

'Perhaps the French.'

'Yes, so I have heard. And even the Swiss.' He let that one sink in. The guy was obviously so far ahead of me on everything, I decided to keep quiet. 'Why should the Swiss do that?' he asked.

'They are very cautious. When international trouble brews, they trust no one. Not even the Americans.'

'But why? Has it anything to do with . . . sequestership?'

Now that surprised me. I am supposed to know about those things; but the Shah of Iran?

'Yes. In fact, it must. Yes.' I said.

'But explain.'

'Well, it goes back to what happened in 1941. On June fourteenth, 1941, to be precise.' Now I was showing off. But what the hell. I knew this stuff. The title of my doctoral dissertation had been 'Sequestership : Its Application and Effect During World War Two.' You have to look very hard for dissertation themes in any area, including international economics. I had searched, and had found that one.

'Yes?' from Pahlavi.

'Well, on that day the American Executive Order 8785

was applied to Switzerland. In fact, to all of continental Europe.'

'Why on June fourteenth, 1941?'

'I don't know, but I can guess. That executive order was originally issued in April of 1940, two days after the German occupation of Norway and Denmark. But it only applied to countries actually occupied by the Nazis. Maybe in mid-June of the following year Roosevelt had reason to believe that the rest of Europe would soon suffer the same fate. As you may recall, it was eight days later, on June twenty-second, 1941, that Germany attacked Russia.'

'I don't want to interrupt, but how do you know these things so exactly?'

I told him.

'All right,' he said, awfully pleased with himself for some reason, 'now what does all that – or did that, I should say – executive-order stuff mean?'

'Well, it meant that the United States on that date sequestered – seized, grabbed, you can call it what you want – all the assets of all the countries in Europe. Except England's, of course.'

'It actually seized them? You mean, the Swiss banks could not get their money back from America?' He was really worked up. And I had assumed he knew all about this.

'Exactly.'

But he would not let it go at that. 'Wait a minute. Let's say a Swiss bank owned stock. Say, of General Motors. And they wanted to sell it. Do you mean that after the application of that executive order they could not?'

'No, I didn't say exactly that. Sure, they could sell. But the proceeds would have had to stay in New York. Blocked for the duration.'

'What do you mean, duration? In June of 1941 the United States was not at war. Neither with Germany nor Japan nor anybody else?' No dummy, our Shah.

'Yes. You are right.'

Now he was shaking his head. 'But on what possible

grounds could the American government have done that to the Swiss?'

'Look,' I said, 'it was not just the Swiss. It was everybody: the Belgians, the French, the Norwegians, the Swedes. Everybody.'

'With what justification?' he persisted.

'I can almost quote the reasons given by heart.'

'Do.'

'OK: "To prevent the liquidation in the United States of assets looted by duress or conquest" and "to prevent the use of financial facilities of the United States, in ways harmful to national defense and other American interests," and "to curb subversive activities in the United States." That enough?'

'Incredible!' said the Shah.

'Yes, wasn't it? Considering that the United States was completely neutral at the time,' I answered.

'But I must come back to one point. You say this was applied to all countries, and banks of those countries in Europe, including Switzerland.'

'Yes,' now a bit wearily.

'But as you know, many people from outside of Europe use Swiss banks to invest for them in the United States.'

'Of course.'

'That means that the real ownership, the beneficial ownership, of such investments was not Swiss, nor European. They merely acted for, say, an investor from Brazil or – Mexico.'

'Yes.'

'Surely *such* assets were not seized by the Americans?'

'They were. And were not released until 1949. Eight years later.'

'My God!' said the Shah. '*Now* I understand.'

At the time I did not quite get what he now understood. But it came out later.

'Let us, just for discussion's sake, say that a war started. Say in the Middle East. And say that, at least initially, the United States was not involved.'

'Yes.'

308

'Could they seize the assets of every nation in the Middle East under that old executive order?'

'Yes, I assume so.'

'And those of Europe?'

'Well, that would stretch things a bit. But Washington stretched things very far indeed in June of 1941, wouldn't you say so?'

'Yes, yes.' He was wholeheartedly in agreement.

'Why do you ask such a question?' That, suddenly, came from Ursula.

'My dear,' he said, 'we were talking business.'

'I know full well what you are talking about!' she replied, vehemently.

'Now, as I was saying, Bill—' he went on, turning his back on Ursula.

'You are planning on starting a war, aren't you?' Ursula shouted. 'And you are afraid for all that stolen money you have hidden through Swiss banks, aren't you?'

'Ursula,' I said, 'take it easy.'

'I will not take it easy.' Now she glared at the Shah like a Swiss tigress. 'You have involved my father in your dirty business, haven't you? With your crazy idea of having atomic weapons. And all you do is sit here and worry about your money.'

Jeezuz!

'I think,' said Pahlavi, 'that it is time for you to go, Dr. Hitchcock, and to take that Jewess with you.' Then to Ursula: 'I know about you. You Jews are all the same. Troublemakers. But not much longer.' He stood up.

'You are insane,' continued Ursula. 'You are just a simple-minded peasant who has gone crazy because somebody was stupid enough to make a Shah out of a dirty Iranian peasant!'

'Out!' yelled Pahlavi.

'And you are even afraid of the words of a Jewish woman,' she continued. 'You are not only an insane peasant, you are also a coward.' And I swear to God, she spat at him.

We left. Without even getting those hot toddies.

In the two minutes that followed, the Shah did something that eventually affected all of us – although Ursula more than most people.

'Barami,' he bellowed, once the door had closed behind us. 'Barami!'

The general came flying into the room, gun in hand.

'Put that away, you fool,' said the Shah. Then : 'You are to proceed with those bomb racks.'

'What, Your Highness?'

'Listen when I address you. I said that you are to equip six Phantoms with nuclear-bomb racks. You hear? And I want that done the first thing – the *first* first thing – after we return to Iran. And we will return tomorrow. All of us. You are to inform the empress. And prepare. We leave at nine.'

It took us almost a full hour to climb back up the path leading from the grounds of the Suvretta House to our chalet on the Chantarella plateau. Ursula was silent the entire time.

When we got back, she went straight to bed. I stayed up. I had a few telephone calls to make. First I called Randolph Aldrich in New York. I got him at the bank. It was only four in the afternoon there. I told him what lay ahead. The problem was no longer the Saudis' money. Hell, that could be managed. What I feared was a general exodus of European capital from the United States' financial markets. That amounted to over $100 billion. Aldrich would not buy that. I explained the sequestership theories which were obviously starting to make the rounds. I told him that the thing to do was to get Washington to shut things down for a few days until the situation in the Middle East cleared up.

His answer : 'Look, Hitchcock, we got everybody into that mess with the Saudis to begin with. Our advice today is worth nothing. Go to bed and get some sleep. We'll luck through. We always have.'

I did not go to bed and I did not go to sleep. It was well past midnight, but I managed to get the number of the U.S. ambassador's residence in Bern, and I even got the person who answered the telephone to get Sinclair out of bed. We had never met, but he must have known who I was.

'I am extremely sorry to call you at this hour,' I began, 'but I have some information which I feel is of extreme importance to our government.'

'Yes?' he said.

'There is no doubt in my mind that Iran is planning to attack its neighbors on the Persian Gulf.'

'Perhaps,' he said. 'What makes you say that?'

'I have just spoken to the Shah.'

'Yes. So have a lot of people today.'

'But the real point I want to make is this: I know – you hear? I know – that Iran has nuclear weapons, and intends to use them.'

'I suppose he told you that,' answered Sinclair.

'Of course not. But I have absolute evidence from other sources.'

'Are you in the intelligence business, Mr. Hitchcock?'

'No, for God's sake. I know, because I happen to know who has developed these weapons for the Shah, where they are being built, with what. Everything.'

'How?'

'From the daughter of the Swiss scientist who is involved.'

'Swiss? Come now, Mr. Hitchcock.'

'Look, I . . .'

'Mr. Hitchcock, I am afraid that this conversation has gone far enough. If you wish to tell me more about this, put it on paper and in an envelope, and send it to me. I will be glad to arrange for one of my men to follow up.' With that, the connection was broken.

Ursula had come out of the bedroom during this conversation. She stood watching me as I looked up from the dead phone.

'Dill you tried. Thank you. Now go to bed. You look very tired.'

'And you?'

'I can't sleep.'

'Ursula, you surely must realize one thing. If your father – the Swiss, really – had not helped the Shah, somebody else would have. Another Swiss or a Frenchman. Somebody.'

'I know, Bill.'

'There is nothing more either of us can do. I am afraid he has beaten us all. And we will all now just have to live with it.'

'Go to bed, Bill.'

'OK, I'll go. But let me tell you one more thing, Ursula. It's not much. But I know one guy down the mountain who will not go to bed for a while after the going-over he got from you.'

Wrong again. For the Shah had a system for getting things off his mind just like the German chancellor. Or, I guess, some past American presidents. Nothing wrong with that, as long as you can get away with it.

The Shah was well placed in that respect. He did not have to sneak off like his German counterpart. No; every winter when he came to St. Moritz he stocked the east wing of the Suvretta House with a variety of women. And why not? It was not just a modern tradition by any means. The Old Testament is full of emperors and kings who did the same thing : Solomon, David, Ahasuerus, to name but a few. And the Shah was a great believer in tradition – in the *obligation* of tradition.

But what was eerie that particular night was *whom* he had lined up. She was waiting for him – in Room 316, just a few down from the room of Mr. Khamesi, who was the unofficial keeper of the harem.

She was Trudi Schneider. Remember her? The Adler Hotel in Baden, Room 24, between six and eight on Friday nights after work? Of course. But it had been on a Wednesday night, back in November of 1978, when she had first been fucked by an Iranian – Fawzi Tehrani of SAVAK. And it was he who had introduced her to the Persian position. She liked it. In fact, she loved it. Trudi actually dreamed of it. So when Teherani had finally called her

312

again, after months, suggesting a rendezvous in St. Moritz, she damn near came while on the telephone. It had been easy to arrange. Her boss and his wife were going to St. Moritz at the same time, to a party in that very hotel where she was going to stay. The good Dr. Suter suspected hanky-panky, but was going to do nothing that could possibly end his Friday-night recreation. So she had come down with him and his wife, in the back seat of the Mercedes. And now she was waiting for Tehrani, paging through a Swiss illustrated magazine, the *Sie und Er*. Finally, well past two, came the knock.

She opened. And there stood – not Tehrani but the Shahanshah of Iran.

'My dear,' he said, as she gaped, 'you are even lovelier than Fawzi told me. And you are Swiss.'

'But . . .'

'No time for buts. The Shah closed the door and reached for Trudi. She struggled.

'Was denkst du eigentlich?' she yelled.

But she was already on the bed, and he already had her nightgown off in one rip. And a few seconds later, he was in her. Ten times, hard. Then he turned her over. And took her, not in the Persian, but the Greek position. It was brutal, because he was big, and angry. In one minute it was done.

The Shah rose, placed a one-thousand-franc note on the bed, zipped himself up, and left without a further word.

Probably about this same time – the middle of the night – I woke up in my bedroom, alone. It was Ursula's voice that did it. She was speaking on the phone, obviously to her father in Iran.

'. . . and then he called me a Jew. I guess he knows about me from the SAVAK people. But after that he said – can you hear me, father? – good. Well, then he said, "You Jews are all the same. Troublemakers. But not much longer." Do you understand, Father?'

A short pause.

'Did you think about what I told you that night before I left?'

Another pause.

'Did you find another solution?'

He must have said yes.

'Oh, thank goodness. And you promise?'

He must have again said yes.

'Father, I love you. And Father, you must save yourself. Can you?'

A long pause.

'Father . . .'

Then I could not listen any longer. I put a pillow over my head. Ten minutes later she slipped into bed beside me. I did not move. For I could not help her. At least she had been able to talk to him before the lines to Iran were also cut off.

At nine that morning, the Shah, his dear wife Farah Diva, and their beloved children left St. Moritz, bound for Teheran. Ursula and I once again witnessed their passing through town, since we had decided to ski early that day and try to forget.

Neither of us even commented on it. For there was nothing either of us could now do, except hope that 'something' would happen which would reverse the path of history. It was, I guess, exactly what most people had done in August of 1914, or October of 1929, or September of 1939, when their worlds started to fall apart. Only this was March of 1979, when that sort of thing was not supposed to happen ever again.

But it did.

Three days later, on March 19, 1979, the Shah of Iran attacked.

CHAPTER TWENTY-FOUR

The Four Day War began at 6:30 A.M. on that Monday in March. The Shah's astrologer had approved of the date, and his court historians had concurred. Their calculations, using the Persian calendar, indicated that it was exactly on this date, in A.D. 226, that one of the Shah's predecessors had declared the establishment of the Sassanid Empire, an empire that had included all the lands bordering on the Persian Gulf on the east, west, and north, and one which had lasted for more than four centuries. It was the reestablishment of the glory of ancient Persia that was the goal of the King of Kings in 1979. For he was fifty-nine, and time was running out.

He had arrived at his command post the evening before. It was located in a bunker, twenty feet below the surface of the airfield on the outskirts of Khorramshahr. It was from that airfield that the first strikes were made. It was right out of the Israeli book : one hundred Phantoms and fifty French F-1's which had been flown in just the day before – the Phantoms equipped with Phoenix missiles, the F-1's carrying Matras – made low-level dawn raids on the eight Iraqi military bases. Thirty-three of Iraq's 285 combat aircraft were destroyed on the ground before the sun was up, thanks to the remarkable accuracy of the air-to-ground missiles and to the skill of the Iranian pilots, all of whom had been schooled by the United States Air Force. No Saudi Arabian aircraft were destroyed, since none were there.

The second air strike, ordered by the Shah one hour later, was directed at Umm Qasr, the port city just off the Iraqi-Kuwait border, where the Russians had built a naval base for the Iraqis designed to guard the mouth of the Shatt al-Arab River. One hundred and twenty Northrop F-5's leveled the place within an hour. By 8:30 A.M.

315

battalion after battalion of Iranian troops were landed by helicopter. It was a walkover.

'Well done, Barami,' said the Shah, when the reports of this success began to arrive in the command post.

The bunker itself was a marvel of modern technology. It had been constructed by Bechtel Corporation of San Francisco and equipped by Raytheon, Westinghouse, Litton Industries, and Texas Instruments with the very best in communications equipment. Nothing in either the Pentagon or the White House in Washington even came close. Not only was it perfectly equipped; it was only ten miles from the Iraqi border and fifteen miles north of the Persian Gulf. A risky place, perhaps, for a commander in chief. But the Shah envisioned himself as another Patton, not an Eisenhower.

Thus, at eight forty-five it was not one of his generals who gave the next command, but the Shah himself.

'Now, Barami, we take them out across the river.'

'Now?'

'Now.'

The third air strike that resulted was one in which both Phantoms and F-5's were employed, and it was the most massive of all. It was directed at the artillery and missile sites just across the Shatt al-Arab from Khorramshahr and Abadan. A great deal of napalm was used – with devastating effect.

The Iranian air force was proving itself the most efficient in the entire Middle East, exceeding even the Israeli performance of the earlier 1970's in terms of turnaround time and operational techniques.

By eleven o'clock that March 19, when all three air-strike operations had been completed with stunning success, the Shah was ready for his most elegant military play.

'Shabanah,' he said. 'We shall begin.'

What began minutes later was what military historians today refer to as 'the Shatt al-Arab end run.' It had been conceived and was now implemented by Brigadier Shabanah as the first major military offensive based primarily upon the use of Hovercraft. The idea was tailor-made for

316

the geography of the area. Remember all those Iraqi tanks in the corridor between the Tigris River and the Iranian border? Well, behind them, to the west, were the swamps of the Tigris-Euphrates delta – impassable terrain from the military standpoint. Impassable, that is, for every military vehicle known to man except the Hovercraft, which could move on top of its air cushion across anything that was reasonably flat – water, swamp, or beach – and at a speed of 40 m.p.h., fully loaded. These remarkable machines (all built for the Shah in Britain, the world's leader in Hovercraft technology) could move an entire armored battalion : in their cavernous bowels were tanks (Chieftains, also British built) and armored personnel carriers (BTR-50's and BTR-60's of Soviet origin) plus a full complement of military personnel in the wings and on the upper decks. They had a range of 150 miles. But they could not move until the naval base at Umm Qasr had been put out of action, and until the Iraqi fire power on the west bank of the Shatt al-Arab – the gateway to the Tigris-Euphrates delta – had been eliminated. By 11 A.M. that had been accomplished. Thus the Shah's command.

The scene that followed on the beaches of the Persian Gulf, just to the east of Abadan, was a spectacle that no participant ever forgot. At 11:05, the wild howl of hundreds of these Hovercraft engines began to fill the air, producing an incredible torrent of sound. Then, slowly, the mechanical monsters began to rise, as the air pressure built up within the skirts beneath the vehicles. Then, in columns of five, they began to move off the beaches and onto the shallow waters of the Persian Gulf, creating cloud after cloud of swirling mist. It was as if the devil himself had conceived the operation. For as these grotesque weapons of war moved around the corner, row upon row, and up the Shatt al-Arab channels, the scene resembled a Martian invasion.

Only two hours later, they began opening up their ramps on firm ground to the rear of the Iraqi forces. At the same time the main body of Iranian panzers, which had been grouped between Dezful and Ahvaz, began a frontal assault

317

from the east. It was nothing less than a massacre. Already by early afternoon the vast majority of the Iraqi forces chose surrender.

The men in the bunker in Khorramshahr spent the evening hours of March 19 planning the regrouping of their forces and plotting the activities of the next day on the huge battle map that covered the east wall of the bunker. One by one they went down the targets for the following day : Kuwait, Bahrain, Qatar, Abu Dhabi, Dubai, Oman. Already by eight their plans were complete.

CHAPTER TWENTY-FIVE

The Crash of '79 probably really began that same time – at noon on March 19 of that year in New York, which was eight time zones behind Iran. For by noon of that day, the big boys in that town started to realize that an irreversible economic phenomenon was developing : a financial panic.

Measured analysis, tempered by the time that has passed since that day, surely indicates that it was not the war in the Middle East that caused it. No – the news of the beginnings of that conflict in the early hours of March 19 indicated that it was just another border clash between Iraq and Iran. To be sure, this time they were doing a lot more than just lobbing a few shells at each other. But it was strictly a local affair. No Americans were directly involved. No Russians. No Chinese. Not even any Saudi Arabians, or Egyptians, or Israelis. So the beginning of the Four Day War was hardly the cause.

But it was perhaps the trigger. The only historical parallel which even comes close was the assassination of Archduke Francis Ferdinand in the capital of Bosnia in July of 1914 : it kindled the blaze of World War One, but only because the fire had already been laid.

The point is that the entire financial system of the West, but particularly of the United States of America, had reached a degree of vulnerability unprecedented since the 1920's. The condition of the banks was, of course, deplorable; that of America's largest banks represented a latent bomb. Already back in 1976, the two largest New York banks – the First National City and Chase Manhattan – had been declared problem banks by the controller of the currency. Sure, they tried to correct the situation. They were even taken off that list. But in 1978, the folly of lending long and borrowing short, of lending good money after bad to avoid having to write off bad loans, of pouring billions upon billions into the developing world, lending to governments which could not possibly repay in this century, or maybe even the next, of purchasing the notes and bonds of essentially bankrupt municipalities to keep the politicians in line – all such practices had left the banks wide open for a run on their deposits.

But runs never occur in an atmosphere of general prosperity and confidence – especially confidence in the institutions of government. For healthy governmental institutions can save anything in the public mind : even the banks. However, by 1979, public faith in public institutions was approaching zero. The cities, the states were all in a condition of essential paralysis, because they had overspent for so long and borrowed so much that their credit was nonexistent. They could not take care of themselves, much less bail out anybody else.

The key, however, to the conditions of confidence in early 1979 was the condition of the Federal Government. It now owed a grand total of $879 billion! And it was being forced to borrow an additional new $3 billion each and every week just to keep going. If you added together all the debts that had accumulated in the United States by early 1979 – that of the Federal Government, of the states, of the cities, of the corporations, of individuals – it amounted to trillions. Not a trillion. But trillions.

But so what? That is what the economists said. Debt in a productive society is a healthy thing. In fact, without the instruments of debt, America would never have become the world's greatest economic powerhouse. And it was a powerhouse with an output which grew at a rate that consistently outstripped the rise in debt. Yes. But it was a powerhouse that was fueled by energy. And oil was the most important source of such energy. And America, where oil and thus energy was concerned, was just as vulnerable, just as prone to disaster, as were the banks. Operation Independence was a total, absolute failure in 1979. Soon half of America's petroleum needs would have to be met by imports. The continuing operation of the powerhouse now depended upon – foreigners.

And that is where the ultimate vulnerability of the American economic system lay: in its international exposure. Not only did foreigners control the energy sources, but they also controlled a strategic segment of the American financial markets.

Not a massive proportion. Not even a large proportion. But a strategic proportion. They held about $80 billion of short-term U.S. Treasury notes. They held about $95 billion in corporate bonds and stocks – meaning paper of American corporations. And they controlled another $75 billion on short-term deposits with the American banking system. All told, just a couple of hundred billion out of those trillions of American debt. But it was enough to provoke the beginnings of a panic when it started to leave America.

And on that Monday, March 19, 1979, it was leaving. Oh, how it was leaving! Of course, the Saudis were pulling out at the rate of a couple of billion a day by then. The French were liquidating their entire holdings of American governmental paper. The Swiss – and they controlled tens upon tens of billions of dollars of foreign investments in the United States + joined the exodus in full force that day. They did not begin to sell, they began to dump: T-bills, AT&T bonds, General Motors stock. They pulled their deposits out of the New York banks, and out of the branches of the New York banks in London. And out of the Chicago banks, and their overseas branches, and the California banks, and the Texas banks. The Germans were the last to join the crowd. And they were as dangerous to the United States financial system as were the Swiss. For they had lent the American government almost as much as the Saudis.

Why? Why this massive liquidation in the United States? Because the foreign community had been building up a growing mistrust of the stability of the American financial system for years. Because they had been building up a growing mistrust of the American dollar for years. Because they knew that neither the system nor its currency could forever survive the effects of runaway fiscal policies; of ever pyramiding debts; of irresponsible, even irrational, banking methods.

But the ultimate trigger was the war – the Four Day War. The Europeans knew that America had barely survived the 1973–74 embargo, when it only imported 15 percent of its petroleum. Now that it was approaching 50 percent, anything could happen, including the response which the French, and then the Swiss, and then everybody else feared : that the Americans would block all foreign funds in the United States; that a panicky Washington could revert to the type of controls and, yes, even sequestership, that it had used in 1941. For a real blowup in the Middle East would lead to global economic warfare. And then anything was possible.

So they started getting out.

At noon on March 19 the New York Stock Exchange volume had already reached 50 million shares. The Dow-Jones was down 56 points. The bond market was in shambles. The average price of AAA industrial obligations had fallen $105 for every $1,000 face amount in two hours. The Swiss franc had closed against the dollar the prior Friday at 33 cents; by noon on Monday it was 38 cents. The D mark had started at 31 cents. It was now 37 cents. The yen had started at 300 to the dollar. It was now 260. It was estimated that the foreign liquidations in the first two trading hours of March 19 equaled $12 billion, and were continuing at the rate of $5 billion an hour.

The New York Federal Reserve Bank was helpless to prevent the massive flight of capital. Sure, it was charged with maintaining an orderly market in foreign exchange. It was charged with the international management of the dollar. But at the insistence of the American government, the dollar was a floating currency. Anybody could buy or sell it at will, and at a price which supply and demand in the market determined. And at the insistence of the American government, under the revised rules of the International Monetary Fund no foreign government was obligated to come to the aid of the American government when this run on the dollar began. So they did not.

At eleven o'clock on March 19, the first Americans outside of New York joined in. Sure, the professionals in the Big Apple and elsewhere had started getting out at the opening – just as I had a few days earlier. But it was not until late morning that the little guys in the hinterland caught on to what was happening.

The first place where it went wrong was Fort Wayne, Indiana – at the main office, on Calhoun Street, of the Hoosier National Bank. It was 11:15 A.M. when the lineups for withdrawals at the three teller windows filled the lobby and first slopped over onto the sidewalk outside. Mid-March in the Midwest that year was cold; it was no more than 25 degrees outside on Calhoun Street. But there they stood, three abreast, waiting for the line to push forward.

'You heard?' were the words said again and again. And usually they were voiced by a woman, since at least two thirds of the people thronging to the tellers' windows were women. They had heard on the radio. About the markets in New York, about the Ayrabs, the French, the Swiss, the dollar, the war. And they just wanted to be careful. People in Fort Wayne, Indiana, were not the panicky type. It was a small city, populated by people of good German Lutheran stock, many two generations removed from the Indiana farms, or Valparaiso, or Indiana State, or Michigan. They were fifty years removed from the happenings of 1929. Most had not even been born then. But they had heard the stories, told over and over again, from parents and grandparents.

'If only we had gotten our savings out a bit earlier,' the stories always ended, 'then we could have made it through the 1930's fine.'

These women were not going to have to go through the 1980's that way. So there they were, lining up on Calhoun Street in front of the Hoosier National.

Not that the Hoosier National was a bad bank. Quite the contrary. It was a very solid institution. No lending to the Congo, no wild real-estate schemes in Florida, no New York State bonds. Its lending was to the Zollner corporation – bearings, pistons, a big supplier to the Big Two in

323

Detroit. And to Timkin, the company that made gasoline pumps. And to the farmers in the surrounding counties. And the merchants in town. Solid. Sure, it had a lot of Treasury bills, but so did every other bank in the country. The problem was that like any other bank, solid or otherwise, anywhere in the United States, or the world for that matter, the Hoosier National Bank never had a great deal of cash lying around in the vaults on any given day. Especially since the mass use of credit cards and checks, that had never been necessary. Compared to how Hoosier National used to operate, even back in the 1930's when the last catastrophe had occurred, it was extremely cash-poor.

The manager was Fred Willis. A good man. Fifty-five, married thirty years, a veteran of the Korean war, a staunch member of the choir at Concordia Lutheran church, a prudent, honest man. But by eleven thirty he was scared.

He hovered behind the three tellers' windows, monitoring the outflow. And then he went back into his office, and called in Marty Kohler, his number two.

'Marty,' said Willis, 'we are going to run out in an hour. Get the First National of Indiana to send a million over. In small bills, if they've got them.'

Marty phoned, while Willis was outside, watching the lines grow still longer. Marty Kohler was soon beside him. 'Mr. Willis,' he whispered, 'they can't. They say they're running short themselves.'

'Marty, stay out here and keep everybody calm. I'll get the Fed.'

The Federal Reserve Bank closest to Fort Wayne, and the one that controlled the territory, was in Chicago. After a lot of switching around inside the bank, Willis finally got the chief cashier there.

'Mr. Rogers,' he said, 'this is Fred Willis at the Hoosier National in Fort Wayne. We've got a slight problem and need a couple of million in cash – preferably small bills – right away.'

'A couple of million?'

'Yes. And I think the best way would be to send it out to the airport and charter a plane. We'll pick up the cost.'

'Willis, that's impossible.'

'What do you mean? Isn't that what you're there for?' 'Why all this?'

'Because we've got a run, that's why. Certainly you are aware of what's happening in New York.'

'Of course. But that's no reason to panic. Look, Willis, just go out and talk to those people. These things require time. Now, what collateral can you provide us with?'

'We've got very good loans outstanding. You know that. We will pledge the very best. But . . .'

'Fine. I'll send a man over tomorrow.'

'Goddammit,' said Willis – the first time he had probably sworn in years – 'I need that money, and I need it now. In cash. Today!'

'Don't yell at me, Willis. I'll send a man over tomorrow.' And Chicago hung up.

'Well, Fred Willis had tried. He called for everybody in the bank lobby to listen. And he told them that there was no need to withdraw any further money today. The Federal Reserve was sending a very large shipment of cash in the morning. The Hoosier National was one of the best banks in the country. It had always met its obligations – even fifty years ago when ten thousand other American banks had been forced to close their doors – and it would do the same now.

It did not have the slightest effect. At one fifteen the Hoosier National ran out of cash, and at one twenty it closed its doors.

So much for the Federal Reserve System that day. Within the next hour, two more banks in Fort Wayne closed, one in South Bend, two in Indianapolis, and one in Bloomington – a total of seven in the State of Indiana. All were solid banks. But none could pay off their depositors – because they had run out of cash.

For some reason, Indiana stood very much alone that Monday. There were a few other isolated closings – in Iowa, Utah and Nevada. But none of the big states were hit. Every bank in New York, Illinois, Texas, and California closed the day intact.

By five that afternoon, the White House was in a state of utter chaos. The head of every department, agency, authority in town wanted to see the President. But only four had made it into the oval office : the Secretary of State, the Secretary of Defense, the Secretary of the Treasury, and the chairman of the Federal Reserve Board.

Money, not war, had the priority at 5 P.M. that day.

The chairman of the Federal Reserve had just finished summing up what had happened in Indiana. And the President had asked his Secretary of the Treasury for his views.

'It's not our fault,' the Secretary of the Treasury began, though he had not been asked that. 'It's the banks, accepting all that goddamned foreign money.'

'Look,' said the Secretary of State, 'it is by no means just the banks. Your department sold those foreigners eighty billion of your own notes.'

'And what were we supposed to do, for Christ's sake?' answered the Treasury chief. 'You try to finance this government.'

'Well, all I wanted to point out is . . .'

'Enough of that,' interjected the President. 'What about the market for Treasury bills?'

'It is in an absolute shambles,' replied the Secretary of the Treasury. 'Now even the Germans are dumping. It is scaring the bejeezuz out of everybody. I can understand those folk in Indiana getting upset.'

'Well, goddammit,' said the President, 'what do we do?'

'I'll tell you. We have no choice. The Federal Reserve is going to have to move in. With everything they've got. If the French and Saudis and the Swiss and the Germans are selling our bills, the Fed is going to have to buy them. Nobody else will. In fact, as sure as we're sitting here, the big banks in New York and Chicago are going to start dumping our paper. Probably starting tomorrow at the opening. If we are not in there buying, the market will collapse. Totally.'

'That's impossible.'

'Of course it is.'

'But hold on,' said the chairman of the Fed, 'do you both realize what you are talking about?'

'I think so,' replied the Treasury man, who regarded his colleague at the Fed as a financial caveman.

'I don't think you do,' came the reply. 'If we start buying up Treasury paper, it will simply flood the market with cash.'

'Well, for Christ's sake, isn't that exactly what we need?'

'Do you realize what you are talking about? This is not money that we are getting from taxes or from borrowings. You are talking about us simply printing up billions and billions of new money, and distributing them in the market.'

'Exactly.'

'Do you realize where that could lead to? Do you remember what happened in the 1920's in Germany, in Austria, when their governments tried that? The inflation that resulted was . . .'

'Listen,' said the President, 'I am not interested in hearing any more theories about inflation, or money printing, or any of that stuff. I want action. I will not accept any collapse in the markets for the securities of the government of the United States. Period. And I will not accept one further bank failure in this country. Do you understand?' And his finger jabbed so close to the Fed chairman's face that it damn near shoved his pipe down his throat.

'I . . .' was the start of the response.

'You,' thundered the President, 'do exactly what I say. Otherwise I will have your ass. If you are not lynched first.' The President, theoretically, had no power over the Fed. But if he went public with his case, and if the situation deteriorated, there was no chance whatsoever that the chairman would survive the mob reaction. It was better that he temporarily meet the demands of these economic illiterates and survive, to restore sanity at a later date.

327

'It will take at least fifteen billion dollars of new money – our money – to stabilize the market for government securities tomorrow. And we'll have to dole out another ten to the banks, probably, to keep them liquid enough. That's twenty-five billion of cash created out of thin air.'

'We know,' said the Treasury Secretary. 'But you turn around the government market, and all the rest will follow, including the New York Stock Exchange. Then our troubles are over.'

'We will probably have to charter some aircraft to distribute these funds before the opening tomorrow,' said the central banker.

'Look,' said the Defense Secretary, 'why not use some of our planes?'

'Good idea,' said the President. Then to the Fed, 'Can you start on that right now?'

'Of course. But I would like it on the record that I do not agree with these policies.'

'It's on the record,' said the President. And the central banker left.

'What about the dollar?' the President then said to the Treasury Secretary.

'It's falling like a rock. But I say, let it fall. When this is over in a few days it will come back on its own. There is simply no sense in trying to meet this run by borrowing billions and billons of francs and marks and yen. We will only have to pay them back later. Once the Fed does its stuff tomorrow, those guys in Europe will cool off.'

'All right,' said the President, who knew nothing about foreign-exchange markets. 'Now, what have you got on the Middle East?'

'Nothing is clear yet,' replied the Secretary of State. 'We know that the Iraqis are mixing it up again with the Iranians. There have been some very serious air strikes. It is our belief, according to very reliable information which we received a few days ago from our ambassador in Switzerland, that this affair was instigated by Iraq. That all the Shah is doing is retaliating.'

'And I don't blame him,' said the Secretary of Defense.

'So it is strictly a local affair,' said the President.

'Most probably,' answered the Secretary of State. 'But the whole situation in Saudi Arabia remains a puzzle.'

'What does our embassy say?'

'They know nothing more than we do. The embassy is in Jedda. The Saudi government is in Riyadh. And Riyadh has been sealed off like a tomb for five days now. We believe that Prince Abdullah is in charge. We know that there have been massive changes in their economic policy vis-à-vis the United States. As you know, they have withdrawn their funds just as abruptly as they placed them in this country.'

'And started all this,' added the Secretary of the Treasury.

'But,' continued the Secretary of State, 'we have no proof of any other overt act against us. I talked to the people at Aramco just an hour ago, and they tell me that the Saudi oil is still being pumped into their tankers in the Persian Gulf.'

'So what do you suggest?'

'I think we must wait and see,' said the diplomat.

'I have put both the Sixth and Seventh Fleets on alert,' said the Defense Secretary, 'as well as the Third Army in Germany.'

'Has the Shah appealed for any aid?' asked the President.

'No,' answered the Secretary of Defense. 'But if he does, I think we should provide it. He is the only stable partner we have in the entire Middle East.'

'What I can't understand,' said the President, 'is what blew up this entire storm. What on earth is causing the Europeans to panic in this fashion? Don't they realize that we can control any situation on this earth – in the Middle East or wherever? If the Russians were involved, I could understand it. What are they saying?'

'I tried to get both the chancellor in Bonn and the premier in Paris. Neither was available,' replied the Secretary of State.

'Should I try?' asked the President.

'Well, now it's a bit late over there,' answered the Secretary. 'But there is one thing we might do.'

'What's that?' asked the President.

'Get Israel on the hot line.'

'Israel? Why?'

'Well, just to keep them informed. After all, they are our only other reliable allies in the area.'

'Forget Israel,' replied the President. 'We've got more important matters to consider.'

With Israel forgotten, the President then laid out his master strategy for coping with the crisis. 'All right. Look, I want continual surveillance of the entire Middle East, using both our satellites and aircraft if necessary. We'll meet again first thing tomorrow. All of us. At nine. I have the feeling that by that time the entire affair is going to start to blow over.'

Actually, the President could not have been more wrong. At 6 A.M. on March 20, Middle Eastern time (or 10 P.M. Washington time on March 19), the Iranian takeover of Kuwait, Bahrain, Qatar, Abu Dhabi, Dubai and Oman began – the second step in the progressive encirclement of the real target, Saudi Arabia.

The Kuwaiti operation was simple. The Iranian forces, which now completely controlled the entire southeastern corner of Iraq, simply turned south. By noon Kuwait's 3,000-man army surrendered. The next place to go was Bahrain. For years, the large and powerful Iranian minority in Bahrain had been demanding *Anschluss* with the mother country. On March 20, the local Iranians – who in the meantime had been welded together in a well-organized and superbly armed paramilitary force – took the country over. No more than a hundred shots were fired.

The takeover of Qatar, Abu Dhabi, and Dubai involved a combination of betrayal from within and invasion from the sea. In all three sheikdoms there were large numbers of Iranian immigrants who had brought with them the skills and work ethic necessary for the building of a modern economy – attributes which the local Arab population lacked. These immigrants, who had been organized along Bahrainian lines, occupied the strategic military points at dawn. When the Iranian regular troops arrived from the islands of Abu Musa and Greater and Lesser Tanb, they had very little left to do.

In Oman no invasion was necessary. Starting in the mid-1970's, the Shah had generously provided the Omani government with military assistance to help it counter the Dhofar rebels in the strategic northern tip of Oman. By 1979, Iran had five thousand paratroopers and one hundred and twenty-five helicopters in that region. In addition, the majority of the Omani army were Baluchis, recruited for the most part from southern Iran. The paratroopers and the Baluchis simply got together and ran up the Iranian flag.

While all this was happening on the ground, a major redeployment of Iranian air and sea forces was taking place. It involved a massive shift of equipment of the new naval air bases at Bandar Abbas, which guarded the mouth of the Persian Gulf from the west coast of Iran, and was situated almost due west from the principal potential military targets in Saudi Arabia. A further buildup was focused on Chah Bahar, situated on the Iranian coast, just west of the Pakistani border. Chah Bahar was by far the largest military base anywhere in the Indian Ocean. It had been built by American contractors in the early 1970's at a cost of $1 billion.

The bases at Chah Bahar controlled all approaches to the Persian Gulf; those at Bandar Abbas the mouth of the Gulf. The Shah now had that body of water, and its surrounding countries and sheikdoms, completely sealed off from external interference by sea. As an added measure of deterrent, both the *Kitty Hawk* and the *Constellation*, carrying ninety Phantom aircraft each, were in the Indian ocean, and at full battle alert. Perhaps the United States had supplied Iran with almost all of its military potential, ranging from the bases to the aircraft carriers to the Phantom jets – but it was the genius of the Shah and his two principal military advisers that had employed Iran's military resources in such a brilliant fashion during those first two days of battle in March. In just one more day, according to the plan, the war would be over, and the Shahanshah would be complete master of the most valuable real estate on the face of the earth.

The Secretary of Defense had telephoned the President at 3 A.M., Eastern standard time, with the first news of the expansion of the war to Kuwait. At four, the entire White House was ablaze with light. At four thirty the limousines started to arrive, carrying the Secretaries of State, Treasury, and Defense, plus the chairman of the Joint Chiefs of Staff, and the head of the CIA.

The CIA man had the latest. It was not just Kuwait that was now involved, but all the sheikdoms on the west coast of the Gulf. It had been a totally unprovoked attack by the Iranians. The CIA man's judgment was that Iran would completely control each target area within hours. For once the CIA was right.

'Do all of you realize what this means?' asked the Secretary of the Treasury. 'I'll tell you,' he continued. 'The Shah of Iran now controls all the oil in the Middle East, except for that of Saudi Arabia. And there is no doubt in my mind – none – that he is going to now grab the Ghawar oil fields. That would give him one hundred percent.'

'Get a map,' said the President. He had no idea where the Ghawar oil fields were. The map came. He saw. They were only thirty miles from the west coast of the Persian Gulf.

'OK,' said the President, now addressing General Smith, head of the Joint Chiefs of Staff.

The general frowned. 'Sir, what exactly did you have in mind?'

'The Marines, the Navy, I don't care. We've been completely double-crossed by Iran. I want the Shah to pull back. All the way. And right away.'

'Uh, that's going to be a bit difficult. I mean, doing it right away.'

'What do you mean?'

'Well, actually, sir, we've got nothing in the area. Our closest strike force would be the Sixth Fleet, I guess. But that's in the Mediterranean, of course. And the Seventh Fleet's off Formosa right now. If we moved either one, it would be about a week before we'd be ready to hit the Gulf. But even then I'm not sure we would want to do it.'

'Why not, for Christ's sake?'

'Well, the Shah has an enormous amount of firepower ready to go against us. He's got two of our carriers – you know the ones we leased him a couple of years ago – cruising off Chah Bahar. They've got about two hundred aircraft aboard. You know, those Phantoms we sold them. Then there's Chah Bahar. He's got a bunch of F-14's there – more than we've got in all of Europe, come to think of it. And take those missile sites on Abu Musa – that's a little island in the Gulf, sir. Assuming we could get into the Gulf, and I'm not so sure we could.'

'Do you mean to tell me that we, the United States of America, cannot take on the Shah militarily?' thundered the President.

'Well, we could. But our casualty rate would be astronomic. And then there's something else to think about. In order to get the Shah back out of the Gulf, we'd have to mobilize a type of landing on the scale of Normandy in World War Two. With the exception that our supply lines would not be fifteen miles across the English Channel, but about five thousand miles from Western Europe. I'm not sure that course of action is to be recommended.'

'Wait a minute,' said the general's boss, the Secretary of Defense. 'Look, we're approaching this whole thing the wrong way. Forget the Seventh Fleet. Sure, it will have to set sail for the Gulf immediately. But something's been overlooked. We've *got* a military presence in Saudi Arabia. Three thousand regulars, a lot of technicians, plus those guys from that corporation in Los Angeles that the Saudis hired a few years ago to guard those goddamn Ghawar oil fields. Plus a whole bunch of guys with Aramco. We must have eight thousand Americans in Saudi Arabia. Not only that, but thank God, during the past couple of months we have been shipping enormous quantities of weapons to the Saudis. You know that, Mr. President. You and I implemented that policy. With that fellow that runs the Saudi army – Sultan Abdul Aziz. All we have to do is reinforce the Saudis from Europe. From Rhine-Main air base in Frankfurt. We can move in twenty-five thousand men within forty-eight hours. With the best equipment we've got in Germany.'

'By God,' said the President, 'you've got it!'

'Hold on,' said the Secretary of State. 'You're forgetting about the Saudis. We don't know for sure, but we have every reason to believe that your Sultan Abdul Aziz is dead, along with the entire pro-American clique in Riyadh. And that left-wing radical, Prince Abdullah, is now in charge—'

'So what?' said the Secretary of Defense.

'Exactly,' said the President. 'If the Shah attacks them, the Saudis – and I don't care of what political bent they now are – will take help from any place they can get it.'

'And the Russians?' asked the Secretary of State.

'Have they made any moves?' asked the President.

'No.'

'Then let's just ignore them. It's too late for them to interfere.'

'OK,' said the Secretary of Defense. 'So what we've got to do is get that airlift going from Germany.'

'What about the formalities?' asked the President. 'Don't we have to inform NATO and the German government?'

'Yes,' interjected the Secretary of State. 'But that's a pure formality.'

'Well,' said the President, 'then let's get it over with.'

It was late morning in Bonn, and he had a connection with the chancellor in his office there within three minutes. Within another three minutes, the President had explained the situation and had made his request concerning the use of the Rhine-Main facilities by the American Third Army. When he had completed his pitch, there was a long silence on the other end.

'Mr. Chancellor,' said the President finally, 'are you still there?'

'Yes.'

'Well?'

'I am afraid, Mr. President, that I cannot give you an immediate reply.'

'What?'

'Our national interests are involved, as you understand. I shall have to consult with the full cabinet. I am afraid that it will take a few hours at least to get them together. The Bundestag is in recess at the moment.'

'But this is a matter that cannot wait!'

'I understand your position. You must understand mine. I shall come back to you as soon as I can. Goodbye, Mr. President.' And he left the President of the United States of America dangling on the other end of a broken connection.

'It is unbelievable,' the President finally said, phone still in hand. 'That fucking Nazi is stalling.'

'There is a further alternative,' said General Smith, breaking the quiet.

'What?' asked the President.

'We've still got those B-52's in Guam.'

'And so what?'

'Well, they've got the range. We could bomb them.'

'Ach,' interjected his boss, 'that's absurd. Sure they've got the range. But only if they damn near fill the planes up with fuel. There'd be no capacity left for any payload that would have any effect whatsoever.'

'I'm not talking about a conventional payload, sir.'

'You mean nuclear?'

'Yes. But you do not understand me. I do not propose that we drop any nuclear bombs. I merely suggest that an ultimatum be put to the Shah, vaguely threatening their use. He would start pulling out the moment the B-52's appeared over Iran.'

'No,' said the President. 'That is completely and totally out of question. Do you think I want to be impeached?'

'Sometimes you guys in the Pentagon astound me,' said the Secretary of the Treasury. 'In what kind of world do you live? I have never in my whole life heard anything so absurd.'

'I agree with you,' said the Secretary of State. 'But perhaps the concept, though absurd, is not entirely remote.'

Everybody knew that the Secretary of State liked to talk in riddles, so they just waited.

'I received a report from Ambassador Sinclair in Bern, three days ago, informing me that he had received a call from an American banker called Hitchcock.'

'I think I know him,' said the President. 'Didn't he work for the Saudis?'

'Yes. Exactly. Well, he correctly predicted – three days ago, mind you – that the Shah was preparing to launch an attack on his Arab neighbors. He was correct, of course. Although Ambassador Sinclair did not believe him, and neither did I.' A pause. 'What is disturbing is that he also suggested that the Shah had nuclear weapons and was prepared to use them.'

'How could he know that?' asked the President.

'Apparently from a Swiss source.'

'Maybe he has a nuclear capability,' said the President. 'But he would never use it. Just as we cannot. I know the Shah. He is a reasonable man. And I think I have the solution. Yes, I shall send an ultimatum to him. Withdraw immediately or we shall intervene. And we shall get the Seventh Fleet under way immediately and make sure he knows it. In the meantime, all we can hope is that the Saudis can hold him for a few days, if he does attack. By that time we can start the airlift from Germany.'

The Secretary of State was instructed to draft the message to the Shah. It should be sent within two hours, at most.

The men all got up to leave. Dawn was beginning to appear outside the windows of the Oval Office.

'Fred,' the President said, now rather wearily, to his Secretary of the Treasury, 'can you stay just another minute?'

'Sure.' He sat down again, as the other men left.

'What is this going to mean today?'

'In the markets?'

'Yes. And with the banks.'

'Mr. President, we're prepared for the worst. Don't worry, we'll handle it.'

While quiet reigned on the Persian Gulf, it being night there and the battles won, it was anything but quiet in the United States, where a financial battle of immense proportions had begun taking place.

It's impossible to explain, even in retrospect, but somehow the masses in the United States began gradually and collectively to reach a decision : enormous trouble was brewing in the world, the foreigners were losing faith in America and getting out. Now they also wanted out with their money. Out. Which meant out of stocks, out of bonds, out of savings and loan associations, out of banks. And into cash.

What no one had ever really thought about in the United States up until that time was the unbelievably huge volume of liquid assets in circulation that could be traded in for cash. Just the value of those shares traded on the New York Stock Exchange amounted to $850 billion. The amounts of Federal Government securities in the public's hands in 1979 represented another $879 billion. The corporate bonds in circulation yet another $750 billion. Deposits in banks – $1,000 billion. Plus the public's holdings of bankers' acceptances, of commercial paper. Etc. Add it all up, and in 1979 there were perhaps $4 trillion in assets which, theoretically at least, could be converted into cash instantaneously.

What would happen if even 1 percent – just *one* percent – of these assets were sold, traded in, withdrawn for money – in one day? Well, we found out on March 20, 1979. Chaos. The scenes were frightful on the exchanges in New York, Chicago, San Francisco, and in front of the banks in almost every city and town in the United States. But the system held. Because the central bank had anticipated the run. By dawn of that day $25 billion in new cash had been distributed around the country to thousands of banks. This,

337

together with the normal cash holdings of American financial institutions, was sufficient – barely, in some cities, but sufficient to meet every demand of every person who wanted cash.

Even the Hoosier National Bank in Fort Wayne, Indiana, was able to reopen its doors at 9 A.M. that day. It doubled the number of withdrawal windows. And it stayed open until normal closing time, although at the end of the day only $4,335 was left in its vaults.

At six o'clock that night, Eastern standard time, when the California banks had also survived the day intact, the President appeared on national television on all three networks, and his speech was carried directly by every major radio network in the Western World. He patiently explained that the situation in the Middle East was strictly a regional affair. That the great powers were not involved. That conversations were under way aimed at establishing an immediate ceasefire. That panic was in no way justified. That the American banking system had proven beyond any doubt that it could meet any run. And that it was time for the American people to come to their senses. When he was finished, no one in America turned off his set. Because the first films of the Four Day War had become available – from a Canadian team that had been in Abu Dhabi doing a documentary for the CBC. They got them out by hitchhiking a ride on the Lear Jet of a local sheik who was getting the hell out of the way of the Iranians at the very last moment.

By eight that evening, the telephone system in the United States began going berserk. Because fathers were calling sons, mothers daughters, clients the homes of their brokers, bankers each other – and all were asking the same question: 'What do you plan to do tomorrow?'

The other 99 percent of those $4 trillion in liquid assets were still on the sidelines.

One hour later, the now week-long silence from the capital of Saudi Arabia was broken. In a message issued jointly by King Khalid and Prince Abdullah it was said that two

338

hours earlier Saudi Arabia had been attacked by Iran. The Saudi forces, it said, were holding. Then came an appeal to all the Arab brethren for assistance in the struggle against the Aryans from the north. There was also an appeal to the United States. Saudi Arabia would welcome direct military assistance from its American friends.

So there we had it – finally. All the rumors were wrong. Despite the bullshit, King Khalid was still alive and, at least jointly, in command of Saudi Arabia. And the Saudis were attacking nobody. The Shah of Iran had suckered us all.

Within the hour, Colonel Qaddafi of Libya had dispatched one hundred and twenty Mirage III fighter-bombers to Saudi Arabia. Egypt had begun its first flights to Riyadh – Russian-built transports, carrying the 'elite' paratrooper battalions of the Egyptian army. The king of Jordan pledged that he would personally lead his armored division across the desert against the enemy. The United States said that the Seventh Fleet was heading toward the Gulf at top speed, and that discussions were in progress with the NATO allies with regard to the possible use of the Third Army stationed in Western Germany.

The Shah had anticipated this. Perhaps not to such a degree, but still, he was a realist. Thus his entire strategy was based upon his ability to finish the war in three days. He would then control all of the Middle Eastern oil fields before a counteroffensive could be mounted. And then he could hold up the world for ransom. Hands off, or he would blow them up.

His strategy was working perfectly. On the morning of that third day he had two armored divisions closing on the Ghawar oil fields, and had five hundred aircraft operational overhead. All in all, he had over a quarter of a million men on the battlefield. The opposition was pathetic. The Saudis had a total of 61,000 men, including both the army and the national guard. A ratio of four to one. A walkover.

But he had badly underestimated the equipment buildup that had taken place at a frenzied pace in the early months of 1979. The Americans had made massive deliveries, especially of tanks and aircraft. In fact, the Saudi air force was the equal in every way of the Iranian. When the American air force personnel started taking over the controls of these aircraft – there were 1,800 of them there to serve as instructors to the Saudis – the Saudis soon developed a marked superiority. In fact, before the first direct clash between the Iranian and Saudi armor, at least 25 percent of the Iranian tanks had been knocked out. That the Shah had not foreseen. He had also greatly underestimated the Saudis' air defense system. The Americans had been working on it for four years, at a total cost of $7 billion. On January 1, 1979, it had become fully operational. It was the best in the entire world. And it was manned completely by American personnel. The Iranians lost 120 aircraft during the first four hours of the battle.

By two that afternoon, Middle Eastern time, the Iranian advance had been brought to a total standstill. And at the same time, the reinforcements from Egypt and Libya had begun to arrive. The Jordanian armor was already on the move. And the Seventh Fleet had rounded Singapore.

When darkness brought the battle to a lull, it appeared that – and the cliché was inevitable – the Saudi David had stopped the Iranian Goliath, and stopped it dead.

When news of the developments on the battlefield of this third day of war reached Western Europe and the United States, it was soon followed by other glad tidings. The Saudi authorities had officially announced the cessation of any further repatriation of funds from the United States. The Western European banks, which by now had taken $35 billion out of the United States, seemed to markedly slow their dumping of the dollar. The volume on the New York Stock Exchange, which had reached the panic level of 80 million shares, dropped to the semi-panic level of only 57 million. And the lines at the banks, though still large, were not growing. It was still a very touch-and-go situation.

Then, late that evening, it was announced that NATO

and Western Germany had approved the use of European-based American forces for intervention in the Middle East. The first Hercules aircraft, loaded with the best military personnel and equipment the United States possessed, would soon start off on their four-hour flight from Frankfurt to Saudi Arabia. Europe had gotten off the Shah's bandwagon. For it now appeared that it was going to be the Americans who, directly or indirectly, might end up controlling the Persian Gulf.

The world, it seemed, had gone to the brink. But no further.

CHAPTER TWENTY-SIX

It was 4 A.M. on March 22 in southern Iran. The Shah, General Barami, and Brigadier Shabanah had not slept for forty-eight hours. Their grim, unshaven faces were those of men on the verge of collapse. In spite of the hour, the bunker was buzzing with activity, as messages came in from the fronts in Saudi Arabia, as new orders were dispatched.

But the Shah, seated in his commander-in-chief's chair, had not stirred or even spoken a word for the past half hour. For it was then that word had come through that the first American Hercules were starting to lift off at Rhine-Main airfield outside of Frankfurt.

'Your Majesty?' It was Barami.

No reply.

'Sir, I believe it is still not too late to stop them!'

'Barami, shut up. I'm thinking.'

'Your Majesty, we must talk to the Russians. They will not allow the Americans to invade the Middle East.'

'The Russians agreed to nonintervention. They will not take on, openly and militarily, the entire Arab world. Do not be stupid, Barami.'

Again the Shah lapsed into silence. He sat completely upright, his eyes now closed. He was in full uniform. 'Get the professor.'

'Pardon?' said Barami.

'The professor. Get him. Now!'

The Shah's eyes remained closed as he shouted these orders. And they remained closed until Barami returned twenty minutes later with Professor Hartmann. Both men stood silently before the Shah's command-post chair.

'Professor,' the Shah finally said – and now he opened his eyes, and fixed them on the Swiss – 'I am now going to ask you one more time. Are you positive? Are you absolutely sure?'

'Your Highness, I have told you many times, I am sure. They will work.'

'Barami.'

'Yes, Your Majesty.'

'Are they mounted?'

'Yes. Six. The aircraft are on standby with their crews.'

'All right. Arm the bombs.'

'Now?'

'Now!'

The general and the professor went back to the elevator which would return them to the surface of the airfield at Khorramshahr, where the Phantoms awaited their attention.

'Shabanah!' Now the Shah addressed his tactical commander.

'Yes, Your Majesty.'

'Order an immediate withdrawal. All the armor. All the personnel. And I want them to pull back at the greatest possible speed.'

'Yes, Your Majesty.'

Now the activity in the bunker rose to fever pitch as the orders to retreat were radioed out to all the Iranian field commanders poised north and to the west of the Ghawar oil fields in Saudi Arabia.

Thirty minutes later, General Barami returned with Professor Hartmann.

'They are armed, Your Majesty.'

'Excellent. Please get some coffee, Barami. You, Professor, come sit beside me here.'

The Swiss professor did as bid. The old man showed not a trace of fatigue. In fact, his face and eyes were alive with anticipation and excitement.

Barami returned with the coffee. The Shah drank it slowly.

'Now,' he said, 'the following communiqué will be issued. It will be transmitted directly to the governments in Riyadh, Washington, and Cairo. Do you understand, Barami?'

'Yes, Your Majesty.'

'It will read as follows: "The Shahanshah of Iran,

Mohammed Riza Pahlavi, hereby advises the government of Saudi Arabia and its allies to immediately surrender all troops in and around the Ghawar oil fields. Nuclear devices will be dropped within two hours near that area. No one will be killed if they immediately abandon that area. However, anyone who remains more than twelve hours following the detonation of the devices will face lethal radioactivity. We demand that all military equipment be abandoned, as is, on site. If any further military action of any type be taken against Iran from this time on by any party in the Middle East, further such devices will be employed against the offending nation. I know that the liberation of the oppressed peoples of the territories surrounding the Persian Gulf will be welcomed by all responsible governments, and that mankind everywhere will welcome the permanent restoration of peace to the Middle East." '

'That is all, Your Majesty?'

'Yes. Send it.'

Then : 'Professor Hartmann, how many devices should we drop?'

'I would suggest three. All to the west, of course, of the oil fields, say about ten miles to the west. And they should be spaced ten miles apart, on the north-south axis. I have set the devices to detonate at five thousand feet.'

'Excellent. We will keep the other three Phantoms ready and armed, on standby.'

Barami returned. 'It has been sent.'

'Excellent. What is the flight time to the target area?'

'Forty-two minutes.'

'You will order them to leave in exactly one hour.'

'Yes, Your Majesty.'

'Now, Hartmann,' the Shah said, 'all of these bombs have magnesium as the contamination agent?'

'Yes, Your Majesty, exactly as you instructed.'

'So my troops can move back to occupy the area within one week.'

'I would say ten days, to make absolutely sure.'

344

'They will have enough to do in the meantime rounding up those Arabs and getting them into camps. Perfect.'

'May I leave now, Your Majesty?' asked Hartmann.

'No. Remain here.'

The Shah rose. 'I am going to sleep now,' he said. 'Wake me in one hour and forty minutes, Barami.'

The King of Kings disappeared into his private chambers in the rear of the command bunker.

At 6:30 A.M. Middle Eastern time, the Shah returned to the command room, rested, shaved, and clad in a fresh, immaculate uniform. His two principal aides, General Barami and Brigadier Shabanah, were huddled in front of the main communications panel. The rest of the room was hushed.

Then out of a loudspeaker came, in Pharsee, the voice of the pilot of the lead Phantom. 'We are one minute from target. No problems.'

Then, at 6:32: 'Bombs released.'

Thirty seconds later: 'All three devices have detonated. Returning to base.'

The Shah motioned for silence. Then he spoke. 'With the guidance of Allah we have won this glorious war. I hereby declare the establishment of the new Persian Empire.'

After that, the command bunker was in a state of pandemonium. But the Shah, a man of destiny, wanted his triumph recorded for history in every possible fashion.

'Barami,' he said to his commander, 'I want complete aerial photographs of the target area. Our children must be able to see, with their own eyes, what we have done. I want you personally to fly this mission. Immediately.'

'Yes, Your Majesty.'

The general bowed before the King of Kings. Beside him stood the Swiss professor, silent, but with an expression that approached ecstasy.

At 6:57 A.M. on that Thursday, March 22, seventeen Phantoms led by General Falk, air attaché of the American Embassy in Riyadh, flying the lead Saudi air force plane, approached Khorramshahr from the east. They had

345

crossed the Persian Gulf far to the south of Abadan and then looped around over the desert, flying at 1,500 feet. It was the second end run of the Four Day War.

Seven minutes later, at exactly 7:04 A.M., their murderous attack on the Khorramshahr air base began. At 7:06 one of the three Iranian Phantoms that still stood waiting on standby on the tarmac, loaded with now armed nuclear bombs, was hit. The explosion triggered the bomb's detonator. And the resulting atomic blast triggered the armed bombs in the other two planes microseconds later.

The airfield, Khorramshahr itself, disappeared from the face of the earth. The crater at the center of the blast was seventy feet deep. The winds were blowing from the north, and later shifted to north northeast. The radioactive cloud engulfed all the oil fields around Abadan, as well as the city itself. Driven by an ever stronger wind, a few hours later the radioactive dust began falling on Kuwait. The population in Khorramshahr was, of course, dead. That in Abadan fled to the desert; in Kuwait, to the open sea.

The King of Kings had won his empire. But now it lay under a cloud of lethal radioactivity; its people were either dead, dying, or fleeing for their lives.

And nothing whatsoever remained of the Shah or Iran. His command bunker – and he – had been vaporized.

The middle East was eight time zones ahead of New York. Thus it was about 11 P.M. the night before on the calendar that the first intimations of the happenings around the Persian Gulf began filtering through to the media centers in that city, too late for most of the regular late-news shows. But CBS, with its unparalleled news sense, suggested to its remaining viewers that something very big was breaking. Their news center in New York was not closing down that night as usual.

Already at eleven thirty, Eastern standard time, the first people began to form small groups in front of the New York banks. By midnight, it was estimated that over twenty thousand had already gathered. Those who had just been watching the events of the week and hoping for the best were now also going to 'get out' while it was still possible.

At 1 A.M. on Thursday, March 22, the White House issued a very brief communiqué. It stated that atomic weapons had been employed in the Middle Eastern war. It was not clear who had employed them. But all signs were that hostilities had ceased. American military personnel were arriving in the capital of Saudi Arabia at the rate of three thousand men per hour. It was thought that they could stabilize the entire area within only a few days.

At 3 A.M., upon direct Presidential orders, two teams of nuclear scientists were airborne from Los Alamos, bound for the Middle East. Their mission : to determine when it would be safe for the men of the Third Army to begin occupation of the oil fields around the Persian Gulf.

At 4 A.M. it was decided that the banks in the United States would open as usual. To do otherwise would merely provoke unnecessary panic, and perhaps rioting. It was a logical decision. And the logic behind it was explained by the President in his speech to the nation at 7 A.M. that morning. He summed up with the words : 'With incredible luck, it is we, the United States, who have won this terrible struggle for the oil fields of the Middle East. With our Arab friends, we shall insure that free and open access to the immense resources of the Persian Gulf remains forever. And now, my friends, it is time that we all return to our business. For America – its great banks, its great industries – will remain open for business. Today and every day.'

Nobody believed him.

It is estimated that on that Thursday the American public converted well over $100 billion in liquid assets to cash. And on Friday another $125 billion. Within a span of just one week, the total money supply of the United States had been artificially increased, by printing of new money in the amount of $250 billion. Thus the money in circulation in America had essentially been doubled – but not one bank failed. And, with the weekend at hand, there was no reason to believe that the tide would not turn. People would realize that the system had held. And on Monday, very sheepishly they would start putting their money back where it belonged : in banks, not in their pockets.

But that Friday, and that Saturday, and that Sunday, a new phenomenon developed. Cash in vast hoards was now being converted into tangibles – food, – clothing, gasoline, shoes, houses, horses, furniture. Twice the normal money in circulation was now chasing, in full fury, the same amount of goods which had been there before the madness began. Soon price was no longer an issue. It was a classic case of instant hyperinflation. It was not the banks that were first forced to close. It was the Safeways, the Searses, the Levitzes. They simply ran out of stock. And on Sunday afternoon every McDonald's in the land closed. For their proprietors realized what was slowly dawning on everybody else : the dollar had become a worthless commodity. It was insanity to accept any more. It was the same with the yen, the mark, the pound, the lira. The amounts of these currencies in circulation had risen explosively as a result of the flight from the dollar. Then, as the 'American madness' spread, governments everywhere had been forced to flood their countries with even more currencies. Now they also were worthless.

The banks did not open on Monday. In fact, the majority never opened again. For they had been broke long before all this happened. The run merely brought this truth into the open.

Peace, however, was maintained. The National Guard was out in full force, nationwide. Still, dozens of banks were burned and hundreds of stores looted.

That Monday, Ursula and I, safe in St. Moritz in ever-orderly Switzerland, decided to get married. It was, perhaps, a marriage of convenience. For Switzerland was now deporting all foreigners. It could no longer support them under the new world conditions, it was said. Anyone married to a Swiss could stay. Ursula was Swiss, and we both wanted to stay, at least for a while, until the rest of the world cooled down. But we fully intended, later, to go to the United States. For there was no doubt in my mind that after a while that resource-rich land would be the only sensible place in which to live. And, after all, I owned thousands of acres of the best ranch land in California, fully stocked. There was also no doubt in my mind that America would soon adopt the xenophobic policies of the Swiss. But they could hardly keep out the wife of an American citizen. Besides that, I guess we needed each other.

It was a civil ceremony in the small office of the local mayor. Herr Meier, of the Swiss Bank Corporation – now also closed, so he had lots of time on his hands – was our witness. At three thirty it was over.

At four that afternoon we went to Hanselmann's for tea. They accepted gold coins, and I had lots of them.

'I wish your father could have been here,' I said.

'Yes,' said Ursula.

'But perhaps he preferred it this way. I think we both understand why he did it. The Arabs are through. And if there is a winner in this whole mess, it is Israel. They are now safe.'

'Yes,' said Ursula, 'safe. But for how long? Maybe a few years. And that is what bothers me.'

'Bothers?'

'Yes. My father – you hardly knew him – was a very thorough man, and the most honorable I have ever known. And he promised me.'

Thorough? I did not say it, but I certainly wondered: How thorough could a man get. And promised? What had he promised?

We all found out later that week. Not only had American nuclear experts gone to the Middle East, but those from a dozen different countries of Western Europe. Their conclusions were unanimous: That madman, the Shah of Iran, had inexplicably used cobalt as the contamination agent in the six nuclear bombs which had exploded in the Middle East. Cobalt has one of the longest half-lives of any substance known to man. The oil fields of Saudi Arabia, of

Kuwait, of Iran, would remain totally inaccessible for at least twenty-five years. The Arabs were through as a world power – and as a threat to Israel. Of course, the Western industrial powers were through too.

The professor and his daughter *had* been thorough. But this time, the Israelis had gone too far. And I sometimes wonder if that son of a bitch Ben-Levi is still alive and happy with what he started.

For the world was now forced to live with a bank system that lay in ruins, with monetary chaos, and with the prospect of having to survive on half its former oil reserves. The lights, everywhere gradually began to flicker and fade.

The Crash of '79 was complete.

A selection of Bestsellers from Sphere Books

SARGASSO	Edwin Corley	95p	☐
RAISE THE TITANIC!	Clive Cussler	95p	☐
STORY OF MY LIFE	Moshe Dayan	£1.50p	☐
THE CRASH OF '79	Paul Erdman	£1.25p	☐
EMMA AND I	Sheila Hocken	85p	☐
UNTIL THE COLOURS FADE	Tim Jeal	£1.50p	☐
MAJESTY	Robert Lacey	£1.95p	☐
STAR WARS	George Lucas	95p	☐
KRAMER'S WAR	Derek Robinson	£1.25p	☐
THE GOLDEN SOVEREIGNS	Jocelyn Carew	£1.25p	☐
THE INVASION OF THE BODY SNATCHERS			
	Jack Finney	85p	☐
GOLD FROM CRETE	C. S. Forester	95p	☐
THE GOVERNANCE OF BRITAIN	Harold Wilson	£1.50p	☐
MIDNIGHT EXPRESS			
	Billy Hayes with William Hoffer	95p	☐
CLOSE ENCOUNTERS OF THE THIRD KIND			
	Steven Spielberg	85p	☐
STAR FIRE	Ingo Swann	£1.25p	☐
RUIN FROM THE AIR			
	Gordon Thomas & Max Morgan Witts	£1.50p	☐
DAMNATION ALLEY	Roger Zelazny	85p	☐
FALSTAFF	Robert Nye	£1.50p	☐
EBANO	Alberto Vazques-Figueroa	95p	☐
MY CHILDREN AND I	Margaret Powell	95p	☐
FIREFOX	Craig Thomas	95p	☐

All Sphere books are available at your local bookshop or newsagent, or can be ordered direct from the publisher. Just tick the titles you want and fill in the form below.

Name...

Address...

Write to Sphere Books, Cash Sales Department, P.O. Box 11, Falmouth, Cornwall TR10 9EN

Please enclose cheque or postal order to the value of cover price plus:

UK: 22p for the first book plus 10p per copy for each additional book ordered to a maximum charge of 82p

OVERSEAS: 30p for the first book and 10p for each additional book

BFPO and EIRE: 22p for the first book plus 10p per copy for the next 6 books, thereafter 4p per book

Sphere Books reserve the right to show new retail prices on covers which may differ from those previously advertised in the text or elsewhere, and to increase postal rates in accordance with the GPO.

(10:78)